PERILOUS POWER

"I don't know how to ⟨...⟩ feeling for you," Lucas said. "I ⟨...⟩ any man I ever met."

Megan gave him her lips as an answer, and he easily answered her questions there.

"How simple you must find me," Megan said. "You have only to kiss me to set all my doubts flying."

"And I have only to step away to send them flying home again," he replied.

"You know what I mean," she said more sharply. "You have had so many women."

"I know how to touch women," he agreed, his eyes glittering, "and how to take their bodies. It's a great sport in many lands I've lived in. An art, in others."

Lucas and Megan. Each had power over the other. Yet neither of them could trust it. Or resist it.

THE CRIMSON CROWN

by

Edith Layton

AN ONYX BOOK

ONYX
Published by the Penguin Group
Penguin Books USA Inc., 375 Hudson Street,
New York, New York 10014, U.S.A.
Penguin Books Ltd, 27 Wrights Lane,
London W8 5TZ, England
Penguin Books Australia Ltd, Ringwood,
Victoria, Australia
Penguin Books Canada Ltd, 2801 John Street,
Markham, Ontario, Canada L3R 1B4
Penguin Books (N.Z.) Ltd, 182–190 Wairau Road,
Auckland 10, New Zealand

Penguin Books Ltd, Registered Offices:
Harmondsworth, Middlesex, England

First published by Onyx, an imprint of New American Library, a division of
Penguin Books USA Inc.

First Printing, December, 1990
10 9 8 7 6 5 4 3 2 1

 REGISTERED TRADEMARK—MARCA REGISTRADA

Printed in the United States of America

BOOKS ARE AVAILABLE AT QUANTITY DISCOUNTS WHEN USED TO PROMOTE PRODUCTS
OR SERVICES. FOR INFORMATION PLEASE WRITE TO PREMIUM MARKETING DIVISION,
PENGUIN BOOKS USA INC., 375 HUDSON STREET, NEW YORK, NEW YORK 10014.

For Norbert,
for teaching me that *vincit qui partitur*

How dreadful knowledge of the truth can be,
When there's no help in truth!

—Sophocles

Foreword

For almost thirty years, from 1455 to 1483, England was at war with herself. It was a war between powerful ruling houses, and although common men were physically untouched by it, fierce battles were waged for and by noblemen throughout the country, throughout those years. Unfortunately, the conflict has become known in history by the foolish, misleadingly charming name "The Wars of the Roses." But these were acrimonious, hard-fought, bloody, bitter wars—as wars between relatives always are—for they were between cousins, the Plantagenets (the house of York) and the Tudors (the house of Lancaster), for the crown of all England. The wars weren't waged over great ideologies, because as in all family arguments, now or then, the issues are never so important as the personalities involved. But they changed the face of England, and of history.

Still, in truth, all but ardent students of history find the wars confusing, since the crown passed so rapidly from head to head. To further complicate matters for modern minds, most of the men involved were named Edward, Richard, or Henry—and their wives and daughters all seem to have been named Elizabeth, Margaret, or Catherine. But they were all very different men and women, and their stories are worth remembering. One, in particular, has been called "the greatest English murder mystery."

Edward IV, a genial, pleasure-loving Plantagenet king, died young (some say of his excesses) in 1483. His elder son and heir, Edward, was only twelve at the time, and was king for only a space of days because his uncle promptly put him and his younger brother under arrest in the Tower of London, proclaimed them illegitimate, killed their supporters, and made himself king—Richard III.

Within months, both princes in the Tower were gone, never to be seen again.

A year and half later, Richard himself was deposed, killed in battle at Bosworth field by his cousin Henry Tudor, who in turn became King Henry VII. To ensure peace, Henry married the lost princes' sister, thus blending the houses of York and Lancaster, mating Tudor and Plantagenet, and ending the "Wars of the Roses." But it was an uneasy throne, for ghosts of the defeated continued to walk.

In 1487, thousands died at the Battle of Stoke, trying to wrest the crown from Henry for Lambert Simnel, an adventurer pretending to be a rightful Yorkist heir. Then for years Henry was harried by a claimant who said he was the younger prince in the Tower: escaped, grown to manhood, and ready to reclaim his throne. Henry threatened war with various kingdoms and went to war with France and Scotland, as well as with some of his subjects, because of their support of the youth, until he was captured in 1497.

The prisoner confessed to imposture, stating his real name was Perkin Warbeck. But his supporters never believed his rack-induced confession. The issue wasn't dropped, although Henry insisted that the princes had been killed by their uncle in the summer of 1483. To end the matter, in 1502 he tried an unlucky surviving gentleman of Richard's court for doing the deed, and executed him. But he couldn't kill the controversy. As the Tudor line grew stronger, only feeble attempts were made to impersonate the two princes and the living issue finally died, but the questions never did.

Some agree that Richard was the villain; Shakespeare's *Richard III* illustrates that theory. But Horace Walpole and Mary Shelley, among others, have disagreed. As the princes' bodies were never proved to have been discovered, every explanation for their disappearance has been postulated over the years—from their natural deaths and secret burials, to their deportation, to murder done by Henry himself.

What did happen to the two unlucky boy princes? The conjecture has gone on for five centuries, despite the fact that no new facts have come to light. There are precious few old facts. Between the efforts of two clever usurping kings—Richard and Henry—and the natural depredations of time, most of the records have been lost or destroyed. The years 1475–1500 are a virtual black hole in history.

But it can't end there—both nature and novelists abhor a vacuum. Where facts won't speak, fiction must—and may sometimes come closer to the truth.

Part I

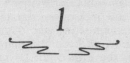

1

April 1498

Cold. Intemperate, unseasonable cold. Colder still because it was so late and lonely and growing later. It was an indecent hour and an embarrassing situation and certainly no place for a decent man to be. But then, kings never sent for decent men at this time of the night, unless they were dying. And Henry wasn't. He'd summoned this man because he wanted to delay that unhappy state, the messenger thought, dancing from toe to toe in place as stealthily as he could as he waited. The corridor was cold, and his boots not only encrusted with ice, but thin, and thinned further from hard travel, and the stones beneath them held the chill of centuries. If not eternity. This was said to be a damned place.

But then, that would have made it hot, the messenger thought, welcoming the thought of eternal damnation if only because of the idea of unblessed warmth and then the hot flush such heresy brought to his cheeks. There were fires burning in every great room in the castle, heavy tapestries were flung against the walls and piled underfoot, the walls of hewn rock were five stout men thick, almost as thick as the fog he'd just come in from, and yet nothing defeated the damp or held back the wind that came in off the sea. Nothing attempted to in the long chill corridor in which he waited. Even the flaring wall torches bent to the constant draft; it took all his years of training at court for the young messenger not to do the same.

And yet the man who finally came walking toward him through the gloom seemed to carry a May morning on his shoulders; he sauntered down the gray corridor with springtime in his step, no more aware of the cold in this

godforsaken rock pile than the devil would appear hot in
hell. He was so damnably impervious to the moment and
the season that the messenger refrained from crossing
himself only by remembering who the man was. He was,
after all, as famous, wicked, and dangerous in his own
mortal fashion as the Prince of Lies himself was in his.
And fully as fantastic-looking, the messenger thought,
gaping at him.

He was tall, slender and fair as ice, with deceptive
bitter-blond hair that glowed like a daffodil in the torchlight, then grew pale as moonlight when he passed from
beneath its leaping glare. Pale and graceful and elegant
as a swan, the messenger saw, just as they'd said, and as
they'd said, his light eyes were as glittering and cold as
the night's cold, for all he smiled and smiled.

It was astonishing that his face was the first thing
noted, because his costume was foreign, lavish, and as
exotic as it was extreme. His cape was yellow and red, flung
over a wide-shouldered amber velvet doublet slashed with
yellow and white on its puffed sleeves. Beneath, his hose
fit to his legs like yellow-and-black skins, and his shoes
were soft: he lacked only bells to make him the very
image of a madcap jester. But there was nothing amusing
about him. The body beneath the colorful raiment was as
strong as it was shapely, for though he moved like a
dancer, there was little doubt he knew how to use those
muscular limbs for more than dancing, as well as how to
ply the long sword that swung so lightly at his hip. No,
colorful and graceful as he was, he was easily as dangerous as a bright-colored snake such as came, they said,
from the tropical lands where he'd lately been.

"Lucas Lovat?" the messenger breathed for the form
of it, for he'd no doubt of it. His words were a white mist
in the dank air as he swept into a bow and presented the
paper he'd been charged with.

The brilliantly clad man held the paper to the torchlight and read the words, and the messenger stared at the
light as it shone on those bright eyes until he was done.

"Ah. Henry wants me now, or even better, yesterday.
Do you want me to ride with you tonight?" he asked in a
low, mocking voice, as though he expected the answer to
be amusing, as though he knew it would not be.

"Tonight?" The messenger's breath caught in his throat,

exactly where his heart had leapt. Only a madman or a determined suicide would travel by night in the dangerous darkness, where evil men and less-than-human influences might flourish. Well, and if the gentleman were a madman, or even in league with the spectral horrors of the night, what could a poor servant of the crown do, after all? He had the king's seal of authority, but not the ordering of this journey. It was the gentleman's game. He swallowed.

"Marry, it's as you will, good sir," he managed to say, as he consigned his soul to the care of God. He froze at the thought of leaving equally as much as staying in this dank corridor now, but decided whatever would be, would be God's will, after all. And if it came to be that he had to leave this cold sanctuary for the darker dangers of the unknown, at least the open air might dissipate some of the unreasonable glamour of this man, and this night.

"Tonight, then, I think," Lucas Lovat said. "Ah, me. My lady will be outraged. But her husband might be more so if I stayed," he added, as if the messenger and all the castle didn't know what bed he'd been roused from. "Good Henry won't rage if I'm late. But kings don't have to—a waggled finger can do more mischief. Ah, well, make ready, and be easy, the fog will be warmer than this. I'll warrant it can't be colder."

There was a hint of fellow feeling in his rueful smile. And such was the charm of that half-smile that when he turned away it was as though the one bit of warmth in the castle had died. The messenger didn't know he'd been basking in it until it was gone from his view, and then he shuddered, as he suddenly felt the chill he'd forgotten. Oh, aye, he decided, shivering with twice the cold now as he watched Lucas Lovat disappear down a turn in the long gray hallway: that was a very dangerous man, just exactly as they'd said. Or not at all a mortal one, as he began to suspect.

Whether it had been rest or sport that Lucas Lovat had been interrupted at (and given the repute of the gentleman, and the fame of the lady of the household, it wasn't hard to guess which it had been), the messenger resigned himself to a long wait in the chill. But it wasn't long before the gentleman appeared again. He came so swiftly and silently, hooded and soft-booted, carrying his cases, but with his cape flowing like the shadows of the night about him, that for a moment the startled messenger worried that the figure drifting so lightly down the long corridor was one of the ghosts rumored to infest the ancient hold. Truly, the shaken messenger thought as he walked out into the night after his new companion, it was marvelous how the man conjured up the most unholy images.

But mounted on adjacent horses that stepped off the courtyard's cobbles to follow the hard-packed earthen road, they were soon equals: both eerily secret as phantoms in the mist. Lucas' sigh was the first human sound to breach the dreaming night, and his voice was filled with mockery and wonder.

"April in England! Faith, what a charming season! Snow on the buttercups and frosted lilacs. The grass was green just yesterday. Look now, it's white with more than fog tonight."

"It will pass," the messenger said defensively, as though he and not his land was being insulted. "The morning sun will burn it off."

"Oh, aye, I remember," Lucas said softly, "I'd just forgotten that I did. It's been years since I've seen an English spring. I've got used to plucking fruit from the trees for my Christmas puddings. I hadn't expected such a cold welcome home. But now, I do remember, it is fitting."

And his self-mocking laughter was the last sound he uttered for many miles as they rode out into the deepening night.

The night was well-advanced and they'd carefully followed the rime-encrusted track for many hours when Lucas spoke again. The messenger was so lost to the cold that he swore his neck creaked as he turned it to hear what the gentleman had to say.

"The horses weary. And there looks to be an inn ahead. Unless things in England have changed entirely since I left her, I doubt we'll see another until long after daybreak. I think Henry will forgive us for sleeping a few hours, how say you?"

The messenger couldn't answer. It wasn't his place to, for all that he'd have given up a few years of his young life for a little warmth and a lot more safety now. He only nodded, for fear that his longing for a stopover might make his voice break if he spoke, as he made his horse follow the gentleman's into the courtyard and began to flex his gloved fist, wondering if his frozen fingers would ever move independently again.

But Lucas Lovat jumped down from his saddle with ease, before the young messenger could dismount, and strode into the dark stable to rouse an ostler as if it were already morning, and a sunny one at that. And when the yawning landlord guided them up an inky, crabbed and twisting stair to his last vacant places, Lucas followed after, his face in the landlord's candle's light alert and bemused, before they were left to the relative darkness of one meager candle . . . and, the messenger noted with sorrow, only one rude bed. He sighed, and knelt as he took his cape and rolled it up so that he could get two widths of it together to lay upon the rushes on the floor.

"There's room for two," Lucas said as he lay on the bed, his arms behind his head. "Do travelers no longer share beds in England? Or do you fear foreign fleas?"

"God save you, sir, I'm just a page," the messenger said, stiff with cold as well as protocol. "I was given this task because I'd know the road even without eyes. I was raised not far from here. I'm not even a proper messenger yet. I don't mind the floor."

"I do," Lucas said absently, "I mind it too well. Take your side of the bed for your own safety. I've just come from the land of the Borgias and have learned to sleep lightly, but I do sleep. And rouse to strange noises that I cannot see the cause for with my sword drawn, and question their sources only after I've silenced them. It would be a pity to never achieve the glory of being a full messenger because you chanced to stir in your sleep below my line of vision, wouldn't it? Take your side of the bed, boy. I'm not famous for minding whom I share my sheets with either, you know."

Well, and that was true enough, but it was hardly his place to laugh, or disagree with anything the gentleman said either, the messenger thought, brightening. So he took his silent place on the bed, fitting himself along its outer edge precisely, as though he'd found a special slot marked with his name to lay his cold and weary body in. He pulled his cloak over himself, and found his consciousness closing in with his eyelids when the voice beside him spoke again.

"What is your name, lad?"

"Philip, Philip de Lacey, sir," the messenger answered slowly, fighting sleep with newfound worry, wondering if he ought to have introduced himself, for although he was new at his elevated task, he knew his insignificance very well, so the matter hadn't occurred to him before.

"Ah, and how old are you, Philip?"

"Nearly eighteen, sir," the messenger answered promptly, deepening his voice to give it authority, for he was suddenly more awake than he'd ever been, wondering what sort of vices English gentlemen might pick up at foreign courts.

"And all of those many years at court? Or at least the last few, so that you can tell me a thing or two before we arrive there?"

Ah, it was gossip, and only that, that the gentleman was after. The messenger sighed and let his lids drift down as he answered with pride, "Eight now. I came to court, by the king's grace, when I was nine. My father's Sir John de Lacey, a Gentleman of the Chamber."

"Eight years," Lucas said thoughtfully. "The better part of your young life, the wandering portion of mine. Tell me, young de Lacey, have things changed that much? In my day Henry had as many spies as this bed has vermin. I'd heard he'd even more now. Why, he's the envy of the Borgias for all his hired ears and eyes. Why summon me, do you suppose?"

The voice had been soft, musing, and companionable in the quiet of the room, and the messenger had just begun to lose its meaning for its cadence when the import of the question registered with him. His father's son, he knew better than to speculate aloud on any question that had the king's name in it, especially to such a man as this.

"I don't suppose," Philip said abruptly, and for all it was true, and a really remarkably clever thing for him to have said, he thought, it ended the conversation, as he'd wished. He discovered, to his amazement, in the ensuing reproachful silence, that he was sorry that it had.

"You're known to be very clever, sir," he said at last,

grudgingly, into the darkness, unsure if his listener was awake to hear.

"Ah." The answer came soft, but not at all sleepily. "Am I? But if I were, would I be here?"

The messenger stirred, and fell silent. And though Lucas waited, wide-eyed, there was, of course, no answer to that but the eventual morning light.

Refreshed, warmed within by the landlord's breakfast and fresh ale, and without by strengthening spring sunlight, they rode out into a dazzling morning. As they rode, after a while, as the sun climbed in the cloudless sky, they spoke to one another, and the messenger found himself replying without caution, and not fearing to do so. The sun showed him many things clearly, and not the least was his own foolish nervousness in the night. Lucas Lovat might have a certain reputation, but even if half of it were true, the matter was surely exaggerated.

For one thing, daylight proved Lucas Lovat younger than candlelight had hinted. Not above thirty, for a certainty. He hadn't registered the cold of the night, and neither did he comment on the newfound warmth this morning, but now he rode with his face uplifted to the sky, and with his face in full sunlight it was clear that the enviably smooth fair skin wasn't creased anywhere, except by laughter, around the full, well-cut lips. And beneath the thin curved brows the arresting large turned-down almond-shaped eyes that dominated the face could be seen to be heavy-lidded by nature, not dissipation, because they were as transparently blue as the spring sky overhead, and their white surround faultless. He wasn't handsome in the exact sense of the word; the nose was straight and thin but too strong, the pugnacious chin too prominent, as were the long bones that made his lean cheeks seem hollow beneath them; nor was his long thick hair actually flaxen—it was lightest brown at the roots, burnt by the sun to straw above.

But charm and magnetism obscured the observable features, and if his wasn't a classic face, it was far better, for it was a mobile, fascinating one. Moonlight had made him seem spectral; daylight showed him no less exotic, but also engagingly mortal. So if the fellow had a name as a lady's delight, how could he help it? Why, he could make even a mere messenger feel flattered by his complete and unswerving regard.

And I, Lucas thought as they rode on to London and he watched young Philip de Lacey relax under his warming smile and begin prattling about his position, and his father's, and all his expectations and hopes, was never, never so young—no, never.

Soon, for all he continued to smile and nod, he stopped listening; there was no new thing for him to hear in the boy's eager reminiscences. He'd already found out far more than young Philip could know about his court and his world even as he'd sailed across the sea and back to England once again. Back to England! That was the fact that his mind keep turning on as Philip rattled on, as they rode on through the countryside. It was England beneath his horse's hooves, it was her very air he breathed, and for all he'd left sunlight and laughter and lovers behind him to come on what might prove to be a fool's errand in this cold country where he'd too few friends and too many terrors awaiting him, he couldn't help but be awed and glad of that one fact—this was England. He was home again.

But it had changed, even as he had. He had to discover how much. There was an adjustment to be made before he could judge what had altered most—himself or his native land—in these past years. Even the landscape seemed more alien than he remembered. Surely there were more enclosed and cultivated fields now, even though there was more forest than he was used to seeing in the ancient lands he'd lately come from. He was accustomed to landscapes where each acre was marked and busy with labor or growth: patches of orchards, neat grape arbors, stands of olive trees, even orderly rows of sunflowers, and everywhere, peasants clothed as gay as the bounty they harvested. Here there seemed a dearth of people in the fields and lanes, and those that were there were all in peasant's brown, as commonplace as the flocks of sparrows that they scattered in the fields they tended.

To his overstimulated eyes, England seemed dull, drear brown and gray now, with just a faint wash of promising green over all, as though even the spring was less loudly generous than the ones he'd got to know. He needed to use a process of reduction in order to see the truth, he realized. For here he wouldn't be greeted with theatrical embraces and smacking kisses, loud laughter and as much ado as he was used to, either—although it might yet be that he would eventually be more warmly welcomed here than anywhere else on earth.

But laughter covered over many things, and the widest embrace could be the one that concealed a dagger up a sleeve. He'd known men to toast their hosts from a poisoned cup even as their health was drunk to, and who better than he knew how deeply love and hope could be buried from view? No, for all he missed the gaiety and ease of life abroad, he was home now, and if there was a just and merciful God, here he'd stay until he was one with his native soil. . . . Only not too soon, please, he thought as he automatically smiled at something young Philip was smiling at, because he'd learned long ago how nicely a mirrored expression made up for lack of attention.

Who better to know such artifice? He'd been in the king's service since his nineteenth year, and so he'd had eight years of secret servitude to the crown now. And most of them abroad, because he'd passed most of his life away from this gray little island of his birth and first youth. He'd not noticed any lack of sun and color in that childhood, because his life had been warm and exciting enough for any lad—until he was just turned twelve, the night his father died. Then, despite his resolve to be brave and endure, complete darkness had set in. Because his brother was gone soon after, his family shattered, his home vanished, he'd been betrayed at every turn by the damnable double turns of fate and war. He'd resisted leaving even then, vowing to fight against the tide. But he'd been beyond fortunate to have found a foster father wise enough to overrule him and send him away to heal beneath the warm sun of Italy. To heal, to grow, to bide until he was old enough to return and volunteer to serve the king, so as to be able to live in hope of revenge.

And what should a clever, bitter, nobly born, and well-bred boy burning for justice do to earn favor in such an age, at such a court as Royal Henry's? Why, spy, of course. It only needed money, and his adoptive father had that. And a safely noble name, which he'd been given, and a way about him, which God alone had granted.

And the king's goodwill, of course, without which he'd have neither home nor life.

Then, he thought wryly, a hopeful youth must go back to Italy and visit France—traverse the Continent, and charm and deal and delight; be a trader and make a fortune in goods, and a vaster one in information. What are the Medicis, the Orsinis, the Fuggers, the Borgias, and their cousins doing? No matter, what are they planning to do? Never mind God's anointment, merchant princes are the making or unmaking of royal ones; a clever man soon learned that. So travel the old spice and silk and gold routes as one of the unseen army that traveled from market to palace, from bed to board to dark meeting places so as to whisper to tell the king how his friends and foes went. And now and again, return and bend a knee to the anointed king so that he might remember your face when you arise and leave again. And so that you remembered never to forget his.

Aye, Lucas Lovat thought as he continued to seem to smile at the young messenger's story, the very way to win success. Do all of this until you are as rich as you desire, and sick to the heart at how no one trusts you, as you trust no other man. Then go on until you are richer than you care, and no longer care if you have a heart at all. Then, and only then, you are ready to return. It only needs the summons. And now he had that.

He focused on his companion again, and sighed. The boy was young enough to have grown an inch in the night, and his fine clothes were disgraced at ankle and wrist by mute testimony to just such a rapid pace of growth. He'd a thatch of unlucky red hair, and beneath it, an open face with an embarrassment of freckles. God save the lad, Lucas thought in wonder, what had that supposedly wise father been thinking of to bind such as he to service in wily Henry's court?

"Westminster Palace?" Lucas said suddenly, frowning, belatedly paying attention to a word he'd caught in Philip's tangled tale to do with another page who'd begged for the honor of his escort, and lost. "I'm expected at Westminster? But I thought the king rested with the queen at Greenwich—she'd a babe due by summer, I'd heard."

"Alas, that came to nothing—a month past, poor lady,"

Philip replied. "She's still there, with the children and her ladies. The king's at Westminster, and charged me to bring you to him there. He often stays there without her."

"Stays there, and everywhere else, without her," would be the truer statement, Lucas thought, but said no more, too secretly pleased and grateful that he'd be spared the sight of his queen and her brood to comment further.

They paused for a brief meal and took to the road again, riding hard now, anxious to get to London's walls before the night fell, riding onward even though the dusk grew deeper gray, and a worried look replaced Philip's usually amiable smile. He knew that the nearer they came to the great city, the greater the danger of man-made mischief on the road, for robbers, like spiders, set their webs where there was most frequent passage of their prey.

But "They say these roads are difficult by night, sir," was all that he dared to say, though his eyes constantly slewed to the edges of the road as more and more cottages came into view, and less and less daylight showed around them.

"Sooth, I'll be more difficult than anything we chance to meet if I have to wait another night before I arrive," was all Lucas said, but he said it harshly. It quieted his companion, and when he glanced at the silent boy, he saw admiration, and not fear, in Philip's awed eyes.

It wasn't courage; he really felt the need for speed more than he felt fear. He seldom felt fear in any case. He didn't count himself brave. More likely, he thought, when he thought about it at all, he'd learned to ignore fear, since living with it intimately for so long had blunted it for him. For now he no more felt the force of it, even in danger, than he'd notice any other omnipresent sense of his, such as touch or taste. But he did feel those things. In fact, he noted that the hour was late because he became aware of hunger. He disregarded it, as always, but as they took a bend in the road and he saw what lay ahead, he couldn't ignore the sudden surge of a different hunger, more acute and overwhelming than any he'd felt in a very long time.

As they came into view of the city walls, he was gripped by a wave of longing and joy and a tumult of other emotions he'd forgotten, so moved that he actually saw his own hands shaking on the reins. His mount missed a step and lost its steady, even beat, even as his own heart did. It was only for a half-second, but that loss of control of his horse and himself almost entirely unmanned him. Philip saw nothing but the horse's little dance of distraction, and the tightening of his companion's generous mouth as he reined it in. But Lucas was shocked at himself. He hadn't expected to be so overset. He'd returned to London only five years past. But now at last there was the possibility that he might never have to leave it again, and surely it was that which had thrown his heart into his throat and made him bereft of breath.

Still, there was no excuse for such a lapse—at least, he wouldn't allow one. And so he rode on, his face set grim and cold again, as though, Philip de Lacey thought apprehensively as he eyed him sidewise, he really was transformed into a different creature at the coming of the night. They rode side by side and silently as they came into London, riding in beneath the great crenellated western gate before it closed, and entered the town in the last hour of the dying day, in the last hour of lingering light.

Lucas looked about eagerly, and yet as they rode into the heart of the city, his spirits fell. There was a time when he'd thought this city the pinnacle of modern man's attainments. But now, to his tutored eye, it seemed less beautiful than that queen of graceful cities, Venice; less civilized than her learned brother, Rome; less elegant than clever Florence; and not half so sophisticated as envious Paris. Even now, on this longed-for return, even in the gracious flattery of twilight, the city seemed diminished. After all his travels, this, his beloved lost home, seemed primitive, backward, awkward in style and civilization, compared to the great cities where he'd lately been.

But, he reminded himself, a boy's home, however noble, always shrinks when the man returns to it. And also, it was the twilight hour—the least typical time to see this city, too late for respectable trade, too early for the sport and commerce of the night. Even now the last few shop windows were being boarded over as the merchants and guild members of London ended their long workday. Only moments before, there would have been traffic and noise, masses of people on foot and on horseback, and the usual tumult of London's main business—business—would have deafened them. More than seventy-five thousand human souls crowded together within the walls of London, but now there were few passersby in the streets. Only an occasional robed apprentice hurrying to his master's bidding, or a cowled monk hastening to his, was abroad to note their passage. For the several hundred scents of London's dinners rode high in the air.

Young Philip knew his way, and Lucas followed without comment. It was difficult for him to remember which districts they rode through now, with the usual gaily colored trade signs obscured and the bustle of commerce stilled. But an observant eye might note the guild arms on the houses they passed, and if not, Lucas decided on a smile, even the dullest nose could remark the differences between the streets of the goldsmiths and the grocers, the skinners and the ironmongers. But those scents, however rank, were yet familiar, and brought him ever closer to his home.

"Westward even now, young Philip?" he asked in surprise as they rode past a perfectly decent inn that he'd expected to stop at. "Is that wise? Henry knows I've traveled leagues to reach him, but do you think he wants to see evidence of it on my boots and face? Surely it would be best to stop and wash and rest awhile. Kings, like battles, are best faced fresh in the morning, don't you agree?" he asked.

Philip's face was dim in the growing dusk, but his voice was sure. "I warrant it's so, good sir, but I've my orders, and for all I'd welcome respite, they are clear. 'At once,' he said, and so I must take him at his word."

There was a moment's pause and then the young voice asked more hesitantly as his horse slowed, "Marry, sir, but now I wonder too, how say you? I'truth, I hadn't thought to ask, but to appear in all my dirt before the king? I'd thought to bring you to him at once, since he'd said at once, but now . . ."

"Be easy, lad," Lucas said, smiling. " 'At once' means 'before you possibly can' to a king, and so you're right to hurry. Never mind my doubt, I can wash in a palace as well as at an inn, if needs must."

He rode on, glad to be home again, pleased to be at

is journeying, curious as to his king's sum-
prepared by training and by habit to let the
fold in its own due time. It was too dark now to
t much but the forms of the wood and stone and
thatched houses around him; even Philip was only a
caped and crouched silhouette beside him now. But above,
the sky retained a last glow. Glancing up, he saw a
purple sky streaked with gold that foretold a good mor-
row. His smile faded as he noticed what dominated the
skyscape, looming over all London that lay beneath its
stone feet. And so he looked away at once, turning his
head abruptly from the outline of the Tower, and rode
onward toward the dying light, to Westminster Palace,
his king's pleasure, and his fate.

Now, here, Lucas thought, is majesty at last. Men
came running to take their horses from them as quickly
as they'd been challenged and passed into the palace
courtyard. Torches blazed in many hands, and more atop
each parapet and wall, so many that they made the night
sky insignificant, driving it back, making it a mere background for the works of man. The palace itself, in all its
size and glory, stolid and forthright as its outer wards
were, was so vast and richly furnished, Lucas thought as
he and Philip were led down gilded halls and through
frescoed passages, that it was fit for any sovereign, and
ranked with the best in any land he'd visited. But his
admiration for architecture was stilled when he saw who
awaited him in the anteroom he was led to.

The well-dressed, short, gray-bearded older man and
the round-faced elderly lady stood side by side and stared
at him with growing but tentative smiles on their faces.
Lucas came forward at a rush, surprise and delight in his
incandescent eyes.

"Father!" he cried, and took the older man hard by
the shoulders as he looked down into his smiling face.
"You never said you'd be here. And Mother!" he added
gladly, releasing the stocky man and taking the diminu-
tive lady into his arms in such haste that her wimple was
set askew. "How long has it been since I've set eyes on
you, my lady?" he asked in a wondering whisper, before
he added, more loudly, "I just saw this rogue yesteryear,
in Amsterdam. But you! Let me look at you. Faith! Why,
the rascal must be feeding you on potions of powdered

bats and topaz. They say that's what preserves eternal youth. Confess! You're bound to him if you want to remain so wondrous fair, aren't you? Fie! I see it now. The knave! Why else should you stay with him, when every gentleman in the land must be clamoring for you? It can't be mere loyalty or habit—I've never seen such steadfastness given for so little cause," he said, laughing at last as he hugged her closer, and she tried to encompass him in her arms in turn, trying so hard that the bottoms of her little slippers left the floor.

When he set her on her feet again, her eyes were red, and her husband had to run his sleeve under his nose for a moment and pretend to help his wife straighten her coif before he spoke. Yet, Philip thought from where he watched in the shadows, although the three of them stood mute for a moment, it seemed only the elder pair was struggling with their emotions. Because pleased as Lucas appeared to be, it was hard to tell if he'd been moved, aside from the warmth of his words. In no way, then, neither face, nor form, nor attitude, was he like his parents, but still they gazed at him with love that bordered on reverence. For himself, Philip thought, he'd like a son whose face and figure showed exactly who'd begot him. But then, noting the age of the doting couple, he saw that Lucas was obviously their consolation child, got at the eleventh hour. And too, he decided, staring at the graceful form of the tall figure before them, any parents might dote on such a son, however unlike themselves, maybe *especially* unlike themselves, at that: so tall, so fair, so quick of mind and body—for all his fine lineaments and narrowness of bone, a champion at the joust and ring; for all his caution, a master of diplomacy—and much renowned. And with the special blindness of parents, they might make themselves unaware of the other things he was said to excel at too.

"Well," Sir Charles Lovat of Ilchester said a shade too heartily, in an attempt to disguise the way his voice trembled, "try to keep her away when she'd heard you were coming. Rode all the way up to London without a murmur; not a word of complaint if it was to see her darling boy."

"Whereas if she has to travel so much as to town on a festival day, her laments can be heard throughout the

land: 'Faith! The road's all muddy . . . look out, there's a
ditch . . . God keep us! Blockhead, can't you keep your
horse steady?','" Lucas cried in an uncanny mocking
falsetto. "Oh, I do remember," he added as the lady
colored up and hid her face, and her husband laughed
loudly.

"Marry, it is good to see you. How well you look . . .
but your hair," his father said, staring at him.

"Aye, so fair . . ." his lady put in tremulously as she
raised a hand to touch it.

Lucas caught that quivering hand and kissed it. "It was
not just the fashion, but the sun of Italy," he answered
lightly. "Only a Moor remains dark in that clime. I'd be
much remarked on if I had," he explained.

"Oh. Well, it's no matter," Sir Charles said. "What is,
is how long we can keep you with us. Do you stay long
this time?" he asked, and a sudden quiet descended on
the room, as if, "Do you stay for good this time?" had
been the question asked instead.

"I am, as always, at the king's pleasure," Lucas answered gently.

And as if he'd been standing waiting, listening patiently for the exact moment at which to enter, a liveried
young page came up out of the shadows, and after making a deep obeisance, said, "Good sirs, lady, God save
you masters, the king wishes to see Lucas Lovat, and
now, by your leave."

The lady made as if to catch at her son's sleeve, the
older gentleman started, but in a moment both had recovered their composure. This time, Philip de Lacey was
surprised to see it was their son who reacted. For although his face was just as calm as ever, it had suddenly
gone white, as chalky as if it had been carved on a
sepulcher for himself, and it seemed he no longer breathed.

And then he moved, drew in a breath and laughed,
and was his poised, immaculate self again.

"By your leave, Father, Mother, I go now. I'll see you
as soon as I've discovered what it is our king wants of
me, for in all his haste to summon me, he didn't say."

"By my faith, I don't know either," his father said
hoarsely. And because his face was in no way like his
son's, and either had no guile or had lost the knack of it
due to his age, there was nothing but fear in his expres-

sion then, as there was nothing but dismay in his wife's eyes.

"Wait for me. I doubt I'll be long. Come, Philip, and take your bow for your swift pace and the successful completion of your first errand," Lucas said as he moved to the door.

As Philip stirred himself, lifting his back from the wall he'd rested against, the page stopped him with an up-lifted hand.

"Only Lucas Lovat," the boy said softly.

Such was the silence in the room, they all heard. But by the time they looked to see Lucas' reaction, he was gone from them.

2

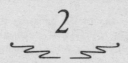

He went down to one knee and bowed his glowing head until it touched that bent knee before raising his eyes to see the signal giving him permission to arise again.

"Sire," Lucas said, all obedience, all dignity.

"Lovat," Henry said, as though that were greeting, welcome, and explanation enough.

But this king was scant with words, so each one weighed heavily. Lucas stood before his sovereign and gazed at him and held his tongue, for it wasn't his place to ask the questions most natural to him, and he never forgot himself in the presence of power, wielded worthily or not. They studied each other in silence.

Henry Tudor was tall, almost Lucas' own height; almost youthful, only a decade or so his senior—although he appeared much older, and thin, with a narrow and pinched face that spoke of some terrible impoverishment in boyhood. He'd long thin drab hair and a long thin mouth, and small gray hooded eyes beneath his scanty brows—everything about him spoke of thrift as eloquently as he did not. Despite his black velvet finery, he looked more like a miser than a sovereign, more like a merchant than a king. But so he was a frugal, watchful, careful man. He was nothing like his predecessors: there was none of the golden splendor that had been the easy, affable Edward about him, nor even a trace of the powerful, restless, nervous tension that had marked ill-fated Richard's presence. But there was clever calculation within this almost invisible king, for those who could sense it, and Lucas could always sense danger, however concealed it was.

"You are come in good time," Henry said at last, after he'd studied his guest.

"You have young de Lacey to thank for that, sire. He wouldn't stop to tie his breeches. I don't doubt that if you'd ordered him to more speed, he wouldn't even have stopped to make water. A conscientious lad, that," Lucas said, all at his ease, all affability.

"I don't remember you as being so fair," Henry said, fixing his gaze on Lucas' bright hair.

"Ah, 'tis my folly to be fashionable," Lucas said on a sigh. "Alas, but what's fashion there is bizarre here, I see. I changed my hose to these drab black ones this very morning so as to be more acceptable. Still, all Englishmen see is my hair. My parents, too, remarked on this yellow crop before they so much as noticed me. But it's utmost style in Italy, sire. The sun and a judicious application of saffron or onion skins will do it for any man, unless he's got a touch of the Moor. I didn't care to smell like a dinner pot, so it was the sun and some lemon for me. Both Italian ladies and their gentlemen sit outdoors until you'd think their brains would bake like pies, in order to achieve the golden crusts they seek. The ladies guard their skins, so they wear straw hats with holes poked in them, and pull their hair through. I thank some unknown ancestor for the ease with which mine bleached. It made me very much admired . . . why, your own lady's golden tresses are famous there, and spoken of most enviously too, your majesty," he added.

But as if that last reminded the king of the trivial nature of their conversation, or Lucas' easy smile did, Henry looked away before he spoke again. As his king paused, Lucas gazed about the room to which he'd been summoned. It wasn't well-lit, at least to a man used to the radiant palaces of spendthrift princes in lands that were in love with the sun; it seemed ill-lit and dull. But it was undoubtedly a room a frugal man could feel comfortable in, with only a few torches and candles and the hearth fire for illumination. Still, that intermittent rosy glow showed riches befitting a king: some of them inherited from less lucky monarchs, no doubt, but others just as fine, and new. Because for all his care with a coin, Henry knew what befitted a throne, and whatever his own tastes, was wise enough to know that men tend to value a king only as much as he himself seems to do. And so Lucas noted in one swift bright glance that there were several ornate hangings, and fine carved chests to fit up against them, along the painted walls, and thick colorful tapestries beneath his feet as well, and heavily carved chairs with embroidered cushions that he'd not yet been invited to rest himself upon. Then he noted one dark shadow behind the king, and he froze, and stood arrested in his place. That one small lapse from his studied ease was noticed by Henry at once. He smiled, and turned his head for a moment to look at the form behind him as though he'd just seen it himself. Then he glanced back to Lucas.

"Oh. You hesitate?" Henry asked. "No need. This is Brother Robert. Pay no mind, Lovat. He's often close by me. He's a grey friar and a very holy man, and is by way of being a confessor—a confidant of mine, because his only confidant's not in reach of any lesser man."

Lucas bowed from the waist. "Your pardon, good brother, if I seemed startled," he said sweetly. "I'm lately come from the chambers of his excellence the pope himself, and his confidant's his son—and any wench his delighted eye happens upon that day."

The friar didn't move or speak; his face remained concealed in the shadows of his cowl. Lucas was reminded of the tomb of Henry the Bold that he'd seen in France, shown to him by the delighted Henry himself before he'd come to occupy it. It had been a carved representation of a band of hooded monks, black as death's deepest night: eyeless, faceless beneath their great cowls, they struggled into eternity with the heavy casket that rested on their obsidian shoulders. They'd personified death and grief to him, just as this lurking friar did—as did all men who hung in the shadows behind kings.

"Popes are infallible," Henry snapped, with a trace of temper, "or so we are taught. And this is England. Be grateful I'm no theologian, Lovat, to debate or to deny you your freedom to. Howbeit, Brother Robert is no pope, no ordinary man either. He's pious."

There were both threat and finality in that, and so Lucas swept into a deep and gracious bow again.

"By your grace, forgive me my rude tongue, sire, brother. I'm a contentious, thoughtless fellow. Forgive my casual comments on holy matters, I pray you. I forgot myself. Where I've just come from, no one takes His Holiness that seriously, except to his face, of course. I'm too used to his son's twitting him; my friend Caesar was forever teasing his father—our holy one—you see."

It was too smoothly said, too charmingly made an apology for the thin suggestion of a threat to be taken seriously. This was too clever a gentleman to really believe that the possibility of his injury or death on English soil would roil international waters. Yet the reminder of powerful friends and excellent service to the crown because of those associations was well-taken and drew an appreciative half-smile to Henry's pale lips. He nodded. The friar remained still.

Lucas smiled back seraphically, but for all his smiles, he was troubled. Henry was a religious man, but he'd never known him to be a stupidly devout one. In Lucas' opinion, any man who trusted a priest was a fool, because priests, when all was said, were only mortal men, and Lucas had never trusted any of them implicitly either. Henry swore allegiance to Archbishop Morton, that was true, but the bishop was a man who'd helped put him on the throne, and was as good a politician, spy, and tactician as any Lucas had ever met. But he'd never met a holy man, in any guise, and so doubted the reason given for the presence of the friar. Lucas had rested in some of the most labyrinthian courts in the world, and never doubted this was one of the best of them, despite his king's solemn manner and holy demeanor. If he insisted on Brother Robert's presence, it only meant the man was another element of danger to be taken into account, for Henry Tudor had one of the best spy networks in the world. He should know, Lucas thought wryly, being a part of it himself, and yet having survived to this day.

"What do you know of Perkin Warbeck?" Henry asked suddenly.

But he didn't catch Lucas off-balance, for all he'd been expecting anything but that question. After a life of deceit, he was quick on his feet, and was ready for Henry, and men like him, at all times. He paused to think—not only of his truthful answer, but of the one best to give, the reason for the question, and how he fitted into the matter. He spoke up almost at once, deciding that in this case, honesty could do no harm.

"The pretender? But his career is ended. You've caught him, confessed him, and hold him fast, last I heard."

When he got no answer, he shrugged, understanding that Henry wanted more than what he'd heard.

"We all knew of his confession, in Italy," Lucas went on. "An impostor, like Simnel was, only not merely claiming to be a nephew to Edward Plantagenet, as Simnel did, but instead swearing to be Edward's lost son: Richard of York. And trained in his paces by the same bitch, Margaret of Burgundy, to punish you for succeeding her brother Edward—or to spite you for overthrowing her brother Richard. Sooth! Who can fathom a vengeful female mind? Another year, another claimant to royal blood. And this one a resurrected prince, no less. 'Hohum,' says Italy. But they hear it's a plausible impostor with the mark of the Plantagenets on his face and form, and on his honeyed tongue. Neither is that unreasonable, since Edward sowed bastards as his peasants did grain, and so say all who support you. As always with these impostors, sire, those who champion you applaud his defeat and call him rogue. But those who bear you a grudge or malice persist in proclaiming him the rightful king, and would if Christ himself—begging your sweet pardon, Brother Robert—came down off his cross and swore to his falseness."

Then, faintly disappointed to see no reaction at all from the friar, Lucas added with genuine curiosity, "Does he still live?"

"He does," Henry said. " A pleasant fellow. He ornaments my court here."

Oho, Lucas thought, twist and twist again, King Henry. Well done. A dead pretender, especially such a plausible one, might become a dead rightful king in time. And such a man, however much dead, can yet overset a throne. A live pretender might yet dwindle to a fool.

"Ah, and does he tend the turnspit in the royal kitchens, as does his brother-in-ambition, Simnel, as we heard in Italy?" Lucas asked. "That would be a lovely touch.

Why, sire, you're the envy of the Italian courts for that jest. To take your would-be usurper, defeated in honest battle, and put him to work—not fertilizing your fields from beneath them, but turning roasts in your kitchens? Sweating over the preparation of your dinner meats instead of your downfall? And to have him earnestly grateful for it, as they say he is?" Lucas laughed. "A masterstroke, sire. They're all admiration and envy for that in the courts of the Borgias and the diminished ranks of the Medicis, and only wish they'd thought of such a revenge for a foe first."

But now he'd gone too far, and knew it. Henry's sallow face grew cold and his eyes narrowed. Before he could speak, Lucas spoke up again, lightly. "Indeed, sire, that's the face they put on it in the corrupt courts from which I lately come. It's to be hoped, of course, that your humanity and forgiving nature, your forbearance and the great generosity of your act, impress themselves upon them and serve as an example to them in God's good time."

Clever, quick, capricious Lovat, Henry thought, and smiled his thin smile as Lucas waited, wondering if he'd been swift enough to save himself. For no matter how adroitly he danced, he never forgot that seemingly slow Henry was as quick with his wits as he himself was with his tongue. Henry was the sort of man who might never think to make the jest, or find it very funny when it was made, but only a fool forgot that he'd always understand it very well. Henry Tudor's was a different sort of mind, only that, but just as keen, and perhaps, Lucas admitted, even a more circuitous one than his own.

Royal pardon was made as quickly as the retraction had been, and bore the same sort of sting within it.

"So it is to be hoped. I have enough enemies as it is, and don't need to count mere mistaken men as new ones."

Lucas inclined his head, but kept his eyes open, for he saw the monk move into the light. For all the good it did, he thought without humor as he saw the monk speaking softly to the king, since the folds of the cowl obscured his face entirely, so that not even brightest noon would pierce that shade. He'd seldom met such a heavily cowled friar, but had heard of them. They lived in the world, counted themselves teachers and helpmeets of men, but however much they abandoned the isolation of the monastery, they took the cloister with them just as a snail carried its home on its back. Their veiling signified total sacrifice of self for the sake of purity.

Here indeed was humility, Lucas thought wryly: to hide one's face, whether it was a beautiful or beastly one, from the sight of mankind forever, lest temptation show itself in any way—by flattery, or lustful glances, or even pity. Such mendicant monks hid their identity from all but God. They claimed to be friends to all, and answerable only to God, vowing lives of utmost poverty, chastity, obedience, and anonymity.

And very clever it was, too, Lucas thought with genuine admiration, for out of his billowy grey habit, Brother Robert could be any man, anywhere. He seemed slender, but such a wealth of sacking tied at the waist could make any shape it chose, and though he seemed tall, any sort of footwear beneath the long skirts could achieve that. For he was as anonymous as the darkness he stepped back into now, and even his voice had been so soft that Lucas' quick ears caught only the susurration of it before he was done speaking in secret with his king, as he supposedly did with his God. Lucas would sooner trust a hangman with his shoes than this so-humble holy friar of Henry's with his least thought.

"I see, it's as I was told," Henry said, as though there'd been no interruption. "But what do you think of Perkin Warbeck, Lovat?"

"I?" Lucas asked, using that extra heartbeat to formulate his answer, again deciding on the truth, since he saw no harm in it for himself. "I think it is exactly as it is said."

And then, hearing the silence, and realizing Henry wanted still more, he gave him all. "After all, I've seen him close, and often, as you might have guessed, sire. Well, and if a gentleman claiming to be the lost Richard of York, and so now King Richard IV of England, was roaming about Europe, gathering crowns to back him up, as well as lists of common men ready to take his hand, it would hardly be reasonable for me not to arrange to have a look at him, would it?"

"Crown, and lists of men to help, as well as to be rewarded if he succeeded, I heard," Henry said dryly.

He hadn't been asked to sit, Lucas realized, because a man's legs sometimes told truths his face and voice would not. And something so decisive was being asked, and judged, that he could feel it in every bone in his body. But he was as much an athlete as he was a courtier, so he continued to stand straight, and moved nothing but his head to the side, and his lips in a smile, as he raised his arms in a gesture of helpless submission as he replied.

"In sooth, sire, is there need to ask? If I'd been one of those men, you'd have known it by now, I'm sure. And I'd have known you did, of that I am certain. No, I saw him at Frederick's funeral in Vienna, marching with a royal guard as befitted the station they decided it prudent to agree he was; I watched him at court in France, in Flanders; I even spoke with him awhile once, a long time since, in Amsterdam. But I never pledged anything but his health in a toast as we drank. I marked how he took in the courts on the Continent, marry, I could see how he could have enchanted the Irish, and beguiled even someone as wily as Scots James. For he's beautiful, daring, princely, and charming, with Plantagenet eyes and a facile tongue, but whoever he is, he is not Prince Richard returned to us. On that, I would swear my life."

And since that was entirely honest, and since all three men in the room knew that was precisely what he was being, there was only a second's more consideration before Henry unbent, seated himself, and waved Lucas to another, albeit lower, chair nearby.

"Much the same could be said of you," Henry said as he settled himself, and Brother Robert stepped into the gloom behind his chair. Lucas sat, lifting mild, inquiring eyes even as he did so, as Henry added, "Especially with that hair, I remark it now, except for the nose, and the fact that you've less flesh, you've much the look of him . . . and the sound of him too, at that."

"Aye, I and a few hundred others," Lucas said as he reached out with a steady hand to take a cup of wine his king proferred to him, "for though my mother was faithful to my father, I can't swear to her grandmother, can I?

And we know how successfully inconstant some of the
gentlemen of that line were," he added, and waited for
Henry to appreciate how adroitly worded that had been,
incriminating the Plantagenet males, with never a hint of
a word against the females of the line, since one of them
was his own queen.

When the king nodded at Lucas with something very
like bitter humor in his thin face, Lucas said more seriously, "But I only seek to serve the throne, not sit upon
it. As you well know, sire," he added, greatly daring, for
he knew the time of inquisition was past, and the moment for the other reason for his being summoned was
near, "else I wouldn't be here, would I?"

It was too true to even comment upon, and as Lucas
sipped at the overly sweet wine that Henry favored,
Henry spoke again.

"Perkin has a way with him. I hold him prisoner.
Here. He's known the force of my army, my anger, as
well as my forgiveness. Because he's unimpaired. He
only kissed the rack and we had his confession, whole."

Lucas sat quietly, swallowing down the sticky wine
with the same calm forbearance as he did the story, since
he doubted "Perkin" was even the impostor's name. It
was more likely a thing gotten with the rest of the confession they'd written and instructed him to sign when they'd
shoved it beneath his pain-blurred eyes.

"Which doesn't surprise me, since he proved such a
warrior at Taunton," Henry said with a sneer in his
voice, for he himself was a tireless fighter, and couldn't
understand how the impostor could have fled the field
that day. What he understood less became apparent as he
went on. "But although he ran from the battle and into
my arms, he rests too easy here. Why? It makes me
uneasy. Yes, I give him his freedom, he runs tame here
in my household, but he must know he could just as
easily have remained in the Tower, or in an unmarked
grave within it, and yet . . . and yet," Henry said harshly,
with some strong but unreadable emotion beginning to
show in his tense face, making Lucas reconsider the
reason for the dimness in which he kept this room, ". . .
and yet, still, knowing this, he acts as though he were
himself king here. And so although I'm certain he knows

his every breath is taken at my charity, I don't trust him."

"He's hardly 'free,' sire," Lucas said softly, thinking of the weight of the pretender's invisible fetters. "He is, I understand, kept apart from his lady, is he not?"

Henry relaxed. "Trust you, Lovat, to think *that* the hardest trial a man can suffer," he said on an indulgent smile.

"I have my preoccupations," Lucas answered lightly, as if the thought of his reputation as a seducer didn't sting. "As do most men," he added, as though he never knew that Henry's constant distance from his queen wasn't much remarked upon, even as his odd fidelity to her was, "for, having a lovely wife, as they say he does, most men would find abstinence bitter punishment, even the good, chaste brother must see that."

"Punishment? Say simple sense, instead—should I help him breed a race of pretenders to bedevil my Arthur with in his time?" Henry asked, genuinely angry, rising to his feet in his agitation, even as Lucas leapt to his, wondering whether his hand had been too heavy on the needle for once, if he'd struck too deep, and gone too far this time.

He seldom miscalculated, but the oblique reference to Henry's relationship, or lack of it, with his queen, had nettled the king more than he'd have dreamed. It was a political marriage; there was little reason to think it anything else, indeed, there was much evidence it was a difficult thing for Henry to accept even so. A usurping Tudor bonded in wedlock for the sake of expediency with a Yorkist daughter—the victor wedding to the departed but well-remembered and beloved golden Edward's daughter, and she also the niece of his defeated bitter enemy, Richard, must be a bitter union for both. For the lady—to be wed to a stranger-conqueror, even though that was a woman's lot; for Henry—to be compared to one predecessor and then the other by his wife as well as by the nation, and likely to be as despised by her as her line was by him—it was no wonder he was wary of her. Indeed, it was a wonder he dared turn his back on her in the marriage bed when he was done with breeding with her. Which must be why he so seldom did. He always left her

soon after his efforts in that tense bed began to bear
fruit—each time, and from the first.

In fact, it was secretly jested that Henry dared meet his
queen only like that—face-to-face, in bed, when she was
bare, with no place to conceal weapons. It was said that
holding a disputed throne, he remained faithful for fear
of offending the nation, not the lady, for he showed little
desire to please her. He'd even withheld her coronation
until he'd gotten her with child, and nothing seemed to
have changed since that first year. Although he treated
her with courtesy, he never stayed with her for very long,
except to get heirs on her, or inspect them when they saw
the light, or bury them if they failed to survive infancy.

Or so they said. Now, belatedly, Lucas realized the
folly of disregarding one of his chiefest rules, for he
never acted on common knowledge, preferring the witness of his own eyes. And he'd never seen the king and
queen together.

But Henry didn't remain angry with him long. Or else
it was that he needed him more than he was vexed with
him. In either case, a murmur from Brother Robert
distracted the king, and when he sat again, he looked at
Lucas expressionlessly. Then, though Lucas showed no
more emotion that his king did, he was genuinely alarmed,
knowing it was just as dangerous to be needed by a king
as it was to be useless to him.

"I have discovered almost every hand behind the pretender's schemes," Henry said bluntly, "and have had
their heads for it. Dean Worsley, Lord Fitzwalter, Lord
Stanley, Lord Audley, the lawyer Flamank, Lord Stanley
. . . many, many, too many others." His voice dwindled
and he grew still. Lucas knew Henry was genuinely moved,
for he seemed not to have noticed that he'd named the
perfidious Stanley twice, although that unlucky nobleman
had had only the one head he'd lost for his crime of
supposedly saying, when Perkin Warbeck first appeared:
"If the lad is indeed Richard, then he should indeed be
king." For all that brave Stanley had fought side by side
with Henry on Bosworth field, he'd lost his life for that
one mis-saying, and it might be that the king regretted it.
Although, being the man he was, Lucas thought, it was
more likely he regretted the necessity, not the deed.

"Too many others," Henry went on abruptly, "and too many others I can't reach abroad. But I know them, and know they'd intrigue to put a crown on a pig and call him rightful heir, if they could. Margaret, of course, will hate me until she dies." Then he paused, and smiled, as though he admired that. "And Charles of France?" he asked. "Why, France never loved England, and Flanders will meddle where she will, as Rome, or any ambitious land in Europe. And Ireland, where it all began? She's ever ready to make mischief for us. Scotland? But I can see why James took this impostor so close to his bosom—going so far as to war for him, and giving him a wife from his own house. He and Perkin are of an age, and he's just such a dashing, impudent, rash boy himself."

Henry's cold, thin voice was trying to be warm; he almost chuckled, as though the war on his borders was nothing but a boyish prank. Such divine forgiveness, Lucas thought, amused, as if no one knew that James and Henry had begun to repair the rift the war for Perkin's rights had started, and had opened negotiations for wedding Henry's half-grown daughter to the hot-headed Scot.

"As for the others here, I know there are those who loved the house of York and will until their last breaths. Shall I hate them? I admire loyalty. I hope to satisfy them with children of the union of our houses. If they can never love me, they may be more comfortable with the idea of the king to come after me: my Arthur. If not, it little matters. I have their names, and their directions. All, I think. But I prefer, of course, to know absolutely. I thought that if I had a clever, smooth young fellow, a new face, from abroad, but at my service," he continued as Lucas listened closely, knowing the line had been cast and his fortunes hung in the balance, "and one with a way with ladies, who might make himself pleasant to some females in strategic places—why, then I would know all."

"Ah," said Lucas, and bit back a bitter smile at the sudden thought of how he was to be used for his sex, in his own way, just as the queen was, in hers. Although he'd almost forgotten the unmoving figure in the gloom behind the king, he was surprised to find himself almost as embarrassed for his presence as he suddenly was for his own reputation.

"Such confidence in my . . . charm—I'm flattered," he said dryly.

"Oh, I've heard you've other—more prodigious, shall I say?—tools," Henry said, and the twist of his lips showed he was well aware of the play on words, and perhaps even of Lucas' distaste for his opinion of his assets.

"I see. So you'll give me the names of those ladies you hope will be susceptible here?" Lucas asked with not so much as a grimace.

"No," Henry answered, "I've no need for your services here. You may stay the night, or two. Refresh yourself, make yourself comfortable with your good parents. You might even be well-advised to renew your acquaintance with Perkin and try for his friendship. But then I want you to go to Greenwich, where I've sent Lady Katherine, Perkin's wife, to be part of the queen's court."

"Lady Katherine!" Lucas was genuinely surprised. His great eyes opened wider and he whistled softly. "I fear you hold me in too high a regard," he sighed. "She's said to be as great a lady as she is a beauty, highly born, a connection of James himself, as lovely as 'The White Rose of Scotland' they call her. And unhappily, said to be entirely faithful to the pretender. Faith, sire!" He shook his head. "You rate my charms too high, to set me to seduce a lady said to make patient Penelope a cheat by comparison. Unless," he mused aloud, "being a mortal female, she tires of longing for him now, and you think that because I bear some small resemblance . . ."

"No!" Henry snapped. "Not her. You are to leave her alone. She is, just as they say, virtue and beauty personified."

There'd been more than admiration in that explosive command. Lucas looked at his king with sharpened interest. But the traces of temper were gone from Henry's face and voice as he went on, "There are other females in her train, in that household. Women say things to each other that they might not say to men—except to some clever one, in their pleasure, in the dark of night. It's those sorts of confidences I'm after. A man such as you should be able to discover what I'm after. And that is: is there to be any more trouble from Perkin Warbeck? And if so, from whom?"

Lucas sat silent. It was a simple-enough task, so simple he knew there must be more to it. He'd have to discover what other purposes Henry had in mind, in time. But it was no difficult thing he'd been assigned to do; he'd done as much on his own, many times in the past. He could do it. He would, in fact. But he'd no taste for it. Or more accurately, he realized, he'd little stomach for the realization that this was what he'd come to, as well as what he'd come to be thought of.

"What? Surly silence now?" Henry asked in heavy tones that he doubtless thought were teasing. "Marry, I'd think you weren't pleased. You're known for your way about bedchambers. Isn't that flattering?"

"Hardly," Lucas drawled, and then, grinning like the buffoon he decided he was being played for, added, "If you'll forgive the pun—hardly, at all. It's my pride, sire. A fellow wouldn't like a reputation of being led about by the nose. I don't enjoy being thought to be led about by another, lower member."

"Ah, but we know that's not true," Henry said seriously, "as we know you're not guided by any feelings at all, for that matter. It's that which makes you so valuable."

"Thank you, my gracious lord," Lucas said with every evidence of sincerity.

It was only when he'd bowed himself out of the room that Henry spoke again, without turning around.

"Done. How say you, brother?"

"Only," the monk answered in a slow, sure voice, "that I would have thought such a clever young man too clever to be a spy, sire."

"Would you? Aye, so would I. So, you see, I try to catch two birds in one snare."

But as he turned about, the king caught the glimmer of eyes shining in the recesses of that overwhelming cowl, and he looked away, discomposed.

"Ah, well, and but you know, Robert, it's only common sense. I'm an economical man, that's all."

When there was no reply, in motion or in words, he added gruffly, looking down to his hands, as though the words were pulled from him, "I would, I vow, rather find nothing."

Only then did the friar nod, and the king relax again.

Henry's next audience was briefer.

"Watch Lovat," he told the tall young man.

And received a nod, which was as good as a bond. When the monk turned his head to him after the young man had gone, Henry shrugged.

"I never do anything by half-measure, Robert," he explained.

Which might have been another reason why the monk hesitated a moment as he left the chamber, when he saw who awaited audience with the king he'd just left.

The archbishop was still frowning after the monk as he painstakingly settled himself in a chair.

"I know you dislike him," Henry said immediately, "but Brother Robert has his uses."

"I don't dislike him. I don't know him. And so I distrust him," John Morton, Archbishop of Canterbury, said.

Henry smiled his thin smile.

"You, my friend," Henry said with rare warmth, "procured a throne for me, and my gratitude is endless. He procures my ease of mind. And wants nothing from me but my salvation. So I do believe. All London spoke of his saintlihood, and testing it, year after year, I have found it to be so. I share him with the lowest prisoners in the Tower, as well as the rabble in Cheapside. Imagine that! I know you've little use for my piety," he added on a slight laugh, "but it's part of me, you know that too. I need this friar, John. Marry, but you know this. I've no doubt that if you'd ever heard otherwise of him, I'd know that too."

"Aye, and you would," the old man, his lord chancellor, agreed on a long sigh. "But I don't trust him—but then, you know I trust no one but myself when it comes to you. I leave for Canterbury in the morning. Why have you not done anything about what we last spoke of?"

No man on earth, not even the holy friar, spoke to Henry Tudor so, but then, no man was as responsible for the throne he sat upon. Morton was old, older than almost any man Henry knew, but every breath in that old body was his, and he knew that as well. Morton mightn't do a thing for his soul, but no man on earth was as preoccupied with his earthly safety.

"Don't fret. I've begun. Do you think I passed fourteen years in exile only to let a pretender strip me of my crown? Or threaten my Arthur's future? I yearn to end him." Henry's dark face grew taut with anger. "Seven years, John! Seven years he's deviled me. Now I have him, and he plagues me still. I itch to remove his head now I have it beneath my roof. But you're right. If I destroy Warbeck now, I feed my enemies. They'd proclaim him king the moment his head was off his shoulders, saying I'd done it because he was truly Richard of York—his death at my hands without good cause would be his coronation."

"And so?" the old man asked.

"And so I will have good cause. Cause enough, at least, to cage him well and keep him from sight until either he's forgot by the world or I've time to find a better reason to put an end to his pretensions. I've been busy of late ensuring that Perkin himself will give it to me. He's here, his lady's there—in between, I'll see to it that there'll be a dozen temptations to err in every direction, and I've a man—and one behind him—in each to catch him when he does."

The old man remained passive.

"He has two cravings," Henry said impatiently. "One for the crown, and the other for his lady. Given the nearness of one and the distance of the other, he's bound to make a misstep soon, and fall to me."

"And if he doesn't?" John Morton asked.

"He'll be pushed," Henry said coldly.

"Ah." The old man smiled, and relaxed. "And what of Ireland, now?" he asked, sipping his wine.

And so reassured, they discussed mere politics.

After the first courses, when the meats and fowls and fish were done, when the edge was gone from hunger and the mind ready to receive its share of the king's pleasure, there was music. A cart with a cut-out castle upon it was pulled into the main dining hall by men dressed as horses, and when the laughter stopped, a dozen boys came out of the castle onto the platform and began singing, as a dozen little girls answered them from the cut-out windows, and threw flowers down upon them. It was a simple thing, and charming, and delighted the guests. But when it was wheeled away, and the jugglers entered, it could be seen that the king turned his attention away, and the conversations at the several tables rose up again.

"Don't worry for me. Sooth, your face, dear Mama, is enough to give the king second thoughts! He's treated me well, given me an easy commission. When I've done it, I'll come to visit with you." Lucas held the lady's little hand and sighed as he looked to his father, seated on his other side. "What's to be done? She believes nothing I say. See how she looks at me," he jested, "as though I'll march to the block, not our home, when I'm done here."

But there was too much to worry about in what he said for his father to laugh with him. His wife stared at Lucas with her heart in her eyes, those anxious eyes going from his blond head to his face, and then darting swiftly toward the king, as though she thought her sovereign might any moment stop speaking, rise, and put down his knife—in her dear boy's heart.

"Her thoughts were ever in her face," Sir Charles said sadly.

"Ah, so that's how you summoned up the courage to ask for her hand." Lucas laughed, but his father went on, shaking his head, "And when I tax her with it, it grows worse. Best we leave in the morning, lad. She frets for you, but you don't need everyone knowing that."

"That my love for you should be a cross to bear!" the lady cried, tears welling in her eyes, "Oh, my dear lord—"

"Mama," Lucas said, after he'd quickly covered her trembling lips with his own for a moment to gain her silence, "if Father says he's needed at home, you must bear up. I know I'm only a youth you worry about leaving alone in this wicked court," he added, his eyes sparkling as he smiled at an interested couple across the long table, who'd obviously been caught by the drama of the moment, "but trust me that I'll do well for myself by being chaste and gentle, as you taught me."

As everyone in their vicinity grinned at his statement,

his mama smiled back. When a lady nearby gained all attention with her gossip, his father arose, and laying his hand on his son's broad shoulders, said lightly and with a hidden tremor, "It's off to bed with us now, lad. We'll see you in the morning. We country folk rise with the barnyard, if you remember. So don't stay up late, because we expect you to bid us good-bye then."

"Now you sound like Mama," Lucas said on a laugh as he too rose and gave them good-night.

After his parents left, he walked down the long lines of tables, and sought the lowest of them. There he took his sweetmeats with young Philip de Lacey, who was both proud and astonished at the honor paid him, and flushed red as his crop of hair as his companions gaped at the sight of him being so honored by a gentleman.

Only when the tables were being put up, and the men settling on which games of chance to play, and the ladies on whether to game, go to bed, or chance their luck with a gentleman, did Lucas leave Philip. Then he began to walk the great hall, as though aimlessly, but always in the direction that his eyes had sought, as though looking for diversion, all night.

Even in such a crowd it had been as impossible to overlook Perkin Warbeck as it was easy to understand the king's discomfort, and everyone else's interest, in him. Aside from the allure of the man himself—and it was considerable, even from afar—there was the fascination with the situation. It was a wonder that they'd been seated in the same room; with any other king, in any other court, the pretender, if he still lived, would have been seated beneath this dining hall, in the dungeons. For his own reasons, Henry had kept Perkin Warbeck not only breathing but also eating and drinking with his other guests, not ten body-lengths from his own table. He might have thought the irony of it amusing at first, it might have begun as a jest, or a testimonial to his mercy, or it might even have been true mercy; anything was possible. But now, it couldn't be clearer that whatever the impulse had originally been, unless it was to show how unkingly this Henry was compared to his would-be usurper, it had failed.

Because wherever he sat, no eye could have failed to

note Perkin Warbeck in his splendor. That majesty had
little to do with his clothes, although he wore them well.
Well, but he would, Lucas thought, remembering the
man had first been noted when he'd arrived in Ireland as
a model for the shirts his master sold. Then, they said,
his princely ways were so obvious that all knew him for
what he was, whatever he pretended to be. Lucas had
heard such tales in his nursery: the princess obvious even
as she posed as a goose girl, the stolen prince shining out
from the rags of the Gypsies who'd stolen him—the myth
of royal blood so golden pure that it sang out when it was
spilled: "Hold! I am the king." All of it was just that—
myth. He'd known too many kings who looked like swineherds, and too many princesses who didn't look as good
as goose girls, to credit that. But even he, with all his
special wisdom, almost believed it again as he gazed at
Perkin Warbeck now.

It went beyond the pretender's height and breadth of
shoulder and well-made body. It was the way he carried
that gracious form, the way he inclined that noble head
when he was spoken to. The rack had indeed left no
mark upon him, for he was all fluid grace, and had none
of the characteristic floppiness, the disjointed movement
and stumbling gait of those who had stayed overlong, at
the king's grace, in the bowels of his Tower.

Remembering Warbeck from brief observations in previous years, Lucas thought that he was being flattered
when Henry had remarked on his slight resemblance to
the impostor. Now he realized he'd been mocked. The
youth had attained a glorious manhood. Perkin had skin
of creamy, milky purity; his eyes were slumberous and
azurine, his long and shining hair was a dulcet shade of
fresh churned butter, his cheeks full, his nose retroussé,
his chin, though pronounced, with a slight slurring hint of
a double beneath it, determined. In all, it went beyond
good looks, for his imperfections didn't matter. He was
larger than life, and more regal than a common man
should be. He looked more than the culminating flower
of generations of the handsome Plantagenet line: he was
the very image of a prince of fable. Better, for his was
warm, approachable, and living splendor that nevertheless breathed welcome as well as glory. So had Edward

looked, and he had been a king. What was this Warbeck, then?

Lucas hadn't felt heat or cold or pain or true joy in a very long while, but he felt an odd thrill of something he'd forgotten run along his spine as Perkin looked up to him with mild, inquiring eyes. He bowed as he came to the table where the pretender sat at his ease among several gentlemen, not a few of them there to guard him, not a few come to mock and stayed to admire him.

"I doubt you remember me," Lucas said, "but we met years ago, in Amsterdam. I am . . ."

"Lucas Lovat. I recall you well. You traded in wool. We drank to the health of England," Perkin said in his warm, rich voice.

Such a memory was the hallmark of kings, Lucas thought with a start, before he remembered that it was also the trademark of spies.

"I'm flattered," he replied, "and pleased to see you, and so well, again."

"Come sit with us," Perkin said, moving a hand so that the gentlemen made a space for him.

As Lucas sat, he had to use his utmost self-control not to glance to the end of the room, where the tall, thin, gray king sat in the shadow of the impostor. For Perkin's welcome and his easy acceptance bore a grace that Henry could never achieve. Only born kings knew how to make a man they gave no thought to feel so worthy. Only born kings and a few gifted men could make a frozen man feel such things as Lucas began to feel again now, even though he knew it was all facade and that he'd be gone from Perkin's mind a moment after he'd been registered upon it. He doubted Henry could ever make a man he loved—if he could love—feel so welcomed as Perkin made a stranger feel.

"I remember you said you traveled. Are you returned to England for good?" Perkin asked as though he cared, as though he'd a right to know.

"Ah, not for long," Lucas said, realizing he'd lost his glibness, realizing the statement sounded naked because it hadn't been ended with a "your grace" or "sire."

Confused for the first time in many years, and angry for it, he added, "Alas, no. It seems to be my portion to be a wanderer. I go to Greenwich Palace next, on business. Ah, but . . ." He hesitated, and so as to retain a portion of himself until he could reason out this unreasonable joy he felt in Perkin's presence, and to further his own interests even as he began to despise them, he added quickly, "Greenwich . . . is that not where your lady waits now? But then, how fortunate! Can I be your messenger? Have you word for her?"

He had thought the man glowed. Now it was as if he had poured spirits into a flame. Perkin's eyes blazed up and his joy was so brilliantly reflected in them that Lucas almost shrank away, feeling like some thing of the darkness that must scuttle back into the cracks of the floor so as to save its small life.

"I knew," Perkin said as he laid a warm hand over Lucas' cold one, "I knew that you would do me good someday."

3

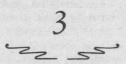

The lady sent her maid from her with an impatient wave of her hand, although the woman still held her comb poised as though to give the gleaming hair one last touch, as though the image before her wasn't already perfection.

"Enough, enough," the lady said as she glanced at the reflection in the glass, nodded, and began to pace the room. "Now, go below and see if there's any word, and come back to me as soon as you hear."

"My lady," another young woman in the room said softly as the maid left to do her bidding, "there's no reason to think that it is he—indeed, there's every reason to think it's not, because—"

"—because you don't believe Henry has a heart?" the lady interrupted. "But, Megan, child, I have seen his charity, this letter itself is proof of it," she said, holding out the piece of paper she hadn't released from her keeping, waking or sleeping, since she'd received it.

The girl sighed. She knew the words on the paper as well as if they'd been written to her, although she knew she'd never receive such a message herself, for all it was her fondest, most secret dream. For who should ever write of her, or to her, that her face, ". . . bright, serene, gives splendor to the cloudy sky"? Because even if she should ever be so fortunate as to meet a man capable of poetry, he would have to possess more imagination than poetry to write such to her, or so she decided with a secret wry grin. Whereas anyone looking at the lady before her would know that the words were only truth.

Lady Katherine was beyond beautiful. Everyone said so. Even dour Henry had paused in the face of her beauty, and named her the "White Rose of Scotland"

and sent her to his queen for safekeeping—at the same time he'd sent her husband to be chained, pilloried, and racked for daring to claim that he was born under the sign of England's white rose himself. But it was more than bitter irony that he should punish the man for calling himself what his wife was dubbed, Lady Megan Baswell thought as she gazed at her mistress with a mixture of love and envy; it was simple truth.

Because Lady Katherine Gordon, Perkin Warbeck's lady wife, was tall and slender, with masses of ink-black hair, and skin as white as a ewe-lamb's. Her face was perfection, no less than that. Someone at court had said that it was a living model of classic ancient beauty and could be used as a model for all future beauty, since not one of its perfect features was a fraction of an inch too long, too wide, or too high. Nor was it only a matter of shape and form, for the personality that animated that perfect face was no less charming; it shone through her eyes, and those eyes—the next line on the paper praised them for being "brilliant as the stars," before going on to say the sight of them could make "all pain to be forgotten, and turn despair into delight."

That, Megan thought, turning her own eyes aside from the bit of paper that wounded and enchanted her, was to say more than she would. But it must be so, for it was written by an expert on both pain and despair. Because who in this sad world knew more of pain than the noble man who had composed those lines? Or more of the depths of despair than he?

"Whosoever sees her cannot choose but admire her, admiring, cannot choose to love her, loving, cannot choose but obey her . . ." because, the letter vowed as it continued, Megan knew, as she closed her eyes and yet continued to see the strong pen strokes as though they were written in the blood-red dark before her, the lady was ". . . not born in our days, but descended from heaven."

Well, her mistress was certainly mortal, but it was a tribute both to her and to the man who'd written that, that he felt so. As if he needed more tribute, she thought, as if Perkin Warbeck weren't already perfection in his own fashion.

"No," the Lady Katherine said with barely restrained excitement, "put off your pained face, Megan. If the rumor says we're to have visitors from Westminster to-day, he may yet be among them."

"My lady . . ." Megan paused, for she'd opened her eyes to see her mistress alight with anticipation as well as impatience, and seeking a jest before she spoke dismal truth, she said merrily, "Oh! Do you really think I can put it off? Why has no one told me before? Do you think I would've kept it on for so long if I'd known?"

She waited for encouraging laughter, but Maeve, the other young woman in the room only frowned, and Lady Katherine looked at her unsmiling. She sighed, lost her own smile, and went on carefully, "He wouldn't come by himself, my lady. He couldn't. And if the king were on his way, we'd have had word of the royal barge by now. But nothing like it's been seen on the river today. Guests may be coming from Westminster to Greenwich, but if they come by road or boat but not in state, none of them are likely to be your husband, Perkin."

"My husband, *Richard!*" Lady Katherine said fiercely.

"Oh, lady . . ." Megan began, biting her lip, but Maeve cut her off to say, "Now, now, my lady. You know better than to say that—even in our presence. What if Meg here's a spy for Henry?" she said on a laugh, and as Megan flushed and began to stammer a hasty, shocked rebuttal, she went on more sternly, "Oh, tush, sweet Meg, leave it, I only tease. Lady, you know Henry has spies at every door. Loyalty is grand, but such mis-sayings might cause your lord more grief than joy."

Lady Katherine's shoulders drooped, but even in de-jection she was magnificent. A second later, she lifted her head, and her eyes sparkled. "You're right, my clever Maeve. And so are you, Megan. Rest easy. I'll not look to see him today. But I'll seek word of my dear lord instead. Because whoever comes may yet do us some good, for if he comes from Westminster, he'll have seen my lord, and that will at least be something. But I can't wait here like a caged thing. I'll go below now. Join me when you will," she said, and catching up her long skirts in one clenched hand, swept out the door and left them alone.

"Oosh!" Maeve said, plumping herself down on the high bed and fanning her face with one hand. "I have had easier duties."

"You did well, you did very well," Megan said in earnest admiration. She was grateful for Maeve; buxom, blond, pragmatic Maeve, who always made them laugh, when she wasn't making them sigh for her commonsensical hardheadedness. Then Megan shook her head in sorrow and said softly, "I'm sorry, it seems I can't say a word right today."

"You," Maeve said as she stopped swinging her shapely little legs over the side of the bed and looked hard at her, "are too wrapped up in my lady. *And* my lord," she cautioned. "Ah, don't look so," she said a moment later, as Megan felt the heat rising in her cheeks and struggled for the right, careless word to say. "As if it mattered. As if you'd do a thing about it, even if you could, poor lass. I only hope Henry sends you a husband soon. You're both too old and too young, and too pretty, all together, to be cloistered with our Lady Katherine. You need a man of your own to give you grief."

"As you say," Megan said, smiling now, "I'm too old, and thank you, because only a friend would say I'm too pretty. But 'too young'?"

"Too young to know that another's lover is easily made perfect," Maeve said, hopping off the bed and straightening her skirts. "When you've had a husband and a lover or two, or three, like me," she laughed, "you'll see the difference between dining and hearing of a feast, and know that any man of your own is better than stories of another woman's, however grandly they're told. And she does him proud. Lady Katherine's a dreamer too—but not like you," she said seriously. "She lives out her dreams. You only dream them. You take care, Meg."

"Thank you, Mama," Megan said, grinning. "Only, how you managed to have a daughter when you were only four, I do not know."

"Lady Katherine and I are of an age, but we're both a hundred years older than you."

"You've both been married," Megan answered.

"Bedding doesn't bring wisdom. If it did, I'd be Solomon by now," Maeve said, but as Megan began to laugh, she added, "You're as handsome as she is, in your own way, but you don't know it. You're more tender than either of us, and you let everyone else see it. There's danger for you." Maeve's round face became uncharacteristically solemn as she stared at Megan. "All of nineteen and still with a heart as virginal as your body," she went on seriously, "and with too much conscience and too little opportunity to change either case on your own. You need to be gone from this place. You take care, Meg," she repeated as she walked to the door, "that you don't bleed to death of another woman's wounds." And as Megan stood frozen in place, without an answer at the ready, she added, "I'm fully dressed, I'll go to the lady, you join us when you will."

When I can, Megan thought, trying to cover her embarrassment as Maeve whisked through the door, leaving her standing alone except for her reflection in Lady Katherine's glass.

Everything Maeve said was true, she realized—except for the part about her being handsome. She'd never greatly admired her own looks, even less so since she'd come to serve here. Brown hair and brown eyes were dull and commonplace compared to jet hair and blue eyes. If she comforted herself that her own skin was just as white as the lady's, it didn't show up very well with dun hair; and imperfect features, however they might be called "piquant," were blunted ones compared to classical perfection. Smaller, slender, but with a figure that was nevertheless fuller than what she daily saw as ideal, it seemed to her that she was the literal shadow of the beautiful lady she constantly attended—a shadow cast exaggerated and dimly perceived behind her.

The part about any man being better than a dream of one was untrue too, she decided on a righteous sniff as she set the veil on her gabled hood straight. Because Perkin Warbeck was the living embodiment of a dream. She knew, because she'd met him.

Lady Megan Baswell waited upon Lady Katherine Gordon Plantagenet—or Warbeck—at the order of his gracious majesty Henry VII, and had done since the day the lady had fallen to his mercy. It was Megan's duty to attend the other lady: sing for her when she was bored, bathe her temples with cool water when she was ill, tell her stories when she needed distraction, run her errands, and see to her every wish—except for any that had to do with seeing her husband. She was only four years younger than her lady, nineteen to her three-and-twenty, and just as wellborn, well-bred, and well-educated as the woman she served so diligently. But however menial her tasks, she served without complaint. She was beyond glad to have the position she held because she'd neither family nor fortune in back of her any longer, and without these things, she might as well lack life as well. Even the lowliest peasant girls had more freedom, if only because they could more easily find a place in life than might an impoverished wellborn female who lacked family.

Because her widower father had supported the wrong man before he'd been deemed the right one when another one gained the throne, and had lost his head in the confusion at that time, she'd been left without resources. Her older sister, married to a man of simple position, gave her house space in the brief time before her fortunes turned. For Megan's petition was put before the king, her father's name remembered, and she was lucky enough to be made one of his wards, for his charity. And he'd been charitable.

As Megan had been told when she'd been taken from obscurity to serve, she could as easily have been married off to either of two neighbors of hers, both of whom had asked for her hand: one of whom was fat, fifty, and flatulent, and the other, although ten years younger than his rival, anxious to wed a third time, believing his seven children weren't enough to leave to a grateful posterity. There was no dowry for a better match, and none for a place at a convent either, even if she'd had a calling. She could just as easily have been given in marriage to any number of men, of any age or condition. Dowered ladies seldom had say in how they were disposed of in wedlock; undowered ones, none at all. But it was true that well-loved daughters could sometimes speak their preferences. Lady Katherine had been a famous beauty in her native Scotland, and had turned down many matches until the day her cousin, her king, had received a gentleman claiming to be the rightful King of England. But king or no, from the moment he'd stood before her, as she so often said, there'd been no further questions in her mind. She'd taken his hand and followed him on his wild journeys for three years. Only cruel fate, and stern Henry, had ever separated them since.

But that was the way of a great beauty with indulgent

relatives. Megan's own father, like most noblemen, believed his daughters were negotiable properties to be intelligently disposed of. And so for all she'd lost her home, she knew she was very fortunate to have gotten the king's notice, and this position. Lady Katherine mightn't be too interested in a younger girl, and as she'd been a great lady, was accustomed to ignoring all those who served her. But she wasn't cruel or hard to suit; there was another lady-in-attendance—and Maeve Constable was a delight; and the past months had proved the job to be simplicity itself. If, that was, she could just ignore her one other task.

Because, as Megan never forgot but always tried to, there was one other duty, this one to her king and not her lady. And that was to tell King Henry everything she saw and heard and thought in the course of her service to her lady.

And so she did. Everything—except for two things: her shame at her duplicity, and her great love for Perkin Warbeck.

From the moment she'd seen him, she had been lost. She had, after all, she'd discovered, a calling. He'd stood tall though he'd stood in shackles. He'd been dragged through the streets of London, pilloried, forced to read his confession east, west, north, and south. There was that about his beautiful mouth that spoke of what he'd endured on the rack, even though he never breathed a word about it. Tall, fair, and graceful, even in his chains he was a kingly figure. Humiliated and captive, yet still those lucent eyes had sought out his lady, and he'd managed a smile for her. No wonder Lady Katherine, having heard his confession, and being told of his crimes, had nevertheless raised her head and said that whatever he was, he was noble enough for her, and that she was, and wished to remain, his wife. They said he was nothing but a boatman's son. They showed her his signed confession, showing he was scarcely worthy of looking at a king, much less being one.

"He is king enough for me," she said.

The court had stilled as she'd come to stand at his side in that moment of public trial. They couldn't touch, but their closeness was visible. They'd gleamed, they'd glowed, they'd outshone everyone else in the great hall. And then, abandoning all dignity, she'd gone down to her knees before the king to beg for her husband's life. It was like seeing a white rose bowed down by the rain. The king had sighed, as had all the tender ladies, if for different reasons. The lady had been given a place of honor in the queen's own household, with ladies-in-waiting, as though she were indeed herself a queen. The impostor had been spared. But soon separated from his lady wife. And yet perhaps someday . . . If men were taught to wait for the coming of their redeemer, as Lady Katherine said later, why then, how much easier to wait upon the kindness of a king and the arrival of a mortal man.

Now Megan waited too. Even though he'd had nothing but a smile for her, as his lady's helper, it was enough. It was, in fact, just right. She'd great stores of untapped devotion and passion she could draw upon.

The odd thing, even to herself, was that she never actually believed he could ever love her, indeed, she mightn't love him if he could—because that would mean he'd betray his lady, and that wasn't the way a noble man would behave. And if she sometimes idly imagined what might happen if he were suddenly freed, not only of his prison, but also, by some stroke of fate, say, plague or childbed, of his wife . . . Shocked, she'd shake herself from such cruel daydreamings and remember the way they'd looked together—bright and dark, tall and fair, well-matched in everything—and see that she could never fit into that glowing picture.

The most peculiar thing, even to herself, was that she realized that if she envied anyone on earth more than Lady Katherine, she supposed it might be their infant daughter, Margaret.

It wasn't very much to expect from life, but then, she'd not known very much love since she'd grown, and didn't dare dream she'd find more anymore. There were many handsome, charming men at court, and they'd noted her as often as they'd given up on her when she'd denied them. But she'd little choice. She'd nothing to offer them but herself, and if she gave that before marriage, she'd forfeit her future. Wellborn girls were supposed to be virgins until their wedding night, but a well-dowered one from an influential family had assets enough so that her bridegroom might overlook her one lack. A portionless bride could be cast out naked and homeless into the cold morning after her wedding if her marriage-bed sheets stayed as pure and unsullied as she was supposed to have been before her wedding—even if it had only been her own husband who'd sampled her prematurely to their vows, and changed his mind.

No, she'd had to learn to suppress desires for all but continued life. Virginity was her only asset, and so her impossible love was the best one she could have found. She was wholly devoted to it, though it gave her as much pain as if it had been reciprocated.

Megan adjusted her hood and veil over her thick brown hair, and realizing how much time had passed, rushed out of the room to find her lady and resume her work.

"It's only a messenger from Henry and a guest from Westminster, newly come from abroad. They're closeted with the queen," Maeve whispered to Megan when she joined her in the garden, where Lady Katherine was pacing.

"Ah," Megan said as they followed along behind their lady. "Only more of the same," she sighed, as disappointed as her lady likely was.

Messengers and guests passed between the two palaces every day. Henry might keep separate from his queen for his own reasons, but for those same unknowable reasons, he kept as close watch over his private domain as he did his public ones. But then why was Lady Katherine so agitated? Now the lady's face had high color, and her eyes were bright and seemed to be seeing far beyond this little bit of tamed land. She paced down the garden paths, unseeing, not noting the newly swollen buds and first tender flowers of spring any more than she did her own little Margaret, toddling in the wake of her nurse, as excited by the unexpected sight of her mama as she was by her first flush of success at walking.

There must be something more to these visitors, Megan decided. Messengers came and messengers went, but such was the nature of their world that by their names and appearances their directions were as well-known as the stars that wheeled in the sky over the palace every night. But such was the nature of their world, too, that the advent of an uncommon guest might be made known all

over the palace by the simple reason of his coming, as a
comet might be observed in its unusual flight.

The brief brightness of the spring day fled in clouds, but
only when a dank drizzle began were Maeve and Megan
given the excuse of interrupting their lady's thoughts, to
beg her to go inside. Megan was chilled and damp, but
even though bright beads of rain decorated her lady's
dark hair, the lady seemed unaware of them, and as the
day wore on, her feverish energy was so high that only
Maeve's cool hand laid on her brow proved the fever
came from her mind, and not her tense body. She stalked
and spun about her room, sending her maid into despair.
"It must be hard to dress a running deer," Maeve commented, to get her to alight in one spot long enough for
the distracted maid to get her clad for the evening.

But in all, it took so long that Maeve and Megan had
only minutes in which to dress so as to join their lady. As
Megan did up Maeve's gown first, she scarcely looked at
what she was doing as she scrambled into her own. She'd
not that many to select from, but the four she had were
more than less-fortunate ladies owned. Still, her usual
toilette included time for a choice of different under-
dresses so as to give the illusion of vaster choice, as well
as nice decisions to do with which of her two vials of
scent to dab on, which of her small selection of belts and
hoods to wear, and what veil to wear behind her hood.

She wore her russet wool gown because it had a heavily paneled skirt and needed no underskirts. But she'd
gotten overheated in her haste, and as the bodice was
tight and the sleeves tighter, by the time she'd struggled
into it she'd no time to do more than push her heavy hair
up under her gabled hood. When she was done, she
paused for a second's regret that she was. As ever when
she knew she was to join the court and meet new company, she wished she could meet them as herself. Whoever that had been.

She'd begun to wonder what had happened to that girl,
or if she'd ever really existed. Once, surely, she'd have
wanted to wear sunset-scarlet or peacock blue, something
as fine as it was dazzling. Once, certainly, she'd have
hurried, laughing, down the stair to meet the company,
ready to try to win them with her wit and her charm. Or
so it seemed she must have done, since she found herself

wishing to so often lately. But it had been so long since she'd been free to do as she pleased that now she wondered if she had either wit or charm anymore, or if it had only been the dream that she did that she'd had.

Unless she could successfully practice self-deprecating wit and a matronly air of worldy wisdom such as Maeve did, a lady-in-waiting had to be demure. It would never do for a great lady's attendant to try to rival her, or attract the notice of her gallants, even if she could. The thought was laughable, unthinkable. No, even Maeve knew when to shrink back into the shadows. Although at first it had been as hard as fitting herself into an iron garment, such as the armor knights wore to carry out their duties, Megan had practiced to be quiet and modest, self-effacing and discreet, deflecting attention from herself, lest she give offense. Ever watchful, fearful of putting a foot or a word awry, like her mistress only in that she chafed at her restraints and waited for the day when she'd be set free. But now she began to wonder if her days of servitude might not stretch into years, and that if her day of freedom ever came, she mightn't find that all she had suppressed had been lost. If, indeed, she thought again, she'd really ever had the power to attract a man for more than a night, or an offer of a brief meeting in the night.

She heard voices in the corridor and started, remembering that dreams were too expensive for her now. She hastened to follow Maeve from their room and join their mistress.

"I hope I'm fully clad, at least," she whispered to Maeve as they carefully made their way down the long stone stairs together in Lady Katherine's train. "You'll have to tell me if my coif is straight, and I'll have to hope they all take the bird's nest on my head for a style I was attempting."

Maeve looked at the heavily waving hair that escaped from everywhere beneath Megan's gabled hood, and grinned.

"You look like you've just been tumbled," she whispered back. "You'll be the most popular lady at dinner tonight. Whereas I," Maeve continued softly as they wound down the long stair, "have been, and no one would guess it."

Megan gasped, but held her tongue. She'd be teased if she were shocked, whether it was true or not. Maeve *had* been gone for an hour in the afternoon when their lady was resting, and with Maeve, the claim might well be so. She was a widow, in waiting to Henry for another match, for her late husband had fought for the king. A widow had as much freedom as she wished, and Maeve seemed to wish for all of it. Whether her brief liaisons were with wedlock in view or for the sport of it, Maeve never said, and Megan certainly couldn't guess. But if they were in hopes of snaring the gentlemen for more permanent bouts, they were remarkably unsuccessful, for she'd no constant admirer. If they were for the sheer pleasure of it, they were a triumph, for it seemed Maeve was always smiling. It might be that Megan could know, if she ever dared ask.

When they arrived in the great hall, even the question was put out of her mind. She stood behind Lady Katherine where she'd stopped short, and she stared, as did Maeve, as if her ladies-in-waiting were in duty bound to copy even their lady's expression.

There was a crowd of people in the hall, as always, for it was a great palace, and the queen, although a quiet-loving lady, had her own court even when Henry wasn't with her. But one man stood out from the rest as he paid court to his queen. He was tall and graceful, and sensationally clad as he was in rich violet doublet with great slashed sleeves, with a golden pendant gleaming on his chest, a patterned brocaded short coat over all, and dark violet hose, the glory of his clothes was surpassed by his face. Or was it his presence? For his eyes were so large they could be seen to be azure even in torchlight, and his smile was as warm as the glow from his long bright hair, hair so fair it was almost the same shade as that of his queen.

The air hissed out of Lady Katherine's lungs as she breathed again. After that split second of shock, she saw that for all he was very like, he was, for all his splendor, only a shadow of her own lord. Although very well-looking in his own style, he *was* in his own style. The gleaming cap of hair was pale as moonlight, not the dazzling hue of sunlight she knew so well, and though muscular, the man was slender; his cheeks were hollow, his nose too long, his chin too pronounced in that lean face: he was very like and nothing like her master.

But he could not be a coincidence. It was that thought that gave her back her confidence, even as it frightened Megan, who stood rigid behind her. They each, after all, had their secrets to keep, but only Megan felt guilt for hers. And only she knew only too well that however much she might want to protect her love, she had no one else in the world to protect her but herself.

When Lady Katherine arose from her deep obeisance to the queen, she found herself the object of the gentleman's cool, delighted regard.

"My Lady Katherine Gordon," the queen said softly, ever politic, ever gentle, ever able to feel pain, perhaps because she always recognized fellow sufferers, "I give you Lucas Lovat. He's lately come from Italy, France, Flanders, all the lands you may remember. He stopped at Westminster before he arrived here, and wished to meet you. Perhaps, sir, you'd wish to take Lady Katherine in to dinner? You two might have many acquaintances in common."

"It would be my deepest pleasure," Lucas Lovat said, bowing, as he would have said even if his queen had asked him to dine with painted savages.

Nodding, the queen drifted away. She received guests, dined with them, and discoursed with them, but it was as if she never noted them. Something in Lucas Lovat's face had wakened her briefly from her constant dreaming, but it had soon faded. Pale and beautiful, with the Plantagenet heritage clear in her coloring and fine-featured face, and the sensuality of her father in the lines of her mouth and body, yet she was like a fairy queen in some children's tale, waiting to be awakened. Royal orphan, pawn to kings, and loved by her people, she seemed never to forget the blood that lay between her and her crown. She did come to life with joyous pleasure when she was with her children, where she passed most of her time, and roused to something else when her king was near her, which was seldom. Now she smiled absently, and went in to her dinner with an old knight, an old friend and courtier.

Lady Katherine was all soft smiles and pliant grace with Lucas Lovat; she said little and laughed a great deal, hiding her white teeth behind a white hand when she did, as a lady should. But that was her way with all men, even her husband. She allowed herself to be cross, or tense, or agitated only when alone or with her ladies. As for the gentleman, he was as charmed and charming as one might expect him to be when dining at the queen's table, and with a lady as fair as his dinner partner. They had eyes only for each other, though no one thought there was a grain of love in it, and everyone's eyes were on them every moment. Especially at the lower tables, where Lady Katherine's ladies-in-waiting and other lesser beings dined.

"Italian manners," Maevc whispered, poking an elbow into Megan's ribs and causing her to almost drop the bit of bread she held. "See? He takes that . . . forked thing from his pocket to use on his meats. I suppose they don't trust knives in each other's hands, or hands on their food in Italy—and in Italy," she sniffed, "who can blame them? But look at the cut of that doublet, will you? Very fine. And look at the man beneath it," she sighed, so captivated she stopped chewing.

"Any man can have shoulders like that in a well-cut jacket," Megan answered repressively, though the breadth of the slender man's shoulders impressed her every bit as much as it did Maeve.

"God save us!" Maeve cried, so loudly that several other ladies at their table stared at her. "A holy miracle! The girl notices shoulders at last," she went on in a loud whisper. "In time she may look lower, hey? But see how he looks at our lady now, how exciting, how frightening, like a falcon sighting its prey," she said, so engrossed in watching the couple again that she put a huge bit of mutton in her mouth and was silenced by it.

"Yes. Very frightening. Very like the way you're watching him," Megan said, but Maeve was too occupied with swallowing to notice, and as soon as she had, she went on breathlessly, "Much good it will do him, well-made as he is. But if he's a man of the world, he knows it and will look elsewhere for sport. Ah, look. Ah, by cock! Look. She turns to old Sir Reed to have a word, he looks about and looks . . . at you. And smiles. Damn! God's teeth! That," Maeve said in disgust as Megan looked up, startled, to see those bright, amused eyes meeting hers so levelly even from such a distance that she had to look down at once, "isn't that the way of it? Those who have no need, receive. You've about as much use for him as a nun has for a teething ring. Ah, well," she said, plunging her knife into another bit of mutton, "he has to go somewhere to warm up when you freeze him solid, doesn't he?"

But when she looked at Megan again, she was even more disgusted, because from the way the girl was blushing each time she found Lucas Lovat's eyes upon her, which was every time she dared peek over to where he sat again, it looked as if the man was more likely to be burned than frozen by her.

"Yes, my little Megan is lovely, isn't she?" Lady Katherine said softly when she saw where Lucas was looking, as she turned back from speaking with the elderly peer she'd neglected on her right, for in this great raucous hall, normal conversation could be heard only head-on, "but as I said, homeless, save for the king's good grace, even as I am now."

"You have family in Scotland, my lady," Lucas answered gently.

"My home is with Richard . . . Ah!" she said suddenly, as if she'd cut her tongue, and looking around quickly, said, "I mean to say 'Perkin.' Odd—a simple child's name, yet I can't accustom myself to it. It's so hard to remember that the man I wedded and lived with for three years is supposed to be called 'Peter' or 'Peterkin' or 'Perkin' now," she apologized prettily, as if she didn't know every nuance of what she was saying. "But no, I have no other home any longer, only with him. Where he abides, I do live. I have no home, no resting place, no place at all without him."

"As he, as I've said, says of you, my lady," Lucas replied. "The situation is a grievous one to anyone with a beating heart." He spoke low as he gazed into her eyes. "If there is any way I can be of service," he whispered, "from carrying your words to each other, to . . . to any other errand I may perform to your benefit, my lady, I am here, you may call upon me. For that," he said, and paused significantly as he noted she ducked her head and lowered her lashes over her eyes, "or for whatever else you would of me," he added with a slightly roughened edge to his voice.

Now she looked straight at him, and there was certain knowledge in her clear, cool, assessing eyes. "I would that you be *our* friend, Lucas Lovat, a friend of Rich . . . ah, Perkin's, and of mine."

"But I am," he said at once. "Forgive me if I hinted anything else."

"Oh, I do," she said quietly. "He once said that I must not take offense at such, for it's only that a man must know. And if he's a man, how is he to know unless he tries?"

"He's a wise man," Lucas said, smiling now, "and you a forgiving lady. Now I know, and now I will let it lie. I beg you to believe me. Please consider me always at the service of you both—you and Perk . . . ah, Richard's."

Her eyes widened, she paused, and then she smiled.

4

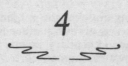

The lady was a fanatic. Lovely, yes. She had a legendary beauty. But there was that in the depths of Lady Katherine's sparkling blue eyes that he'd seen in the eyes of men going singing to the stake. He admired her and her beauty enormously. But something within him shrank at the thought of intimacy with such a woman. And because, therefore, doubtless something outside him would shrink too, Lucas thought merrily, it wouldn't be just Henry's edict that would keep him from her.

Oh, but she was attainable, for all her piety. Lucas knew enough of fanatics to know how willingly they'd sacrifice themselves, and how much faster they'd do it if they thought their god was in danger. And since Lady Katherine worshiped at her husband's shrine, she'd do anything for him. But for all her beauty, Lucas wouldn't dream of testing her loyalty, and not because of doubt of his abilities in the matter. He'd done much that wasn't to his taste in his life, and was all too familiar with sexual congress that had little to do with desire. Nor was it only because he wouldn't enjoy having a god sitting somewhere just over his shoulder as he made love. For that was where her eyes, her heart, and her mind would doubtless be fixed, and he'd never cared for merely occupying a lady's body. No, he'd leave the lovely lady to fate, or Henry, or her maker, or even to her husband—although that was her most unlikely destiny, he thought—because there was no point to her seduction. She'd never give up confidences even as easily she'd offer up that lovely body if she had to, however cleverly he insinuated himself into her good graces.

Now, if Henry wanted to test his rack, this would be

the lady to do it with, Lucas thought, because she'd take her secrets to her grave with her. And with his goodwill, he decided, looking out over the garden and beginning to smile, since there was always another way. And perhaps even a better one. Legendary beauty wasn't always as satisfying as the warm, human sort. A fallible maiden was far more desirable, since lack of self-control, no asset in a conspiracy, was delicious in a close embrace, as well as being profitable during the sort of drowsy, seemingly aimless conversation made after that embrace was done.

"Ladies," Lucas said, sweeping into a bow as he presented himself before the two women he'd intercepted as they strolled down the path, "you grace the landscape—I'd give you good morning, but you'd shame my poor pretensions, having already embellished the morning beyond anything I've seen in many long years."

Megan and Maeve ducked into curtsies, and Maeve, the first to recover from his gallantries, or the last to be overset by any gentleman—except literally—Lucas decided, eyeing her as he rose from his bow, said immediately, "Oh, are you in the habit of going about with your eyes closed? Fie, sir, but we've heard of how beautiful the Italian ladies are. How can I compare, even in jest? . . . Oh, you jest, sir!" she cried, putting out one little hand to tap him on the shoulder.

From "we" to "I" in the space of a breath? Lucas was impressed at how quickly the little blond lady was drawing her quarters and including her lovely, silent companion out. This one would be simple prey, and she loved to talk. Pretty, too, and lively. Whereas the other was beautiful but wary, and already beginning to distance herself by taking a step away. But he didn't want it to be too easy, because he didn't consider the getting of female bodies, and then confidences, a worthy profession. If he had to do it, he might as well make it interesting, and a certain degree of difficulty, which he anticipated from the guarded look in the silent girl's wide watchful eyes, might allow him to test his skills to the point where he'd be able to forget momentarily his reasons for using them.

"Ladies," he said with an admiring look that included both women, before he gestured to the garden they were in, "you behold a man starved for springtime in England, and most of all for the look of her subtle flowers—beside which, believe me, all foreign blooms seem overly ornate, overperfumed, and overdone."

"But most important, overseas," he was sure he heard the brown-haired one breathe *sotto voce*, but when he looked her way, her face was polite and still.

He grinned. It transformed him, making him entirely human, if not one less whit exotic. Maeve sighed. Megan, seeing the look that crossed over the little blond woman's enrapt face as she stared at him, sighed herself and took another tiny step aside, deciding that if things went as usual, they'd want to be alone quite soon.

"Now, that's something I'd forgot," Lucas said, relaxing. "Italian ladies expect their compliments to be like their desserts: rich, sweet, and served up often. I'll warrant I sounded like a cozening knave, all overdone and overblown myself. Your pardon, my ladies."

"Oh, but I thought it was charming," Maeve protested. "Do tell me just what sort of flower I remind you of, sir."

"An English rose, of course," he said lightly, before he halted Megan's small and steady backward pace with a smile as he added, directly to her, "and a nettle. Which I deserved."

Megan smiled despite herself. This gentleman was entirely too much for her, as well as too little, and she was wise enough to know it. He was all in shades of gold and green today, with a light brown cape thrown over his green doublet. His long light hair was a shade darker, damp and subdued, as though he'd lately washed it. As he stepped closer, she could discern the slight scents of lemon and sandalwood that most court gentlemen used, but it was mingled with some other, more exotic Eastern essences that must be his, as they were altogether too heady to have come from the first few blossoms of this spring garden.

There was still that about him which reminded her of Perkin, of course: the hair, the stature, the intense blue eyes—although his were larger, even as were his nose and chin. But the more one looked at him, the less they looked alike. It wasn't a matter of features. Both men had the same easy grace, the same knack of looking at people and making them feel as though they were the only ones worth looking at in the world. They had the

same ineffable glow, that air of distinction and importance that lay upon their shoulders so lightly one wondered if they even realized how set apart they were from
the common run of mankind. So many similarities, despite the fact that this man was leaner, and sharper in
subtler ways.

But Perkin didn't frighten her.

She glanced away from his searching eyes.

"Now, there it is—if I'd been pinked now and again in
my wanderings, I mightn't have got so homesick," Lucas
said thoughtfully as he gazed at Megan. "Englishmen
need trimming back sharply every so often, you see, if
they don't want to grow weedy . . . if you'll forgive my
continuing botanical trend of thought," he added as Megan
fought back a tremendous desire to giggle.

Suppressed laughter became her almost as much as he
thought outright merriment would, he decided, eyeing
her with admiration. Graceful, tilt-eyed, snub-nosed, full-
lipped, with what would be clouds of waving brown hair
when it was loosed, and what would be a magnificent
form when he freed it from the tight-bodiced gown it was
confined in. A combination of imp and temptress, all
rigidly held in by the force of her will. He liked the
thought of what would happen when she unfurled herself
to him far more than what he'd seen already openly on
display in other women of this court. And there were
scores of them here. The queen had a dozen ladies-in-
waiting, and Lady Katherine only two. But Lady Katherine's two were the ones who'd know more of what he was
seeking, and of them, this one would have caught his eye
even if he hadn't been ordered to seduce her. He smiled
at how nicely the processes of reduction worked, how
neatly he'd convinced himself of his duty.

He noted peripherally how the blond lady, noting his
attention to the other one, shrugged and slowly, regretfully drifted away, even as he offered his arm to the girl
he'd selected and asked, "Will you walk with me for a
space, good lady? I'm in desperate need of cutting, you
know.

"I can speak of other things than flowers," he said as
they walked on in silence for a few moments.

"Ah, but can you speak other than flattery?" she asked
quietly as she seemed to scan the path she was treading.

There were other gentlefolk out walking this lovely early morning. A warm, sunny spring day was too rare a thing to miss, and the gardens were lovely. There was no reason to feel ill-at-ease or as inanely nervous as a green girl, as she did, Megan thought, simply because she was so close to this strange gentleman. After all, she'd been brought up in a noble house and had been at the noblest house in all England for almost a year. So she raised her head to see as well as hear his reply, and only the greatest force of will allowed her to keep looking at him when she gazed into his eyes. It was, she thought in confusion, scarcely hearing his answer, like looking into a mirroring glass, only one which weighed her soul as well as her corporal form.

"Not flatter you? Why, you set me to a hard task, lady, and I wonder why," he mused.

"Because," she answered, looking away, "because flattery tells me nothing: nothing about myself, even if I did believe it, for then I'd only agree, and nothing about you but that you think flattery will please me."

"And what if it isn't flattery, but only that I truly find you so enticing that I must comment on it?"

"Then how many times must you comment on it?" she asked pertly, feeling more secure now that she wasn't looking at him, now that their discourse was becoming just that—discussion. "It's hardly flattering if you think I must hear it over and again in order to understand it."

"Ah, but what if I think you must hear it until you fully accept that I'm overwhelmed, and then take pity on my suffering?" he asked lightly.

"And if I pitied you?" she asked.

"Then I might ask if you'd consent to heal me," he answered very softly.

"Then I might bid you a good morning, sir, for such healing is beyond my own poor capabilities. But I should be willing to guide you toward some other lovely ladies, those who are more accomplished healers than I," she said, vaguely disappointed at ending the flirtation so easily, more disappointed that it had been only that, that he'd only wanted the same thing as the other gentlemen she'd met here at court. For it had been more than his chance resemblance to Perkin. Something in that crystalline gaze had hinted at a rare intelligence. And yet it had turned out to be no more brightness than reflected light, she thought on a sigh.

"Such sighs—dare I hope it's because you expect me to leave you at once in pursuit of those more charitable, experienced . . . healers?" he asked. "Then if so, pray don't waste another breath. It might be that it's a different sort of healing I'm after. After all, a kiss on a wound is a pretty gesture, and may be effective if it's a mother's on her toddler's bruised knee. But if it's a mortal one, on a grown man's heart . . . ?"

"Oh, please, sir!" she said impatiently as she stopped walking, losing her nervousness in the face of his foolishness. "No one is smitten to the heart on a moment's notice! And certainly not by me. Perhaps the ladies in Italy might think such vows overwhelming, but I—"

"—am not overwhelmed, nor neither 'overseas'—yes, I remember that," he said blandly, watching her color rise for reasons of embarrassment as well as vexation now, before he patted her hand and grinned down at her again, "which is why, you'll recall, I asked to walk with you. I've tried, and dismally failed, with the usual gallantries. Please accept that I began in perfect form, however imperfectly it turned out for us. But I'd like a happier ending—or beginning. Now, then. Faith! What can I say? No flowers or flattery or importuning will do for this lady. Mistress, I'm at a loss. What shall we speak of? And be sure," he said quickly, "that I want to speak with you, to know more of you than your lovely face— and that's no flattery, unless you say truth is flattery, and then I'll warrant you'll speak to no man unless he lies."

She laughed aloud. There was no other answer.

And he looked down to see a flash of how white and even her teeth were, for she laughed outright, not bothering to conceal her mouth beneath her hand any more than she hid her wholehearted delight, and he lost his smile for a moment before he laughed with her.

"Well begun in laughter, very well," he said, nodding, "but I'm not a jester, so I'll have to go on with the mere truth about myself. Although that might make you merry enough, God knows," he said ruefully, before he went on. "Now, then, lady, my name is Lucas Lovat, as you know. I'm a trader and a traveler, lately come from Westminster Palace, via France, from Italy, as you may have heard. But I was raised in the southwest, in Devon, by the sea. I have some education and no brothers. One sister survives, and she's given me a score of nieces and nephews, or so it seems, since I find more, in too many sizes to keep count of, each time I return home. I have six-and-twenty years to my credit—or disgrace, as you will—and I've used the later part of them trying to increase my good father's fortunes. I trade in wool and what-have-you. I speak a few tongues, write a fair hand, and sing very like an angel. And you?"

She laughed again, but this time so as to give herself enough time to recover from his words. Because they were like the ones she'd wished, for so many lonely months, that a gentleman might someday speak to her. But still, she trusted him no more than her reaction to him. So when she spoke, almost the first thing she told him was the reason why she doubted him.

"I am Lady Megan Baswell," she said, "and I've been at court since November last. I was given the position of attendant to Lady Katherine by the grace of King Henry. I like it very well here, no one could be a better mistress than my lady, although I do grieve for her and for her most grievous separation from her good husband . . ."

He saw the look in her eyes as she paused, before she rallied and continued, "I was raised in the west, near to the river Wye, when I was so young it looked like a sea to me. But I haven't been there in many years. You see, my father supported York in Edward's day, and was thought to do so still when Richard seized the throne, when he really was devoted to Tudor's cause by then, but he was representing that he was one to deceive the other—or so I think. It's all a muddle to me. What I've been told and what was, may be different things anyway. I can't remember well because I was too young to understand, not that I'm in any better case today, it was that complicated." She raised her hands in supplication. "Still, for whatever reasons, he is no more, nor is his house or his lands, nor my brothers, nor anyone from my house remains but my sister and me. And she was wedded and gone from our house before I was as old as her youngest is now, for she's knee-deep in children now, as is your own sister."

She grew still, but before he could speak, she grinned

and added, "Marry, but I thrive. I have almost twenty years to my name, and all the education a lady requires, or so they say. I play at the guitar, as all well-brought-up ladies do, and speak a little French, as we are taught to do, and sing very like a bird in the treetops—a crow, my good sir. And," she said, cutting across his chuckle, "I am not wedded because I have no dowry, nor anything but Henry's goodwill."

That was plain speaking, he thought, bemused. She was warning him off as kindly as possible. No family, no fortune, and no illusions about how marriageable that made her. But he wasn't seeking more than she could offer him.

"Then I believe I'll have to sing while you play the guitar," he said, and smiled. The more so when he noted her startlement, and then her smooth recover as she tried to hide the extent of her pleasure at his words.

They spoke of many things as they strolled through the garden, most of which she couldn't remember an hour after she'd left him. But they were things that made her laugh, and made her think, and made her forget her fear of him. Which would have been disastrous, she knew, if he didn't himself remind her of how dangerous he was every so often, by looking at her with something entirely different from the benign words he was saying, and if he hadn't spoken about Lady Katherine and her husband once more.

She never remembered exactly what had brought it up, but she thought it was something that ought not to have, in the general way of casual conversation. So it was as if she'd been suddenly wakened from some pleasant reverie when she heard him ask, "And so you've met him? The most famous man in England? And what do you think of Perkin Warbeck, lady?"

"You've just come from Westminster," she said. "Surely, then, you've met him as well."

"Of course," he said smoothly, with no indication of his annoyance at himself for forgetting she'd know that, for forgetting his usual planning because of how she'd diverted him, "but I wondered how a lady might feel about him. It's said that if the nation was composed only of women, why, then, he'd be made king in a day. But hist! Keep that close, please, for there's a treasonous jest!"

He spoke up at once in suddenly loud accents. "Henry's handsome as an Adonis, or so they do say all over the Continent!"

She smiled at the way he was pretending to speak to invisible company, and almost forgot the disquiet she felt at his question.

"So is Perkin Warbeck handsome," she finally said in answer, although she added, loudly, as he'd done, "But sooth! Not so much as our good King Henry, 'tis the very truth!"

Then she said, in lower tones, as he grinned, "But what else can I say of my Lady Katherine's husband? I met him only a few times when he was first . . . brought to London, and I to my lady's service. Perkin Warbeck? He is well-looking and well-spoken, and she loves him very well, that's all I can say."

Liar, he thought tenderly. For you only a little while past said no one could tumble into love at a moment's notice. How many moments had you with him, then, for I doubt you'd more than that, my poor besotted lovely liar? he wondered, even as he said approvingly, "Ah, well, and a well-considered answer that is, too. You were born for court life. Tell me, did you have many guests at Baswell House before you left it? For I warrant you've teethed on diplomacy. Had you any royal guests there?"

She thought, and then spoke of a dim remembrance of one of Royal Edward's sons and his party's visits one autumn day, and laughed with him at her clearer, envious fragment of memory of a fat pony that had been in their company. And then they spoke of Baswell House again, or rather, she thought, she did as he listened. She found that if she avoided his too-encompassing gaze as they walked, she could speak very well, and rest easy in his company. In fact, the more he prodded, the more she spoke of things she'd not in years, and felt a bit of her omnipresent homesickness ease at the sharing. In his company she discovered that she could not only speak of her lost home but also swallow more easily as she did, for the lump in her throat shrank and her chest didn't ache quite so much when she recalled the house and gardens and family that were all gone, except for the memories which recreated them again for him and herself. It was such a luxury that she might have continued walking and talking with him, heedless, lost to her memories and his presence, long after the hour when she was needed in her lady's bedchamber, if a cloud hadn't passed over the sun before then.

Then a fresh wind promising the usual damp conclusion to a bright English morning made her skirts and his cloak flutter, even as the hint of cold rain on its breath at her neck made her shiver.

"A goose walked over my grave." She laughed, and as he cocked a thin eyebrow at her, she explained, "That's what they say in the countryside when you shudder for no reason."

"Then you must have been buried in a gooseyard, you're trembling so. Come, we've gone far afield, but I'll have you back before the first raindrop falls. I think it's those black clouds and not the fowl that account for your shivers. Take my cloak," he said as he pulled it from his shoulders and wrapped it about hers, careful to let his fingers brush her neck as he did, pleased at the faint but visible quake that brief contact produced in her.

"But won't you be cold?" she asked, ducking her head as if it were the wind that made her shiver again. And then, so he wouldn't take it for insult to his manhood, she quickly added, "I mean to say, because you're not used to English weather."

"I? No, I don't feel the cold," he answered truthfully, for he didn't, no more than he felt the heat, or any temperature changes in the air about him. And had not since the day he'd returned to England. Or, more to the point, since the day he'd had to leave, so many years before.

"We talked about . . . about . . . why, me!" she said.

And then Megan bit her lip in vexation. Because she hadn't been able to answer most of Maeve's questions about Lucas Lovat.

"What a green girl!" Maeve cried. "Don't you know you're supposed to let them talk about themselves? That's all men like to hear in a maid's company," she said, before her voice trailed off. "Marry, I'm a fine one to be giving you advice. It wasn't me strolling through the gardens with him all morning, was it? Mayhap I'll start giving the gentleman an earful of my woes, opinions, and ideas when we meet. Sooth!" she said with a snort. "And after that five minutes, what will I say? Never mind, go on as you are, and you'll have him sooner than you can say it."

"Have him for what?" Megan asked softly.

"God keep you, Meg! What else? But if I have to explain country matters to you now, we'll never get to our duties today. Didn't they teach you anything at home?"

Megan laughed, as she was expected to, then hurried on in Maeve's wake to wait in attendance on their lady. But there wasn't anything humorous in the thought that the question hadn't been answered, or at least, if it had been, then not in any way she wanted to hear, or believe.

This afternoon Lady Katherine chose to bear the queen company. She was always welcomed in the queen's apartments, but although she seemed to enjoy being in the queen's undemanding presence, and pleased to have her own little Margaret keep the young princes and princesses company when they were summoned to wait upon their mama, often as not she'd pass her afternoons pacing and dreaming, apart from the others in the palace. The weather had deteriorated, and so all the ladies and children were indoors, in the queen's quarters, as were most of their guests at this hour.

So Megan was surprised to see Lucas Lovat the moment she came into the queen's rooms. He knelt on one knee before the throne as he spoke to the littlest princess, Mary, while the other towheaded infant girl, Lady Katherine's Margaret, perched on his other knee. Although the room was crowded, the three fair heads clustered together made a strikingly handsome picture as they subtly lit a portion of the rainy-day-dim chamber.

"Faith! He fascinates females of every age and condition. The man's a marvel," Maeve breathed in Megan's ear.

But she hadn't spoken softly enough, for Lady Katherine, two steps ahead of them, laughed and added, "Mayhap, but more likely it's because he reminds my Margaret of her own father."

"And the little princess of her own brothers, aye, I see it," Maeve agreed, looking to where young, slender, light-haired Prince Arthur was standing, as usual engaged in earnest conversation with his mama. Shy, fair young

Prince Henry played at her feet, as smug Princess Margaret, with her superiority of two years, watched him indulgently, as though she'd nineteen years instead of a full decade less to her credit.

These chambers were never empty at this hour, but they seemed more populated than usual today, or perhaps, Megan thought, it was because she was seeing them as though through Lucas Lovat's stranger's eyes. The robed men by the windows were the princes' tutors, the one holding court among them, the princes' physician, John Argentine, no doubt visiting his charges today because of rumors of a rashy pox in the town. It was spring, and spring meant coughs and spots, sniffles and measles, and all manner of childhood complaints. Even if it weren't worse, it was troublesome enough; there was no such thing as a simple disease, not for children. Hadn't young Princess Elizabeth, fairest of all Henry's daughters, died of just such a minor ailment only three years past, when she'd only three years to her own brief mortal span?

The various ladies of the court sat in another corner, gossiping, giggling, and missing nothing that was going on before them, even if nothing very much was, except for their favorite thing: gossip. The children's nurses occupied themselves in their own niche, as did the maidservants of the queen's ladies-in-waiting in their own customary place. Knights, nobles, and gentlemen of the court were clustered together; a knot of foreign visitors were deep in conversation a few feet away, their attendants nearby, in just as tight a circle; the guards stood in all their stations ringed round the great room. Naturally, then, Megan reasoned, she'd seen Lucas Lovat first, for he alone, as the most recent arrival, and being alone, had no customary place to take. But he did, she granted, take the eye.

Even the queen glanced at him with her sad, sweet smile in place as she watched her infant daughter being charmed by him. As Megan watched, she saw that there was, in that one moment, something in the queen's mild eyes that was a question, a brief puzzlement, and it seemed she would speak to him about it, before the thought was gone and forgotten when something in Arthur's words called her back to him, for she never strayed far in thought or distance from this, her first-born boy.

Lady Katherine joined the queen when Arthur had done speaking to her and had turned his attention to his younger brother. The two women sat in close conversation, looking over to Lucas and their daughters every so often. In time, Lucas straightened, the girls scampered off, and he, sensing the summons in the queen's glance, dusted off his knee before he bent it to her once again.

"Majesty," he said as he rose gracefully at her command, "not in all the courts in Italy have I seen such charm. And the littlest princess is but an infant! She will carry the world before her one day." He shook his head, as though too astonished for words.

The queen inclined her head at the compliment. But Lady Katherine smiled with almost too much animation, but that might have been, Megan thought uneasily, only what she read into that bright look the lady shot to Lucas before she looked away, swallowing transparent glee. For the queen only smiled her usual sad smile and asked for news of her lord, and never noticed, as perhaps only Megan and Lady Katherine did, that by not naming her, the gentleman had not said *which* child was the princess he meant.

No, not possible, not so, Megan thought when Lucas had done with his audience with the queen and was beckoned over to join the gentlemen. She read too much into every movement her lady made, and now she watched the gentleman far too closely too. There was nothing exceptional in Lucas' demeanor to give credit to that wild surmise. Now he stood in quiet conversation with a group of notable men and courtiers: merry John Andrews, and Prince Arthur's constant champion, Sir Reginald Bray, grave Giles Herbert, Thomas Black, and some courtiers from London, were among others she knew, or tried not to know, all too well. And here today too, Megan noted, as her heart froze, a man Lady Katherine looked at not at all, or stared down if their eyes chanced to meet: Lord Daubeney, chief commander of Henry's improvised army that had defeated her own husband's pretensions. A lesser woman would have been overwhelmed, Megan thought, but not Lady Katherine: sister to an earl, cousin to a king, and wedded to a man she still believed to be king, she carried herself with dignity and grace in this hall filled with enemies.

Maeve went to join the queen's ladies; Megan followed absently as her eyes continued to follow Lucas Lovat's tall figure as he moved from group to group and finally paused to speak with the physician Argentine. It was only when she felt a painful pinch on the soft flesh of her upper arm that she spun around, turning her gaze from him to stare in hurt affront at Maeve.

"God's wounds! Lobcock! Will you have every cat in the courtyard mewing about you and the fellow? Then where will you be, eh?" Maeve hissed at her. "For be sure, sure as I know men, that one's only out for sport, and who'll take his leavings, eh? It's not like you've an excuse for clean sheets on your wedding night. If you want to play and dare to risk it, for sweet Christ's sake, do it cleverly. You've been goggling at him as though he just slipped out of your arms—aye, blush, that will make it better—now they'll only think he's just slipped out something tighter in your bed," she said with disgust.

"You go too far, Maeve," Megan said in a harsh whisper. "I wasn't even thinking . . . of him, I was daydreaming, and if you dare to pinch me like that again . . ." She paused, seeing Maeve grinning.

"Ah, better," the smaller woman whispered. "Now they'll only think we were fighting—and I won't give you back the needle, because it was mine to begin with," she said loudly.

The other women, who Megan finally noticed had been staring at her with avid expressions, looked disappointed before they looked away.

"Ah, my thanks," she sighed. "I'd forgot. Nothing done in this place goes unremarked, even if nothing *was* done. I don't know what came over me."

"Nothing," Maeve said merrily. "It's what you wish would come over you that's the problem."

She skipped away before Megan could reply, leaving her glowering after her as convincingly as if they'd had a terrible row.

But Megan couldn't stop looking after him. She did it discreetly now, as though she were adjusting something on her shoulder, or brushing at something on her sleeve, or looking at someone just to the left, to the right, to the side of him. She detested herself for doing it, but couldn't stop, any more than she could stop thinking of him.

Because he spoke as fair as he looked, and he looked at her with more than pleasure and less than brute lust. But when he looked at her, to find her looking back to him, he smiled. Only that. There was no malice, or gloating, or preening in his expression before he turned away to continue with his conversation. But then, she knew it would never do. If she showed a lack of pride, it might turn his thoughts—if, that was, she realized, she even knew what they were.

She didn't look at him again that afternoon, though she'd vow that her very skin warmed when he was anywhere nearby, and cooled when he walked away. But now she remained resolutely ignorant of his expression. Because he'd given too little to receive so much of her time—though God knew, she thought, she'd time and to spare to give. And, she reminded herself sternly over and again, her attraction to Lucas Lovat might merely be like young Margaret's: because he unwittingly echoed that face and form she couldn't forget, any more than Lady Katherine could.

Why else, she asked herself when she sat down to dinner that evening and looked to the high table, would her lady choose to dine with him again?

"How long do you stay?" Lady Katherine asked Lucas as he handed the cup of wine to her.

"Long enough to rest, long enough to learn, long enough to know enough so that I may go back and give a good report to your husband, lady," he answered. "Try this wine, it's not so sour as the last, or perhaps the last has killed my taste. How say you, lady?"

She gazed into his bland face and nodded.

"I say I shall see," she said, accepting the cup.

"It is all I ask," Lucas answered, as unsurprised as he was disbelieving. She'd never trust him unless her husband ordered it, and how should he do that? But something was afoot, although he'd heard nothing in all his several conversations to even hint at it. Rather, he felt it, as he'd learned to do. Collusion was thick in the air. He glanced to the lower table, where Lady Megan sat. Lovely, restrained, straining to be free as much as she was to conform, stealing glances at him as she had all day, all night. He raised his cup to her and drank, smiling, after he saw her lower her eyes in pleased alarm at his gesture. And smiled the more, into his cup, when he saw Lady Katherine's eyes narrow as she wondered how she could make use of his obvious infatuation.

Lucas wandered from group to group in the dining hall when the dinner ended. He had a word with carrot-haired Elizabeth, and shared a jest with stammering Joan, and drank the health of jug-eared Mary, and passed a pleasant moment with vain Alys, Sir Harold's grasping widow, and three giggling ladies who were all determined to spite each other. And then, when he knew he'd not insulted any of the other ladies, as well as making Megan wonder if he was ever going to come to her, he sought her out at last.

He was convinced Megan was the most desirable woman in the room. He'd had too many women to count in his time, and every time he prepared to woo one, he convinced himself of that. This time there was no persuasion necessary. She was well-made and well-spoken, and if there was any luck left for him in this world, she'd be well-advised on what was going forth with her mistress and her husband.

"So now," he breathed as he came up behind her, "I've visited a dozen others first so as not to embarrass you, my lady. I think I do deserve your company now."

She whirled about to face him, her obvious, instant joy causing his smile to slip, before she recovered herself and said with due modesty, lowering her lashes over the pleasure in her chestnut-brown eyes, "My company? You don't ask for very much, for you have it, sir."

"Do I?" he mused. "But what if I want it exclusively?"

She seemed puzzled. "You have that too," she said. "Maeve's left my side, and as you see, there's no one else there."

"Ah, but where's privacy? Or is that a foreign notion? Come. The singers are tuning up their instruments, the gamesters are rattling their favorite dice and marking their best cards. There'll be music and laughter to add to the noise, and dozens of pairs of eyes to watch our every movement. I don't call that exclusivity. Come. The rain has stopped, come out into the gardens to stroll with me again? Or," he said softly, stepping closer to her, his breath making the strands of hair at the sides of her face sway, "better, come with me to my chamber. I'm honored here, for I share with no one, and it's a long night ahead."

He saw her answer in her face before she could speak.

"Have I a rival?" he asked innocently, as though he didn't know, as though he hadn't spoken of the man all night with Lady Katherine.

She shook her head in denial. "I hardly know you," she said.

"How long will it take to get to know me?" he asked.

"I don't know." She turned her head.

"Shall we see?" he asked gently, touching and testing one brown curl that had escaped her coif, near to her ear, as though he was fascinated with it.

"No, no," she said at once, as if that touch had awakened her and she'd just heard their conversation. "However long it would take, I could not. I cannot," she said, gazing up at him with confusion, as well as entreaty and sorrow. "Not I. I'm sorry."

"That I asked? Or that you cannot? Both? Never mind. I understand. Forgive me. I'm used to foreign ways. No, don't flee me," he said as his hand grasped her wrist the second she began to back away. He held her still beside him, seemingly beguiled by how small the bones in that slim wrist were, because it was a moment before he spoke again, and then it was lightly, charmingly.

"If Henry were here, we'd have a tournament, and I'd wear your favor on my helm. You smile. But I can ride to the ring. And joust. Would that impress you into my favor, I wonder."

"You carry your mail and your helm and your warhorse in your traveling bags?" she asked, fighting for control as his fingers continued to slide over her wrist as though he hadn't captured it, stroking it, shaping it, measuring it and her pulse.

"I can make do. You doubt me? You ought to have seen me in Flanders. I wore so much cloth of gold that I blinded three opponents before they could so much as raise their lances. Even their horses blinked."

She didn't smile, but only looked away.

"Good lady, forgive me. Please," he said seriously.

She nodded, because she couldn't speak. And he loosed her wrist. They stayed, and spoke of the dinner, the

entertainers, the company, and the night, until she saw
Maeve gesturing to her, and looked toward her to see
where Lady Katherine was standing, preparing to with-
draw. Then, never knowing whether it was an hour or a
moment that had passed since Maeve had left her, she
curtsied and gave him good-night. He watched after her
for a moment when she left him before he began his
seemingly aimless wandering about the room again.

At the end of the night, it was the king's physician that
he'd spoken with earlier that he spoke to at last, before
he retired to his own chamber again.

"Another consultation, please, good physician. My heart
pains me, and I seem to have lost my allure," he said,
placing one hand on his chest as he came up to the other
man.

The doctor gave a rusty chuckle before he sobered and
said softly, "Take care, my Lucas. Take care. I misgive
this. I've thought on it, little else all night, in fact, and
for all you say, I do misgive it. Do you really think this is
wise?"

"I really think it is necessary," he said as somberly as
the older man had, before he went on lightly, blithely,
"But what am I to do? Not only is the lady lovely, and
one of Lady Katherine's confidantes, but I have been as
much as ordered to seduce her by my king. Now, what
could be more pleasant? Except for the bothersome fact
that I seem to have lost my way with Englishwomen.
Although I grant I only met her just today—that usually
is time enough. Now, give me your learned opinion,
good doctor, what do I lack?"

"Sense," the other man said bluntly. "She's virtuous."

"Why, so were all women, even Mother Eve, once,"
he replied.

"She has too much to lose to play at your game," the
older man answered with a worried look.

"Why, so we are a match made in heaven. For so do
I," Lucas answered on a light laugh that had no humor in
it, and was not returned.

5

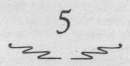

Some days they were merry, some nights they were somber, in the mornings they gossiped about the night before, in the evenings they reviewed their day. Megan had never realized how little time she had to herself before, and yet since she'd met Lucas Lovat, she'd never known how much time there was to lie heavy on her hands when she wasn't with him. They never seemed to run out of things to discuss. They giggled about the foibles of others at court, even as they compared their feelings about them, and it constantly amazed her that he seemed to enjoy hearing her impressions about her own mundane experiences as much as she loved to hear him talk of his travels across the world.

Sometimes, in the mornings, they'd pace the gardens and talk about trivial things that became gloriously funny as they spoke on.

"Yes, they do eat frogs and snails, but not toads—hush . . . silly wench," he said as she made an exaggerated face to show her revulsion. "Didn't your mistress ever tell you what she sustained herself with on her travels?"

"She's not in the habit of gossiping with me. I'm her lady-in-waiting, not her friend," Megan said, suddenly sober.

"But you knew about the fashions at the courts of Rome and France, and said you'd met Polydore Vergil, Tom Bell, and John . . . What was his name?" he asked idly. "You know, the one with the long nose—one of those who was friend to your lady and her husband when they were abroad."

"Oh, yes," Megan answered, smiling. "Long nose, indeed! I only said 'imposing nose'—Sir John Fordyce, it was. But that was only because my lady introduced them to me in passing, and I overheard them reminiscing."

"Ah," he said, "not about snails, obviously."

"I don't like the thought of eating things that slither," she said disdainfully.

"No, you prefer eels and cockles, crabs and whelks," he said when he'd done laughing, "things with a bit of bounce to their slither, eh?"

And they'd laugh until Megan looked at the sun and remembered the hour, and left to go with her lady again.

Sometimes, in the quiet of the night, when they found a darkened corner, they'd speak about music, or dance, and matters philosophical, and when they were done with that, they'd talk about themselves again.

"The thing about traveling," he mused as they sat in a window embrasure and heard the music drifting from the great hall beyond, "is that when everything is new to your eyes, you never expect to see a familiar face, and so never feel lonely if you don't—or, that is to say, lonelier than any other traveler. Whereas, if you were at home, you'd feel odd about not seeing a friend for days. That, I think, is the lure of constantly seeking new lands."

"Oh," she said, her heart constricting at the note she heard in his voice, keeping her own voice neutral and her gaze on her lap as she murmured, "that does make sense."

"Aye, but only for some, that is. I'd warrant your lady sought friends even as she traveled, aye, and made many too. Indeed, I wonder why she sees so few from those days now."

"Ah, well-a-day," Megan answered thoughtfully. "How can she? So many are in the tower, or slain—those from Ireland, certainly. And those from other lands who weren't English are not welcomed here."

"She doesn't even correspond with any of them?" he asked, as though diverted.

But when she looked up at that, momentarily disturbed, as if at some bothersome intrusive thought, he smiled down at her. And then reached for her, drew her to him, and kissed her hesitantly, and then with more conviction. His lips were warmer and softer than she'd thought they'd be, but their very gentleness stirred her more than she'd believed they could, and his hands were so tender she became confused at the way she felt both stimulated and comforted. But the excitement she began to experience was enough to make her feel endangered. Even as she recalled herself and began to pull away, he released her. Her lips tingled, but she restrained herself from touching her hand to them, and kept her eyes cast down, fully expecting to hear his apology, or his request for more. She was trying to decide which to accept, and so was astonished to hear him laugh with genuine merriment instead. Her eyes flew wide.

"Sooth! Is that how Englishwomen kiss now? I wonder that they're still begetting Englishmen! Why, lady, kissing with a closed mouth is like dining without swallowing. Interesting, but nothing to the point."

She lost her shame in her fury, as he'd expected. "English *gentle*men don't expect more from unwed ladies," she raged, feeling foolish as well as wounded, "and those who take without asking have no right to expect more."

"Ah. So that's why they withhold their tongues in kissing, so they can use them to stab their gallants for trying to please them?" he asked wonderingly. "Sooth, I beg pardon, lady, and you've my oath not to try more, if you wish it. For I shudder to think how they use that which I most desire, in more advanced love play."

She bit her lip, and then pursed them, trying hard not to laugh.

"Oho," he said wisely, "and then they look as though they'd sucked on lemons to discourage more attentions. My admiration for my fellow countrymen grows by leaps and bounds. Surely they must be the bravest of men. Lady, can I try again?" he asked, suddenly contrite, suddenly serious, even as she broke down and laughed up at him.

He'd tried, and succeeded, again and again. At little embraces that slowly grew more bold, as bold as their brief times permitted. As the time went on, she became both more alarmed and more gratified at how brief their times were. Because for all he'd become so important to her, still, there was her future as well as his past to consider, and for all it was so much, when she'd time to consider, she'd realize it was much too soon—only handfuls of days and nights for all it felt like it had been forever.

Yet each new day she looked forward to the night, and each night their talk became less, and their embraces bolder. Tonight, as soon as they were alone in a corridor after dinner, no matter how she tried to distract him, he'd speak of nothing else after he'd tried to do nothing else but embrace her.

"A troubadour, then. Yes," he sighed, running his finger along the edge of her gown from her neck to her shoulder, "with a ragged doublet and one leg striped and the other decorated with triangular patches, a lute over my shoulder and a song on my lips. How the ladies sigh for them in Italy. I shall certainly have to try that next. What else is left to me? You turn up your nose at the thought of me, magnificent in my armor, riding off to the joust for you. You giggle when I so much as mention seeking out dragons to slay, yes, and there you go again," Lucas said in great mock disgust. "So how can I win you?" he asked, his voice suddenly serious, and waited for her answer, as all merriment fled from her eyes.

"Lucas . . . I—" Megan began.

"—am not interested," he said flatly, interrupting. "Then please tell me so, and I'll go."

She looked up at him without speaking, but everything she had to say was clear to read in her face, even in the wavering torchlight. It was that, her complete lack of artistry at something he had mastered long ago, that made him speak again, paining her more, twisting that curious pang of pain in his own breast more deeply.

"Say it if you must, my lady. I'm a man grown. I'll not mope, or lie across your doorstep, or cast you long hurt looks every time we meet, I promise you. And as for that—why, I'll leave this place soon enough and not trouble you again. *If* you say me nay. But say it. For sweet Christ's sake, and mine own, lady, cut me loose if you won't have me. Do not look me 'aye' and say me 'nay.' I'm no boy, to live on looks and sighs."

No, it wasn't fair. He knew it very well. But neither was life, he thought savagely. Long days and longer nights of his intensive courtship had passed, and still she wavered, and yet she paused before bestowing her final yes.

And then he didn't wait for her to answer whatever it was she was desperately trying to, but only pulled her into the shadows of the corridor, drawing her into a niche in the great stone wall, and his back against the cold stones and his heart against her warmth, he put a hand on either side of her head and brought his lips to hers. And now he felt no shame, but only heat and yielding sweetness, and that, he thought, was surely evidence of his several small hard-won victories in this siege against her denial of him. He'd never met a more resistant maid—or at least he'd never tarried so long to try a more resistant one. It had become more than a challenge, more than his mission. He'd begun to doubt she'd anything to tell him about Perkin and his lady that he didn't know, but there were other secrets he wanted of her now. So many moments, in so many days, and more in hidden retreats and odd encounters in the furtive moments of so many nights. It was as gratifying as it was disturbing; he was unaccustomed to denial and frustration and half-measures, almost as much as he was by the little doubts he was experiencing.

Her lack of experience meant little to him; all knowledge must begin somewhere. Her lack of guile meant more. He seldom preyed on the helpless, or was it, he was beginning to wonder, that he seldom realized he did? No matter. He wanted her for a host of reasons. And not the least, although the most unusual, and so the most confusing, was his desire for the special taste and feel and scent of her. He'd known expert and generous lovers, and she gave nothing without a struggle against herself as well as him, and knew nothing but what he'd taught her. A devoted admirer of the breed, it was the variety, never the particular specimen he'd always desired. Unless that was the crux of it, he'd thought as he sought sleep at the height of his unusually celibate nights; it was the very fact that she was so elusive that beguiled him. He might need what she might know, but he'd almost forgotten that in his more basic need of her.

It seemed that he'd begun to admire her honesty as well as her breasts, he thought mirthfully, and her sense of humor just as much as her sensitive lips.

Now he forgot just why he admired her as he enjoyed her. For now she opened her mouth against his, and by reaching up her arms about his neck, opened her body to his touch. He relaxed against her and sighed into her

mouth. This was homecoming; this was his field of expertise, his sport, his comfort, and his delight. His hands
drifted down from her face; sweet smooth high breasts, a
ripple of ribs, a slide of supple waist, a small roundness
of bottom, damp heat here now, beneath his questing
fingers, so like to that beneath his lips. And then, of
course, as always, it was all abruptly withdrawn from him
again.

He stood still and closed his eyes, mastering himself so
that he wouldn't do what he was tempted to: pull her
back into his arms and spin around so that he could hold
her up against the wall and force her into it, and be done
with the cursed unaccustomed ache in his body. But then
he'd lose the other thing he was after, and as he opened
his eyes to her obvious despair, he was no longer sure
that thing was the confidences he was sure she'd share
with him after.

It was simpler to rage, and probably more beneficial to
his cause.

"God's precious wounds, lady!" he hissed. "A nibble
today, a tickle tomorrow. Today I can touch this breast,
can I? Next week the other? Next year your heart? Have
done with this teasing and backing and filling. I am not a
boy. Nor you," he said with deadly aim as she opened
her lips to answer, "a girl."

"That's true," she said in a shaken voice after a pause.
"That's . . . that's very true."

How to say that she knew it too well, but for all that,
she'd never known what it was to want what she knew
she shouldn't have? This was nothing like her love for the
man he resembled so slightly. This was a painful physical
yearning to share more than her mind. But how to tell
him that she'd never known that desire could follow so
swiftly on the heels of friendship, just as she'd never
guessed that she'd feel such a strong kinship to a man?
And how to say that she dared not reject him—almost as
much as she dared not accept him? Or that she was as
overjoyed as horrified to discover that a glance at him in
company brought the remembrance of more than their
many conversations to her mind? For just the look of him
across a room brought the feel of his shoulders beneath
her hands back to her. She'd never made such a close
friend so quickly, and she could swear he was a friend,

and yet she could scarcely hear his words anymore for looking at his mouth. He was new to her, everything about him a revelation. But what was that against the wisdom she'd lived with all her life? Yet, still, she couldn't bear his anger or dislike for her, any more than she could bear her own.

"Forgive me," she said in a small voice. "You're right."

"Then come with me, down this hall and up a stair, and into my arms, and now," he said tightly.

"I cannot!" she said. "Because . . ."

She hesitated. How could she say "marriage" now? For all he could speak of was lovemaking, and did when he instructed her in the preliminary arts of it when she was in his arms, and it sounded entirely right then; the word "marriage," the demand for lifelong security for momentary pleasure, seemed an obscene thing to say now. Especially since she feared saying it would dismiss him forever.

There it was. To lie with him would be to gain pleasure and give him pleasure, but might be to lose her future and even his love. Because for all she knew him, it had only been a matter of days. And for all they'd spoken, and she knew his thoughts on art and life and laughter, yet—and this was the most confusing thing—still she knew she didn't know him very well.

"I cannot offer more," he said roughly into the silence between them.

It was hard to say which of them was more surprised at what he'd said.

But he reacted first. He took her hand as she turned to flee him.

"Stay," he said. "Don't leave me."

She paused, wanting to stay so badly she knew she must go.

"We'll let it be, for tonight," he said as he drew her close and simply held her. "We'll talk, I think," he said as he put her away from him, since it seemed his body wasn't being as reasonable as he was, "for a while. But stay, please, lady, stay, until both sleep and friendship— even when we're apart—seem possible again."

She didn't creep into the bed she shared with Maeve until dawn was worrying at the edges of the night sky outside their tiny window.

"Ho!" an exceedingly wakeful Maeve said as soon as she felt the slight body settle next to hers. "So he finally won, did he? The more fool you," she said with a trace of envy.

"We only spoke," Megan said softly, wonderingly, as she realized she couldn't recall what they'd said.

"And I danced with the king until dawn," Maeve scoffed. "Please credit me with the wits of a maw worm. You even smell of him, you know."

"We kissed. But then we only talked," Megan said, aware of the lingering scents of lemon and spices upon her, and grateful for the memories they brought her.

"The more fool you," Maeve sighed, and fell silent.

"Yes," Megan agreed absently, until she heard what she'd said, and realized she'd meant it.

Then she woke from her reverie to fret and stare at the ceiling until true light.

"Shall I be losing my Megan to love, I wonder?" Lady Katherine asked.

Both Megan and Maeve stopped still in their places at her words. They were alone with their lady, but their lady was one who'd learned how to be alone when with them. Her words were as surprising for having been spoken as they were for having been thought. It was the shank of the afternoon, a time when the ladies at court were dismissed from the queen's company, when Lady Katherine had long since dismissed Margaret to her nurse and her dinner, a time when she customarily began to wonder what to wear down to her own supper. The most she ever addressed to her handmaidens at this time was orders—as at most other times, Megan thought, bewildered.

"Why, no, my lady. Why do you say so?" she asked.

"I'm not blind or deaf, Megan," Lady Katherine said simply. "He waits upon you, you sigh after him, you two can scarcely keep your eyes off each other."

Maeve took pity on Megan's dismay and cackled loudly in her best imitation of licentiousness incarnate. "Ah, but she swears that's all he's put off—or on—her, my lady."

"Which is as it should be," Lady Katherine said. "Do you think he'll ask the king for you, Megan? I shouldn't be surprised if he gets consent. He *is* in the king's good graces, isn't he?"

"I . . . I think so," Megan said, before she added quickly, "But there's no thought of that, my lady, no, none at all. He's never said it," she said, reddening at the lie, for he'd just spoken of it—to soundly deny it—but how should she admit that and yet admit that she still bore him company? "And I doubt he will. We are just . . . just acquainted."

"Don't be foolish, Meg," Lady Katherine said, fixing her with a chill blue stare. "Men like Lucas Lovat are never 'just acquainted' with women your age. He means either marriage or mischief. Which is it?"

"Neither," Megan blurted. "Or, rather, I cannot say, my lady," she said, for she couldn't, any more than she could fathom the reasons for the lady's sudden interest in her future.

"You should be able to say," Lady Katherine insisted, as Maeve, recovered from her surprise, began to nod agreement. "Unlike Maeve here, you cannot afford the luxury of pleasure without reward." And as Maeve gave her mistress a new and considering look, she went on. "What have you learned about Lucas Lovat, then?"

Megan marshaled her thoughts, wondering whether to begin with his love of horses or his knowledge of foreign lands. She decided to repeat his glowing descriptions of Florence. She smiled.

"He's an only son, we all know that," Lady Katherine said before she could speak. "Why has he not wedded yet? Or was there a previous contract that went awry—and if so, why? He's all of six-and-twenty, I'd say, easily my husband's age. And my Perkin was unwed when we met three years ago only because of his extraordinary position." Her voice softened before she said more harshly, "He's a trader, but how successful? He speaks of powerful friends abroad, I've seen him speaking with some at court, is his power all in his speech, or is there money there? Or must he find it in a wife? Can he wed where he will? What does he know of your condition? Indeed, what do you know of it? Will Henry dower you extravagantly?

"Well, Megan, where are your answers? You pass hours with the man, you've grown shadows beneath your eyes thinking of him—or staying with him throughout the night. Have they seen nothing but his handsome face?

Have you heard nothing but his dulcet voice? Or is it,"
she asked in a quieter voice, "that when you meet, you
two speak only of you and your life?"

"We . . . we speak of many things, my lady," Megan
said hesitantly, her spirit rebelling against the neccessity
for being civil to her mistress now, even as she knew she
must be more than civil to her. "It's true he speaks more
of his travels than of himself . . ." Her voice faded. But
then she went on. "He . . . he's never mentioned his
fortune . . . but I consider that modesty," she said, raising her head as she thought of how to excuse each point
of ignorance. "Nor has he asked after my expectations,
and I think that only a kindness, for I've no idea of what
they are, or if they are anything at all. I don't know if he
was ever betrothed, but he has never asked me if I was,
and . . ." she said, her spirit flagging again, as her voice
lowered, "and it does not appear that he will speak of
marriage to me—or to the king."

"And what does he ask about your life, then?" Lady
Katherine asked, her lovely blue eyes kindling.

"We speak about . . . about my likes and dislikes, as
we do of his, and of what happens here at court, and . . .
and . . ."

"Twaddle," Maeve put in, "lovers' piddle-paddle, I
think, my lady," as Megan yearned to throw down the
clothing she held in her arms and run away from their
searching stares.

Lady Katherine seemed to relax, but her voice remained sharp. "But what are you thinking of, Megan?"
she asked. "You can't afford the luxury of a lover. What
if you prove successful, and he leaves you? I can't keep
an unwed girl who is increasing, and neither will Henry
have a care for you if you start breeding like a careless
peasant. And don't think it altogether unlikely, even if
you know enough to practice the arts Maeve does. It isn't
a matter of frequency so much as potency and chance. I
gave my husband our Margaret almost nine months to
the night of our wedding. And however it has turned
out," she said, her blue eyes glistening with unshed tears,
"he stayed with me until they dragged him from my
arms. *That* is love, *that* is what you should seek, not
careless play.

"Oh, go and wash your face, Megan," she said on an

aggrieved sigh. "Return when you're recovered. I didn't
speak in order to reduce you to tears, I only sought to
caution you, to tell you what love is. It's different for a
man than it is for a woman. Only when it's the same is it
good for a woman in your condition—only then is it
noble. That's the only worthwhile love. Hold your tongue,
Maeve," she cautioned as Maeve began to smile. "Do
not jest about the joys of lust when the girl's whole life
hangs in the balance. Or is it lust, or even love, at all?
Think. You're very lovely, Megan, but so are many other
girls at court. But they aren't in my service. Never forget," she said sternly, "the nature of this court, for I
never do. Never forget who it is that you attend, and who
they are who might be interested in knowing more about
me and my husband."

Even Maeve's face grew still at those words.

"But you . . . you pass so much time with him yourself, my lady," Megan stammered.

"Dolt!" Lady Katherine spat, showing a fury no man
had ever seen and her ladies had only ever guessed at,
before she saw their shocked faces and calmed herself.
Then she said bitterly, "Of course I have. How else
should I know who he is and why he is here, and so
suddenly interested in us? Ask yourself who Lucas Lovat
is, Megan, and what it is he really wants of you," she said
in the same tones in which she'd ordered her to wash her
face, although now Megan's hot tears of embarrassment
had been dried by the chill of a new small fear. "If you
know that, you'll know how you should go on, and even
if you decide you should not, at least that's better than
blundering into whatever it is you'll find with him. I have
loved, and I do love, and there is nothing more beautiful.
And nothing so loathsome as deceit. I've known that
too—faith! I have—but never at my husband's hands."

"And never at mine, my lady, I vow it!" Megan cried,
and clasped her lady's hand hard, before she bobbed a
curtsy and fled the room to seek a corner of her tiny
antechamber and the time to think alone.

Had she thought him like to Perkin? Now Megan saw
him coming to her across the room and saw that they
were actually little alike. As she had always thought
herself a poor thrown shadow in the light of Lady Kath-

erine's perfect loveliness, now she saw that Lucas Lovat was himself a strangely distorted replica of her lady's perfect love. And more, in that one instant she saw that their relationship was in itself a parody of the love that Perkin shared with his lady. The one pair united in holy wedlock—the other grappling together in lust.

Lady Katherine and her husband were stately twinned souls. It was painful now to think of the contrast: the proud, vivid, highborn lady and her golden, warm, displaced prince, as opposed to foolish, drab, and fearful Megan and her icy, clever Lucas. Here was caricature. Here was a replication too cruel for comedy, too sad for satire. For she herself was neither so brave nor so beautiful as her lady. And Lucas? Whereas Perkin's hair was beaten gold, Lucas' was the greenish cast of envious citrine; whereas Perkin's eyes were warm and caressing, Lucas' were mirrors reflecting whatever she wished to see in herself: every fine feature of Perkin's was exaggerated in Lucas, except for his gallantry. For whereas Perkin would surely give his life for his love, Lucas wouldn't even give his word for it, and whereas Perkin had pledged himself for eternity, Lucas wanted only heated moments in her arms. The only similarity she saw now was that she knew neither love could ever be hers.

Yes, now that she'd thought on it, his questions often had to do with Lady Katherine and her husband. It could have been mere curiosity. But no, now that she considered it, whether he dallied for the sake of spying or amusing himself, she couldn't go on with him. The sound of his voice was as much of a lure as the taste of his lips, but she saw now there'd not been truth in either. She almost gagged at the realization of what she'd been attempting. Pretending she was a virtuous lady, and then thinking of writhing in the sheets with a man who reminded her of another, vastly his better? There was the ultimate mockery: Megan and Lucas, as opposed to Perkin and his Katherine—the purity of holy love, and a tawdry, vulgar echo of it.

Apart from all that, there was another simple basic truth, Megan thought as she watched Lucas approach her. Her life was a matter of loss and gain, and she simply could not afford him. She hadn't the price to pay for a counterfeit love.

Lucas bowed over her hand and raised his eyes to see all the doubt and disgust she thought she concealed.

"How now?" he breathed. "Who's been calling me thief? Or murderer? By my faith, I haven't drowned any kittens since we last met."

She flushed, and stricken, lowered her head.

One finger beneath her chin tilted it up to him again.

"Let me at least hear the charges before you hang me, lady," he said seriously, his clear eyes denying everything she'd thought. "What is it?"

"Nothing, a fancy, a nothing, forgive me," she said, stumbling into the light of his smile, forgetting almost everything she'd imagined in the dark of his absence from her, finding it absurd, counting it a dream, as everything seemed to be when she was not in his presence.

"Anything," he said, "even if there were a thing to forgive. But now you must be as good with me. I cannot stay to hear the charges read. I must go in to dine with your lady. But I will see you after. And I will know the cause of this momentary 'nothing' then—it's only fair, my fair lady."

And bowing, he left her to the same dark thoughts as before.

"Good sir, have you been trifling with my little Megan?" Lady Katherine asked lightly.

Lucas swallowed down the bite he'd had in his mouth and was glad he'd not been drinking when she asked that.

"Good lady," he answered as gently, when he could, "has she been complaining of me?"

She bent her head, and when she raised it, she'd only the same gentle smile she usually wore.

"Well-said," she sighed.

They dined, and spoke, and laughed as usual. But now he detected a distance in her attitude to him, and decided that as much as he knew of this lady, it wasn't fear for her "little Megan" that was causing it. No helpless creatures in nature survived. For all her submissiveness and lack of weapons, he never doubted Lady Katherine was purest steel. Like the gentle rabbit who could hear the slightest noise in the brush and sense any lingering shadow overhead, though she'd neither fang nor claw, she would survive. There were a great many more rabbits than hawks in the world.

So that was the reason for the lady's "little Megan" staring at him tonight as though he'd sprouted horns and a tail, he mused. Her mistress had picked up something in his demeanor that had alerted her, and for all he thought he could talk the lovely Megan around it, he respected her lady's heightened senses and fervor too much to ignore it. In truth, he'd lingered overlong. He'd been beguiled, and be damned to it, it was more than his vanity snubbed and his body aching; he was too old to linger for kisses like a stripling boy. He'd learned nothing from the lady or her Megan, and now it was time to try harder, or be gone. It was past time to stop dallying, time to press Megan to the limit. For all he knew, he might just as well lose as win her by it, and he welcomed the decision. It was very sweet in her company, and there was danger in such sweetness. It was time to partake of the sweet, or leave it, or take it and leave it, and so be done with it in either case.

It was also time to throw some dice with the Lady Katherine, he thought, glancing at her sidewise from beneath his lashes. Sometimes giving a little gained a great deal.

"I hear," he said as he sipped his wine, "that Henry's coming here in state, perhaps so soon as later this week."

It may have been that she stopped breathing. When she did again, for all she still sat straight, he could see her breast move, almost as much as her fingers trembled on the glass she held.

"In state?" she asked. "Ah. But, as you seem to know so much of him, do you think he'll bring my husband with him?"

"I doubt it, my lady," he said, although he patently disbelieved it. "You know he feels it's in his best interest to keep you apart, as yet. But I'll be going back to Westminster before I take leave of England again, and I'll be happy to bear your lord news of you. And it is good news. For I'll tell him the truth: that I found you comfortable, treated well, and well content to wait for him. Never fear, lady," he said softly, "Henry treats him as well as he does you, and not just because you're a beautiful lady. He holds all his onetime foes in velvet chains."

"Does he?" she asked, and looked at him with glittering eyes, although he saw no trace of tears. "Does he, indeed? I think you and I have an amusing thing to do if you're done with your dinner. Your dalliance with my lady attendant will have to wait. No, better, bring her too. It will look odd if we go off alone. But come, I have the most interesting thing to show you. Have you never had a tour of Henry's kitchens here?" she asked as she rose abruptly and beckoned to her ladies to follow.

Lucas gave her his arm as Megan and Maeve followed them out of the dining hall and down a stair, and they walked on through long corridors and past sentries, as the music being played in the great hall faded away behind them.

"Not many guests here now, I see. Ah, well," Lady Katherine said as she walked forward eagerly, her skirts held from skimming the stone floors, clasped near her knee in a bunched knot by one white-knuckled hand, "I don't wonder at it. However entertaining, all sport palls when it becomes commonplace. I understand there was a time when these halls were clogged with curiosity seekers. Now only foreign guests seek it out. Aye, but come, it will be worth the walk, I promise you," she said gaily, as, instinctively, now that he understood where he was being led, Lucas shocked himself by hesitating a step, because all he wished to do was to dig in his heels before he turned and fled.

The kitchens were vast, and filled with smoke. It was hot, and grease seemed to hang in the heavy air, even as the stinks of various foods, cooked too long, for too many successive years, did. The various cooks and maids and butchers and scullery boys scurried about, ducking quick bows as they ran if they chanced to see the noble company, but Lady Katherine ignored them, and walked on, determined.

"Ah, good," she said brightly, though it seemed she spoke through clenched teeth. "He's not done with his chores yet. For the servants haven't eaten, and work isn't done till all's done, isn't that so, Lambert?" she asked the turnspit who attended the sides of cow at the great hearth she stopped in front of.

"It is so, my lady," the turnspit said as he quickly rose from the chair he'd been seated in by the side of the roaring fire. He bent his head and then raised a heated sweaty face to them. Megan mightn't have been the only one to gasp aloud as he did.

For they were clear blue eyes that looked back at them, above an aquiline nose, and the full lips that quirked up at them were set above a strong, pronounced chin. That flushed skin must have been fair as alabaster for the heat to fire it to brick red, that darkened sweat-soaked hair was yet so light it had to have been lighter than the brightest shades of the fire before he'd begun his chores. There'd been grace in his movement as he stood, as there was a sense of composure in the man even as he hid reddened hands in his stained leather apron.

"A popular model, indeed, since it seems they made so many of us, fellow," Lucas breathed. "I give you good evening, Lambert—it is Lambert Simnel I address, is it not? They didn't exaggerate when they said you bore the mark of a prince, did they?"

The man only ducked his head again, and murmured, "It's I, and it's long since, and past, good sir—I am Prince of Turnspits now," and he raised his face to show a shambling smile, the sort that dogs give when they want a scrap.

"Almost a decade past," Lucas said, staring at the man as avidly as Lady Katherine did. He grew still, not wanting to say the obvious—the things that this man had heard countless times before, and perhaps still dreamed on every night of his wretched existence.

Because thousands of men had died for this pretender. Some said four thousand, some said five had died on the battlefield at Stoke alone, bristling with arrows, bleeding Irish, English, and German blood onto England's green fields. They'd marched from Ireland, where he'd been originally hailed as heir to the throne, and had been joined by some from every part of England where he'd stopped, proclaiming himself the rightful king. Not prince. For he'd only claimed to be the dead princes' cousin, their uncle the Duke of Clarence's son: Edward, Earl of Warwick. Such had been the temper of the times that even though Edward had been shut up in the Tower since the day Henry had taken the throne, and even though

Henry had immediately paraded the true young Edward of Warwick through London to show him to the people before putting him back, still London was a world away from Ireland and the rest of England. And so this man had convinced his supporters that he was the last legitimate male Plantagenet, the living, rightful king.

Not this man, Lucas corrected himself. He'd been a boy then, and hadn't the wit or ambition. His supporters. Hotheaded defeated Yorkists, the damned impatient bitch Margaret, brooding in her exile across the sea, as well as the Irish, who hated any consent in England, the Germans, and too many others to name: the ragtag assortment of men always drawn to conflicts, the sort who thrive on confusion, gambling that they can use it for their own gain. Most were dead, or fled now. Except for their king, Lambert Simnel. Who now proclaimed himself Prince of Turnspits. Which was probably far more honor than he'd expected when Henry seized him. And more, Lucas thought, with growing nausea, far more, than most men could bear.

"And are you well, Lambert?" Lady Katherine asked sweetly.

"Yes, my lady," Lambert answered.

"This gentleman has the king's ear, Lambert," she said. "Have you any message for him?"

"I give him continued thanks for my health and my life," Lambert answered in his calm beautiful voice that was so at variance with the man.

"Velvet chains, just as you said!" Lady Katherine said gleefully as she turned to Lucas. "Now, come, Lambert, don't be so shy. I know you have other ambitions still. Come, you may trust me, tell my guest what they are."

"I should like, one day, to be permitted to be a falconer, my lady," he said with a sudden glow in his eyes, as though he saw the cool green fields in which he could stand, as though he felt the powerful beating of wings that could fly over castle walls. Then he grinned that singularly pleasant-unpleasant, unbefitting grin of his again. "I have a way with birds—and not only roasted ones," he added, showing white teeth as he laughed.

Then he went through his paces, answering her questions to do with his duties and his pleasures, as though he'd done so a thousand times before, as he had done, until they gave him a coin and bade him good night.

"Why, you are very still, sir," Lady Katherine said as they walked back to the great hall.

"You've made your point, lady," Lucas said as he strolled back with her, "and believe me when I say that I am at your service."

"Oh, yes," she said.

"Lambert's really remarkably happy," Maeve whispered to Megan uneasily, because no one else was as merry as she thought they should be. "After all, he could be long dead—drawn and quartered as a traitor years ago if it weren't for the king's mercy—couldn't he be?"

"Yes, that's so," Megan said, wondering if she'd ever be able to forget the sight of those rough reddened hands twisting and turning in the folds of his apron.

"Now, then, Megan . . ." Lucas said as they stood in the shadowed hallway where he'd stopped her, each of his hands flat on the wall beside her, sealing her into an improvised velvet-barred prison before him. "Now, then, before we rejoin the others—no, they know we've stolen this moment, so be easy. Now, I think, an answer, please. You looked at me with loathing just before. Why?"

"I don't know," she lied miserably. "A thing was said, I listened, and . . . Ah, what's the point? I disbelieve it now."

"Enough to come with me now?" he asked. "Or, if we must, a little later, when your lady is abed?"

"Where?" she asked, though she knew.

"Where?" he mocked, and leaned forward to touch her lips with his, before he drew back just far enough to graze her brow with his lips again. "Where? Oh, you may not know the 'how' of it," he whispered, "and that will be my pleasure to teach you. But I'll swear you know the 'where,' my love."

She looked at him steadily, and he stopped placing light breathy kisses on her face and studied her, as she did him, in silence.

"I cannot," she finally said bleakly, and knew it for the certain truth only when she said it, and that was in her voice as she repeated it, so he didn't argue.

"Ah, well," he said softly, dropping his hands to his sides, "I'm sorry. I am, you know."

"Mightn't we . . . couldn't we remain as we are?" she asked as he stepped back from her.

"No," he said with a sad smile. "No. I can't afford that. Good night, my lady, and fare thee well."

And as she watched him, disbelieving, shaking his head, he backed away from her to go back to the company in the great hall, and then he never glanced back.

But she could not leave off watching him all the rest of the evening. As the night wore on, he joked with some and chatted with others, and then, by slow turns and infinitely measured degree, she realized he was steadily making his way back toward her. She knew, she thought, with a blaze of triumph that misted her eyes, she knew he couldn't simply drop her, pretend she no longer lived, just because he no longer believed she'd lie with him without marriage. Not he. Oh, not Lucas.

So she'd a trembling smile on her lips when he paused in front of her and smiled, and bowed, and then turned his head and spoke a light word to Maeve. Who answered him as pertly as she ever did a handsome gentleman, and fluttered her lashes as he said some other things Megan couldn't hear above the roaring in her ears. But she could see them well enough when he gave Maeve his arm and led her off to a corner of the room with him.

It was hard to miss him, clad in yellow velvet as he was. Maeve was in blue, so it was easy to see when that bright-colored arm eventually stole around that dark blue waist. And easy to note that bright head as it dipped to hear what Maeve said, and easier still to see when Maeve's head leaned against that broad shoulder, and simplicity itself to watch and note, even from across the room, when that long-fingered hand began to play with the bright curls at the back of Maeve's short, bare neck.

"Come with me now, Megan," Lady Katherine said from behind her. "Maeve can join us when she wills, if she does. She knows what she's doing, God help her."

But even in the dark, in her bed, as she waited for the night to crawl by and Maeve to return, Megan saw them. And still saw his clear eyes fixed on Maeve's plump lips, as though all truth and beauty resided there. And then saw more than she'd seen: his lips on Maeve's lips, and

his long body on hers, doing all the things she'd seen
couples doing in the shadows of castle hallways and corridors and peasant middens since she was the girl who'd
asked her nurse what dance those two swineherds were
doing on the grass. And heard the echoes of the laughter
she'd heard then again, although this time it made her
cry.

Her tears were long since dried when she finally saw
the shape in the fading darkness at her door and scented
the familiar, achingly delicious odor of lemons and sandalwood and Eastern spices. Maeve stepped into the
room and pulled off her gown and lay down to sleep in
her underdress, and the scent grew stronger.

"I'm sorry," Maeve said in a strange flat voice, breaking the dark silence, speaking in tones as clear as if
they'd been talking for hours. "I couldn't help myself.
Well, I wanted him. You've never wanted anyone either
of us could have had before. It may be," she said grudgingly, in a tight little voice, "that I wanted to best you. It
is possible, though I don't dislike you. It is my way,
though. There it is, but I'm sorry now for it."

Megan didn't speak or breathe or move.

After a moment Maeve spoke again, nevertheless.

"He was very good. Very good. He knows much about
women. He was everything I expected and wanted."

Megan didn't reply, although she tasted the salt tear
that slid down her face, nor would she sniffle, though it
seemed she'd choke.

"I have had a dozen dozen men," Maeve said dis-
tinctly, "and enjoyed most, but he was best. But I never
felt such a filthy sow before. I'm sorry."

It was no consolation. Megan still refused to speak or
move her head, though she did believe she was drowning.

"He asked me about Perkin. When we were done, of
course. He picked up a lock of my hair and slid it through
his fingers, and he rested on his elbow and looked down
into my face and talked about Lady Katherine and Perkin.
How I felt about them, and what I knew of him, and
what did I think the lady would do if Henry didn't give
him back to her soon. Had I heard anything, and so on.
And do you know, Meg, if the lady hadn't warned you, I
wouldn't have known? His hands and his voice were that
good, even then, when I was so comfortable and weary.

He wouldn't talk about you, though. Not a word. Only Perkin and the lady. I don't think he listened when I talked about myself. I don't think he cared to know whom he was pleasuring. Oh, aye, he did that. But do you know? There was something new. Something I never knew in a man before. For all he kept me at it until I finally had enough, for once, I don't know if he felt anything at all. I really don't," she laughed.

"You were no fool, Meg," Maeve said finally, softly. "You were very wise."

Megan finally spoke.

"Oh. Yes. Very wise." she said, and knew she'd been.

But she'd known that before he'd killed her, she thought, and turned her head into her pillow so that the scent of lemons and spices was only in her mind, and not her nostrils, and waited wide-awake and dry-eyed, until morning, as Maeve did, without speaking again.

6

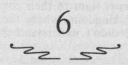

By the time the king's barge came into view, all the preparations for his arrival were done. Children stood waiting, their handfuls of flower petals already squashed and wilted by the heat of their hands; the knights and nobles had their best smiles firmly in place; everyone in the palace—from minstrels to cooks—was turned out on the grass leading to the waterside. The queen and her children were positioned, dressed in state and waiting with calm expectancy even before the first sweet strains of music being played on the royal barge were heard wafting downriver.

Lucas Lovat stood apart from a group of gentlemen, and smiled to see the spectacle, smiling the more when he thought of how soon his task would be done.

"It's thrilling," Philip de Lacey exclaimed, before he remembered whom he was talking to and added sheepishly, "I expect you've seen much finer."

"No, it is thrilling. One never does get used to the spectacle of power," Lucas said softly as he watched the bold banners on the barge glide into view.

"Probably next to nothing to what you've seen abroad," Philip insisted.

Lucas remembered the pageantry of the pope, the splendor of his son when he rode out in company, the finery of the competing noble houses of Italy as well as the dazzle at the courts of Charles and Maximilian: the extravagant numbers of richly caparisoned horses, the heralds in costumes that would shame the dukes he saw here, the gilded fountains splashing wine, the gleam of gold festooned everywhere, the tapestries and banners, the singing, the rare perfumes wafted on the open air. He

recalled the glamour of all those courts where impressing
the citizenry was important to their continuance, as opposed to this tiny kingdom, where the freed men and
minor noblity still didn't understand the full extent of
their own power.

"No," Lucas said truthfully, "nothing compares to this
for me."

The musicians on the barge gave way to those on the
shore after the heralds' trumpets were blown. The barge
docked, the petals were tossed, the nobility moved forward and stepped aside before they bowed low, creating
an aisle for the king to walk down to his queen. He
raised her up and she stood with him, accepting the
applause of their subjects. Lucas was too far away to see
their faces. He scanned the company still leaving the
barge and was surprised to find himself relaxing: there
were no drab gray cowled gowns in that gala company,
no shadowy holy brothers attending the sunlit king. Henry's thin figure moved on along the line to greet those of
Greenwich Palace who did him obeisance. Lady Katherine, all in shades of rose, curtsied low, as did the two
graceful figures behind her. Lucas turned away, restless,
impatient. With luck, Henry's arrival signaled his own
departure.

In the days that followed, the king was seen everywhere, from the kitchens to the gardens to the highest
towers. Such appearances were politic, but most in his
court knew the real business of this king went forth in
private, where he arranged to see almost as many of
them singly as had seen him severally since he'd come to
Greenwich. He sat at the highest table now, served by his
yeoman guard, and almost half of the company in the
hall before him relaxed and ate with gusto, having already been called into his presence and account pri-
vately, while the other half glanced at him and then at
their dinners, wondering when and if they'd be called. It
was too bad, if only because they couldn't fully appreciate the feast that had been set out for them.

The king's visit to Lambert Simnel in his kitchens must
have inspired his staff, because the food served this night
was memorable. The courtiers ate until they groaned.
Pies and minces, roasts and stews, tender first spring

greens in salads and vegetables, fresh fish that scarcely needed their sauces, baked meats and stuffed poultry, and wines and ales to get them down the faster. By the time the sweets were sung out by a host of angelically white-robed children, the seated company was replete. But not so much so that they couldn't enjoy seeing the huge carved sugar barge that had been borne in destroyed so they could taste the creams and first fruits and other honeyed treats that had been its cargo.

"You have hardly eaten," Lady Katherine said.

"I've had my fill. But you?" Lucas answered.

"I await mine, sir," she said, lowering her eyes.

Did she expect it from Henry? Lucas wondered. And in what form? For the king, only a few feet away, did glance to her from time to time, and when he caught Lucas' eye upon him, that wide thin-lipped mouth twitched into something that might be a smile. But for all Henry obviously admired Lady Katherine's beauty, there was nothing but a colder sort of speculation in his narrowed eyes when he gazed at her. Still, she was the only female he seemed to note; most of the time he only looked with pride and pleasure on his son Arthur. He ignored his queen, at his side, but she scarcely seemed to mind, since she also paid all her attention to their firstborn.

Small wonder, Lucas thought. He was their one successful compromise. Neither could claim ascendancy there. At twelve, Prince Arthur was already tall and slender. His smooth, clear light skin and light hair showed his mother's influence. He'd his father's eye color, and his narrow features, but they weren't pinched, nor did they sit ill on his gentle countenance, and so looked aesthetic rather than meager there. Poetic and charming, studious but observant, shy but forthcoming when spoken to, Arthur was a gracious youth. Henry had got what he most desired in this child—a true Plantagenet, yet stamped with his own distinctive brand. Prince Henry was still a pink-and-white boy, his mother's ewe-lamb. The princesses, however comely, were, after all, only game pieces to be placed in whatever marriage beds would most profit their father. Arthur was all to him.

Until, of course, another such came along, for Henry was not old, and Elizabeth still fertile. Henry could have more heirs. That was, in fact, likely why he'd paid this visit. The queen had only just got over losing another babe. But that had been weeks ago. Time for the king to call again, Lucas thought, his own mouth tightening with distaste at the idea of such expedient lust. No better than I, majesty, he thought with sour amusement, eyeing his sovereign. Not a whit better than I, eh, sire?

Because he knew what duty was too. Tonight he avoided looking down to the lower tables, just as he'd done last night, and the night before, ever since the bleak night he'd taken the wench Maeve to his bed. Megan would have given him nothing for a long while, and he'd no time for nothing, no matter what his taste had been; and whatever his taste, she'd been priced too dear, however much time he'd had. He'd used her, nonetheless, in his own way, thinking of her while he'd had the other, until the thinking was no longer necessary for the doing of it.

Now the sweets were done, and the sweet wine drained to the dregs. The king arose at last, and the company got to their feet to let him pass, and their night begin. Lucas made his bow to Lady Katherine. When she beckoned to her ladies, he turned to avoid being pressed into conversation with the one he'd lain with, and turned again, to avoid so much as seeing the one who still lay so heavily on his mind. He'd caught her eye only once since that night, and then he'd been the one to look away, lest he look too deeply and see his own disgust again. But he'd not forgotten one gesture, one word, one moment he'd passed with her, for all he'd known so much more of the other, and yet remembered only her name and faceless white body moving beneath his. Even that would soon be forgotten, for it transpired that she'd given him nothing of value at all, after all, for himself or his king.

Lady Katherine found a sympathetic earl and his countess to pass the evening with; Maeve discovered a likely old knight with a purse almost as heavy as his paunch, and Megan was left to another evening in which to test how successfully she could avoid noticing Lucas Lovat. She passed her time not watching him talking in a group of gentlemen, after not listening to him jest with two of the queen's ladies. When she felt a light touch on the back of her arm, her shoulders leapt, and she spun around. She had to look down before she saw who'd accosted her.

"Lady," the little page boy in green-and-white livery said softly, "I'm sent to tell you that your confessor awaits. Will you follow me?"

Her shoulders went up higher, and it seemed her heart was caught in her throat; she was a very small cog in Henry Tudor's wheel of state, and it had been weeks since she'd last reported to him. But she had to earn her keep. She nodded, drew in a breath, and followed.

The king received her in a small chamber, with only a fat, bored priest as witness. Henry sat tall and straight, his thin face impassive, watching her with hooded eyes, his jewels of office glittering in the dim room. As always, she felt as though she should kneel when she was done curtsying to him, for this was, in a way, very like a confessional, except that she seldom left these meetings feeling either clean or easy in her heart and mind. She swallowed her distaste and fear and tried to be as brief as possible, telling him everything that had happened in her life in the past weeks that she thought he'd wish to hear. Fortunately, as ever, there was nothing harmful she could see in it, and as ever, it wasn't very much, so she was soon done with her report.

"Yes. But why no word of Lucas Lovat's advent into your household?" Henry asked when she was through.

She started, feeling the blood rush to her cheeks, until she calmed herself, realizing her mistake: the king would have little interest in the mistaken love of a lady-in-waiting.

"Lady Katherine has eyes for no man but her husband, sire," she said softly. "She welcomes Lucas Lovat because she bids him be her messenger when he sees Perkin Warbeck again. But she only sends Perkin her love, as always."

"She gave him a message, ah, but what did you give Lucas Lovat?" Henry asked.

When she didn't reply at once, he prompted her by musing, "More than a message, I'll warrant. You passed much time with him."

She paled, remembering how many others had come to this room before her.

"Nothing, sire," she said at last, since for all she knew, he already knew even more than she did. "I could not. He only wished to sport with me."

"Why is that, do you think?" Henry asked, as though

he were only testing her, as though he already knew, implacable as God in this confessional of his.

"I cannot offer him very much," she said carefully, at length, voicing the explanations for Lucas' betrayal that she'd reasoned out during the last long, empty days and nights. As she recalled his wit and his face, his worldliness and vast experience of life and women, she added, "No, not half so much as he needs or wants, sire," she concluded sadly, accepting herself as she was, at last.

"Your father was a friend to me. As you have proved to be," Henry said, watching her closely. "Didn't you know I'd dower you well? Shall I tell the fellow?" he asked.

Her eyes flew wide. She was astonished. He'd misunderstood her for the first time since she'd come into his service.

"Oh, no, I pray you," she cried, "No, sire, please."

"Very well," he said, instantly bored, as though it scarcely mattered to him, any more than she did, and told her to keep her eyes and ears open, as always, before he dismissed her.

She fled the room, as guilty and amazed as grateful to discover that for all she'd given, for once she'd left an interview with him with something of her own intact, because despite all he knew, her king knew nothing of her heart.

"Nothing, sire. Nothing at all," Lucas said. "Lady Katherine longs for her husband, but we knew that before I came. As to what she'll do after I leave? I think she waits upon fate and your discretion. I regret I can't say for certain. I do doubt that staying on will profit me more, since the lady already wonders at my gallantries in the face of the fact that I know her to be supernaturally faithful." Lucas chuckled and then shrugged. "Perhaps another may be able to discover more," he said lightly, and was still, waiting for Henry's reply to his report.

His bags packed, important farewells made, he stood ready to leave; if this report was taken in the spirit it had been offered, he'd be free. Free to return home, and then to decide what it was he must do—could do—then. But Henry took his time, so Lucas stood before him with an easy smile on his lips, as though the answer were of no importance to him, as though he only waited to be told to sit, or say on. They were alone except for a priest, an explicable one this time, a round-faced cohort of Archbishop Morton. Lucas disregarded him. He was a petty man known for his political ambition as well as his loyalties to king, archbishop, and church, in that order. God alone knew how many others Henry had interviewed late into the night and then this morning, Lucas thought idly, and then had a better idea when he spoke again.

" 'Nothing . . .' " Henry mused, "although you were busy enough. You courted one, and bedded the other, and befriended the lady herself. And 'nothing,' you say now. So you think there's no danger from Perkin Warbeck now?"

Of course, he'd have set a spy on his spy, Lucas thought; he'd expected as much, and so didn't know why the certainty rankled now, but none of it showed in his face as he answered, "Ah, but I never said that, sire. I only said that so far as I know—and that isn't so far as you can see on a cloudy day—the lady has no plans for acquiring his freedom—beyond your good graces. Because she does seem to eagerly await . . . your grace," Lucas said just blandly enough to cause a high and sudden flash of color in those lean and sallow cheeks.

"She will wait, then," Henry murmured, and then fixed Lucas with a considering eye. "You left the one you courted just as you found her . . . an innocent. Surprising."

"Is it?" Lucas asked negligently, biting back his anger. "I'm pleased to be known for my skills, majesty, but was I expected to carry on like Lust on a pageant wagon? I'd no idea. What a missed opportunity. As it was . . . no, I don't despoil good little virgins"—he shrugged again— "unless there's a compelling reason. She knew less than nothing, about many things."

"I am prepared to dower her well someday," Henry said, watching Lucas carefully.

"Indeed?" Lucas said with as careful a show of indifference. "She deserves it. And a good husband, as well."

"And the other? The one who fell into your lap? Not much security for Lady Katherine, having such a light lady-in-waiting, should you say?"

"Not so light, surely! Think of my feelings, sire! I thought you granted my expertise in such matters," Lucas protested, one hand on his breast, not letting a fraction of the distaste he felt show through. "Security enough, I'd say, since she told me nothing."

Henry nodded, and studied Lucas.

"And now?" he asked suddenly.

"And now, if you've no further use for me here—and I don't see how I can aid you any longer—I'd like to go home for a spell, sire. Unlike me, my parents grow no younger."

"Home to stay?"

"Only for a time. I did promise the lady I'd return to Westminster Palace to see her Perkin once more. And I shall. Whatever I learn, I'll send to you at once. After that? Faith! I don't know," he said truthfully. "Home again, mayhap to stay. But every time I think on it, my heels begin to itch again. If I leave the country, you'd know," Lucas said with a smile for the truth of that in every way.

"And if you stay, you've no use for a virtuous, well-dowered wife?" Henry asked.

Something in Lucas' eyes lighted, turning them to the burning blue shade of the core of a flame, before the spark died down again. Games on games—how else can he tell value but by seeing what he's bid by your face, fool? he told himself angrily. He quenched the sudden hope that had sprung up, unbidden, by reminding himself that even if she were really to be a gift from a grateful king, her price would still be far too high for him.

"I think my father has the matter in hand, sire, and has for many years," he said, since that seemed a reasonable thing to say. "Which may be why," he added, laughing, "I keep taking to my heels whenever he starts muttering about banns."

"Go, then," Henry said, but instead of merely waving his hand in dismissal, he arose and did Lucas the singular honor of walking to the door of the chamber with him.

Side by side, they seemed to be almost of a height, although Lucas had some few inches more. He was slender, but he'd shoulders and breadth of chest; Henry was so lean overall that he appeared taller than he was. But even in his finest robes, the king was eclipsed by his courtier. Lucas was all gold and graces, the king dim and sallow and thin of hair and flanks. Which was why Lucas

disliked walking with him. This was a king who dressed
his guard as resplendently as he did himself, knowing the
people needed a show of grandeur—well aware he lacked
it in himself. He'd clothed his yeoman guard in brilliant
red and gold because of that, and fed them with best beef
and ale, to show their robust splendor. A dark usurper
from a flint-poor land, a fatherless boy who'd been a
foreign beggar awaiting his chance to come home and
seize what he'd never had, he always felt the lack of glory
of the house he'd overthrown, and never forgot the look
of kinghood—and that with all he'd got, he'd never have
it.

The door to the chamber swung open before them.
The queen and her children held court in the room beyond.
The queen conversed with Lady Katherine. The golden
lady wore her usual sad and gentle smile. She was gowned
in white trimmed with ermine and glazed with gold,
although she scarcely needed the gilding, with her bright
hair all about her fair white face. Lady Katherine, dark
and bright, was night to her pastel sunrise.

Lucas had to pause at the king's side as Henry halted.
He wanted nothing more than to be allowed to step
aside. He'd enjoyed standing shoulder to shoulder with
emperors and popes, but here, with this king, comparisons could do him no good, and potentially much harm.
He looked to Henry for his cue to leave. But Henry, who
never forgot anything, had forgotten him.

For the king stood and stared into the room before
him. In that instant his thin face was still and grave, his
usual sidewise clever look entirely gone. Instead, there
was nothing but hunger to be seen in his pale eyes,
nothing but a terrible, bottomless, painful longing etched
into every lineament of his pinched face as he stared
unblinking as a beggar boy at his queen. By the time she
looked up, as though she'd felt the force of his gaze—in
the time it would have taken Lucas to blink to be sure
he'd seen aright—Henry had his grim half-smile in place,
and was himself, Henry Tudor, King of England, again.

But Lucas was momentarily rigid with shock at the
glimpse he'd had at Henry's secret. It made the king a
man he'd never seen. Henry loved—think of that! Lucas
thought in astonishment, and worse, loved what he could
never have, for he could never trust her, or himself,

enough to admit to it. And how terrible it must be to always spy on the one he loved, to look sidewise in order to see her, to wait until the depths of night when she lay sleeping in his bed in order to admire her and wonder that he had her. How much more terrible to hold his love in the ultimate embrace and dare not breathe a word of his longing for more, even as he gave himself to the ecstasy of having what he could of her.

They said Henry had hidden behind a screen at her coronation, watching her receive her crown alone. They'd thought him uncaring, just as they did every time he impregnated her and then left her. No one guessed how he must long for her to be less fertile. Perhaps not even she herself. For if his face had told the truth he concealed, he held her to be worthier than himself, but could never tell her so, for fear she'd agree, and betray him with the knowledge of it. Perhaps she did agree, and would, at that—who knew anything of the thoughts of the sad and lovely lady? Last of her line: her father and uncles dead, her mother shut up in a convent, her two younger brothers slain by unknown hands; she'd scarce had time to weep before she'd been taken as a prize by the new king, and made to bear his child before she could wear her crown. But was her lord in any better case? A king who spied on his wife and feared her as much as he loved her? It made him a figure of fun as well as pity. But it made him a man, for all that.

Now Lucas thought he could understand Henry's sudden offer of a well-desired, well-dowered wife. Who better than he would know that a man with someone to love becomes a man with a handle to hold him by?

Lucas liked nothing of what he'd discovered in that one unguarded instant.

Then he noticed the queen gazing at him, and saw the faint troubled look grow in her eyes again. He bent into a deep bow to end the moment; to distract her and himself and Henry from all that was passing, unsaid, in this strangely intimate moment between them.

"My lady," Henry said, "I give you Lucas Lovat for the last time for a while. He leaves us today."

There were little cries of protest from the company—except from Lady Katherine's ladies, Lucas noted with a sidewise glance. The queen gave him her hand, and he

bowed himself away from her good wishes. Then he'd a
moment for a quiet word with Lady Katherine herself.

"I'll see him anon," he said sincerely as he strolled
with her to the windows, "after I've passed some time
with my good parents."

"When will you see us again to tell us of him?" she
asked eagerly.

"I'll send you word," he said gently. He saw her disappointment in her suddenly lowered head. Then he added,
to the veiling at the top of the shining black masses of
upswept hair, "Marry, lady, am I a bouncing ball—to go
from Westminster to Greenwich, to Westminster to Greenwich? Have pity, please. I'll send word by one who's
reliable as any I know in the land—young Philip de
Lacey, the red-thatched rogue over there, the one ogling
your ladies with such poorly disguised enchantment. He's
as transparent as glass in all things as he is in his admiration. Never fear him."

She raised softened blue eyes to his. "But what . . .
what if what you send needs less . . . transparency, sir?"
she whispered.

Oho, Lucas thought, and I said "nothing" to Henry?
before he said, with sincerity in his voice, "Why, then,
lady, I become a bouncing ball for your sake, and gladly,
believe me."

"I do," she said softly. Her lips quirked as she added,
"But I fear my ladies don't, anymore."

"They are not you, in any way, my lady," he replied,
bowing over her hand after seeing the pleased look come
over her face. They all had one weakness, he thought
wearily; hers, of course, was vanity, as was most of
woman- and mankind's.

But I never found yours, he thought as he straightened
and his eyes met Megan's before she could hastily look
away.

It was only a moment's work for him to corner the
woman he sought after he left Lady Katherine.

"Forgive me," he breathed to Maeve when he found
her to a side of the room where she'd retreated. "It was
poorly done of me not to further our acquaintance after
. . . I'd got to know you. But I was a coward. I knew I
had to be going soon, and knew there could be no more
for us. I didn't want to court pain," he said simply, fixing

her with a wide luminous stare. It was easy enough to say; he'd said it so many times before.

He knew why again when she colored up, and hesitated before she spoke, swallowing down all her reasonable objections before she did.

"Fie, sir," she said in pretty confusion, "I'd have understood."

"Do you?" he said, holding her hand, forgetting her face even as he gazed into it. "Then I am content—for your sake—even if I can never be for mine own."

"Oh, what a pretty rogue you are." Maeve laughed. "It was worth it if only to have memories of such a subtle liar. Go to, sir, and with my good wishes. You're a rare one, all right," she chuckled.

She went up several notches in his estimation when he saw the rueful knowledge in her eyes as well as her words.

"Lady," he said, and sighing very dramatically to raise another giggle from her, bowed and left her.

And waited.

He circled the room several times, making unnecessary good-byes, until he saw her from the corner of his eye as she slipped from the room. It was simplicity itself to follow, and stop her in the corridor a second later by seizing her by the arm. Megan's overbright brown eyes glittered with fury and hurt, but not from his grasp, as she turned on him.

"I'm sorry," he said, only that. "I couldn't afford you. But I won't forget you. I'm sorry," he said again before he released her, and left her before she could run away from him, because there was so much else and nothing left to say.

When he returned to the room, he saw young Philip de Lacey standing near the door, looking uncomfortably aware that he'd been caught peering down the corridor after him. But then, Lucas remembered, he'd looked just as ill-at-ease when he'd been discovered riding to Greenwich on the same road after him when he'd first come here. Poor young Philip, he thought, who'd grown so much older in so many ways since he'd met him, but mercifully, not in all.

"Well, lad," Lucas said heartily, "now we part company at last, don't we? I do go to my own home now," he added, as Philip's face grew red. "Ah. I see. You do too, is that it? Well, then, come along, there's room enough there, it'll save me sending for you when I want to go to Westminster again. And save you from sleeping rough in haystacks near to our manor, I suppose. Come along, and stop trying to invent a reason, I know what duty looks like when it calls." He clapped the boy on the back and noted how nearly his young face matched the hue of his hair now.

But sooth! Does Henry know he's hired a chameleon for a spy? he wondered, chuckling to himself, before he grew grave again, realizing that of course Henry knew, that was part of the game, they were very much alike after all.

He was to think that again when he'd his traveling bag in hand and was striding down the corridor for a last time, and found himself looking back to see if he could see her somewhere in the company he was leaving, without her knowing that he did.

But she watched from a hidden corner of a window, and so could look her fill of him, at last, until she could see no more.

"It's not a castle. Nor is it precisely the manor house it seems," Lucas said as they rode down the long road past the churchyard and the high turrets of his home came into view. "It has fortifications, in among the roses," he added, as though young Philip didn't know it. "The view from the topmost story of the tower goes on for miles, and the only way to reach it is from the drawbridge. The wall round the whole would take a legion to breech, and those inside could hold tight for months, if need be. But for all that, it's small as such holdings go, although the great hall is fine enough for anyone, with enough windows to let out anything the great hearth can hold, and the solar's my mother's delight. Aside from all the garderobes, that is. She will not go out of a night, nor does she hold with chamber pots—and my father indulges her unmercifully. There's a window in every one of them too, there's a reason for all the roses—the woman has an uncanny and fretful nose. So prepare to bathe, and often, lad, will you, nill you. That was my cross to bear as a boy . . .

"Ah, Edgar," he said to the rangy rustic who was

opening the gate they approached, as he reined up his horse, "how many years now? And still you grow? Faith, has my mama been spreading manure on more than her posies? Say her nay, man, or you'll top the trees before you know it."

The lanky peasant grinned a gap-toothed grin as he tugged at the front of his hair and went down to one knee. "God save you, master, I be Edgar's son, Arnald, by y'r leave."

Lucas' blithe smile faded as he stared down at the man in the blue smock.

"Edgar's son? And he and I teethed on the same bones? Give him my greeting, Arnald. But first open wide the gate. The prodigal son returns."

The lord and lady of the manor greeted Lucas with as much joy as if he'd been the prodigal son, yet with as much courtesy as if he'd been not only their son but also an honored guest.

"By my faith, it gets more beautiful each time I return," Lucas breathed as he looked about the long hall before him, taking note of the chests and tapestries, tables and chairs.

"I'd hope you think so. You've stocked it well for us," his father said proudly. "Tapestries from Bruges on the walls, vessels from Rome on the tables, with lace from Flanders and cloth from France—even on his mother!" As they all laughed and his wife glowed with pleasure, he added, "Why, tonight we'll bring out those Venice glasses you sent to us, not a scratch on a one—our son doesn't even drink from pottery or wooden cups anymore," the stocky older man confided to Philip with as much pride as wonder, as he continued to gaze at his tall, graceful son.

"And so mayhap," his lady said softly, never taking her round brown eyes from Lucas, "you'll stay on here with us if it reminds you well enough of the foreign lands you love."

Before his son could answer with more than a grin, his father put in, "Aye. And for another reminder, we've hired on more serving girls—and we'll have John Wichcomb's youngest, Elizabeth, Peter Grimes's lovely Eleanor, and all three of the widow Graham's daughters here to visit too. They're ripening like cherries—that ought to make you feel at home, eh?"

"Of course. But," Lucas said imperially, before he joined them in laughter, "only if they all fight over me."

"We'll dine together this night," Lucas' mother said with satisfaction when the laughter was done. "But stay, you've traveled long and hard. First I'll call for a bath for you in your room, Lucas. And one for you as well, Master de Lacey," she added, wondering at the merry look her son passed to his guest, and even more at the color the lad then flushed as Lucas grinned at him.

They were all in accord, and all in good humor as Sir Charles led Philip to his rooms, and Lucas' smile didn't slip until he was alone in his rooms. He unpacked his bag as the great canopied wooden bath was brought in to rest near the fire, and stripped off his clothing with the weariness of an old man as the servants poured steaming water into the tub. He was too exhausted to speak to any of the men, and too weary to do more than smile at the wenches when he dismissed them, despite their disappointment at not being able to aid him at his bath. When they'd all left, he lay back in the warmth, his head resting on the wooden brim, inhaling the sweet herbs, the steam caught in the curtained recesses of the bath clouding his vision as much as he wished it would his mind. So it was that he was alert and ready when his father opened the door to his room, and he and his mother came in quietly and shut it behind them.

"I'm done, and I'll come out," he called, pulling back a corner of the hanging sheet to see his guests, as his mother squawked, "Into the chill? And catch your death? Not while I live," she cried as she held a warm sheet up for him. But as he was twice her height, she stood on tiptoe, her small round body almost overbalancing in her efforts, and that brought the first real smile to Lucas' lips since he'd returned home.

When he'd wrapped his long body in the sheet to the lady's satisfaction, Lucas sat with the elderly couple at the fireside, sipping at a cup his father handed him.

"Good," Lucas sighed, stretching his bare legs before the fire so that the light played on the mesh of golden hairs on them. "Ah, sir, you cannot know how good it is to be here again."

"And still we must talk in whispers, in stolen moments," his father complained.

"Not whispers, at least. He bathes now. I sent in a comely, forward wench to bring him warmer water, so he'll be too beset choosing between good manners and her wants to stray from his door right now," Lucas' mother said with satisfaction.

Firelight glinted on Lucas' eyes as he laughed. "If I know the lad, there's no need for warmer water, he'll be heating his bath with his blushes."

"A strange spy," Sir Charles commented, and then grew still as Lucas said mirthlessly, "Does Henry have any commonplace ones, sir? Be easy. The lad may have some twists and turns I don't know yet, but what I do know is simple enough. He watches me. And then tells Henry what he sees. What's new in that? Sooth," he sighed wearily as he laid his head on the back of the chair and stared at the dancing designs of light on the wooden ceiling, "there's nothing new in that. Ah, by God's sake, it is good to be home again."

"You can't stay long," his father said bluntly, watching him, worry as well as sympathy clear in his dark eyes.

"What's this?" Lucas asked, sitting upright. "I come, and you say 'go'?"

"We all say 'go'—this is not a good time," Sir Charles explained. "We thought it was, it would have been, but as it is . . . What news of Perkin Warbeck? And what did you tell the king of him?"

"The news of Perkin Warbeck is just what I told the king. So much as I'd like to see the man dead and buried in four places, there's no sense in lying to Henry, he knows as much as I do. Even if I knew more, there'd be no sense in it. Half the time he only asks questions to test the answerer, not to find answers. Perkin's held loosely at Westminster Palace, and I don't know why. I think it's because Henry wants his supporters to show their hand by trying to free him again. It could be that he thinks that the longer Warbeck lives, the longer the list of enemy names he may eventually compile. It's not because he wishes to amuse himself, whatever you've heard. Henry does nothing for his own amusement."

Lucas turned angry eyes on his father, as his fist clenched

around his cup. "Just who is this damned Perkin Warbeck anyway, sir? Is there anything new on that?"

Sir Charles sighed. "A boatman's son from Flanders. A pretender. As he said in his confession, so it remains. There's not been another word. What do I hear in less-exalted places? A wealthy Jew's grandson. Which explains his cleverness and pride. A baseborn son of Edward's or Clarence's—which explains his air of majesty and knowledge of court manners more than being the son of a merchant or a Jew does. Whatever his besotted wife thinks, none but idiots believe him to be truly Richard of York risen from the grave. Or rescued from it, as he claims to have been. The murderer of his brother took pity on him, he says, and for his vow of silence, smuggled him from the Tower. As if vows meant anything to a desperate murderer and regicide! As if a man with hands wet with the blood of one boy would lay them gently, moments later, on his brother! And that dead brother only two years senior to the saved one, and twice as beautiful besides. Ha!" he spat, bereft of words in his disgust, as he rose to pace in agitation.

He stopped and fixed Lucas with a knowing look. "Howbeit. What do *I* think? A baseborn son of Margaret's. What do I know? Nothing new at all. But what of his foolish lady? We've heard about your friendship there," he said with what might have been censure or worry fogging his gruff voice.

"Friendship?" Lucas smiled. "News to her—and to me. But I do admire her. One has to. The Lady Katherine may be a fool, but she's a great lady who's found her crusade. She believes in him and would sell her soul to see him free, if she could only find someone who has the price to pay for it. I didn't, and didn't pretend to, there was no point to it."

"We'd heard about another lady you befriended. One who was unwedded: the Lady Megan Baswell," his mother put in slyly.

"Unwedded, unbedded, and never to be either by me," Lucas said abruptly.

"But we heard she was lovely and clever and wellborn. I saw her, and she was. And you seemed—"

"God's teeth, woman!" Sir Charles thundered. "Let

be! He can't take such as her, unless in wedlock. Where are your wits?"

"I never meant—"she cried, as Lucas interrupted, rising and taking her trembling form into his arms, for she'd shot up in distress at the rebuke. "No, she never did, I'm certain. 'Let be,' indeed, sir. She could not be more my mother, and like all mothers, only wants to see grandchildren of me—one way or another. And I, sweet lady," he said gently as he kissed her cheek, "only want to see you glad. But I can't take any sort of wife now, you know. Not when I don't even know why you greet me only to hand me my cloak again," he said teasingly. "Now, come, why do you want me gone so soon?"

"Henry keeps Perkin Warbeck to some purpose," his father said flatly, "to lull his supporters, or else to show how little credence he puts in the man's claims. Whatever it is, we don't want you fed upon by accident when the reckoning comes. And be sure it will. No, no, too many people speak of the kingliness, the grace, and the charm of the man for his head to remain long on his shoulders. We want you gone when the trap closes—gone far and gone safe, until you can come home again."

Sir Charles strode a few steps before he turned and faced Lucas once more.

"Go to Italy again—Florence or Rome. We've friends there. Stay until we call. Please," he said as Lucas began to speak.

"I'm tired of leaving," Lucas said softly, though his mother felt his arms tighten about her.

"I'm tired of mourning," Sir Charles said roughly.

"Ah, yes. Well. Selfish of me, of course," Lucas murmured, leaving his mother to face his father. "But, sir, the time may never be right. These are tempestuous times, but when were they not in my lifetime? Or yours? The wars are over. Let the war begin. I'm willing to risk rather than rot . . . Don't turn away from me," he commanded.

As the older man obeyed, he said in gentler tones, "When may I come home and take my rightful place? I do not bask under the Italian sun, you know, no, not for all my jests and all the tales you hear. I chafe, I burn, I . . . Or," he said with a sudden bright look, "is it that I've been gone too long? Have you decided my sister's children would be better at ordering things here than I, after all? Better equipped perhaps to take on my inheritance? It may be, it may be . . . say it, if you think it, and I'll be content. Or if not, for I warrant I won't be, at least I'll know how you feel and be free at last to do as I think best."

His father stared at him, and Lucas was the first to drop his gaze. He gestured with one hand before he let it drop to his side.

"Forgive me," he said, "for the thought as well as the words. I'm really very weary. And now to dress, and dine, and laugh, and tour the house, and do the pretty with the neighboring folk, until I leave again—for London once more. Before Italy, of course. I'll be fine, don't fret. I will, I vow it," he said to his mother's worried look.

"But since I don't know when I'll be able to be alone with you again so soon—even accommodating wenches have their limits," he said with his usual brilliant smile, "one more question. Who is this dreary monk, Brother Robert? The one in Henry's confidence in London? I'll swear he's not what he's said to be, or any ordinary man."

"No monk is," his father said abruptly, "but this one is less man and more monk than most. He's said to be truly holy. Henry thinks so. So do I. He has Henry's confidences, but no man has his, only his God. Don't fear him."

Lucas' eyebrows lifted. "A strange thing for you to say, sir," he murmured. "Well-a-day, if you say so, mayhap 'tis so."

"I never meant to say, 'Trust him blindly,' " his father protested anxiously.

"Never fear," Lucas said, silencing him, "I won't. He won't have my confidences, however holy he is. It's not a matter of religion, but of another sort of observance. For he could be any man beneath his robes, and so then could any man be he—by donning them in his place. I leave blind confession to the pure of heart—I trust only men I can see."

His mother gazed up at him, and he bent to give her another kiss. "And not even them, lady. Not even sweet little Englishwomen, as you so sadly noted."

"I only worry that you are lonely," she whispered.

"Curious," he answered with a quirked smile. "I only begin to worry when I'm not." He gazed over her head to his father, who was nodding his agreement.

"And now I'll dress," he said, walking them to the door, "so send me good James to help—if he still lives, that is. It's been so long since my last visit, I find my boyhood friends' fathers, and their fathers likely gone altogether." He brushed away the gloomy thought, and added merrily, "And then we'll to dine, and I'll tell you all the tales of court: about our old friend John Argentine, and Harry Fairfield and good Sir Bennet. And if you can bear it, lady, and don't split from chagrin, I'll tell you all the gossip about the great success—at the games of love—of the Turners' bad daughter, Jane."

And I swear, not a word about good young women and their failures at those same games, he vowed to himself when they'd gone and he could despair again. Or so much as one syllable about my own.

7

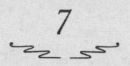

The court had gone to Greenwich with the king, but Westminster Palace was still well-occupied. The business of government ground on even when the king was absent, and so Westminster, the heart of Henry's England, kept beating even when its mind was elsewhere. But Lucas' only business was at Westminster Palace. After that he'd ride to the sea and be gone—for how long, he'd no way to know, so he'd mixed feelings as he rode back to London. Not the least were his reactions to town after weeks in the cool green countryside. This June morning Lucas suddenly discovered London to be too crowded, too noisy, and mostly, too far from Devon—or at least so he jested to Philip as they rode into the city under the arch of Aldergate.

"Don't say it!" he then immediately cautioned his companion. "I know it. If I love Devon so, why did I leave it, and so soon, to pass my last remaining days in England in the north?"

Philip flushed as red as the feather in his slouch hat. Marry, everyone knew what Lucas had been doing at Sir Baldock's home in the north, save possibly for Sir Baldock. Lady Baldock had more tears in her eyes when they'd left her than Lucas' mother had had when they'd left Devon weeks before. Almost as many as the wench at the manor they'd just left had, although it was hard to say if the widow Douglas at the Earl of Auden's estate they had left the previous week, or Thomas Conway's spinster daughter at the manor where they'd previously stopped, had more. So he was surprised to hear Lucas muse, "A man can never be a grown man in his mama's house, unless he has his own lady wife there to do battle

116

for his manhood. So much as I love my mama, it's no easy thing to be scolded for coming late to bed when a man's of an age to make his own bed and lie in it . . . and not necessarily alone."

I would wish, Lucas thought bemusedly as he glanced at his companion's flaring color, that I lived the life the boy thinks I do. But since the only way I've found to keep him from prying is to appear to be busy 'neath sheets, I've led him on to the most astonishing estimate of my abilities. He chuckled to himself, wondering if the king fully understood the boy's morals, for the merest hint of the possibility of catching a glimpse of Lucas at work or play with a female was enough to keep him far from any closed bedchamber door where Lucas was said to be. He'd be a better monk than spy, Lucas decided—mayhap. Because with Henry's men, one never was sure.

But faith! Lucas thought. Had I been as busy as all that in the sheets, they'd be able to slip me between them like a warming pan by now! He grinned, remembering the way his friends and supporters had made mock of that in the long nights when they'd spoken together while Philip paced restlessly in the halls or slumped propped up against them for hours awaiting the end of his nightly vigils, when he could finally see Lucas taking off for his own bed. It would doubtless have been more amusing if it hadn't had to go on so long, Lucas thought, his grin fading as he urged his mount forward from the shadow of the great arched gate and down the narrow cobbled streets.

"But we're going in the other direction," Philip protested as he kneed his horse neatly around a pig that was rooting in the gutter.

"Aye, to St. Paul's. To hear what's happened since we left London," Lucas answered. "I want to catch up on the news. The last time we came, it was coming night, most of the criers had gone, and all the interesting idlers that congregate there had already gone to their evening's entertainment. Come along, lad, I'd like to hear some raw news before we get to Westminster, where even the latest accounts come already chewed so we can swallow them easier."

They made their way through the congested streets of the candlemakers and merchant tailors, ironmongers and

cloth workers, and by going a circuitous route, avoided
the most crowded—the market streets—as neatly as they
guided their mounts around the waste-clogged grooved
gutters in the center of the cobbles.

They took a devious route because they knew they
attracted too much attention to pass through Cheapside
unmolested. It wasn't that they feared attack: few men
would dare losing a hand to the law by raising theirs
against fine gentlemen in this part of the city, and few
cutthroats, however desperate, would dare against the
look in Lucas' eye or the sword at his side. But they
would be entreated to buy or to give charity if they
passed through the teeming market. They stood out, as
Lucas said, like cardinals in the snow. Even if they hadn't
been mounted on fine horses, Lucas, in his gold doublet
and amber cape, and Philip, back in his official court
livery of white and green, would have caught the eye of
every vendor in the street, just as they did every citizen's
they rode past.

For though the streets were thronged with men clad in
every hue, each was clothed according to his station.
Only fine gentlemen could be garbed in such array as
they were: their clothing was the very emblem of their
condition, as was every man's in London. Guildsmen
wore the robes and colors of their trade, their appren-
tices plain jerkins or smocks with only a badge of their
guild's hues to brighten their costume; peasants and common workers were in drab and brown; monks floated by
in gray and white and black; and even the wenches weren't
so richly attired as the two gentlemen—although their
eyes held as much envy as invitation when they gazed at
them.

Lucas guided himself by the great spire of St. Paul's
that dominated the city, dismounting when he came to
the walled churchyard in its shadow. He made his way
across the square to a corner near the wall where the
wooden pulpit of St. Paul's Cross stood. And then he
wandered on foot, leading his mount as he questioned
both the idle old men and fine gentlemen who loitered
there. He listened to them more attentively than he did
the various criers making public pronouncements. Philip
followed and heard all, but couldn't make out which of

the many things Lucas heard were most interesting to him, any more than he could understand why any of it was.

When Lucas was done and they'd finally ridden out and stopped to have a meal at a tavern along Paternoster Row, Lucas explained it all, and Philip understood even less.

"The news? Spain is still seeking alliance through wedlock, but Henry is holding Arthur aloof . . . as yet. Which gives Rome ideas," Lucas reported as he chewed his bit of cheese and bread. "The infanta is ailing, and mayhap mad Savonarola finally vexed too many in too many high places—we shall see, we shall see ." He shook his bright head as he swallowed his ale, before he went on. "Closer to home, there's an earl died in the north who was no friend to me, and another born in the west country—without a head, they say . . . knowing the poor lad's father, I wonder anyone noticed. And there's a mysterious beast been seen in the west that's got half the population hunting it and the other half crossing themselves, although by all reports, all the thing does is slink about as if it's embarrassed at being called a cross between a cow and a hippocamp. Ah, well, the other news from abroad is no less strange: The Portugee Da Gama hasn't been heard of for months, there's word he's dropped off the end of the earth, even though there's odd news of the Italian Columbus claiming he's reached even more new worlds. Much good it does any of us if it *is* true that there's no end to the world in sight even at the edge of the seas, when we can't even order this old one, eh?"

Philip attacked his own meat pasty and nodded knowingly. Never knowing, Lucas decided happily, that the wording of some of these things that he'd heard from all those supposedly unknown men had told him even more—as it was intended to do.

They mounted again and rode out through Ludgate, past the prison, and tried to hold their breath all the way across the Fleet Bridge, to no avail. For the stink, as Lucas said on a cough beneath his handkerchief, was so strong that it came in by the eyes and ears. From there it was a short ride to the Temple Bar, and there, once out of the City again and into Westminster and the little village of Charing, they could relax and breathe deep again, for the grass-edged track brought them past the lawns of the great houses by the river's edge and on through green fields to the abbey and palace.

They came to the palace by the light of a generous June evening, for at this time of year the light faded to a glow and stayed so until the smaller hours of the night, or rain, finally put it out. As they were passed in under the gate and clattered over the wooden road side by side, Lucas spoke softly to Philip, or was it to himself? Philip wondered. Because all he said, on a deep exhalation, was: "Ah. Here we are. Almost done, at last."

Lucas had forgotten the impact of seeing the man, but nothing else about him. Neither had he been forgotten. The moment he entered the great hall, where so many men congregated, he saw that majestic head turn to him like a bright flower turning to the sun. And Perkin Warbeck smiled radiantly and beckoned him in, as though he'd the absolute right to, as if he were really the ruler here and not just a remnant of his power and a symbol of his charity, left living by grace. For he graced this palace far better than Henry ever did, and that would be his tragedy as much as anything else, Lucas thought as he crossed the room to greet the pretender.

"Well met! Gentlemen, this is Lucas Lovat, lately come from abroad, and even more lately, from Greenwich," Perkin said as he introduced Lucas to the group of men he'd been talking with, and Lucas remembered that shy Philip, behind him, needed an introduction as well. When that was done, Perkin spoke again, eagerly. "Come, friend, what is the news?"

"All's well in Greenwich, or was, because I left it weeks past—as I'll soon be leaving here," Lucas answered. "It's true I'm lately come from abroad, but the latest news I bear is that I'll straightly go back there again. This is my last stop before I take to the sea."

Concern showed on Perkin's face, and it seemed real, although Lucas knew this man couldn't really care if he was gone or stayed. Yet for all that, he was amazed to find that it was nevertheless gratifying to see that evidence of consideration for him, however meaningless he knew it to be. Power radiated from Perkin, as well as warmth and appeal. What in God's name was Henry doing letting this man breathe? Lucas wondered again, before he was surprised out of his thought by Perkin wrapping an arm about his shoulder and walking him away from the others, for all the world as though they were oldest friends, met again in joy.

For all that Lucas knew it was a dangerous moment for him, he saw it would be impossible to shake the man off. He was shocked to discover a small part of himself rejoicing at that.

They walked shoulder to shoulder, and were of a height, and Lucas was as uncomfortable as he'd been when he'd walked thus with the anointed King of England. But for opposite reasons. He'd known his own presence had diminished Henry's, but now he felt himself to be cast in the shadow of this man. Perkin, though lissome, was the more substantial of the pair: broader in chest and at waist and thigh. His features, too, were more generous, and his hair thick rich gold, making Lucas' seem dulled silver in its reflected light. It wasn't envy, but Lucas, who never felt the cold, nevertheless felt a chill at his back at being in that shadow. A goose, he mused, walking over my grave? And was as suddenly sobered by the unbidden thought as he'd been amused at it.

"My lady," Perkin said anxiously as soon as they'd walked far enough across the huge hall to be out of earshot of the others. "What of her?"

He turned to face Lucas, and now Lucas realized that majesty was evident in the way that noble head sat on its strong neck and in the way the leonine abundance of butter-colored hair framed that open countenance. Something in Lucas' usually impassive face slipped at an unsought memory as he looked at Perkin; he'd seen kings before. That faintest flicker of disquiet alerted Perkin. Utmost concern on his own face, he gripped Lucas' shoulder hard and blurted, "There's something wrong? It *is* as they've hinted to me? Tell me, man, by God's faith, man, tell me all of it at once!"

"No, no, all's well, I vow it. My thoughts were elsewhere and my face is too much a measure of my thoughts—as always, alas," Lucas lamented, before add-

ing, his eyes innocent and gleaming, "It was but a random thought that saddened me—my sudden sorrow at
the realization that you and your lady can be united only
by such a poor messenger as myself. For she misses you as
much as you do her. And sends you all her love. And
bids me tell you that little Margaret is strong and well
and has learned to say your name, but because of the
way she speaks"—he lowered his voice to a whisper
although there was no one near enough to overhear—
"your name sounds more like 'Wisha' than 'Richard' to
her."

Perkin's mild blue eyes lightened and his full lips curved
in a familiar smile as he beamed at Lucas. "You are
indeed a friend to me. I thank you."

"There's nothing to thank me for," Lucas answered. "I
only wish I could do more. But on that head, what's this
'hint' at ill news you've had, and who are the 'they' who
hinted it? For I'll warrant," he said, glancing back to the
knot of men who still stood in conversation where they'd left
them, "that crew know nothing beyond wiping their own
arses, and speaking on—I'd not trust most of them to
turn their back on me to do it." His voice was heavy with
scorn, even though he knew only two of the men, John
Maxwell and Robert Cleymond, the two in Henry's employ, but of them, at least, it was true enough.

"Well-a-day, some of them I'd not trust. You're right
there. But some are only come to gawk at me, and I
know it." Perkin laughed indulgently, an easy, rich chuckling that warmed the ear. "Some of the others are good
men—there's Peter Cross and John Walsh, true as dies
the pair of them, and no harm in them; Robert Cleymond,
a caustic but amusing fellow; and the two Thomases—
those young peacocks Thomas Asterwood and his friend
Strangways, overly concerned with their hose and cloaks,
yes, but good lads and true, I'd vow it."

It was astonishing how easily he'd been made a confidant, and so Lucas believed nothing he'd heard. But he'd
remember those mentioned until his dying day; that was
his way with names and faces. Was Perkin testing him?
Or, more unbelievably, trusting him? A tiny wriggling
sense of doubt crawled in a corner of his mind. But he'd
a job to do.

"But what of this rumor you heard?" he asked. "What sort of friends would feed you on fears and doubt?"

"I'd heard that . . ." Perkin drew a breath and blurted, with little of his usual grace, "Someone also lately come from Westminster said that Henry said to be sure to tell me not only that my lady was well but also all about how she's admired at court as well: her eyes, her lips, her smiles . . ." He shook his head. "It was nothing, I'm certain, only what was in the tone of his voice as he related it to me, foolishness on my part, to be sure . . ."

"To be sure," Lucas said negligently, "there are a great many men who envy you your lady's steadfastness, and having only the freedom you have not, know it, and use it to revenge themselves upon her for her virtue. But surely you know that. Is there nothing else?"

Perkin relaxed, and smiled. "I'd heard a great many other things, but you're right, no matter."

"Are you sure?" Lucas persisted.

Perkin fixed him with a clear and suddenly keenly assessing look.

"Nothing of any account," he said with certainty.

Well, and there it was. It might be that the man had some instinct for survival, after all, Lucas decided. In any event, for all his efforts at friendship, he'd get no more from him, and in truth, it was enough to have new names to send to Henry, along with word that there was nothing else new to report. Then his job was done here, and then be damned to the lot of them. Henry would have Perkin's heart when he decided it was time, and what of it? It was inevitable, and would eventually be better for everyone—even the noble lady, though she didn't know it—when it was done. And if Henry chose to play with his prey until then through whispers and innuendo, what of it? It might be kinder than the rack, or if not, then at least less obvious, and mayhap even more gratifying. Henry had a mighty grudge to bear against this man; it might be that his death wouldn't be enough for him. Lucas hadn't thought it of Henry Tudor, but then, making one pretender toil as a turnspit and the other writhe with jealousy were subtle tortures, and Lucas' travels had taught him that torture was, after all, the sport of kings.

At least he himself would be off to Italy again now, where they had glorious, gory public executions only for saints. Otherwise they were sudden, efficient affairs. Because there they settled political disputes quickly and neatly with knives and garrotes and poisons, rather than this endless creeping and whispering and poisoning of minds.

All was as it must be, and he didn't know why he didn't turn and go now. But there was this niggling doubt.

So he stayed and stood with Perkin Warbeck as they gossiped about Lady Katherine and little Margaret as though they were a pair of nursemaids around the kitchen fire, as Lucas weighed and wondered at how to ask the questions he needed to be answered for his own sake.

"Tell me," Perkin asked when they'd done chuckling over some tidbit about his baby Margaret and her scorn for little Prince Henry's weak stomach, "what do they say of me at Greenwich? Not my lady, or my friends, but those who don't know me? I'd know what they think of me, please. And now, I pray you, good Lucas, because I'm seldom given this much time alone with any man. I suppose it's because you come from court, but as we've this moment, for whatever reason, will you tell me?"

So as to know what to say to convince them they're wrong? Lucas thought, but nevertheless answered, watching Perkin's expression. "Ah, well, marry, it's the same they say everywhere in Henry's hearing—which is everywhere I've been in England—that you're a bold, adventuresome, romantic youth. They say you court with some, dance with others, jest with the rest, and are acceptable to all. And have the look of Edward and perhaps even a drop or two of his blood"—Lucas studied Perkin's eyes as crystalline blue met mild blue regard—"but no right to the crown at all, because whoever you may be, you are not Prince Richard, and so then not King Richard IV risen from the dead."

"Why don't they believe me?"

Perkin's voice held fury, not pleading; frustration, not sorrow. And the look on his face puzzled Lucas, who held himself a good judge of men, because it seemed that he was being honest.

"Several reasons," Lucas said softly, so his voice wouldn't show his eagerness, for without his having to broach it, they'd got to the germ of the matter that concerned him most. "It's not in your face or form or bearing, but in your story. Faith! It's a strange story, sir! The sticking point is the kindhearted murderer who spared you after butchering your brother. The escape by sea, the vow of silence, your wandering the face of the earth until you were recognized and joyously received by your cousin earls in Ireland—all that is sweet to the ear, better than any ballad. But . . . ah"—Lucas shook his head sadly—"that kindly killer—it does not go down so easy."

"And you don't believe it either?"

"Let us say I have difficulty," Lucas said with complete honesty, before he added, "but for all that, I have this unreasoning faith in you." And then, in a deadly soft voice, he said, "And I've little in Henry, God knows." Then, straightening his shoulders, he fixed Perkin with a wide stare, as though challenging him to use that knowledge against him.

Some of Perkin's cronies had begun to stroll across the room toward them. Perkin spoke hurriedly, turning his head so they wouldn't see his lips as he did.

"Truth for truth, then, and let them get a double ax for both our necks if need be. Mayhap there are good reasons—good people who are reasons—for changing some facts. If you believe in me, believe in that. My brother, Royal Edward, *is* dead. Whether it was by God's hand, or God's hand in the glove of a mortal slayer, I cannot—will not—now say. I saw my brother dead. And was myself spared. There is truth, there is no other."

And for all he stared at him, Lucas could see no other truth. Yet nothing of his sudden frisson of dread and doubt, quickly dismissed, showed in his face as he nodded.

They passed the evening in stories and songs and playing cards. Lucas had the new games from Italy to teach them, and they tried to get their money back at the old games he knew so well. It was as odd as it was comfortable, this gaming with a dead man—for that was the truth, whatever way he looked at it, Lucas thought, watching Perkin laugh as he shrugged off the money he'd lost. They didn't speak of Greenwich again, or anything of any importance, until Lucas arose to say good night, and then Perkin asked too idly, for it didn't seem that subterfuge was built into the man, "The rumor is that Henry comes to Westminster again soon, and this time with his entire court. Is't so?"

"I hadn't heard it," Lucas answered.

Perkin walked with him across the room toward the door to the corridor, chatting inconsequential pleasantries loudly enough for anyone listening to hear. Before they neared the sentries at the door, he paused, as though well aware of the invisible circle that drew him in. He looked long and hard at the man he stood with. Lucas gazed back, only his curiosity evident. But he was seething with anger at himself because he'd stopped here, before all eyes, with the pretender, unhappy with himself for having been maneuvered into another compromising position, although he'd not been able to help it—and grew angrier still when he realized that. His face showed nothing but interest and slight amusement.

"They say you're Henry's man," Perkin said calmly, so calmly that Lucas was taken aback for a second, realizing he'd have to reassess the man.

"They say you are not Prince Richard," Lucas replied, as smoothly.

Perkin nodded, amused. Then all the merriment died from his eyes and he grew grave.

"They say Henry's besotted with my Katherine," he said urgently, and grew still, his eyes searching Lucas'.

There was no reason to comfort the man, every reason to lay a dozen traps beneath his feet or add to his disquiet, as Henry's men had obviously already begun to do, more reason to let him feel the bite of frustrated torment. The pretender stood for everything Lucas despaired of, and despised. But since one of those things was the role he'd been forced to play in this game of Henry's, he answered lightly.

"They say the moon is made of cheese, but I'd not believe it," Lucas said.

And felt not one whit cleaner because of the look of relief, and then easy contentment, which returned to the other man's eyes.

There were gracious courtly things to do at Westminster Palace even when the king and court were gone from it. The gentlemen went out with their falcons of a morning, rode on the wide lawns, or dallied with the ladies in the knot gardens in the shade of the trees, as all around them June opened her roses and lilies and shook catkins from her hair. But Lucas saw no sport in sending a winged killer after the innocent, and had seen greener grass, and was in no mood for ladies, or at least not any he saw displaying themselves before him like flowers on the lawns.

Two days after his arrival he decided it was time for his departure: time to be gone from this place and England herself, before he could no longer bear the thought of leaving again.

He said a light farewell to Perkin Warbeck and composed an innocent, reassuring message for Lady Katherine to be left with Philip de Lacey. He walked to the abbey nearby to leave another for Henry with one of the omnipresent monks who'd be sent to him for that purpose. Westminster swarmed with robed brothers of the church, those from the great abbey, as well as the many others nearby. Mendicant brothers, too, were commonplace in London, but it seemed to Lucas that Westminster had as many monks as spies, and that was to say a great many. They were everywhere in sight as they went about their duties, summer-busy bees in a great hive, Lucas thought, collecting information for Henry as assiduously as they did souls for their other master. But for all he'd looked, he hadn't seen Henry's cowled Brother Robert, or if he had, hadn't known it. Which was one of the reasons why he was eager to be done with this last interview. He fully expected Brother Robert to be the one to receive his message, and disliked facing that eyeless, faceless shadow beneath the cowl, as unknown to him as death's.

He cheered himself with funereal humor as he entered into the cool echoing recesses of the vast abbey. Henry's pious monk, after all, was brother to him—for he himself lived and dealt in secrecy, and the monk only embodied it.

As many times as he entered the abbey, it awed him. As many other great cathedrals as he'd seen, still this one most affected him. He knelt as he waited for Henry's agent to contact him, careless of his fine hose on the rough stone floor beneath his knees. It might even have been that he would have prayed for the first time in many years as he felt the weight of all the vast, solemn space above him pressing down on his back, and the grave weight of the dead buried deep in the earth beneath his knees pulling at him, if the monk hadn't come to kneel next to him almost at once, to speak the few words he'd been told to listen for as identification.

After all his apprehensions, he was almost disappointed to find himself turning to face a stranger. Even with the hooded cowl he lacked, the monk could never be Brother Robert. This monk was a short old man with a wide and greasy face, whose lips moved as he memorized the message.

"Perkin is content to wait. He misses his lady, but waits upon Henry's decision. He's surrounded by idlers, fools, and king's men, and they amuse him as much as he amuses them. There is no danger from him now . . . but . . ."

Lucas paused. Again, as he had all night, he thought of how he could end it quickly. Easily enough. Just a hint of a conspiracy might do it, a word of an overheard plot or a breath about a mad scheme could be enough to part the pretender's head from his broad shoulders now. Then the thing would be over and done. The monk looked up for the last words.

But Henry might know if he lied, he told himself again, forcing the image of Perkin's smiling face away. And Henry would definitely want to know why he had. And even if he'd a plausible reason, once having been doubted, he could end on the same block with the pretender.

". . . but if he is not given something to do soon, he may die of boredom and save our king the trouble," Lucas said quickly as he rose to his feet.

"She's a fine ship," Philip said as he stood on the dock with Lucas, and as Lucas grinned at his air of expertise, reminded him, "I grew up nearby the sea, and have seen many. But they were fishermen, not the size they have here—why, she's the size of a cathedral, and has as many masts as Westminster has spires, and . . ."

"And I'm sure the crew are as holy as monks, too. List! They're speaking of God as they're loading her," Lucas said with innocent wonderment.

Philip paused to listen to the sailors and then flushed to his ears as he heard the cries of "God rot!" and

"Christ's wounds!" and "God's precious balls!" that came drifting down from the ship as the sailors sweated the cargo aboard.

"Never mind." Lucas laughed. "You're right. She's a fine merchantman, and if not a cathedral, then a stout-enough seagoing marketplace."

He was content to have found a berth on the *Cathay*. She was an English vessel, not nearly so elegant as some of the foreign caravels he'd been on, nor half so fine as the great *Mathewe*, Henry and John Cabot's pride, out of Bristol—but then, she wasn't setting out to discover new worlds or defeat old ones, only to conquer known ones, by trade. She was a step above the sturdy squat traders all around her in Dover's busy harbor, easily the match of the Hanseatic trader that had set out yesterday, and even better than the Flemish trader that had limped into port this morning.

"Aye, take a good look at her, as I'm doing. Because that's the most joy I'll have of her on the voyage," Lucas said. "No, I don't suffer from sickness at sea, but for all her fine looks, my berth's belowdecks, her passengers sleep as close as the rest of the cargo she's packed with . . . and right above the bilge water too. I'd sleep in the masts like a tern, if they'd let me," he said on a sigh. But for all that, his lips quirked into a grin and his eyes sparkled as much as the choppy waves did in the glancing sunlight.

The sea did that to a man—the sea, and the knowledge that he'd a berth on a ship that would carry him away to all the other worlds that lay beyond this spit of land, this wharf, this dock, this little bit of England that had caused him so much pain. Of course, he knew he'd never leave England, no matter how far he sailed from her, and he lived only to sail back again. But still the salt stench and the sound of the great sails flapping like bird's wings in the breeze gave a lift to his heart, and he was suddenly as grateful to go as he'd been loath to in the night before this dawn.

The captain's cry of "Ho! Hoist now!" and the sounds of the crew beginning to chant in unison as they dragged sails aloft alerted him to imminent departure. Lucas strode to the end of the dock and stopped. Philip followed him, his cloak flying behind him and the breeze lifting his fiery hair back from his face. Lucas paused. The wind blew his gold cloak around him, flattening it against his back, making it flow forward from his arms like banners of glory streaming from a prophet's hands. His fair hair drifted across his face and the rising sun behind him extinguished the light before him, so Philip couldn't see his exact expression as he spoke. But his words were clear enough.

"Time to leave. Tell sweet Henry that I'll send word of whatever I get word of," he said with laughter in his voice, "and fare thee well, young Philip—here's a parting gift: advice. If you wish yourself well, find another sort of work. You've too honest a soul, as well as face, for what you do, and honest men can't thrive at Henry's court. Be easy, you may tell him that, with my blessings."

"Is there any word for anyone else at court?" Philip asked, trying unsuccessfully to be casual.

"Why, whomever might you mean, lad?" Lucas asked.

"I'd thought . . . the lady . . ." Philip gave up the effort and shrugged.

"I've sent word to Lady Katherine . . . Oh!" Lucas said with mock surprise. "I see. But I think I made all the good-byes a man could to Mistress Maeve before I left. . . . Still not satisfied? Well," he said in a bleaker voice, "I said farewell to the Lady Megan too, after that, and it was a far more final one, at that. . . . How old are you, Philip?" he asked suddenly.

"Nearly eighteen," Philip answered, puzzled because Lucas had forgotten.

"Near enough . . ." Lucas mused. "And gently born, and gently spoken. Well-a-day, then, I don't know just when I'll return, so instead of advice, I think I'll be generous enough to leave you a treasure by way of fare-well, instead. The Lady Megan is kind, gentle, and clever as well as lovely, as you have seen. But she's virtuous. I'll swear to that," he said ruefully, falling silent and grave before he forced a smile into his voice and said, "She could do far worse . . . as to that, I don't see how you could do better. Well?"

"I'm sure that's so," Philip said, blushing to a painful red, "but my father, he's a match almost made for me. My first wife—oh, yes, I was wedded when I was fourteen—she died soon after, with the child, and it's taken all this time to find another lady of family for me . . . so, so much as I admire the Lady Megan . . . he . . ."

"The king will dower her well, very well, tell him that," Lucas said curtly.

"Oh." A new light sprang up in Philip's eyes before he cast them down and stammered, "But the lady, she doesn't notice me . . ."

"She will, she'll have to if the king gives her to you," Lucas said abruptly, "and she's wise enough to know how much less she might have to settle for . . . you're a good lad, and modesty's no crime. Howbeit, do as you will—as you will, I'm sure. I give you good-bye, Philip, and wish you good fortune. I know you did what you had to do," he said more softly, "but at least you did it with grace, and," he added so gently Philip had to strain to hear him, "a grace I lack: the grace to be embarrassed for it."

Philip took Lucas' gloved hand and they stood so, until Lucas clapped him on the shoulder and turned round to bolt up the plank to the ship. But as he turned, he saw the sailors on the deck above him pause at their chores, staring down at the quay. He heard the company of horses and the commotion they'd caused even before he turned back again. And so had frozen in place, his expression impassive, by the time the first mounted guard called out.

"Ho! By the king's grace. Hold! I seek one Lucas Lovat. Is he here?"

Lucas looked down the long wharf to the new-arrived company of black-capped men in red livery, halberds at their sides, their mounts dusty and frothing as they pranced in place and tossed their heads after their hard ride.

"I am Lucas Lovat," he said calmly.

"Then, by y'r leave, sir," the captain of the guard said without a trace of humility to give credence to his humble words, "it is my charge to bring you to King Henry at Westminster Palace, and now."

"And now," Lucas echoed. "And why?"

"I only know the 'now' of it, sir. 'Tisn't my place to know the 'why,' " the captain replied.

"Ah," Lucas said, though he looked to Philip.

"Nor I," Philip cried in anguish. "I vow it."

Lucas took one last look at the ship before he smiled a thin smile.

"Astonishing how what one didn't want to do becomes so desirable when one can't do it after all," he murmured before he spread his hands in supplication. "I'm yours," he said to the captain. "Are there to be chains?"

"Oh, nay, sir!" the captain said. "No, no. At least, not if you come willingly, he said."

8

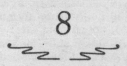

"How have I offended, sire?"

"That is exactly what I want to know," Henry answered.

Lucas remained bowed, his head to his knee. Although the base of his neck was covered over by the drift of his hair, he fancied he could feel the weight of something even sharper and colder than his king's gaze on his nape as he knelt before him.

"Rise," Henry said at length, on a sigh, but his face was still chill when Lucas stood and looked at him.

Lucas spread his hands wide. "The guards were amazingly closemouthed. I heard little but their opinions on England's women and each other's ancestries. My ship sailed without me. I'm a talented fellow, sire, but I haven't the knack of reading minds yet. As I was . . . escorted to your presence here today, I saw people trying not to look at me even as they did. I'm used to attention, but not that particular combination of fascination and terror. That's reserved for traitors and the condemned. Am I?" Lucas asked easily, with a gentle smile, as though he never realized he could be taken from this room and this life at once by a motion from this man's beringed hand.

"Are you?" Henry asked quietly. And then paused to hear something that the cowled monk at his side stepped forward to say into his ear.

"A traitor?" Lucas answered when the monk had stepped back again. "No, sire, and I'd warrant you know that. Condemned? How can I say?"

"You sent to me that Perkin Warbeck was resigned to his fate. That he rested here content to wait upon my grace. Did you not?"

133

"So he was, and so I did."

"Then why," Henry asked in a voice that held no question in it, "did he fly from my good graces here to make for the coast, not an hour after you left?"

Lucas stood absolutely still—as still as Henry's face was, as silent as the air in the room had got to be. He felt the ground opening up before him, and, as ever, when he knew only enough to know that he was in mortal danger, he waited until the shock had been dealt with before he spoke. He paused for the space of three heartbeats, and then he breathed again, and spoke.

"Flown? Escaped?" he asked, and then gave something like a chuckle. "God's blood," he said in a bleak voice, "I did not know. Nor," he added, focusing again on his king, "did I guess. No, I didn't. Something must have happened after I left him. Someone must have said something . . . He was very thick with Maxwell and Cleymond, as you doubtless know—at least by now," he added as Henry's eyes narrowed further. "How far did he get?" he asked, since now he didn't doubt, not for a moment, from Henry's sudden arrival at Westminster, as well as his calm appearance now, that Perkin had only been given an extra length of string and then let out on it before he was reeled in again. So kings played with certain prisoners, as small boys did with caged birds.

"That's what I wish to know—we've not recaptured him yet," Henry answered coldly.

The first thing that occurred to Lucas was the last thing he wished to do, and so, of course, he knew it was the thing he must ask to do immediately.

"May I join the hunt, sire?"

Henry sat watching him from flat cold eyes, while the monk stood silent at his shoulder, his eyes, like his face, as always, in utter shadow.

They'd only to leave the door ajar for an hour and look the other way, and the fool had taken the bait, Lucas raged to himself. But if it were so easy, such a clever trap snapped shut, why had they summoned him back now? he wondered. The answer came to him as swiftly and simply as death itself might. The game was one he knew, after all. However successful their ploy, for whatever reasons they'd done it, heads had to roll for this, expendable ones, for the sake of appearances—and his was to be one of them. With all he'd done! he thought with rising hilarity, and more, with all he'd meant to do, to die before his greatest sins were committed? To die merely as a scapegoat? Laughter bubbled up in him, quickly suppressed. A man ought to go to his doom with dignity, and wild laughter was too close a thing to tears.

Not a muscle moved in Lucas' face, but his eyes showed grim amusement.

"I didn't know," he said again, wondering if he'd have to say that all the way to the block.

"I believe you," Henry said.

Ah, Lucas thought, with no relief, I see, a new game.

"Still, imagine my delight when I returned to find him flown and the palace in great confusion, and you gone too," Henry said.

"No," Lucas said simply, "I'd no idea, not an inkling."

"And now," Henry continued, as if he'd not heard him, "I've his lady wife on my doorsill, weeping. I'd not brought her here myself. No, I'd left her at Greenwich, and had even the kindness to offer her the Sheen Palace until our return there for the summer," he said bitterly. "But now I have her here instead, she came straightaway when she got the news."

"But I saw some of the queen's men too when I was brought here just now . . ." Lucas began, and then his voice dwindled and he fell silent, seeing how the whole thing fitted together. Obviously, Henry had returned to Westminster with all his court and his queen, leaving only Lady Katherine behind. He could imagine Perkin's state when he'd heard that bit of news, and it was simple to think of the next things he'd been told. Asterwood or Sir John, or any of the dozen others had fed him the news that she was to be kept far from him. And then had whispered of the possibilities for it. It would have been enough, aside from whatever else he was told. Captivity was never the worst indignity a foe could inflict; trust Henry to know that some whispers cut deeper than the lash, if a man valued his manhood.

Henry finally nodded, the first of them to move.

"Christ himself knows why," the king said expressionlessly, "but I do believe you. You're too clever for that. I

had to ask, though, I had to see for myself. You may not
love me, Lucas Lovat, but I'd rather have a clever man
about me than a dullard that loves me well."

Useless, pointless to claim affection, Lucas thought, as
he answered, bowing his head, "Thank you, sire. For the
compliment, as well as for letting me continue my paltry
life, after having given you misinformation. But I did not
know. May I help prove it? May I help to secure the
pretender again?" he asked, as if he didn't know the
answer.

"Of course," Henry said. "I need someone with a cool
head to help in the search. Someone," he said with a
small twist to his lips, "who knows it would not be to his
advantage for the pretender to return here lifeless, or
otherwise unable to speak to us—as little to his advantage as it would be if Warbeck escaped altogether. I like
to employ a man with good reasons, as well as good
intentions, for doing his duty," he explained with a smile
that showed all his small teeth.

Your point, Lucas thought bitterly, as he said with the
same sincerity as Henry had, "Thank you for your gra-
ciousness, sire."

"I've new news of him, and have another company of
yeoman guard ready to ride. Can you go with them
within the hour?"

"I can leave as soon as you give me leave, majesty,"
Lucas said.

"You have it," Henry said, dismissing him.

The monk spoke only after Lucas had left them alone,
and his voice held only curiosity.

"If you dislike him so, sire, why do you use him so?"

Henry hesitated. He didn't wish to lie to Brother Robert. Yet the truth, vague as it was, was no more pleasant
than it was fair, or reasonable, even to his own ears.

"There's something about him," he said uncomfortably, trying to see it for himself as he spoke it. "Fair as a
flower and blond as a Viking, he has a presence; whatever his aims, it's impossible to tell his true feelings—
he's only to smile to win his way with most men and
women . . ." he began, pausing as he recalled how very
much that was like his own queen's charm. His reaction
to her was a thing he didn't wish to think about, and so

he thought instead of how the echo of the glittering Plantagenets still plagued him, even as he envied them, and of how Lucas Lovat embodied it in his own fashion. "Sooth!" he said instead, for he'd discovered another true thing, easier to say. "He reminds me of Perkin Warbeck, in a way."

"No man can help his face, he can only hide it if he must," the monk said softly, and as Henry grimaced in discomfort at the words, Brother Robert asked, "Has he ever failed you?"

"Nay," Henry admitted, embarrassed, astonished, as always, that this holy man could so affect him. So he said quickly, "And I've used him for years, abroad. There it is. Abroad, he's a perfect tool. Here, he vexes me. There's no denying that—nor that he makes no secret of his dislike for me in turn, even as he cloaks it in eloquence. It's more than sauciness. I know, good brother, I know— petty and unworthy of me. But a king is still a man, and no man likes to be misliked."

"No man likes to be misliked by one he respects, I think," Brother Robert said, and paused before, with rare amusement in his voice, he added, "Do you know, sire, I do believe you enjoy these skirmishes with him, since I can see no reason for true enmity. Nor do you. So that is what it must be, don't you think?"

"Aye. Aye! That may be so," Henry said, his face clearing at the simple explanation. "So it may be." He nodded, smiling. "Leave it to you, brother," he laughed, "to find the good in a bad business."

"And this business of Perkin Warbeck's escape?" the monk asked, his voice no longer merry.

"That is politics," Henry said harshly, his mood veering, "and not a matter of discussion between us today. Let it be. I know what I risk. Where politics are concerned, brother, I can have no thought for my soul."

The monk made no reply, but his dark cowl fluttered from the force of his sigh.

The guard that surrounded him was composed of grim professional men, as heavy with the weight of their office and this commission they'd been given as they were in flesh. For they were strong of arm and thigh, used to riding and marching in all weathers: the first in any army

the king might have to raise, the last to surrender to any
of his enemies. They were constant in his duty at the
Tower and Westminster, and entrusted with his protec-
tion and that of his court. But not, obviously, of his
courtiers. Because when they first saw Lucas Lovat mount-
ing up with them, they smiled to each other and made
quick wagers as to where and when on their wild ride
they'd lose this foppish, light-limbed, pretty fellow.

They rode out into the mist, and off into a rainstorm,
and rode the afternoon down into a slashingly wet and
windy twilight. But however hard they rode, whenever
they looked to the stranger in their company, they saw he
stayed with them: up hills, across fields, and over beaten
tracks, with his amber cloak and bright hair, like a pale
rod of light constantly moving amidst their own brazen
scarlet-and-gold splendor. Nor did he sweat, as they did
as they labored on, or snarl, or curse if his mount stum-
bled, or seem in the least discomforted from their punish-
ing, pounding pace. Seeing him always in step, and yet
always only bemused, they conceded that though he looked
not half so substantial as the great halberds they wore at
their sides, he was clearly as strong as the steel in their
hafts, and far more supple. And when he caught their
surprised glances, the bright glance in his pale eyes was
as cold and as sharp.

Then, as they rode on, some remembered some things
that had been whispered about one of Henry's spies—
one that looked and acted very like this one. Supersti-
tious as they were brave, they took care to avoid his eyes
after that—until he saw it, and smiled a singularly knowing, companionable smile at them. Then they looked
away, grim and seasoned veterans that they were, realizing that if they looked his way too long, they'd be entirely his.

As darkness fell and the rain increased, the guards'
bright doublets dwindled to mere crimson, and then to
blocks of denser darkness indistinguishable from the sur-
rounding night; with no moon to illuminate them, their
brave gold trim, buckles, and buttons went for nothing,
and they became, all of them then, only a dark and
exhausted company of men riding through a raging night.

"Hold! Here!" the commander shouted into the wind.

"We do nothing but risk the horses now. And if we can go no further in this," he muttered, dismounting, "be sure that whoreson goes no further this night either."

They tethered the horses beneath streaming trees, wrapped themselves in their cloaks, and tipped their hats over their heads as they sat up in a desultory huddle, with the horses and the tree trunks helping to shelter them from the worst of the wind and rain.

The captain of the guard took a deep swallow from his wineskin, and then, noting who had seated himself nearby, arose again, and knelt, offering Lucas a drink as well.

"I thank you," Lucas said, and drank, but stayed the captain with a gloved hand on his sleeve as he began to rise again.

Although his voice rang clear, the captain had to lean in close to hear him against the wild soughing of the trees.

"We rode hard, but left it late," Lucas said. "Shouldn't we go on now, despite the weather? However strong, if the wind sits right, a canny captain might set sail, since steady gusting in the right direction could save him hours at sea."

"At sea?" the captain shouted so loudly his men turned round to hear him. "Marry, sir, so may it be. But what's that to us? We're bound for Sheen, not the sea."

"Sheen?" Lucas asked, astonished.

"Aye, we seek the pretender, sir—that's where he's said to be."

"Ah," Lucas said, and the captain saw his teeth flash in a broad smile. "Aye," he murmured. "Foolish of me to think he'd be where Henry said he'd be. No matter, Captain. Thank you. Yes, of course, Sheen is nowhere near to the coast or the sea."

Lucas watched the captain struggle back to his shelter by the tree, and then wrapped himself tightly in his own cloak, even as all the others had done. Then he lay at his length on the ground, without a murmur, because, just as they feared, he felt none of the discomfort they did, but only because, as they never guessed, matters of mere wind and weather went, as ever, unnoticed by him.

Of course, he thought, staring into the wild night around him: Sheen. Where they'd told Perkin his lady would be. Sheen, Henry's favorite palace and abbey, where none

but monks and caretakers would be now. Where there'd
be no Lady Katherine at the palace, and no sanctuary at
the abbey either, since she'd been left at Greenwich and
had gone to Westminster, and because the monks at
Sheen wouldn't shelter Christ himself if Henry wanted
him back on the cross.

The only question that remained was whether Henry
wanted him to succeed with this mission, or fail. Did he
want Perkin dead? And so then, too, Lucas Lovat? Or
was it a true errand? He refused to debate it with himself
any further, being more weary of reviewing those possibilities than with his mad ride. Such exhaustion was more
dangerous than physical weariness too. He'd do his best
with what he'd been given, as always, and try to stay
alive at any and all costs, as he always had. But the
thought of his destination still rankled, if for another
reason.

Fool! Lucas thought in annoyance, and this time he
wasn't thinking of himself. He felt a faint disappointment
along with his disgust. A man who would be a king had
no right to be such a fool, and for him to be in love was
beyond foolish; it was too costly a taste for a man in
jeopardy, far too expensive for a king. Lucas closed his
eyes and let the night take him; there was no hurry now.
There was no way out for Perkin Warbeck now either,
except death or the road back the way he'd come. And
he was here to prevent the one and implement the other,
and as with most of the things Lucas had done for Henry
Tudor, it would be done, but he no longer wished to
think about it.

They arrived at Sheen with the sun. The rain had
passed with the rising of the dawn, and they stood in the
gray sunlight of first light and looked down to Henry's
favorite palace. The birds had just wakened, and their
tentative song blended with the deep, far-off thrumming
sounds of the monks' morning chant. The men slipped
from their horses, gathering up crossbows and pikes silently, preparing to approach the drowsing palace as
through it were a ringed and armored castle. Lucas' curt
voice rang out in the silence.

"God's blood, man!" he said angrily, rounding on the

captain. "Halberds and bows and spears? We hunt one man, one single man, not an infidel horde."

"Who's to say who his allies are this time?" the captain asked, nodding to a bowman as he slipped into the trees. "The pretender led a force of hundreds at Exeter. I was there to face his men, even if he was not by then. No, he was seeking sanctuary at Beaulieu Abbey as his men bled to death—even as some of my own did. This time, at least," he added on a sneer as he fastened his hand ax to his belt and then slid a dirk up his own sleeve, "I think we will meet."

"I think not," Lucas said coldly, putting one hand on the captain's arm and holding it immobile. The man spun around toward him. The captain was a head taller than his assailant, and twice as wide in the shoulders as well as the waist. The muscular arm Lucas gripped so tightly swelled as it knotted up with tension, but Lucas held it as fast as he did the captain's furious gaze.

"I have the king's seal, and his express command in this," Lucas said softly, speaking each word clearly and separately. "He has said he wants Warbeck back, and back capable of speech—with more than the angels. And so it will be done."

The rest of the guard stood silent, their hands on their weapons as they waited for the next move or word from the pair standing frozen in the clearing before them.

It was a moment before the arm Lucas held grew lax. Then he loosed it. The captain turned his head and spat, cursing as he did.

"I don't say you must like it," Lucas said, "but you must do it. As must I. Come, Captain, you know this— such is the fate of those born to a king's command."

"It isn't fair," the captain finally said, meeting Lucas' eyes with his own angry and confused ones.

"Marry," Lucas said with a sympathetic smile as he shrugged a shoulder and secured his own short sword fast at his belt, "what in all of this is?"

They walked down the grassy slope in two formations: one group of men sent winging to the palace by a motion from their captain's hand, and the other beckoned to follow him along the single track to the abbey. Lucas went by himself, and went more quickly, since he'd a

foreboding as well as a mission now. Because now he
knew he had to find Perkin, and disarm him as well as
protect him from those who might discover him first. If
he'd the time to speak and reason, Perkin might beguile
even the captain of the guard himself. But Lucas doubted
if he'd be left the time or breath to say adieu, much left
treat for his release, if he were found alone by these
men. Lucas hurried to find his twice-hunted quarry, to
save him from escape as well as death, and so to save
himself as well.

He disregarded the palace. For all its comforts, it held
nothing for Perkin if it didn't hold his lady. And if he'd
discovered it didn't hold his lady, Perkin would've known
he was betrayed. He could flee—but the man had a
history of seeking sanctuary in holy places, and Lucas
counted on the fact that he mightn't have learned, even
from his own sad experience, that no sacred place in
Henry's England was safe for any but the blessed dead
now.

Lucas ran toward the abbey. As he approached, in the
first sparkling light of true day, he saw a small band of
monks walking in file toward the entrance to celebrate
their service of gratitude for passing safely through another night. And there, against a gray and fretted stone
doorway, shining out like the morning sun itself, he saw a
man with sunlit hair: tall, broad-shouldered, and smiling
broadly as he stepped out, as though it were a pagan
temple he was inhabiting and he some rural Apollo
risen to greet his worshipers.

Lucas sighed with relief and quickened his pace. And
then from the corner of his eye he saw the sunlight
sparkle, glittering, glancing off water, or ice, or armor,
or some other thing that should not be there, to the side,
beyond a stone and up the hill a length and a half again
away from him.

He ran back up the way he'd come, and down again,
not breathing lest the sound be heard, even by himself,
to distract him. As he ran soft-footed he prayed so that
he wouldn't think. When he came in sight of the bowman
straightening from stepping down on his crossbow to
engage it, he finally let out all his breath to lighten
himself. As the man stood up and sighted down his bow

again, Lucas launched himself into the air as though he could fly as fast and true and lethal as the shaft that pointed in a line true as if it had been drawn to Perkin Warbeck's broad chest.

The bow loosed and the bolt sprang free.

But since it had been jarred as it was released, it flew jagged, landing far from its mark, only near enough to cause that golden head to turn to see, and then turn back and flee within the abbey again.

Lucas and the bowman spun down the slope, tumbling, rolling, locked in each other's arms like lovers, though their passion was to deal each other another sort of oblivion. Lucas lost his grip for a moment as they jolted to a halt, his opponent beneath him. He felt a cool slice in his arm, as if a shard of ice had caressed it, and knew the pain would come after. He forced himself to welcome the insult instead of recoiling from it, and tightened his grip instead of letting go, knowing that he'd still enough strength to break the hold on his arm, and maybe the offending hand that still clutched the knife it had grown, as well. But still he knew words were more effective now.

"Drop it, fool! Ass! Dolt!" he grunted, holding his opponent down with straight arms as he lay atop him. "If you do not, your captain will kill you, if I don't. You left before you heard him agree with me—the king said . . . he must live. Henry Tudor says the pretender must live," he insisted, close enough to his attacker's ear to bite it off instead of gasp reason into it.

It may have been that which convinced him. The body beneath his stopped struggling. Lucas rolled over, laboring for breath even as the bowman did.

"I saved your life, as well as his," he said when he could, as he watched his blood sluggishly fouling his fine silken sleeve. but he didn't say it again as he rose to his knees, holding his aching arm, because by then he was no longer sure.

They stood in a ring around him in the courtyard as a monk finished binding Lucas' arm. Lucas' face was pale as his eyes, and held as much cold determination.

"I'll go in alone. I'll come out with him. Then you can put him in chains. Then. But now, I enter, and remain, alone with him. You lose nothing by this," he said wea-

rily as the captain began to speak. "If I fail, you win as
surely as if I succeed."

The captain paused.

"Aye," he said after a moment's thought, "true. But is
the risk worth it to you, sir?"

Lucas' face brightened.

"Why, thank you," he said, and there was, for once,
no mockery in his smile. "I do thank you," he said, and
put his hand on the captain's shoulder before he turned
and entered the cool, dim recesses of the abbey, alone.

"Perkin," he called into the eternal dusk of the vast
stone abbey, "it is I, Lucas Lovat. And alone. Come
along, sir. I've been sorely tried. I hold no weapon, and
mean you no harm, but it is over, and so you might as
well come along with me, although I cannot bear you to
freedom. No man can now. Believe me. At least I am
your friend."

There was no answer in the high-ceilinged room. There
were rooms beyond this, and above it, and beneath:
roofs and cellars and niches to worship and meditate and
be buried and rot within. But Lucas knew that wherever
he was, Perkin was listening to him. The stone muted his
voice and quickly buried it, but bore it aloft in the silence
first.

"Come, sir," he called. "The monks will not succor
you. There is no sanctuary here. They may not deliver
you up personally, but they'll hide their holy heads and
look away from whatever is done to remove you from
them, if needs be, and pray away the bloodstains after,
believe me. There's a detachment of yeoman guard without, waiting. 'Twas one of them tried to keep you here
forever. I deflected his bolt. He only wished to end the
danger to his king. But Henry Tudor charged me to
return you to him whole and in good speaking voice.
Come, sir, accept it, and do us both a kindness. Come
with me now. If I'd wanted you dead as the bowman
had," Lucas cried into the dark, as annoyed as worried by
the continuing silence he spoke into now, "I'd have sent
them in after you, would I not have? Though returning
you to Henry is no act of friendship, believe that I am
still your friend in this. Although I grant," he said on a
ragged laugh, "that your friends have not given you

much more cause to celebrate of late than your enemies have."

"My friends," Perkin said from behind Lucas, "have at least tried."

"Have they?" Lucas asked quizzically, turning to face him.

"Misinformation given in good faith is no lie," Perkin said, inclining his noble head. "I wonder, is that what this is that you tell me now? Does death await me—us—beyond this door?"

"A fair question," Lucas said wearily, "but what choice have we but to see?"

Perkin stood solid and unwavering, and then he bent his head as if in a token bow.

"Fair enough," he said, and when he raised his head, he was smiling.

They were moving toward the great oaken door when Lucas paused and asked, "Why? Why did you run?"

"Would you not have?" Perkin asked.

When Lucas seemed about to answer, he added, "Only the time was in error, I think."

"And destination?" Lucas asked.

"No, I did not think it then," Perkin said.

Lucas nodded, silenced.

They walked out of the abbey side by side, two fair tall men who bore themselves with regal calm. And it may have been that neither of them drew breath in those first moments. But when the captain of the guard stepped forward, only bearing fetters for Perkin's wrists, both men relaxed.

Perkin didn't speak again until he was mounted on a horse beside Lucas, who'd been given his leading reins. He looked back once at the dreaming palace, Henry's favorite.

"Damn this place," he said dispassionately, but the look in his eye made the captain of the guard look away.

"Mark me, such treachery does not go unpunished. There will be a reckoning," he added in his usual deep commanding tone.

"Oh, aye," Lucas said sorrowfully, and there was that in his voice that made Perkin glance at him sharply.

*   *   *

A detachment of guards took Perkin from Lucas the moment they entered the courtyard at Westminster. There was no sense in protest, or even time for it.

"By order of the king," the guard told Lucas.

There was only time for Lucas to grasp Perkin's shoulder hard and say, "We'll meet again, never doubt it." And in that moment, he could swear he meant it.

They'd had little time for speech on their hard ride back, but Perkin Warbeck had borne himself proudly, riding straight-backed and calm, as a man ought, and a king might. There was that about him which ennobled him, as well as his escort; he'd the gift of making everything done in his company seem significant, even historic. He spoke little, but always pleasantly, and seemed in control of all that was happening, even though it was clear he was not. By the time they'd caught sight of the spires of Westminster, Lucas was not the only one who was both relieved and appalled to come to the end of their journeying, nor was he the only one of Perkin's escort not to know precisely why.

Lucas went to the chamber assigned him, and saw that it was his alone. Noting, but not rejoicing in that mark of favor, he washed and dressed and made sure all his possessions were secured in his traveling bags once more before he went below to seek audience with the king. He hadn't wanted to see the lady who came to his side the moment she saw him entering the great hall, but he'd somehow known he would, and yet had known no way to avoid it. He was only surprised to discover that he hadn't wished to see the lady in attendance on her even more. So he kept his eyes only upon Lady Katherine's fervent pleading ones as he spoke to her.

"He is well," he assured her, "unharmed. He's in even better health than I," he said wryly, thinking of the thick bandaging beneath the silken sleeve she put her trembling hand upon, never knowing she was more reassured by the blue, faintly bruised-looking skin beneath his clear cool eyes that spoke more eloquently of sleeplessness and a humanity that he'd never shown before.

"I kept him safe, upon my word—and upon Henry's orders," he added, and saw the hope spring up in her face again, for it seemed she could not yet speak. "I go to report to Henry now, and then I'll be gone, gone away, and truly this time, lady."

But at that he looked up to see Megan at last, and saw the hope in her eyes flicker and fade, even as her lady's flared, before she glanced away.

Yes, gone, and away, and not a second too soon, he thought as he left them to meet with Henry—although he'd begun to wonder if it were not already too late. But he knew all the tricks of survival, and so knew that if he'd embraced pain in order to free himself before—in his mad struggle with the bowman—now he must run from it if he wanted to save himself. So he composed his face, and his speech. And disguising the one, as ever, he gave the other, the moment he was given leave to rise from his bow to his king.

Henry listened, and let the silence go on a second too long when he'd done speaking. So then Lucas knew the answer, in part, before Henry spoke.

"You may go," Henry said, "but not abroad. As yet. There's another commission I'd have of you."

There was no disappointment in Lucas' face, nothing but a bright, hard look in the lucent eyes that watched Henry, and saw him have the grace, after a moment, to lower his own gaze to a parchment he held in his hands.

"I see, a man who's barked his shins walking in the dark is less likely to make another misstep," Lucas said. "Who is it that you'd have me carry back to you now, sire?"

Close, very close, he steps over the line and defies me to cry hold! Henry thought, as amused as he was annoyed, as always, by the elegant nobleman—just exactly as his holy monk had said—he realized as Brother Robert stirred at his side.

"The same man: Perkin Warbeck," Henry said, in better temper because of the newly explicable nature of his outsize reaction to his devious spy. "You did well there, recovering him without a scratch—on him. He loves you well—enough to walk into your arms without ado. Too bad, that. Mayhap if you'd stayed on a day longer before he broke for the coast, you'd have known all then, and so not have needed to take this last wild ride at all."

Lucas smiled. That deserved no answer. They'd waited until he'd left to lure Perkin forth, and Henry knew he knew it now.

"You rode back here so quickly, you'd hardly time to let the horses piss, much less speak with him . . . and yet, was that wise? I'd think he'd love you even more now," Henry said musingly.

It wasn't hard for Lucas to guess what this next errand would be. There was as little sense in trying to escape it as there was in allowing Henry to have the pleasure of assigning it to him. The sooner it was done, the sooner he could be on board a ship with his face to the clean wind and his back to England and this man. He spoke up before Henry could go further.

"Aye. So be it. I'll see him again, and speak to him once more. But I doubt I'll learn more, sire. Is he back in his apartments here?" he asked, subduing the impulse to sigh.

"Here?" Henry's laugh was like other men might sob; even Brother Robert's heavy cowl turned toward the uncommon sound.

"No," Henry said. "Once tried, only once freed. Now he bides in the Tower. I'll give you my seal so you may see him there. But not tonight. Or tomorrow. When we are done with installing him there."

Lucas stayed silent, his face set and white, but it seemed he swayed in place.

"So squeamish, then?" Henry asked curiously. "But don't fret. He'll be done with the rack by the time you arrive, and in his new apartment in the Garden Tower. Odd," he added with a thin smile. "I'd heard you'd skewered men like rats when you were in a temper."

"There it is, majesty," Lucas said sweetly. "I like to wreak my own revenge. Tying a man down while others pull his limbs off is not to my taste."

It was unfair. They both knew it. A king could not do personal battle with an enemy except in war, and Henry had done that, every time, and bravely too, without shirking. It was Perkin who had run from their one chance at an armed confrontation, at Taunton, the year before. It was foolish too, Lucas thought, for now Henry's face was as white as his own. Still, there was the hope that his anger would make him reconsider the mission.

"Speak to him as a friend," Henry said abruptly. "Find out who his allies in this were—and are."

Then he turned his back on Lucas and began speaking low to Brother Robert—or whatever dark-cowled monk it was who shadowed him today, Lucas thought.

Lucas bowed and left. It wasn't until he'd gone down the corridor and found a place where he could be alone, a place that had been recently cleaned, where the floor was strewn with fresh rushes, so he could hear any footsteps nearing him, that he stopped. And bowed his head, and leaned against the wall, and hugged himself hard, and allowed himself to shudder until he could no more, at last.

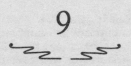

9

"I'm too old to bucket about like this," the archbishop complained.

"Indeed?" Henry said with a show of interest. "And so? I never sent for you."

"You ought have . . . or have you got yourself another counselor?" Archbishop Morton asked sharply.

"Have I grown myself another head?" Henry answered. "There are many who think themselves counselors; you know better. Or should. Marry, all this bile because I didn't summon you—all the way from Canterbury? How could I, and still count you friend, my friend?" Henry said, with a slight smile.

"Whelp," the old man commented, staring into his wine cup, "you knew I was in London."

"Who else is left to call me 'whelp'?" Henry asked, as though amazed, shaking his head. "Do you wonder why I have a care for you?" He chuckled. "But you show my age as well as yours, John, when you say that. Although, in truth, I was a lean-shanked boy when we met. Yet you saw what could be made of me—you brought me out of exile, to glory. I could not have had a better friend and counselor all these years." He shook his head in amused remembrance.

"And see how you remember me? By not telling me about this last mad start of yours—this foiled escape of the pretender," the old man said pettishly.

"But it was not big enough for you to concern yourself with—and you said you were bound for Canterbury, last we spoke," Henry explained with outsize innocence.

"There were things to do in London before I left," the archbishop answered gruffly.

"The very thing I was going to ask you about," Henry said.

The old man's eyes glistened with more than an old man's rheum as he looked hard at the king.

"Nay. Not I. I took no hand in it. Ah, marry, 'tis true," he admitted with a wave of a freckled hand, "I stayed on to see the thing through, after I got wind of it. But I didn't interfere. Why should I have? It went smoothly enough. The men spoke as they were bidden, he ran, Lovat collected him up for you. A nice exercise. But what did it get you?"

"Many little things," Henry said softly. "A nice test of my agents. A nice excuse to lock the pretender away from the world he'd entice to his purposes. Sooth! The man has a way about him! And, not the least, a nice excuse to finish him if ever I should need one to."

The old man looked up sharply.

"You'd need a better excuse than that. There are those who still believe him, here and abroad. He cannot be simply done away with. I thought we'd agreed, it gives him too much credence. A run for freedom is not treason. It is even commendable. I thought I taught you better than that."

"No, it's no treason to run for your life," Henry agreed, "but a man under lock and key might have good reason for true treason, in time. Think of it as a beginning of an ending, if not the actual ending of Perkin Warbeck. I don't need an ending yet. It's enough that I hold him in my hand for now. He may have more names to offer me; he may yet serve me even better in some other way. Lambert Simnel shows the world my patience and his lack of credence by continuing to live. Perkin Warbeck . . .? I'm not so in love with death as you religious fellows." He smiled. "Dead men serve your master, but do nothing for me or my aims."

The old man looked hard at him. Then gave a thin croak of a laugh.

"Did I say I taught you? Marry, you have surpassed me."

Henry bowed his head, as if at a benediction.

"And the rack," the archbishop said as he groped at the side of his chair, seeking a purchase for his fingers so that he could rise, "will give you more names?"

"If not," Henry said as he helped the old man to his feet, and from there, slowly to the door, "then Lucas Lovat will get them for me. If force doesn't work, warmth may. I remember a fable wherein all the raging winds of heaven couldn't get a man to take off his cloak, but the warming rays of the sun could. Lovat has a way about him too. It's not only foolish maidens he's so good at seducing."

"I don't like him," the archbishop grumbled.

"So you've said before, but that's because you don't know him," Henry said, as though bored at the old man's repeating himself, as the archbishop paused in the doorway, catching his breath. But then the old man caught sight of a cowled monk standing in the shadows beyond the door, where he'd been bidden to wait. Henry felt the arm beneath his tremble, and not just with the palsy of age.

"No, nor do I like *him*," the archbishop muttered.

"Ah, but that's because you've nothing in common," Henry said. And saw a faint flush come to the archbishop's speckled, wrinkled cheeks.

"Forgive me," Henry said softly, surprised to find that his jest had drawn blood. "The church needs practical men as well as holy ones, and so do I. God may have put me on the throne, but I doubt whether he could have without your help. It is only that now I find myself in need of other help for when the time comes that I must leave it, and this earth, as all men must one day."

"Aye. There was always that in you. I never understood it. But it gave you strength. So then, each man to his own, Henry," the archbishop said on a sigh, patting his hand, "each man to his own."

The howling was the first thing Lucas heard, the last thing he would ever forget. The lions didn't care for their constricted quarters in the menagerie, and one was complaining to the oncoming night. The first time he'd heard them he'd thought it was all the demons of hell roaring, and then they'd told him it was the lions. The sound made the mount he rode now tremble beneath him, but there wasn't a nerve left to quiver in Lucas' body. He was set for his task, and his task called for him to walk through this life like a dead man in life, with no feelings at all, and he'd got very good at that.

Both palaces and prisons were supposed to be quiet places, but this Tower of Henry's rang with sound. None of it was made by the prisoners. No, the dungeons were deep and stout enough to absorb all the cries they created, and by the time those unlucky enough to receive special attentions there were done with them, they were lucky to be able to let tears trickle down their faces, and that made little enough noise. But the many buildings of the Tower also housed royal family, nobility, well-connected commoners, and honored guests as well as prisoners, and the show of good fortune made more noise than ill fortune ever did.

The peacocks strutting the cobbled avenues and grassy swards between the towers kept up a steady racket, screeching like demons as they attempted to mate, and being randy as goats, shrilled and mewed through the days and nights. Bears moaned and muttered and great horned cattle bellowed; whatever exotic beasts were presented to the king from foreign lands were housed at the menagerie near to the Garden Tower, and they added their own homesick caterwaulings. And the ravens—those omnipresent great black birds of good fortune for the kingdom—creaked and whirred and cackled as they wheeled through the sky overhead. But somehow, Lucas decided as he rode his horse in the twilight shadows of the towers, it was worse when they sat like black stone statues of themselves and watched, quiet as plague, from out of their unfathomable bright yellow eyes.

More than six hundred persons lived within the confines of the Tower, and the best apartments were for guests—willing or not—of rank. The Earl of Warwick was still there, as had been his unlucky father, George, Duke of Clarence, until he'd met his death. Treasonous and treacherous nobility stayed at the king's grace until some monumentally clever mad escape freed them, or ransom did, or, most commonly, the king's favorite messenger, Death, delivered them from it. Kings David and James I of Scotland, King John of France, and Charles, Duke of Orleans, had each rested here temporarily. The earls of Kent, of March, the last Llewellyns, princes of Wales, and only recently, Henry VI, as well as his brother

Clarence, had rested here until rest eternal took them away. Here too, they said, in the Garden Tower, near the Lieutenant's Gardens, the two princes—King Edward IV's orphaned sons—had met their mysterious deaths. And now Perkin Warbeck, a confessed commoner, resided here. Because Henry Tudor, with ironic humor, had housed him as if he really were the long-lost prince he'd claimed to be.

Henry's yeoman guards let Lucas in through the gate at the end of the bridge across the moat, nearby the Lion Tower. Lucas left Philip with the horses and walked soft-booted on. Philip had undergone his own interrogation, and Lucas didn't care to think of what that had been like. It was as painful to think of his betrayal as it was of his innocence. But whatever Philip's interests in the matter, this was a thing Lucas had to do by himself, for many reasons.

That was why, he told himself, his heart constricted when he saw the three women rise to their feet from the bench where they'd been sitting as they saw him walking toward them. He came out from the shadow beneath the arch that led from the Traitor's Gate to the Garden Tower, and they accosted him.

The Lady Katherine's face was devastated, but her beauty wasn't ruined by her pallor and the dark circles beneath her lustrous eyes. Passionate suffering ennobled her perfect features, making mere beauty into magnificence. But Lucas had never desired Medea or Electra, nor did he so much as glance again at the blond woman with the lady. Instead he found his eyes seeking those of the shy, mortal, foolishly young Persephone, standing in the shadow of her lady. Megan avoided his gaze, but he'd enough of a glimpse of her to see that unhappiness didn't enhance her. It only struck him to the heart.

"Thank God. Lucas Lovat. They won't let me see him. You must help us. They've clapped him in chains again. They've taken him down to the dungeons. For the love of Christ, help us!" Lady Katherine cried, taking Lucas' hand hard in hers.

"Lady," he said softly, "God alone must help you. I cannot do more than any man can. But soft," he said, leading her back to the bench, "rest easy. I've been sent to see him by the king. And have been told that he should be out of the dungeons now. God's teeth, madam," he said as he felt her cold gloved hand trembling in his own, "why did he fly from Henry? Did you play a part in this?"

She froze in place, and withdrew her hand from his as she turned her head away, but her words came clear. "I sent to him that we would be meeting again soon. I thought . . ." He saw her unsure for the first time since he'd met her, and then her head swung back to him, and even in the fading twilight he could see the fury spring to life in her eyes. "It was meant that I think thus. But when I discovered I was to remain behind, I sent to him at once to tell him so! And to tell him to have faith and wait. I swear to it!"

"I don't doubt it," Lucas said softly, "nor do I doubt he never received your later message. Lady, let it be for now. You can only make more mischief for him."

"Let it be!" she cried. "Let them destroy him? Oh! How can you say such to me? Only help me," she said, lowering her voice, the fury vanquished, her usual meltingly soft voice back in place, as was her yielding expression, as she deferred to him, pleaded with him. "I attempted . . . I tried to give a guard some coin, Maeve tried to charm them, even Megan tried, but they turned their backs. But you . . ."

"I'd be clapped into chains at once, because I'm no tender beauty, and being of little importance besides, I'd never be loosed. There's the rub of it, lady. Henry won't kill him out of hand. Because in so doing he as well as admits the claim your . . . Richard first made. No. But he will keep him here for so long as he feels endangered by him. The running away was a grave mistake—but not fatal," he added hastily. "There is time. You must give it time."

"Time?" she said bitterly. "Henry will be endangered by my lord for as long as he lives. How long shall he keep him pent here? Because his luster will never diminish. You cannot bury sunlight!" she cried again, allowing the tears to flow unrestrained down her cheeks.

"No," Lucas said quietly, "but you *can* bury that which radiates it. This is no time for poetics or heroics. Your lord is but a man, and one who has made the king uneasy. You do him no service adding to that anxiety.

Go back to the palace. Your charm, your grace, and your soft words may turn a sovereign's head where it only made his guards fear for their own. Good behavior is the best course for you now. The only one," he said bluntly.

"Yes," she finally said, as he knew she would, "I see." She rose and wrapped her cloak about herself.

"I charge you to tell him of my love, if you love us. Tell him that I'll do anything he asks of me, tell him I will wait forever, if needs be."

It will, Lucas thought resignedly as he gave her back a sad small smile. Which faded when he saw the look that Megan shot to him before she left, supporting the lady on her right-hand side. Because for all the things he'd been thought and called in all of his wandering life, he'd never been accused, condemned, slain, and thoroughly despised, all in a glance.

" 'E's 'ere. Came in an hour past. By a back stair. We didn't want the lady to see 'im," the yeoman explained as he led Lucas up the dark and narrow stone stair. And then, as if apologizing for a spark of humanity, or fearful of Lucas' opinion of it, he added gruffly, "Set up a 'owling, she would. Eh, but 'e's 'ere."

But was he? Lucas wondered when they'd opened the heavy oaken door and let him into Perkin's apartment. There were two rooms, and a bed in the one beyond. A washbasin and a small window. A fireplace, and a table and a chair here. And the man who sat in the chair by the window looked at him blankly, scarcely recognizing him, any more than he was recognized by his visitor.

There was no blood. There were no bruises—though doubtless some might show soon on that fair skin on the wrists beneath the sleeves of his shirt, upon the ankles under the hose he wore. The rack left no gore. But the heavy-lidded blue eyes were open wide and blank with shock. There was no expression on the white face, and without one, the face was scarcely familiar, though its features were just as pure and straight. The man half-lay against the wall, and Lucas wondered at the angle at which that lifeless-looking left arm was carried, or rather, was dragged against the slumped body.

" 'Ere, you've another guest, sir. Can't 'ear, I'd warrant," the yeoman confided to Lucas. "They can't do much when they is first brought back, y' know."

But Lucas was looking beyond Perkin, to the shadow that detached itself from the outer room at the yeoman's words. The cowled monk moved toward Perkin with a cup of something in his hands, or at least one cupped and carried within the two long gray sleeves wherein a mortal man might be expected to have hands. The monk went to Perkin's side and touched his shoulder gently. Perkin made a soft low sound, like that of the wind in the trees, and the monk brought the cup to his unresponsive lips, and then stood before him, blocking the view, like Death himself come to comfort him at last after his earthly trials.

"I'll be back later," Lucas said, turning on his heel. When he heard the door close and the rattle of keys told him it was secured again, he asked without looking back, "How long before he will be able to speak and make sense, do you think?"

"You could try again in an hour," the yeoman said consideringly. "Sometimes they come about fast. But 'e was down there for two days—dunno. Eh, the brother's givin' 'im somethin'. Try then. Tomorrow'd be the day, though. Unless 'e's lost 'is wits. It does 'appen, betimes. They pulled one arm out of the socket, they said. Other's nearly. Tomorrow'll tell the tale. You can wait 'ere, if you wish, sir. Want in again, you give me a call. Brother'll wait—may'ap 'e'll spend the night afore 'e wants out, y'know. 'Tis 'is way. Dunno," the yeoman said as he left Lucas and descended the long curving stair.

Lucas followed. But then he paused at the first turn in the stair, and stood alone, leaning against the ragged stone wall, staring blindly out the slit of a window there, just as Perkin had done, at the deepening twilight. He was weak and dizzy, and had gone from hot to cold so quickly he could feel the dew that had gathered on his forehead dampening the roots of his hair. He laid his cheek on the rough stone and tried to drag air into his lungs, and then leaned back and tried to merely stand erect and stave off the darkness that was gathering at the corner of his eyes.

He'd not been at all dizzy after he'd bounded up the stairs coming here. He'd taken them quickly, and had kept his mind close on where he was bound. Not being able to avoid what he feared, he'd learned how to ignore what he did. But he'd let down his guard. Now, leaving, when he ought to have been thinking of Perkin Warbeck and what he'd endured—God's teeth! he swore to himself, that ought to have been enough to keep him from thinking of anything else—now, when he was already on the way to the free cool air of a June night—now it came to him so suddenly he couldn't breathe, much less move away.

He'd seen men racked before. He'd seen them hanged, and quartered, and their bowels ripped out and burnt before their dying eyes, as all of London cheered. But he was well-traveled and so he'd seen men extinguished in so many other various sophisticated and clever ways, seen them taken out of life in gallant armored battle, or by foolish accident, and some simply robbed of life by felons, or disease, or chance. Death in all its force and guises was all about him and had always been. That wasn't what made him sweat and shake now, and clench his teeth against the growing nausea that overcame him. Death was, when all was said, too simple for that. It was the sudden realization of where he was, again, at last, despite all his efforts, that caught his breath and held it. Because for all he'd run, so much further and for so much longer than Perkin ever had done, he was back again too, and every least part of his mind and body rebelled at remembering that.

He'd always loved this place. It had been a place of happy moments and great dreams. But then, when he'd been so young, it had only been another place to visit, a place that was always on the way to another, even happier one. And a place where he'd been surrounded by all those who'd loved him, and whom he had loved. Why, when Uncle Richard had taken him here in triumph that day, he'd ridden in over the moat and surveyed the Tower in its entirety, and had stood in the saddle the better to see its glory and take the tribute its citizens shouted to him.

Distant trumpets and distant tears. Lucas lay against the stone wall, transfixed, blind to the present as the past pressed in on him. What a strange day that had been. How mixed his emotions had been then. Only days before, he'd gone to sleep in his room at Ludlow Castle, miles away to the west, never thinking of London or his place there at all. In fact, he'd likely gone to his bed dreaming of a farther future. It had been his habit when at Ludlow to go to sleep only after staring out his window at the rippling bit of ribbon that was the Avon below, wondering where it would take him someday, for he'd been a boy with romantic notions. Whatever he'd dreamed, it was the last night of his life that he'd ever gone to bed a child.

Because he'd been woken in the depths of the night as a king.

He'd heard the voice of his Uncle Anthony at his ear, and smelling the stenchy tar of burning torches, he'd opened his eyes to see his small room filled with blaring and flaring gouts of light. He could scarcely make sense of his uncle softly telling him the unimaginable, as all the other men's voices cried out: "The king is dead! Long live the king!"

They'd dressed him. And, sleepy, staggering, in pain and in joy, he'd walked out into the damp spring night with them, shivering with the chill and the thought of where he was bound. The wavering torches hissed steam, making the night fade and the stars quiver above them, as they walked with him, before him, behind him, to the great round chapel in the center of the keep. As he'd knelt with them to pray for his father's soul, he'd begun to believe it, and the thought that he'd never see that well-loved golden face again, or hear that warmly tolerant amused voice again, made him shudder almost as much as he was doing now. And when the Knights of the Garter who were with him presented him with a poor crown to symbolize what he'd already become and what he would soon officially become in London, he wept without sound, almost as much as he was doing now.

Then they'd toasted him, and prepared the horses, and packed up his things, and ridden off with him into the night. A company of knights and soldiers and the men he loved most in the world besides his great father: Uncle Anthony, Earl Rivers, Governor of Ludlow, and his older stepbrother, Richard Grey, and old Sir Thomas Vaughn, his lifelong friend and tutor. They'd talked of his duties as they rode by day, and consoled him for his losses as they rode on by night. Because time was everything in these troubled times, they'd explained, and a king dying young and leaving such a young heir gave men too much time to consider alternatives.

Uncle Richard met them at Stony Strafford, near to London. As protector, he took the honor of escorting the new king to London, and bade the rest of the company to go home and ready their affairs so as to be able to meet again, in joy, in London, at the coronation. They'd agreed, but as he'd kissed his dearest friends good-bye and wished them Godspeed, Lucas thought now, he'd never guessed it was to be the last time he'd kiss them, or he would have said so much else to them. Because Uncle Anthony, and Richard Grey, and Sir Thomas Vaughn lost their heads the following week. On order of Uncle Richard.

But he'd not known it then as he rode on to London beside Uncle Richard. Quiet, charming Uncle Richard, so unlike his big amiable brother the king. A dedicated man, a nervous man, with none of his brother's laughter, but with ghostly traces of him in his lean face. They'd spoken of so many things; he remembered that even now: how much they'd both miss his father, how much his mama would miss his father, how hard it was to be king, how much harder for a boy to be king. And he remembered, and he was glad of that stranger boy he'd been now, remembering it, that he'd stopped Uncle Richard then to say: "But I was born to be king, Uncle, my father trained me to it. And I still have my mother and brother. And sooth! If my only crime is youth, I'll escape punishment, for it's a thing I'm growing out of!"

Uncle Richard had laughed. But he shouldn't have mentioned his mother, he was to think so many times later. For she was what Uncle Richard feared most. Climbing, greedy, grasping, he'd said all those things of her—later, of course. It was her ambition he feared, not for his own sake, but for his kingdom's, he said later. Well, and it may have been so. She was an ambitious woman. They said she schemed for the marriage that had gotten him, and schemed for the betterment of all her family then and ever after. But for all she was his mother, and he loved her, he was halfway to being a man and had been raised a king, and wouldn't have let her order his kingdom—and because Uncle Richard knew him, he could never have thought that. He doubted he had, even now. Because even now he couldn't believe it had been Uncle Richard who wanted him dead. His other uncles' deaths—yes. His mother's declawing, yes. But still he'd only banished her to a convent. No, even now, and even here, he wouldn't accept it had been Richard who'd ordered his death. His exile, yes. Not his death.

Lucas shook his head, trying to clear it of yesterday. But the place was so familiar, the very stones knew his name, and had absorbed his essence long before. They'd come into London, been feted at the bishop's palace, and then he'd come here, to the Tower, to await his brother, Richard, Duke of York. For Mama had fled into the abbey at Westminster with Richard, into sanctuary, fearing for herself and him. Which was absurd, Uncle Richard had said, and how could the Prince of Wales take his crown without his brother, York, at his side? And see how all of London had been clamoring his name, and they'd even struck coins in his image. So she'd relented and Richard had joined him. Slight, charming Richard, more like his namesake uncle than his father, a slender and solemn boy, but flaxen-haired, like his brother and as his father had been in youth.

Oh, he knew this place, Lucas thought, sick and despairing and pinned upright to the stones by the force of the suffocating pressure of those lost years rushing back to him. He and his brother had passed the first week of June here, riding, hawking, weeping and laughing and planning for their future.

And then they'd been taken from their apartment at the Lieutenant's Tower to this one. These rooms, they'd been told, were cleaner. The apartment they'd had had looked neat enough to them, but then, Lucas thought with the ghost of a grin even now, what did a boy, even a boy half-man and halfway to being a king, know of dirt, after all?

His coronation was set for the twenty-second day of June.

On the thirteenth day, their father's old friend William, Lord Hastings, was dragged out into the center of the Tower green and beheaded on the spot, immediately after a disagreement with Uncle Richard. Though they'd not seen it, there was no way to ignore it, or the odd looks and whispered bits of half-said things they then heard. But they were still treated with dignity and dined in state, and their tutor still came to hear their lessons, and the physician Argentine still came to see that they were sound. But Uncle Richard came no more.

On the sixteenth of June, on a day just such as this, Lucas remembered, realizing it was more than the bones of this Tower, the memory was steeped in the June-sweet air itself, Uncle Richard declared that his brother King Edward IV's marriage had been illegal, since Edward had been betrothed to another lady before it. And so then, of course, his sons, Edward and Richard, were bastards.

On the twenty-sixth of June, Uncle Richard was crowned King of England.

On the twenty-seventh day, after their lessons, a priest came to hear their confessions.

If he'd been a year older. If his voice had already deepened—if it didn't screech and crack when he tried to command. If his other uncles had only lived. If Lord Hastings had only held his tongue and kept his head. If his brother Richard's wife had only lived—because he'd been married to the Duke of Norfolk's infant daughter when he'd been three—but he'd been widowered at seven, and so there was no help from that quarter. Or any other.

Twelve years old and going on to eternity, he'd stood at the window and watched freemen going about their duties. He'd seen them avoid his eye. He'd raised his hand to wave at his subjects, only to drop it, remembering, but never quite believing, that they weren't his subjects anymore. And his little brother, Richard, so like his uncle in his thoughtful silences, so like his father in his sweetness, had taken that hand and held it and looked up to him and said that it would remedy itself. Villainy would not go unpunished, because God wouldn't have it that way.

At least, thank God, John Argentine and Sir Charles and a dozen dozen other loyal, shadowy noblemen would not.

On a dim night in late June, he'd been awakened in the depths of his dreams again. This time by John Argentine. And dressed, in silence, as was Richard, and taken without a word, down these same damned dark and stony stairs. On the way down, he'd had a glimpse of another pair of flaxen-haired boys going up. Another pair of boys, looking about themselves with wonder—another step-sized pair of pale youths, and well-dressed too. He'd looked his question to the priest that had him by the hand, and had got only a silent shake of the head as answer. If he'd known then, as he'd suspected even then, what would happen to that counterfeit pair in the dark of the night, would he have spoken even so? Lucas wondered again, as he had all his life. For kings learn early to make sacrifices, but this pair was so much a mirror image . . . even if, as he'd learned so long after, they were only common orphan boys staked out as prey for the lion while his real meal stole away.

Away to a village just outside the walls of London. Hiding in plain sight, in a crowded cottage full of children. Waiting for the time to take to the tides and sail away until adulthood, and then come back to right all wrongs, and avenge all wrongful deaths, even unimportant ones—such as hasty and mistaken murders committed in the dark of the night in the damned Tower.

But more than the murdering of kings can go wrong. There was a sickness in the village. Two days before they were to leave again, young Richard began trembling at dusk, and burning by midnight, and at dawn they took him to another room and hid him away, even from his brother. They wouldn't let his brother see him, so when the favorable tide came, he refused to go. For once his voice stayed steady, and there were generations of command in it as he dug in his feet and proclaimed that he'd not leave without his brother.

"There's contagion, we dare not risk it," John Argentine said wearily.

"Come, majesty . . . ah, son," Sir Charles said with difficulty, already beginning his role. "He's right, we dare not."

"I will not leave my brother," Edward-Lucas, the king in transition, the exiled boy king who had lost so much else, said, and there was that in his crystalline-clear eyes that said more.

"It is the pox," another nobleman said as they stood in the dim cottage, prepared to leave.

"I have had such," Edward-Lucas said, "when I was at Coventry, and Richard at Windsor. I will see him, and I will not leave him."

"You had cowpox," John Argentine said softly, reasonably. "Your brother has worse."

"I will see him," Edward-Lucas insisted, and waited.

They went into the other room to waken Richard and make him ready to see his brother, they said. And came out, soon after, weeping openly.

"He is gone," the priest said.

"I will see him," Edward-Lucas said, for there were some things he would not believe.

They'd covered the motionless lump they said was Richard with a peasant's brown blanket. That was the first indignity.

"He is . . . unsightly. Best not . . ." one of the noblemen said as his hand touched the blanket to draw it back—and that was the second indignity.

It was hard to make out the face he'd uncovered in the gloom, harder still because of what still covered all of that once-fair face. Richard looked as though he'd been scalded, boiled until his skin had puckered and blistered and broken open. Only the long pale hair glowed pure in the half-light. And the unseeing open eyes were, even in that light, blue as the summer sky would be after dawn. Then some kind one had covered over his face again, and his brother was glad for it. That was the third and last indignity. For nothing else would ever shame or hurt him again, Lucas-Edward thought as they led him from the house to the sea, to the Continent, to anonymity and freedom.

He came back later, to hide in plain sight in far-off Devon, as son to Sir Charles and his good wife, who'd lost their own sons over the years. And then, grown, he'd gone abroad again. He planned to return someday in triumph, as king. But each time he'd been ready, there'd been another pretender risen to ruin his plans. Lambert Simnel's rash claims had killed his own, unspoken. He'd had to wait until the fool was caught and caged.

Then, even as his supporters were ready to try for him, this damned clever villainous scoundrel Warbeck had begun his march to folly. Eight years waiting this time, Lucas thought. How many men may claim a throne before it becomes a travesty, a clownish melee, with no honor to the winner? And no prize worth fighting for? Henry grew stronger, while his own supporters were vanquished by time and fate. And his lovely vacant-eyed sister kept producing more nephews and nieces to stand between him and his rightful throne. But when he was king again, he'd kill none of them, Lucas vowed to himself . . . before he heard something like sobbing, and realized it was only himself, chuckling at his idiocy: a man transfixed by the terrors of yesterday, hung on a stone on a stair, a man with nothing but his wits and a small estate, coming from a visit with the tortured wreck who'd claimed to be his brother, and daring to plan how he'd spare the king's sons.

He no longer knew if he was laughing or weeping, since even those muted sounds ceased when he doubled over at last, retching against the cold flags at his knees. He tried to be quiet about it, even as his stomach tried to reject everything his body and soul remembered, as he knelt on the stair and wondered if he'd ever be whole again.

A cool hand touched his face, another supported him as he rid himself of the last of the bitter bile. Then he felt an infinitely tender hand smoothing his hair back from his face, so that a cool damp cloth could wipe it. Before he could speak his thanks, as he tried to rise, a cup was pressed into his hand, and he drank something slightly bitter, slightly salty, but clean, like the tears of a child.

When he stood and opened his eyes to see the real world again and thank his benefactor, he found himself staring into the darkness beneath Brother Robert's cowl. He recoiled, and the hands loosed him.

"He is not mortally harmed," a clear, gentle voice said from the depths of the cowl. "He'll sleep to rise to a sane morning. But his arm . . . still, you need not fear for him, he will recover his wits."

It took a moment for Lucas to realize whom the monk was talking about, and then, grateful for many things, but as eager to be away from Henry's strange monk as he was from this place, he said, "Oh. My thanks, I'll be back then. As for this . . . No, no, it was not to do with Perkin Warbeck, something I ate at dinner . . . no doubt."

"No doubt," the monk said.

Lucas took the long stair in a long smooth forward plunge, as though he were falling, instead of hurrying down the steps. Once out into the night, on the cool grass at the foot of the tower, he raised his eyes to the moon and cursed himself for his weakness almost as much as he damned the idiot Warbeck for his presumptions. And prayed for Henry to make a quick end to the damned pretender almost as fervently as he did for a chance, soon, for his own freedom to be himself, win or lose, at last.

He heard a quick gasp and looked down to see the lady standing before him, her eyes wide and fixed upon him.

"What is it?" the Lady Megan asked, terrified.

"Nothing, something I ate," he answered reflexively.

"Ah. Then . . ." She grew calm, her white coif and face shining out of the darkness as she looked up at him. "But he is well?" she asked.

"He?" Lucas asked, disoriented, until he remembered. "He. Yes, he—Perkin is . . . if not well, then well enough," he said.

"But you, sir?" she asked again, because his face was pale as the new moon that shone on it, and drawn with pain besides, and so for all she knew just what sort of man he was, and for all he'd hurt her, she couldn't help the surge of pain she felt at seeing him so stricken. Then she wondered where her wits were when she saw him recover, his usual cold humor restored to his watchful eyes.

"You plan a vigil here all night?" he asked as answer. "Such devotion to . . . your lady. What, I wonder, did you have to promise, in order to be permitted it?"

"No. I've just been waiting for you. She sent me to you," Megan said hurriedly, ashamed that her lady had insisted she come, saying he'd respond to her better than Maeve, since he already knew what Maeve could offer in return for his favor—and suddenly even more shamed to realize that she'd been willing to offer anything to help Perkin. But most shamed of all now that she'd forgotten Perkin entirely when she'd seen this man's distress.

"She wanted to know about him," Megan said breathlessly, "and asked me to tell you that . . . that if there is anything you want that is within her power to grant you, it is yours."

Everything he thought of the offer, and all of its ramifications, was clear in his eyes, and she looked away abruptly before he spoke again.

"There is nothing she can give me that I want," he said softly, truthfully, thinking wearily of what he wanted most tonight: Perkin's death and a place in this girl's arms, both come to him free. "I do not do that sort of trade. I take what I need, not what I want. And I never take charity," he said, grimacing as he realized he lied, since he owed his life to nothing but that.

"You are sure you are well?" she asked timidly, seeing that he'd grown even paler.

"Well enough," he answered, taking in a breath. "Shall I take you home?"

"No . . . no, she awaits, just near the gate." Megan turned from him and then hesitated, wondering how to tell him all those things she scarcely understood herself, things she didn't know why it was so important to tell him now: how the shocking sacrifice her lady hinted at wouldn't have been one, for so many different reasons; how she couldn't have done it, how she'd wanted to.

"I . . . I am my own woman," she blurted, and then fled into the darkness.

"How fortunate for you," Lucas said bleakly to the empty night. "I am not my own man. And have never been."

10

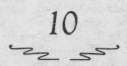

Such an easy thing to say. Just a few words and there'd be an end to it. Lucas paused to frame them. Henry waited.

"What did he say?" Henry had asked.

The room was still. The eyeless, faceless monk beside the king watched as carefully as he did, and Lucas, all grace and insouciance today in impeccable blue and green, the colors of the sea he wished to take to as soon as this interview was over, rose from his bow before them.

"What did he say?"

At first, nothing. The sun had risen high enough to squeeze in through Perkin's narrow window when Lucas had returned to him. He saw Perkin at once, dressed in gold and brown, the sunlight on his fair hair as he sat, as though at ease, in the chair in the outer room, with a paper and a quill before him. But Lucas knew enough of dramatics to know what stage was set before him. There was no way that hand could control a pen so soon after it had been almost wrenched from his body. Still, that knowledge, what he'd seen himself the day before, as well as what he knew had happened, were the only things to show that anything had happened. That, and Perkin Warbeck's eyes.

His face was the same. This time he'd recognized Lucas immediately, and had smiled at him. And there was still warmth and sorrow and wisdom in that smile; the man had lost nothing of his power. But something Lucas could not name had been added.

"Your lady wife sends her love," Lucas had said at once, before he'd even inquired after his health, for that was what the man wanted to hear. What, after all, could

168

a man say to another who'd brought a whole body into this place only days before, so that it might be maimed: "How good to see you well, I'm glad they've not succeeded yet"?

"She's tried everything, save for tipping the earth over, to see you again. She was here yesterday. I saw her yet again on my way in today," Lucas said.

Perkin hadn't answered, only continued to watch him with grave intensity.

Oh, what a great fool you are, Lucas thought, what an ass, how I despise you—to court death by impersonating another, far, far worthier one already dead and lost to me, and by so doing, delaying me, and bringing his death back to me again. Your death would be a favor to the one you're supposed to love, and as for myself, I *need* you dead and gone, Lucas thought, and said, "There's always the chance that she will succeed in seeing you one day. Henry . . . ah, well, such cruelty is not really his way. If . . . List," Lucas said, and bent near to Perkin, but not near enough for his sudden whisper to escape the note of the monk in the next room. And never near enough for it to escape the notice of anyone who might be watching from a concealed chink in the wall of another adjoining room or secret passage. The place was catacombed with them, they said.

"List!" Lucas said urgently. "If you could name some new names for Henry? It might soften his rage . . ." and having said what must be said, he heard what he'd expected to hear.

"I spoke all," Perkin said, and whether it was from the use of the rack or the character of the man, from the tone of his voice, Lucas knew that to be true.

Lucas stepped closer, lowering his voice even further. "If you would but recant—again. Only, this time, with more fervor. And if you would vow to leave this country forever, you might leave it with your life and love intact."

It was easy enough to say, for all that it was never true, and never could be. But the man needed something, and hope was all anyone could give him. And for all that Lucas despised him for what he was, it was impossible for him to hate him when he was with him. After all, he'd thought, uneasy with his charity, hope cost him nothing.

He'd waited for Perkin's reply.

The noble head tilted, the heavily lidded eyes opened to show the intensity of the new cold blue fire glowing there, as the well-shaped lips opened at last to whisper fiercely, "Why? I know who I am."

And then Lucas knew what it was that Perkin had gained in his hours on the rack this time.

He lingered, but Perkin said nothing else to him, except, after a few moments more, as Lucas was leaving, he said again, this time with a smile, "Lucas, trust me, I know who I am."

Well-a-day, and the man was mad now too, Lucas thought as he weighed the words he must say to Henry. So then, saying the needful words could be counted a blessing. Henry needed only a little push in order to end it now. Fear, even unreasonable fear—for a wise king found no fear unreasonable enough to ignore—could be enough to force his hand. And, too, if the defiant words had been heard by this monk, or any other man, Lucas could put himself at risk for neglecting to mention them.

"He said only that he knows who he is," Lucas said negligently. "I'll warrant, then, that his time on the rack was not wasted. He must rue the day he began this mad adventure, if he says he knows who he is, at last.

"That's all I could winkle out of him," he added, glancing beyond Henry to the immobile cowled brother, as though defying him to deny him, and secretly amusing himself by wondering how anyone could fault a man for reporting—and misinterpreting—exactly what he'd heard.

He'd thought he was beyond surprising himself until that moment. But he shrugged it off by reasoning that the thing would end soon anyway, and he'd enough blood on his head as it was—and would be.

"In truth," he added, sincerely enough, "I doubt I'll get more out of him, no matter how long I stay. Sire, my father's got a storehouse full of spring wool clips ready to trade. He's too old to take to the sea again. Now, may I have leave to go . . . and go far, this time?"

Henry stared at him for a long considering moment. For once, there was something other than muted mockery in Lucas Lovat's face. Something infinitely weary.

"Go then," Henry said, surprising himself, "with my good grace."

*   *   *

One passenger stood alone at the rail, and watched, as he had for hours, as the smooth billowing waves swelled beneath his feet, and he rose and fell with the ship as it plowed on toward greener, Italian seas. The day had been sultry, and the evening sea wind was only cool enough to dry the sweat on the bare chests of the sailors on the trader ship *Golden Horn*, but still the wheaten-haired man stayed wrapped deep in his amber cloak.

"Sir," the captain's boy said meekly as he came up to the tall, slender gentleman's side, "I'm to tell you that all the other passengers has et, 'n if you wants yours, you're to come along now."

Luminous blue eyes looked down at the boy, and then the man smiled and said, "Ah, thank you, no. Not now."

The boy didn't bother him again, though dinnertime came and went. Nor did anyone else approach the gentleman, for he stood aloof, and might be dangerous, since it seemed he kept talking to himself.

And Lucas stood at the rail until the darkness took his outer sight away, but nothing removed what he still saw before his eyes.

"I will not come back until I can come home in triumph," he told himself again, his lips moving slightly, as though to reinforce his wish. But he kept hearing Perkin's voice, and seeing Megan's face.

"I will return," he insisted very softly, and though the night breeze only toyed with the edges of his velvet cloak, he pulled it more tightly around him as he stood vigil on the deck, for, he thought absently, it was growing late, and cold.

Part II

11

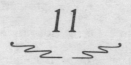

August 1499

The day was just as warm as summer's days had been in the land he'd lately left, but Lucas could feel the difference in the very air he breathed as he set foot on dry land, and England, once again. The salt sea air couldn't disguise it, he was home. It was more than the look and smell of the place that were familiar; even the workers on the dockside called out merry insults to each other in a tongue he could think in, as well as understand. And so he was smiling as he collected his bags and pressed coins into the hands of those seamen that had waited on him on the voyage back, though God knew, he thought as he straightened his shoulders and faced home again, he'd little enough to grin about. Because he recognized the lanky red-haired youth who strode across the dock to meet him, even though he'd changed far more than merely out of Henry Tudor's signature green-and-white livery since he'd last seen him.

"Marry, but you've come up in the world, haven't you?" Lucas asked as Philip de Lacey came up to him.

The difference of a year had changed Philip almost out of recognition. It was much more than the look of the well-fitting russet doublet over fashionable black hose that he now wore, or even the beginnings of a slight thickening to be seen at all of his margins—the new density of jawline, thigh, and waist. It was apparent in the less awkward way his long body now moved: the acceptance of manhood was in the boy's stance, his smile, even in the way his wild red hair had been darkened, tamed and trained to lie neatly against his neck.

"I've done well for myself, that's true, sir," Philip said heartily as greeting, as he picked up one of Lucas' travel-

ing bags. "And you? But I hardly need to ask, need I,"
he said at once, "since your prosperity and health are
easy enough to see."

A courtier now? Lucas thought, eyeing Philip with
ironic amusement. At Henry's court? Alas. That was no
promotion from page, or even scullery boy, at least not
to his mind. But the lad had made his choice, and so
there was no reason to spare him anything any longer.

"Sooth, I'm well enough, and my pockets aren't empty.
Yet you—why, Philip, what a trick to play on me.
You've grown up." As Philip laughed, Lucas added
sweetly, "And what graces you've gotten! Only to think,
to seek me out the moment my toes touch Mother England again in order to welcome me home again. I didn't
know I'd impressed you so. I'm flattered and humbled. I
thank you."

Well-a-day, at least he was still boy enough to blush,
Lucas thought with pleasure, as Philip stammered, "Ah,
well, and but . . . marry, sir, I . . ."

Lucas turned a polite inquiring face to him and waited.

"The king sent me," Philip finally blurted as grace-
lessly as he would have a year past, when last they'd met.

"Ah," Lucas said.

They walked down the wharf in silence, broken only when
Lucas said gently, "At least he sent no guards this time."

"Ah . . ." Philip said, avoiding his companion's eye,
"but he knew you'd come with me."

The continuing silence made Philip look to him again,
and after he did, he said hurriedly, now more than ever
like the Philip de Lacey Lucas remembered, "At least he
said . . . he hoped you would . . . Faith!" he said in
exasperation. "I'm not your equal, sir, and well I know
it. If you decide to ignore me, or challenge me, I haven't
got a prayer, have I? Howbeit, I'm charged to bring you
to Henry at Westminster. Will you come?"

Lucas stopped and looked at the boy . . . man, he
amended.

"You *have* grown up, haven't you?" he asked, smiling
slightly, before he sighed and said, "Yes. I'm yours. As
he knew I'd be."

They sat at the table at the dockside inn and drank to
the evening's first stars. It was too late to ride out to-

night. At dawn, at the changing of the tide, they'd go. But for now, they'd time to sit and talk. Lucas had washed, and for the first time in days been able to dress in clothes that weren't damp, and reveled in the feel of garments that were scented of lavender, not brine. Seated at a table that didn't rock, with a mug of fresh ale in his hands, he felt a curious sense of peace, as though he were any other wanderer returned from his travels, as if he'd no idea of what lay before him.

"Come, Philip," he said as he stretched his long legs out in front of his chair. "A man who stops traveling needs time to become used to it. I'll be sailing in my sleep all night if I go to my bed now. Let's talk awhile. I've some questions to ask."

He hadn't been more than a mere page so very long since, so Philip couldn't help but still feel proud that this man asked for his company—even though he also knew very well that he was the only companion Lucas had to talk with tonight. But the man still had such presence, such grace, he thought, enviously noting the way Lucas' clothes were distinguished by the man who wore them. Because he hadn't noticed more than their richness when he'd first seen them. Only now could he see how handsome the Italian blue silk doublet dashed with gold was, and how fine the lace on the immaculate square-necked white shirt, since at first all he'd seen was how the wearer's pellucid eyes mocked the blue as too blatant, and how the heavy gold was shamed by the purity of the sunchased gilt edges of that long soft hair. Yet it was far more than that; Philip had got used to elegance of clothes as well as manners in the rich and ornate court he served.

No, it was that it seemed that Lucas Lovat smiled down upon him, even though they sat opposite to each other at the table. When Philip found himself the focus of that crystalline amused regard, he felt as though each of the words he uttered was important and he himself was being singularly honored. And so, of course, he couldn't think of a word to say.

"Don't be alarmed, I won't ask you to divulge anything you can't or don't wish to do," Lucas said, deftly absolving him of his sudden awkwardness. "I don't ask for official reports," he went on dryly. "Faith, Englishmen in Italy speak of little else but home—after we finish with business." He grinned wryly and took another sip of his ale, letting Philip understand exactly that the sort of business he was suggesting had little to do with wool clips and silk prices. "I know of all the important things that have happened since I've gone: how Henry courts Spain so that she'll send Arthur his wife, how Spain drops her eyes and pouts for more say in England as her share of the dowry. I know that, as well as what Scots Jamie shouts to Henry across his bloodied borders, as well as what Henry whispers to the pope and what Parliament meekly asks of Henry, and how Henry orders Parliament to be still . . . I know of all the political liaisons here . . . more of the more scandalous ones between men and women—or men and men, for that matter—but it's the little things a man needs to know so he can feel at home again.

"How has the weather been?" he asked seriously. "Were the strawberries sweet this year? Last year there was a plaguey lot of toads in the spring, and this year? Put me in step again. Tell me natural oddities and trivial gossip, the smallest things you've lived through. It's not so much what famous men died, as which promising ones you think have been born. Come, Philip, tell me all—but hold! Start with yourself. I've seldom seen such a change in a lad since the day after I tumbled my first maid. What's happened to you? Because I'll warrant I've got my last blush from you by now, so tell me what accounts for that—more than getting out of Henry's livery, I'd swear to it."

"Aye, and you'd be right. It's getting into my marriage bed that's done it, I think," Philip said, easy under Lucas' gentle words and compliments. "I'm fortunate enough to be a well-wedded man now."

Lucas grew very still. Almost, Philip thought he'd said a wrong thing. But before he could review what he'd said, word for word, Lucas was smiling easily again, although his tightly clenched fist swept his mug of ale round and round, smearing the perfect circle of damp it had left on the wooden tabletop.

"Ah, so you took my advice and wedded, then," Lucas said. "I'd wish everyone listened to me so well."

"She's a beauty," Philip said enthusiastically, for his joy was still so new to him it was a further joy to share it, and a relief as well, since his usual cronies mocked him for never leaving off the subject. "Wellborn, and good, and obedient to me," he said dreamily, thinking of how his wife obeyed him so unquestioningly that by now he'd ceased doubting her submissiveness to him, and had begun to believe the wisdom of it entirely. "We wedded on Lady Day, and by next Christmas I'll be a father, God willing. It's not at all like the first time," he said gleefully, warming to the subject, remembering her arms about him in bed not two mornings past, and how she'd responded, sleepily, but as ever, obediently, to every nuance of his newly risen desire. Now that he was grown and had a wife who was a grown woman too, he found marriage was an incredible joy. There were not so many women in the world as there were men, and being lucky enough to be wellborn and wealthy enough to have one for his own—and a beautiful one, at that, that he could take whenever he wished, for however long he wanted— was beyond wonderful. It was nearly a miracle.

"I'm not so young, nor inexperienced anymore," he explained eagerly, "and so I can please her as well as myself now. She likes—"

"Indeed, how pleasant that your marital rites are no hardship. How thrilling that they were fruitful too," Lucas said in bored tones, cutting him off.

But he was not at all bored. He'd seen the stirred and smoldering ashes of recent lust and satiation in the boy's candid eyes, and found it to be strangely obscene. He, who had dined at orgies with friends carrying on conversations with him to the beat of their every gasp as they took their temporary mates on the tabletop not inches from his soup as he drank it without pause; he, who had seen lust satiated so many times—and too many times lust for things decent men would turn more than their eyes from—was suddenly feeling fastidious, as well as slightly ill at his stomach, at the thought of Philip de Lacey and Lady Megan embracing in their holy wedlock.

He'd not forgotten her. He'd seen and had more beautiful women since. But she'd made him laugh at more than his own cleverness, and talked to him about more than the follies of others, and he'd made her weep real tears because he'd betrayed her, and even so, once, he'd seen concern in her eyes for him. He remembered those tilted, searching brown eyes even now. But now she passed her nights in this redheaded boy's arms. She'd given him her vows, and taken his seed, and carried his baby now too. As he himself had suggested, he remembered. As Philip had no doubt told her.

Lucas yawned, with effort.

But it was a gaping yawn. "The sea air!" he exclaimed, as though surprised, as he yawned again, and stretched, and lazily arose. "My pardon—it might just be that I'm unused to good English ale. But I think that if I don't lay my head on my pillow now, I'll surely lay it on this very table! I give you good-night, de Lacey. I'll see you at dawn. Because even though you share my bed, I doubt I'll see you there if you don't come with me now—I'll warrant I'll be asleep before I touch my pillow!"

But he heard Philip come into the room hours later, and could swear he heard each separate feather in the thin mattress sigh as they bent to Philip's weight as he took his side of the bed. Just as he heard his own heart beat to every second of each hour as the night crept on to dawn, as he lay unblinking next to the hard young body that slept on, with the memory of her body imprinted in its every secret place.

Lucas lay unmoving and endured until the dawn. He was surprised to find that particular loss so painful, but not amazed to discover himself watching out the night again. He hadn't come home to find sleep, after all. But only to discover that which would find it for him again.

They spoke of many things on the road to London. Philip had grown up, but he was still a forthcoming youth and hadn't the knack of secrecy. And so Lucas learned all the little things he'd wanted to know about his homeland before he'd lost his appetite for gossip after hearing the details of Philip's domesticity. He'd known the queen had delivered another heir to Henry, this time another token for him to trade for goods and services: a girl. But he hadn't known that the newest princess was said to already be the bonniest of all the girls; a Plantagenet to her pink toes, fair and white and gold as young Henry, and charming as her late grandfather Edward, too. And although of course he'd known that Perkin still lived, and in the Tower, "unseen by sun or moon," he hadn't known that it was whispered that for a price something other than the sun or moon could see him there.

"That must make his lady wife rejoice," Lucas remarked.

"No, for she's not set eyes on him for a year, not since they clapped him up in there," Philip said quickly. "That I do know. If his jailers are said to be blind at times, for a generous fee, they use their noses to test for her perfume. Or they'd have them cut off. The king won't allow her to see him. So she bides with the queen wherever she is, and when she's in London, haunts the Tower grounds. There's nothing he can do about that. He won't prison her, you know."

"Ah. As to that . . . ?" Lucas asked, raising a thin eyebrow.

"Only rumor," Philip said quickly. "The king admires her—who does not? But only that, I'd swear to it," he said, and as the road narrowed then, dropped behind Lucas. When they were rejoined, he spoke only of a joust at the palace at Sheen, where he'd lately been, and where the queen still rested with the new babe during the treacherous pestilential summer season.

Philip was an amiable companion, and Lucas, having long since learned how to forget that which he couldn't change, silently forgave him for how he'd unintentionally offended. He lessened the offense by never mentioning Philip's marriage again, or so much as speaking the name of Lady Megan. But he did speak of everything else, and by the time they rode into London, he knew what name to put to every severed head impaled on London Bridge, as well as what the climate had been, in every way, on the days that they'd been mounted there. He heard which guild had put on the most elaborate procession on its feast day, which houses had burned down, as well as which minor felons had been hanged, and what the price of butter and biscuits had been. They spoke of every event, both great and small, that had transpired in London since he'd gone.

Lucas asked all he'd needed to know, and Philip had all the answers for him. Yet Lucas couldn't shake off a feeling of disquiet. Because for all his newfound maturity, still there was no doubt Philip was an odd instrument for Henry Tudor to use. The youth could doubtless be trusted, but trustworthiness was never the prime vir-

tue of a spy. It was better to doubt a clever spy than to
wholly trust an inept one.

It was only when they'd parted, after they'd been admitted to the palace at Westminster, that Lucas finally
saw his mistake, and Philip's singular strength.

When Lucas was ushered into the king's presence and
stood before him, and waited as he was pointedly over-
looked, he understood. He hadn't gotten all the answers
because he hadn't asked all the questions. For instance,
Lucas thought as Henry spoke first to his secretary, and
then in turn to a collection of noblemen, as he himself
stood waiting, ignored and expressionless, he hadn't known
how angry Henry was with him. Because he hadn't asked.

Philip was a poor liar. But not mentioning a thing
wasn't lying. And there was seemingly guileless Philip's
greatest worth: the appearance of complete innocence
coupled with the ability not to volunteer an extra word if
he wasn't bidden to. Lucas had a half-hour of standing,
waiting before the king, to silently damn his lapse of
judgment and mull over the possible consequences of his
uncharacteristic impulse to trust.

Henry waited until he could no longer wait for Lucas
to betray impatience. Then he finally turned from a conversation he was holding and not listening to, to regard
Lucas with both eyes at last.

"Lucas Lovat," he said, as though it were a meaningful
thing, and saw the blind light eyes return from looking
inward. Life sprang up in them again before the bright
head bowed and Lucas murmured, "Sire."

"What are you doing here, Lovat?" Henry demanded.

That did get a reaction. The gold lashes dropped once,
in a blink.

It was a further measure of how shaken he was that
Lucas answered, at once, without preamble and with
brevity.

"There's illness in the family," he said. And then,
taking a lesson from Phillip, he waited.

"Your father said nothing of it, last we met," Henry
said.

"I doubt he would. It's not as yet dire. It's a subtle
thing, and if God wills, a misleading set of symptoms.
But if not, I thought I'd do well to return home now. I

sent word of my coming, sire," Lucas offered gently, suave again.

"*After* you left," Henry corrected him.

The other noblemen present listened quietly, as did the knights and priests, monks and scholars, lawyers and laymen and poets, servitors of high and low degree: the various assorted members of this informally met court. They all stood and watched young Lovat as he met with Henry after his absence, and obviously unbidden return, from abroad. Not a few of them saw something other than what they saw, because they were men used to seeing beyond what their eyes reported. Might some fewer still, Lucas wondered uneasily, think they saw an echo of something in his face or stance, especially here in a room of power? This was not a good place to be standing, being nakedly observed. It was the last place he wished to be. But then, he'd passed the better part of his life in just such places. And so he stood, waiting for Henry's next move, for this interview to be over, however it turned out.

He'd never had such a prolonged and public interview with the king—important men and spies never did. He'd never been called before Henry except for secret business. This time it was his own secret business that had angered Henry. Not the business, of course—Henry would think that trivial, whatever it was, if it was his own. No, it was the fact that he'd come home, without being invited, that had subjected him to this public reprimand—or trial.

When he'd decided to return, when he'd been so far away, he *had* been alarmed at a set of ominous symptoms: his own. Troubled by something he'd never had, or had but had buried deeply; then it had seemed possible to act on his own—at least in something so small at this. Now he wondered at his recklessness. None of this showed on his face, of course. Because, he thought, if he lost that ability, he would surely lose all that he hadn't yet regained.

"I notified you after I left, yes," Lucas agreed, and then, inclining his head, he spread his arms to his sides like a man just cut down from the cross, and sighed. "I was too stricken with panic to think, sire. Forgive me."

Did someone in the crowded room titter? Or was that only the miracle of all their same unsaid thoughts taking embodiment at once? The words were exactly right. Nothing else was, and no one could seriously think this cold, clever, reputedly dangerous young man could be stricken by anything but cold steel. He stood before his king, sparkling in his defiance at the same moment he spoke subjection. But he'd begged pardon, and apologized, and really, his sin, as stated, was nothing. Still, the king was a king.

They waited for his answer. As did Lucas, knowing, as Henry did, that too much heat for so small an offense would be as detrimental to a king as to his hapless subject. Still, kings had the right to gamble. Lucas waited.

Clever, clever Lovat, Henry thought, as angry as he was antagonized, as ever with this facile, treacherous gentleman. He'd disconnect the fellow from his life with ease if he wasn't useful sometimes, and if, he thought uneasily, he didn't think that somehow, by so doing, he'd also be putting out a light he needed to see by. Or to see better? he wondered now, staring at Lucas, searching for an elusive thought. A motion, a dark flutter at the edge of his vision, distracted him.

Yes, yes, Henry thought, amused, Brother Robert spoke loudly even in his silences. He remembered how the monk had thought his king enjoyed these exchanges—if he ever had, it seemed incredible to him now. He also remembered the good brother would forgive his king—or any man—anything. But he'd never understand expedient cruelty. Which was why he valued him.

"The next time, Lucas Lovat," Henry said gravely, "if you cannot remember to ask your king's permission to leave a place to which he has sent you, at least remember to tell him of your change in his plans. Now who shall quote me Roman prices for our good English wool?" he asked affably, turning his attention to the onlookers from the man he'd called a wool merchant, even as some of his court smiled, knowing the famous quip about this particular man being a wolf in wool merchant's clothing.

"Sire," Lucas said, "you are generous beyond my merits."

"Yes," Henry said.

But, "Now who'll tell me about the Orsinis, the Colonnas, the Fuggers, the Borgias, and the rest?" Henry demanded when Lucas stood alone with him hours later.

"Da Silva's still in Venice, Fergus in Verona, John Fraser and his likely lads still bide in Florence, and both Polydore Vergil and Thomas Mapes are in Rome now. They all have the same sources I have, and know the same families I do," Lucas answered.

"Yes. They know them. But you," Henry said, "go to bed with them."

Lucas' face didn't change. But he was still. And that, Henry thought, was very unlike him.

"Go home, then," Henry said dismissively, oddly unsettled because Lucas hadn't fought back.

It must be true, then—Lucas thought confusedly as he reflexively bowed, straightened, and strode to the door, only now realizing that the sudden shameful and strange surge of hurt that had silenced his glib tongue had served him well—God does look after idiots.

In his haste to be gone, to be alone, to decide what to do next, Lucas didn't wish to wait even until the safety of morning's light to be gone from this place. He went straight to his chambers and picked up his bags, still redolent of the sea, and then made his way to the stables to find his mount again. He had to summon an ostler from his supper, and they were securing his bags to his ornate saddle when he looked up at the new arrival who appeared before them in the vagrant torchlight.

"In faith! I didn't mean to send you to the stables without supper too," Lucas said on a laugh, forcing himself to gaiety, though he already suspected the worst. "Henry gave me leave to leave, most prettily put and just what I was after," he told Philip blithely, "and so I'm bound for home again, and now. Yes, 'tis odd to travel by moonlight, and even I don't make a habit of it, but no dangers of the dark, natural or not, concern me so much as my worries about my home. It's good of you to come see me off, lad, but no need to fret or make a ceremony of it. I don't deserve such friendship. I'm just a thoughtless knave. I'd hoped you'd take my farewell and good wishes as said, even though I didn't say them. Take my hand on my apologies, then, along with my good wishes," he said, holding out his hand, "and farewell."

"Henry bids me go with you," Philip said quietly, and he looked down to his boot as it dug a hole in the straw at his feet.

Shall I live my life under lock and key as Perkin does, although only one of us is in chains? Lucas thought with a surge of rage that made his hand shiver on the saddle he rested it against. Alarmed and shaken by that display of violent emotion as much as he was by his feeling it, he said in a thin voice, "Oh, surely not! Even Henry wouldn't roust you from a newlywed's bed to come with an old bachelor like me! And to the depths of Devon, as well. And for how long, only God himself knows. What will pretty Megan say? I remember she'd a touch of red in her hair—why, she'll have my head, if not yours, for this. Go to Henry and plead your case, lad, he's in a yielding mood tonight."

His voice must have been more bitter than he'd intended, Lucas thought, because Philip stood and gaped at him.

"Megan? . . . Megan who?" Philip stammered, before he cocked his head to the side and struck it with the heel of his hand as a slow smile grew on his face, clear to see even in the leaping shadows in the dark stables. "Ah. Marry, you thought I wedded Lady Megan, didn't you? God's teeth! Nay, nay," he laughed on a long-drawn-out breath, sounding very like the beasts all about them, "not she! Ah. What a lobcock I am! 'Took your advice,' you said, and so you thought . . . but so I did. I married, yes. But not the Lady Megan. No, I never even asked for her, for when I got home, my father had my sweet Elizabeth for me. The contracts were all signed, save for my mark.

"Elizabeth Foyle is my lady, sir," Philip said, as though savoring the words. "Sweet Elizabeth Foyle, Harry Foyle's daughter, from just outside London Town. You must know the family, they're maritime traders, and do right well for themselves." He grew loquacious in his enthusiasm. "She brought a house, a pocketful of carbuncle rubies from the East, and five and a half shares in her father's ship with her for me," he said, smiling even wider, "and though she's got more than a touch of red in her hair—that's what made them think of the match, they said—she's no more warlike than I. No, she's the sweetest little thing . . . and she knows only too well that the king's command is my command, and she'd not sulk at my absence, though she loves me well," he added proudly.

"And," Philip said, drawing himself up, "I'm not needed at home, since I've already started her summer's work for her." He lowered his voice a little as he explained, with shy pride, "She's sick in the mornings."

Yes, and so then this gawky man-boy wasn't wedded to Megan Baswell, so why then should he rejoice? Lucas thought, tamping down the sudden surge of relief as he asked, "And the Lady Megan Baswell?"

"She's still with Lady Katherine," Philip said, "but they do say that Matthew Lorrilard has his eye upon her, and she does not look away. But he's got rooms in London and an estate in Sussex, and a relative or two with the king's right ear, so he can look however long and hard as he wishes to, they do say too."

Philip racked his brain for more gossip of those old days of a year ago, when he was so callow, and unwedded, as he waited for his own mount to be brought out, pleased that he'd said something that had taken that stark white look from Lucas Lovat's face. Because it was no more pleasant to be a watchman than to be watched, just as he'd told Elizabeth that night in their bed after he'd been given his new duties.

"And that little plump blond Maeve," Philip commented as he rode out into the twilight with Lucas, now glad that he'd something to take his mind off the alarming fact that once more, and with equal unease, he'd be riding out into the night with this man, "she wedded old William Carter soon after you left, and everyone predicted she'd have him in his grave in a fortnight, since he's older than the hills, but she's due to pup before my Elizabeth, so how's one to know? Still, he's got his heirs already, all grown as well, and . . ." Philip stopped talking when he realized that the sound of hoofbeats as his companion spurred his mount would have drowned him out, even if Lucas had been listening to him.

Some things do not change. The sight of the manor house in its wide clearing at the edges of the great forest, the look of it at the end of a journey, so secure on its high hill overlooking the sea, was as welcoming as it had seemed all those years ago when he'd arrived here in equal pain and confusion, Lucas thought.

But that had been fresh pain, and merited confusion,

and this—this was the reason he'd returned again. Lucas slid from his saddle, threw his reins to a boy in the drive before the house, and strode to the door quickly so that they'd see his face first, so they'd say nothing in front of Philip, who followed behind him. He'd ridden as though pursued, all the way home, and hoped Philip would think it was still the angel of death he was racing against as he hurried into the house. It was an equally mortal matter of security.

He had to see his parents first, because there was no way of knowing that the message he'd sent by way of Argentine had got to them. It wasn't the sort of thing he could write in a note.

"I've returned from Italy and am coming home at once because I fear you are dying," would not be a kind or intelligent missive to send or receive. "I'm returned and am coming home with haste because I told the king I feared you were dying," would be no better.

Old John opened the door for them, his surprise and delight at seeing young Master Lucas returned so extreme that Lucas had another moment to worry as to whether Sir Charles's and his good wife's hearts could take the shock of seeing him so unexpectedly—much less the hint he'd have to give them when they did. But they hadn't been chosen to foster him those years ago for no reason.

"Lucas, Lucas, my dear boy," Sir Charles cried as he came at a trot through the door to the hall where his visitors stood. He embraced his tall son at once, wrapping him in his arms, as his wife held her hands together in front of her heart and smiled tremulously at them.

Lucas lowered his shining head so that his soft bright hair fell past his ears and forward over his lips and Sir Charles's ear as he whispered into it, "I've said I've come because there was illness here."

"Ah, Lucas, how I disliked to see you leave your duties because of what some fool leech said of us. As you see, I'm recovered—entirely!" Sir Charles said loudly when he drew back to clap Lucas on the back and stare up into his eyes.

"But he is such a good boy to worry for us," his wife said at once to Philip, before Lucas swept her up and hugged her hard for her cleverness, and because it simply felt so good to trust someone enough to hold her close and not worry about his back in her arms.

"Pray excuse us," she said to her other visitor as she wiped her eyes when she was released. " 'Tis such a happy time. But"—she squinted up at the tall red-haired man who shifted his feet in her hallway—"is it you, Philip de Lacey? My soul! How you've changed," she said as he bowed to her.

"That's because he's wedded now. And expecting another de Lacey by Christ's own birthday," Lucas said brightly, giving his mama a significant smile.

"How fine!" she said at once, patting Philip's hand. "You must tell me all about it. We can't get our son to agree to a match. How did your father do it? Is she beautiful? When's the babe due? Pay no mind to our rogue: 'Christ's birthday,' indeed! I hope he's not punished for his blasphemy," she chided as she slid her eyes to Lucas to see his small approving smile and smaller nod.

"Come," she said, still prattling to Philip, as though he were the most important visitor she'd ever had, far more interesting than the son she'd not seen for over a year, "it's almost time to sit down to our dinner. You'll eat with us, of course. Good lamb, and our own fresh fish, and it's been a good warm season; not only pears, but mulberries and brambles are ripe. And so soon! I'll show you to your room and summon a bath for you after your long ride—we'll strew it with rosemary, that's the thing for relaxing—all the way from London, wasn't it?" she asked as she steered Philip to the stair.

Lucas shot Philip a bright grin, and then shrugged, and watched him taken up the stair and round it, until he was gone from view on the balcony above, out of sight, as well as hearing. When they could hear the lady's incessant babbling no longer, Sir Charles let his smile slide away and fixed Lucas with a long stare.

"Marry, if she sends in that complaisant wench to help him with his bath again this time, she need not bring hot water," Lucas said merrily. "He'll flounder and flush so, his bathwater will steam by itself. He's newly wedded and serious about it—you ought to have seen the way he fled the wench at the inn last night! There's a new plague, a burning rash on the privy parts—it's being spread in

Italy by love's play—but he hadn't heard of it. It's God's shaft he fears if he employs his own without his wife." Lucas laughed, but Sir Charles did not. His dark eyes kept searching Lucas' face, and he saw nothing to smile about there.

Lucas sobered, and then his fatigue was as easy to see as the pallor and the new vulnerable look to his mouth and eyes.

"You told Henry you came home from Italy, and made straightway to London and then came pelting here, because you feared illness in the family?" Sir Charles asked.

"Yes," Lucas said, clenching his hands to keep them from shaking at his sides. "Yes. God's body, yes, my dear father in my exile, yes, I did. I vow it's true. God knows it is an illness. And mine own . . . but not of the body," he said quickly as he saw the older man waver and his eyes fly wide, "only of the heart and mind.

"I cannot stay away any longer," Lucas said bluntly, pacing a restless step away and turning before he said, "There are things I must know now. Now. I'm not willing to hide any longer. There are risks I must take, or lose the chance ever to take them."

"Then be sure it will be an illness of the body soon enough," Sir Charles said dourly, shaking his head, "because it is not time."

"It *is* time," Lucas said in a new voice that Sir Charles remembered well, as he stared down at him.

At that tone, and that bright and angry stare, for all he'd continued to live a life of lies and evasions only by keeping his wits about him, Sir Charles surprised himself by having to exert the utmost control in order not to unthinkingly slip to his knees to kneel before Lucas, as he'd done for his father, so often, so long ago.

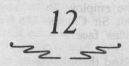

12

"It's an old title, an ancient honor," Lucas said reprovingly. "I'd think you'd cleave to it."

"I'm an old man, I leave nothing behind me but you," Sir Charles said, wagging his finger in order to go on speaking without interruption. "My nephews claim blood, but you have first claim on my soul, and that must be foremost. When you regain . . . what is rightfully yours," he said prudently, even though they were alone where they sat their horses on a cliff on a winding path near the sea, having carefully lost Philip a mile back at a woodsy fork in the track they'd taken, "you may deliver my legacy to another—even one of my nephews if you think he's worthy. A baronetcy was valuable once. But the title Henry hints at rewarding me with will serve you better until then."

"How politic," Lucas murmured, "not to say the obvious—that it may have to serve me until I'm ready to go on to my own reward."

Sir Charles's rugged face flushed as nicely as Philip's downy one did, Lucas thought in sad amusement, before he said in kinder tones, "I know. I must be logical. It may come to that."

"Anything may happen, we ought to know that," Sir Charles said gruffly. "But whatever comes when I'm gone, I'd be happy to know I'd been honored enough to have left you something of value."

"You've given me that already," Lucas said quickly. "I need no title or land grants from Henry to give me more. If it should come to pass that I fail to recover my rightful name, I can think of none I'd be prouder to bear than yours."

Sir Charles turned his head so that Lucas caught only the shining glimmer of the tracks the tears made down his wrinkled cheek. "That I may not call you 'sire' in my lifetime! That I cannot call you my king!" he choked.

There was no answer to that. Instead, Lucas ignored it, saying wonderingly, "Henry thinks to reward you for trade you've brought to England! How like a shopkeeper our sovereign is, to bestow titles for trade where his predecessors did for bravery. Ah, well, but that's the way of the world as I've seen it. I doubt my Italian friend Cesare Borgia could unhorse a man with a lance, for all I've seen him got up in the trappings of gallant warfare when he's on the strut. But he can destroy a man with a whisper of a pen across a debit sheet as well as with a dram of poison, and so he bids fair to rule his world. The world's changing too fast."

"You're much too young to speak that way," Sir Charles said, his own misery forgotten, the more so when he stopped, realizing Lucas had given up his youth long since.

Lucas looked out over the water, the talk of youth reminding him of a thing he'd wondered about when he'd been over the sea.

"How many faithful men are left to me now?" he asked softly.

Sir Charles grew still, licked his lips, and avoided Lucas' too observant eyes when he answered slowly.

"Buckingham's gone, of course," he said ruefully, as Lucas made an impatient gesture, for Buckingham had been long gone, "and Throckmorton and Wainright . . . we lost Lincoln and Fitzgerald and Lovell to Simnel, and North and Brampton to Warbeck—"

"I haven't asked for ancient history," Lucas interrupted. "We've not much time, you know."

The hesitation before Sir Charles spoke again told him more than he wanted to know.

Most of those few men who had been part of the plot that had taken him from the Tower that long-ago night were already lost to him; some to death from age, some to the royal wrath of Richard or Henry. Political men were not long-lived in such times. There were a few remaining who knew he lived, but not where or how. He expected that he'd lost some of them to Simnel's schemes,

and some to Perkin's. But now Sir Charles's silence said
that the same could be said of many more he'd counted
on from those remaining houses loyal to the house of
York.

"I see," Lucas said tightly. "The pretenders have cost
me dearer than I knew, have they?"

"There's still Tyrell, and Guildford," Sir Charles said
quickly, "Suffolk . . . and don't forget or underestimate
Argentine, and Carmeliano, or others like them—sometimes men who work their ways into high places are
preferable to those only born to them."

"I don't," Lucas said ruefully, "nor do I forget that
their senses of honor are more flexible. They've had to
be for them to have been able to attain their lofty places
at all. They're comfortable under Henry," he said before
Sir Charles could protest. "Why should they risk their
lives changing horses now? Especially when they don't
know me? And, too, Henry is more like them, isn't he?
I'd warrant their sympathies would be more with a man
who boldly took what wasn't his more than it would be
for one born to what Henry had to fight to achieve—even
as they had to."

"You are God's anointed and rightful King of England," Sir Charles cried, "and no honest man loyal to
England would gainsay you."

The wind carried away the old man's words as they
were uttered, his anguished cry had flown like a gull's,
but now he looked stricken for his lapse, and peered
around as if he feared Philip would materialize in the air
before him.

"Hush, hush, Father," Lucas said softly. "I know. I
know."

"You were too young when Simnel began his mad
march, and we never believed that Warbeck could come
so far . . . Margaret of Burgundy did her work too well
there, surprising us," Sir Charles explained, almost pleading. "Perhaps we were too cautious. We sometimes think
that mayhap we ought to have applied to her instead
of—"

"No, no," Lucas said hastily, "I saw my father's sister,
I visited with her in my exile, in fact, remember? She's
sick to the soul with hatred. She holds the monument to
her lost brothers and nephews in her heart, aye, and on

her lips as well. It's as though it were still yesterday to
her. Her wounds never stop bleeding; all these years
have passed and her lust for revenge hasn't yet grown
cold. And never will. No, for all her money and influence, I'd not make myself known to my good aunt and
ask for her support even now. She'd be my worst enemy
as my ally. A conspirator can't afford to be hot. No, I
know too well that stealth, deceit, and revenge must be
done—just like murder with a sharp blade—only by hands
that are steady and cold."

"When the time is right, we'll have the men to fight at
your side," Sir Charles vowed. "I didn't think it was
time, but if you're sure . . . ?"

Lucas gazed at the grizzled face of his foster father; the
afternoon sunlight was pitiless. He noted the fine cross-
hatching on the skin that was not wrinkled, seeing how
that weathered skin had taken the sun unevenly, giving
him the splotchy badges of age. He's old, Lucas thought.
And yet ready to die the sooner for me. As are, no
doubt, all those other brave men who let me live so long
ago, as are their young sons, who don't know yet that I
didn't die. But they grow fewer every year; every year,
time and fate take away a few more, as every year
Henry's grip grows firmer.

"I don't know if it's time," Lucas admitted, and couldn't
ignore the relief he saw in Sir Charles's eyes. "I've come
back to see if it is. Father . . . Charles," he said, "did
you see my brother dead?"

The old man looked stunned; he shook his head as if to
clear it.

"How now?" he asked. "What's this?"

"I saw him for a moment only, at the last," Lucas said,
"saw his pox, rather, for I'd eyes for nothing else just
then. And was glad enough when they covered him over
again. But was that diseased thing . . . boy, my brother?"
he asked in a mulling tone, as if he were asking himself.

"Who else should it be?" Sir Charles asked, astounded.

"Were you there with him the while when he was
sick?"

"Why . . . why, no. Am I a healer? No, I . . . I was
told he was gone, same as you. I saw his face when you
did. I . . ." Sir Charles's voice dwindled and the two men
sat in silence for a moment.

Both had lived with deceit for too long to discard any accusation of it, however mad. For they'd both done mad things in order to remain alive. Both had lied to live, and now neither really believed very many things anymore, and none that they didn't see with their own eyes. Neither of them trusted more than three people in the world. And each was one of them to the other.

"Perkin Warbeck was stretched on the rack until nearly torn apart," Lucas said expressionlessly. "I saw him moments after. And he swore—and I know truth in a man's eyes—that he wasn't lying. I've not been able to forget him since. He's been in my mind for over a year now, and his words won't leave me. I've returned to speak with him. He has a *presence*, Charles, he reminds me so of—"

"Don't be a fool!" Sir Charles said in an angry voice he'd never used with Lucas before, just as he'd never said anything so disrespectful, not in all the years he'd known him. "Your brother is dead. Warbeck is merely . . ."

"Yes? Merely who?"

"An impostor. There may be blood there—that might be what calls to you," Sir Charles admitted. "But at most he's a by-blow of your father's—God knows there were enough of them—or an uncle's, or mayhap it is as Henry hints, and he's Margaret's own ill-begotten son . . . it might be. But he is not Richard. Richard was . . . he was light, and laughing, and clever, don't you remember?"

"Don't you remember me?" Lucas asked softly. "I'm no longer that wise, grave boy."

"Why should they lie?" Sir Charles asked. "What would it profit them?"

"What did it profit them to save me?" As Sir Charles remained silent, thinking, Lucas added, "He says he is Richard. And I believe he believes it."

"Madmen may believe they are God. Does that make them master of the universe? I'd an old uncle who believed he was a bear when he reached his dotage. We didn't set the hunt upon him," Sir Charles said, trying to laugh over the new terror he felt.

"He doesn't seem mad," Lucas said implacably, reciting that which had kept him wakeful these long months past.

"God's body, Lucas!" Sir Charles cried. "Mayhap he

doesn't lie! Mayhap they raised him up from youth to think of himself as such! Half of our childhoods are remembered through someone else's tales of them. Why, I'll warrant you know how your father was dressed on his wedding day, as if you'd seen him with your own eyes—although you'd no eyes then, since you weren't born yet. It might be that his own youth was too painful to remember and he was happy to believe the new one they gave him. How shall we know? But I *know* he is not Richard. I saw him in that back room that day, even as you did, and though my eyes were wet with tears, they were keener then, and it was he beneath those pox, I'd take a holy vow it."

"I couldn't," Lucas said softly, "not at all. You would, but do you even know where he's buried?"

"I saw the monks take him away . . ." Sir Charles said, as Lucas shook his head.

"Not good enough," Lucas said sadly. "As a glance was not good enough for me. I must know. Because Perkin will rot to death in that damned Tower, and what if he is my brother? What then? Stranger things have happened, I need not tell you that. I must know if I'm ever to know any contentment. There is a . . . resonance I feel with him . . . a familiarity . . . But be easy," he said quickly, as he saw a familiar figure come riding out of the forest toward them, "I'll learn slowly, and carefully. My doubts will not be the death of me, sir, although my certainties may well be, someday. . . . Ho! Philip! Where did you get to, you mad rogue? That was a pretty wench at Fallow Farm. Shall I tell your Elizabeth that you tarried there?"

"I will no longer blush," Philip cried breathlessly as he rode up to them. "Why, by the time I return home, after all these days with you, I'll warrant I'll never blush again. I took a wrong turn. But what has made you so sad?"

"Not your absence, lout," Lucas said lightly, "nor your presence either, and don't fret, nor were we talking treason," he added sweetly, as Philip gave the lie to his words about never blushing again, "but only discussing a thorny problem to do with words. You see," he said as he nudged his horse forward and the three men rode on up the hill, "it's rumor only, so pray say nothing to anyone"—he paused to smile as Philip's ears grew red as well—"but we hear that my father may soon be elevated—higher than this," he laughed, "by our king, for services done for the crown. Well, and if he is, why, then, he'll need a new motto. '*Faire Mon Devoir*'—'Do My Duty'—is very sincere, and does credit to the stolid Norman who started our line, but it's hardly the stuff to inspire a new earldom or dukedom."

"We thought '*Post Nubila Phoebus*'—'Sunshine After Clouds'—was fit, but Lucas here thinks it inappropriate to English weather," Sir Charles immediately complained, as if they'd ever talked about it before, "and insists '*Deum Cole, Regem Serva*'—'I Worship God but Serve the King'—is too long for future countesses or duchesses to embroider on chair backs." He smiled at Lucas as he said it.

"A lord near our village had '*Odi Profanum*'—'I Hate Whatever Is Profane'—I've always thought it had a good sound to it," Philip said thoughtfully.

"Aye, but if Lucas is going to inherit, it will never do," Sir Charles said grumpily, as they all laughed.

They rode on, throwing up suggestions for slogans, and laughing them down again, as if they none of them had anything else on their minds.

The sluttish-looking kitchen maid opened the door to Lucas' bedchamber a crack and then grinned. She opened the door wider, and tossing her tangled hair back from her bare shoulders, gave her mistress a broad smile.

"Eh, I'll be off now, then, mistress," she said. "More's the pity," she added as she turned her back and with much play of her hips crossed the room and went through to the antechamber beyond it, closing the door firmly behind her.

"Don't frown, Mama," Lucas said on a laugh. "Father's looking after me—and I, him—and he's been here almost from the first."

"Aye. *Almost*," his mama said curtly, staring at the closed door to the antechamber as she mumbled, "Cheeky slut."

"She'd only been here a moment before I came, and I vow the sheets were fresh as when they'd gone on in the morning," Sir Charles agreed.

"And since when were beds the only places for mischief?" his wife demanded, "or don't you remember when you were young? For myself, I feel like a girl again, slipping off in the night to meet my lover," she said as the men laughed and she finally came fully into Lucas' room.

"Ah, you shameless bawd," Sir Charles growled, putting his arm around her plump shoulders and shaking her gently, "now it comes out! I always knew you were a faithless wench!"

"Oh, aye, faithless," she grumbled. "If I'd any sense, I would've been." She pushed him away with the half-pleased, half-angry familiarity of a woman who has lived with the same man for most of her life and is as embarrassed as annoyed that his flattery still gives her pleasure.

"You see what joys my coming home gives you?" Lucas asked merrily as he leaned back against his window and surveyed them. "On any other night you'd be sleeping by now, and wasting the moonlight. Fie, Father! Does it take my homecoming to bring back her youth?"

"If it were a fair world," she said over her husband's chuckling, "I could speak to you in the sunlight." And when his laughter suddenly stopped, she stared at Lucas steadily and went on, "Aye, 'tis very amusing to send you a slattern at midnight so the prim redheaded longshanks who companies you stays far from your door. But it's never right."

Lucas shrugged. "The world is seldom right. I don't mind it. The best intimacies are stolen ones; kings have always had back stairs—my own father used them often enough, or so they tell me."

"And thus the very root and reason you have these troubles now," his mama whispered, "or so *he*"—she gestured with an uplifted shoulder toward her husband at her side—"tells me. 'Tis true you're thinking he in the Tower is your brother? Never think it. Prince Richard was a bright and bonny boy, merry as a cricket, and if he'd lived for life to change him, it wouldn't have shorn his wits. He'd never be doltish enough to take on Henry with only one army of men, and never coward enough to run away from the field they fought on for him . . . whatever his excuse. Not Richard, not he," she said, reminding Lucas that he'd heard once, so long ago he couldn't remember when, or didn't wish to, that Richard had been this lady's especial favorite. But then, when she'd met them, he himself had been a gangling colt of twelve, and Richard, at ten, still babe enough to melt her bereaved mother's heart.

"I wept my fill for him then," she said raggedly now. "Aye, I was there too, remember. A nobleman and his lady and their boy is what we were when we left him and walked out into the light in plain sight of God and man, and no one the wiser, then or now. But it was meant to be *two* men and their wives, and *two* boys going separate paths, to meet again. Mary Hartford, God rest her, was to have the honor to take one of you, and I the other, and it was as well they'd already decided to send you with me, for we didn't know she'd a worm at her breast and would die before another year turned. I wept for your brother then," she said, raising her head to show she'd not finished with that weeping yet. "Have I survived only to weep for you? Aye, for I shall, should you be daft enough to call this base pretender 'brother.' "

Lucas abandoned his lounging pose against the window. He strode across the room to kneel at her feet and take her hands in his.

"Nay!" she cried, aghast, as she tried to snatch her hands away. " 'Tis not fitting that you should bend to me!"

He held her fast with his hands and his eyes. "It is fitting," he commanded, and she ceased struggling. "And save your tears. I'll not die in the attempt to find the truth, or at least I don't think I will. I'm no fool, only a man who wants to be sure. Be easy. I'll take utmost care that your work did not go in vain."

"Aye, well, then," Sir Charles said too brusquely, as his wife conquered her tears, "there's naught to do but bid you luck. But I tell you, as I've told you, it is not he." He heaved a heavy sigh before he spoke again. "And so. Where do you go now?"

Lucas leaned forward to give his foster mother a light kiss on her forehead, which she waved away with a flustered flutter of her damp handkerchief, and then he arose.

"Not to the Tower. I said I'm not such a fool, and certainly not such a one as that. Henry's vexed enough with me. I'll give him time to forget, while you stage a

remarkable recovery—if you don't mind putting up with
me and my young shadow for a few weeks longer. But,"
he said on a grin, "that means you'll have to spare me
more moments with your sweet greasy kitchen wench,
my lady—if we want to meet again by night—because de
Lacey's monkish-minded as his master Henry, but not
half so idiotish as he seems, as his master knows all too
well.

"And then," he went on as both Sir Charles and his
wife began to protest their desire to have him stay for
however long he wished, "I'll visit friends of ours, here
and there, before I return to London with the first breath
of autumn and Henry's return there. He's gone to his
heart's home, Sheen, and from thence to Woodstock or
Greenwich, whichever suits his wandering fancy, but then
he'll be back to London to do the nation's business. It's
then I'll come to him with news of a disquieting rumor or
two about Perkin Warbeck, and ask leave to investigate
it—with Warbeck. In the Tower," he added, becoming
restless and pacing back to the window to stare out into
the depths of the summer night.

"Well enough," Sir Charles commented, though his
wife had caught her breath at the mention of the Tower.
"But why should he send you?"

"He sent me once before," Lucas said, and added,
before they could ask why, for he'd no clear answer to
that and disliked thinking of the possibilities as much as
he knew they would, "I worked hard at being thought a
friend of Perkin and his lady wife, Katherine."

"Ah, yes, the beautiful Scots lady—his first mistake,"
his foster mother said disdainfully.

"First mistake? Why so?" Lucas asked, amused. "She's
clever, beautiful, wellborn, chaste, and wealthy. What
more could he want?"

"Wits, for taking her. Before I'd so much as clapped
eyes on him, that's how I knew he was a born commoner
and no kin to you or your father. The randiness, I understood. But the wedding? He wasn't thinking with his
brain, but with his lesser member—which you gentlemen
are pleased to call your greater one," she answered with
a sniff.

"She's right," Sir Charles said, as Lucas gave her a
bemused and puzzled look. "It was foolish of him to take

her—in wedlock, at least—however tempting she was. Think on it: Spain's looking for a connection here, as is Maximilian, France, Saxony—marry, who is not? Tell me your Italian friends wouldn't like to slip a ring on the finger and then through the nose of the next English king, eh? And here's a lad says he's the king, and straight off he weds a Scots girl? God's cross! Why? Scotland's safe enough, Jamie'll be content to take a king's daughter for himself.

"No. A king lies where he will, and why should he not? But marriage? It's his greatest weapon—for a penniless pretender, a vital one—but as my clever lady said, he must have been thinking with his, not using it. So he's joined with Scots nobility now? Do you see them storming the Tower to carry him to freedom and the throne of England?" Sir Charles scoffed. "Bah. No. A little skirmish, a foray for the look of it, to threaten Henry into giving Jamie a daughter as wife one day, and they left off. Ah, but if he'd wedded to a powerful foreign house instead, you might've had to visit him in a different part of the Tower—the throne room, in the White Tower. Foolish, foolish." Sir Charles wagged his heavy head.

"Ah. Yes. Foolish of me to forget, as well. But then, I wasn't king for very long, was I?" Lucas mused. "Aye. The one and only member a king must keep to himself until it's politically wise to bestow it is his hand, isn't it?"

"Why else did Henry Tudor marry your poor sister in such haste?" Sir Charles asked, expecting no answer.

"As to that . . ." Lucas said softly, "sometimes I think even clever kings can't see the future for the present."

Autumn came in like a lovely lady: cool and lush and fruitful—or so the gallants at Henry's court sang to their own ladies in the gardens. There'd been no plagues to speak of in London, and summer's heat had fled at the first turning of September's moon. Henry returned to court at Westminster and his queen and children followed soon after. The new princess was robust, but they'd lost hearty infants before, and so, the rumor ran, he ordered their presence so he could watch over them and be sure of the latest one's survival. That must be the reason he'd summoned his queen, they reckoned, because, after all, it was too soon for him to seriously expect to get another on her.

There were, as always, especially after the king's long absence from London, a great many noblemen, wealthy men, and average citizens anxious to get leave for a private audience with him. But those waiting this cool autumn day in the great crowded main gallery at Westminster sighed, almost to a man, when Lucas was let in through the wide doors. One look at the tall, slender gentleman dressed in an apple-green doublet with long hanging embroidered sleeves, with white and gold silk and velvet hose on his shapely legs, immaculate from his leather ankle boots to the tip of the dashing, drooping black feather atop the fur hat on his fair hair, told them that however long they'd waited, he'd be admitted before them. It wasn't even so much his rich clothes as the way he entered the room, smiling and interested, as though he was about to give an audience, not ask for one, that convinced them of it. And, too, those who knew the court knew the long-legged red-haired youth at the elegant gentleman's side had once been a page here, so then he'd certainly be one of the first to have Henry's ear.

And so they were as gratified as surprised to discover him left to cooling his elegantly soft-booted heels, as, one after another, they were each admitted to see the king before he was.

"Mayhap," Lucas said as time dragged on, "he's forgot my name."

If he makes us wait so long, then perhaps you'll wish he had, Philip thought, but dared not say as he answered, "Well-a-day, he's been gone so long . . ."

"As I have been," Lucas sighed.

"Mayhap we ought come back tomorrow?" Philip said in a small voice as the hour grew later.

"What? And spoil his game? He'd be even angrier then," Lucas answered, as though amused, as though unperturbed.

It was that same calm, faintly smiling handsome face he showed his king when he was admitted an hour later, and the look of vexation on Henry's sallow face was worth the wait and the trouble he had maintaining his smile, Lucas thought.

But the smile slid off after he'd done speaking, explaining his request to a silently attentive Henry Tudor.

"Yes," Henry said, only that, before he thought a moment and then added, "I've heard things about Perkin Warbeck. There is something amiss at the Tower. Something brewing, and he calls you friend, so, yes. Go to him, go to his lady. Find what you will if you can. Sir John Digby is a trustworthy keeper of the Tower. But no place is inviolate, save heaven, and the Tower's scarcely that. I'm not blind or deaf. I know money buys entry to places I cannot see. But betimes," Henry said in a voice like a warning, "I hear things anyway. I'd hear more. Yes, God has a purpose for all things, Lucas Lovat— mayhap that's why he called you home when I did not, even if your parents still live, by his grace. Go to, then."

But by the slight smile on Henry's narrow face, and the shape of the omnipresent dark monk behind him, Lucas didn't rejoice in his easy success, or in Henry's view of God's plan.

But Henry Tudor was well-pleased, and he was still smiling when Lucas Lovat had left his presence. "An expeditious arrival," he murmured. He smiled again, later, as he penned a note in a crabbed and coded hand, to be delivered to Canterbury, for by then he'd thought of a jest. "I've set idle hands to do the devil's work," he wrote. Then, knowing the old man it was intended for was not so much impressed by humor as by cleverness, and was suspicious besides, he added a phrase that would be deciphered to read: "Lovat's clever, and it serves us well, for he's the very one to let us know should plans go awry."

And smiling at that and his jest besides, he sealed and sent the message.

The complex of buildings called the Tower stood dark against the afternoon light, as though not a shadow had shifted since he'd last looked upon it. This, then, was the foe he must vanquish first, Lucas decided, and it lay within himself as much as before him. He must defeat the power of this inanimate cluster of standing stones, he thought, as his lips spoke a light jest to Philip, for however often he might have to come to this place, his soul would shrink at seeing it, and in spite of all his resolve, he knew now, he would fear it.

But all men know fear, although only the brave can face it, or so he had been taught, and so he must believe, Lucas thought as he sat his horse and looked everywhere but at the view before him. He pretended to be bemused by the sight of a triple-masted ship wallowing like Leviathan as its broad wooden bow made swollen green furrows to each side of it as it plowed the Thames, passing by the Tower. And then, after it grew small in his sight and he'd swallowed down the familiar taste of bile that had risen in his throat at the thought of where he must go again, he turned to Philip and told him to wait.

He spoke before an outraged Philip could do more than start to protest.

"If you come with me, you'll waste both our times. Yes, I know you've Henry's seal on a parchment, and could make our way free, but that would seal up every mouth against me. I'd rather try my luck as a common man—or rather, an idle, curious nobleman," Lucas said.

"But that's impossible—" Philip protested.

"Yes. That's why it costs so much," Lucas said dryly. "The key to his cell is made from ducats, they say, and I have enough with me to choke your horse with. Never doubt gold's ability to permit me to walk through sealed walls—but only if you stay far from me," he said firmly, the more so because he knew what he said was, for once, the truth. But Philip stared ahead, his young face set in unfamiliar stubborn lines.

"God's body!" Lucas said impatiently. "Use your head. You may think you have to bear me company, but think of how often you have! Lad," Lucas said in gentler tones, allowing Philip to retain some illusions, but careful to strip the needful ones away, "you were once Henry's page. Your face is known to be one of a man in the service of the king, while mine is only rumored to be. At that, those who think they know me believe me capable of a double game—at least," he added as Philip ducked his head and looked away.

"If there's a plot afoot," Lucas said impatiently, "who'd be fool enough to spill it with you at my side? If you come with me, I won't be able to so much as begin to bargain with the yeoman I seek. Henry's Gentleman

Pensioners are not averse to earning extra coins in interesting ways, but they're finicking about keeping their heads on their necks."

He gave Philip a moment to think and assemble whatever excuses he'd need to use to explain to Henry why he'd stayed behind. But his logic was clear, and he saw it in Philip's downcast face. He raised a hand in farewell, and left Philip in the shadow of the trees to ride out into the light and over the bridge to the Tower gate.

A word got him in, and another gave him the direction of the men he sought. Then he expected he'd need his gold. If he couldn't buy his way in, he'd use Henry's name, and then he'd see only what he'd come to see, but Henry would wonder about that. He'd thought he invented the tale of mischief afoot at the Tower, and had been staggered when Henry agreed there actually was such a rumor. Whether this was true or only another of Henry's interminable tests, his course was the same. He must investigate the plot he thought he'd invented. And he had to try to pass his first test—Henry was wise enough to know a clever man would never expect to discover a treasonous plot with the king's seal in his hands and his name on his lips.

If, indeed, there was such a plot, Lucas thought as he forced himself to walk over the cobbles toward the Tower he'd already escaped twice, then it would be well to uncover it at once and end the pretender's pretensions, and life, once and for all. If he was a pretender, Lucas thought, pausing in his tracks. That was exactly why he'd come so far and so close to his own pain again. And why he'd had no true rest since he'd left this place a second time. He'd seen that face and heard that voice proclaim the same words over and again in his dreams, awake or sleeping, since he'd first heard them whispered so painfully:

"Lucas, trust me, I know who I am."

But he himself had long since forgotten the word "trust," and it was never only the words, and he knew it.

He wasn't alone today. The pathways were busy. It was a cool but clement afternoon, and because more than six hundred persons lived within the precincts of the Tower, noble persons, wealthy persons, visitors, tradesmen, servants, monks, yeoman guards, and visitors promenaded here on their way about their several businesses.

Passersby glanced at him as he stood immobile. But still, Lucas, damning himself for behaving like a cowering virgin on her wedding night, could not seem to move a step forward, despite his best intentions. He did numbers in his head, like any good lover, to distract himself from reality so he could perform the way he wished to do:

Sixteen years since, they thought to murder me here, he calculated, twelve years living alone, abroad; only one year since he'd spewed up his fears on the cold stones of the long dark stair he was going back to here; how many more years had he to live crouched in the dark waiting for the chance to live fully again?

He stepped forward, to escape himself.

He sought the yeoman guard he'd been told about, but as he walked he searched the parade of faces going past for someone else as well. And since he remembered everything he was trying to forget about the past here, and because he'd already made certain careful inquiries, he was not at all surprised to see her as she strolled by, because he'd been looking for her as well.

Then, it had been night. Then, she had been, even so, as lovely as troubled. She was so again now. The Lady Megan Baswell paused, astonished, when she saw him, and since she faltered in her steps, she caused her escorts to stop with her. The lavishly dressed stout young man and the wan blond lady gazed at Lucas as curiously as they did at her, for her color had risen, and his already fair face had grown whiter. But Lucas had learned how to speak even when he had no words to say, long since.

"Lady," he said, sweeping an elaborate bow, "England greets the weary traveler with sights to treat his eyes. My joy in seeing you again knows no bounds. How is your mistress—if, indeed, you still serve her?" he asked, as if he did not know.

"Indeed," she breathed, when she rose from her curtsy, "I do still, but she rests at home today. Ah . . . Lucas Lovat, may I give you Matthew Lorrilard, who lives here, and my lady's other attendant, Lady Clarisse Colville? Mistress Maeve is no longer with us, she wedded this past year," she added with delicate pointedness, watching him closely.

But the lucent eyes did not so much as blink at the news, or the name; it was as if he didn't remember it, for

he wore a faint puzzled expression in the brief moment
before he began to chat with them.

They talked about the lovely autumn weather, and
how hot it had been in Italy, and bade each other the
joys of the evening and continued good health, as they
were supposed to do, before the trio strolled away, leaving Lucas behind them.

He looked after her and her companions before he
walked on toward the Garden Tower. Although more
subdued, she was exactly as unique, graceful, and desirable as he thought he'd remembered—perhaps a bit thin-
ner, only a shade paler than she'd been as she'd stood
glowing before him, the one luminous light in that last
filthy night. She didn't glance back, nor did he expect her
to. He had expected to see her shock and dismay at
encountering him; her memories of him, after all, could
not be pleasant—it had taken much to express nothing
but polite absence of mind when she'd mentioned the
wench he'd betrayed her with—but neither could they
have accounted for the look in her eyes all the time that
they'd chatted about nothing.

He had, at last, another puzzle, something to divert
him from the task before him. Because that look in
Megan's eyes as she'd stared at him was one he understood all too well as he found himself gazing up at exactly
the tower he sought as he stood in its lengthening shadow—
because it had been one not so much of pain as of terror.

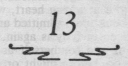

13

Three emotions she hadn't felt in a long while came to Megan one after the other, almost incapacitating her. Foremost, there was fear. The strange thing was that at first, it was only for herself. Everything had been so comfortable. Not good, of course, it had never been that, but these last weeks and months had been so comfortable, if only because they brought no change and she'd begun to understand that when change came, it wouldn't be for the better. But if numbness was comfort—and as she hadn't known what comfort was for so long, she'd decided it was—why, then, she felt comfortable enough, until she saw Lucas Lovat again.

She'd been walking just as she'd been living of late, in a gentle haze of undemanding absence of mind, and then she'd seen the glittering, graceful gentleman bow to her, and recognized that it was actually Lucas Lovat, appeared before her, live and real and urgent as ever, a blazing reminder of all the things she'd escaped in her mind and given up on in her life. So, of course, she was frightened. But a second later she knew enough to know that it was her lady and her husband who had everything to fear—not herself. Oddly enough, her second emotion was a strange and sharp disappointment, and then, of course, it was followed by the one she knew so well: despair.

Matthew hadn't noticed, of course. As they walked on, he kept talking about how much he'd admired the way Lovat had been dressed—except for the difficult peacock-green shade of his doublet, which he'd strong doubts about. When Matthew discussed fashion, he never looked to see her reaction, because he knew his taste was correct and didn't need her opinion. And that, she understood immediately and with a sinking heart, was a thing she'd always known too, but never admitted until this moment, moments after she'd seen Lucas again. Then she knew she'd been right to fear for herself as well as for her mistress. Lovat's appearance might or might not mean danger for Lady Katherine and Perkin Warbeck, but it was certainly trouble for herself.

She'd come to believe Matthew Lorrilard would be her salvation; she'd begun to hope he'd ask Henry for her hand. He wasn't particularly handsome or clever or wealthy. But he was young, and not unkind, and well-to-do, and there was no gossip about his being cruel or difficult. In her empty hours this past season, as she waited for another woman's husband to be set free, she'd decided he was as good a match as she could ever hope to have. Whatever else Matthew lacked, he lacked a wife, and from the first time she'd met him he'd been loudly eloquent on that subject. Lady Katherine had needed places to stay during her daily visits to the Tower when she was in London, as she waited for entry to the one place she wished to visit and never could. She'd befriended everyone she could who dwelt there, and so beseeched Megan to encourage Matthew's suit, if only for the look of it. Soon it was more than appearance on Megan's part.

If Perkin Warbeck had been Megan's dream of perfection in a man, that dream was fading fast, for she'd seen him only briefly, knew him only through another woman's love, and neither of them had seen him in over a year. If she'd once replaced him in her dreams with Lucas Lovat, having imagined that Lucas wanted her for more than a night in his bed, she'd lost him to another woman's other sort of love. And so lost that particular foolish dream entirely. As she hadn't seen him in over a year as well, she'd thought she'd forgotten him, or outgrown the dream.

But everything and nothing had changed. She'd recognized him instantly, although foreign suns had gilded that fair skin and his hair was ashen fair now too. But those same light eyes had looked at and into her, as they used to do. She felt the same hurt and desire the moment she'd looked upon him again, as though no time had passed at all, as though it had been yesterday that he'd deceived her. Only this time he destroyed two dreams, because his mere appearance diminished Matthew in her eyes.

She couldn't allow that to happen, any more than she could let him endanger Perkin. But of course, the only thing she could do was to alert her lady. And put herself on constant watch as well.

"Oh! The hour! And my lady specifically wanted me to remind her! Ah!" Megan said, cutting into Matthew's dissertation on Lucas' hat and hose. "Marry, but I'd forgot. Dear Matthew, could you bring me back to her now, please?"

"Lady Katherine said she and the countess would be well-occupied for the next hour," Matthew said in his high light voice, so amused at her and her pretty air of consternation that he wasn't angry at her interruption. "Don't fret yourself, dearling, I'll have you back to her by then."

"But she herself has then forgot," Megan said, "because she asked me to remind her. Oh, Clarisse, don't you remember?"

But since Clarisse, another pensioner of Henry's because of her birth, and more distinguished by it than her wit, never remembered anything; she only gave her absent smile and looked vaguely confused, as usual.

"Very well," Matthew said generously, "I'll take you back at once. But then you owe me another afternoon," he teased, raising one gloved finger to wag in front of her nose.

Only yesterday she would have been as gratified as reassured by his playful threat, but now Megan felt only a vague sense of distaste at another obligation. So as they strolled back past Lucas again, this time unnoticed by him, since he was deep in conversation with a yeoman guard, she shivered slightly in the autumn breeze, awakened at last to the change in season, awakened to her own life again.

"There's ways," the yeoman finally admitted, "ain't saying there ain't."

"Does this say enough?" Lucas asked mildly, showing his palmful of gold.

The man hissed, and his hand struck out like an adder's tongue to sweep the gold from sight as he looked about to see if anyone was near. But since they stood in a shadow within a dim room, in a corner far from human sight, Lucas appreciated that the taking of this bribe was as stealthily done as the making of it, and for ceremonial purposes only.

"Tonight?" Lucas asked idly.

"Nay, never night," the man said, dropping the coins into his purse and hiding that inside his scarlet doublet. "Night's when things is watched. Night's the time for villains," he said, showing his teeth in a smile, "ain't it? Nay. Here and now, if you want. Daylight's when you walk in with me, bold but quiet, as if you was goin' somewheres different. See? But list! If he don't want you, out you go, and no mistake. And no hard feelings, neither. And I keeps the coin. Because the risk is the same, ain't it? But I don't need him complainin' to the wrong man. If he wants you, you'll have your hour. See?"

"Well enough," Lucas said, stepping back from the blast of onion he received each time the man insisted on a point.

The stair, the damned stair, he thought as he went in the Tower and down a corridor, and around a curve and under an arch: there it was before him again as clear as it had stood in his dreams for most of his life. But if he thought about the man he was going to see as he took the stairs, he could take them as any other, or so he told himself as he followed the guard on the way to see Perkin Warbeck again.

"A guest for you, you want him?" the guard asked as he swung open the door.

But he'd tapped on the door before he'd used his key, and his voice held none of the insolence and craft that it had when he'd spoken to Lucas. A singular honor, to receive honor from your jailer, Lucas thought, before Perkin looked up from the table he sat at, and he remembered what a singular prisoner this was.

He'd wondered what a year of confinement in fear for his future, his life, and his lady wife had done to the man. He'd wondered if Henry had set his torturers to the man again, or inflicted pain more simply by forgetting him and leaving him to rot. And so Lucas was relieved to see that Perkin looked the same, handsome and serene, and his heart was unaccountably lighter as he smiled his greeting to him.

But then, as Perkin rose, crying out, "Lucas Lovat! Well met, sir, come in, come in," he saw each subtle change, and was uncomfortable with them.

The prisoner wasn't gaunt; in fact, he was robust, almost tending toward heaviness; the increase of bulk showed not so much in his form as in his cheeks and chin. There were no signs of ill-usage, except for a slur in his step as he stepped forward, and the hand he gripped Lucas' with had a weaker clasp that it should have had, even as that arm seemed limper and longer than his other when he let it fall back to his side. But none of this was anything compared to his eyes.

The only thing Lucas could think as Perkin stood close to him, watching him, was that those heavy-lidded eyes had intensified, become bluer, more searching—until he realized that might have only been because they were unblinking, as they sought to see beyond what men's eyes can see. Perkin Warbeck's imprisonment hadn't diminished him, Lucas thought uneasily; it had instead intensified him.

His voice, when he spoke, was the same melodious tone, although now it seemed he gave each word special significance and weight.

"Come in, sit down. You may leave, Roger," Perkin said to the guard, dismissing him. "This man is a very special friend to me," Perkin added as the guard nodded and left, locking the door behind him.

"Where have you been? Have you seen Katherine? How is she, and my Margaret?" Perkin then asked at once, but without the urgency such words required, as if he'd known the answers before he'd begun.

"I hear they are well, but I've not seen them. I came from Italy, and from thence to Westminster, where I saw Henry, but she wasn't there then. Then I visited my parents in Devon, and old friends here and there. I've only just now got back to London," Lucas said as he took the wooden chair Perkin indicated. Perkin sat in the other, behind the table, and studied him. Lucas felt as though he were being weighed up, like an aspirant for a particularly good position. He smiled.

"I see you thrive, and I'm glad for it," Lucas said, and was instantly sorry for it and angry at himself for such an uncharacteristically clumsy mis-saying. How could any man thrive in this nightmare place? Or do anything but lament his loss of freedom?

"Marry, I do," Perkin said proudly. "Things," he said, leaning closer to Lucas and lowering his rich voice, "are going well, exceeding well," he added, laying a finger aside his nose and smiling. Then he laughed outright and gave a contented sigh before he looked at Lucas again.

"I have friends," he said, "even in this place. You cannot deny a king, my friend, no—the very earth here has had a surfeit of royal blood. I 'scaped this place once, and shall again, never fear."

Lucas felt his palms grow cold. Again he spoke without thinking, a thing he was not used to do.

"I doubt you should say such things aloud," he said, and then bit his lip, as astonished at himself as he was at Perkin Warbeck—this damnable place seemed to rob him of his experience, even as it appeared to him to have stolen Perkin's wits away.

Perkin laughed loudly.

"Ah, but I feel a bond with you, Lucas. I always have. And see how you've proved me right? Would an enemy beseech me to keep my silence?" he asked before he added gently, as though humoring Lucas, "Very well. I'll say no more, you'll see and hear the rest for yourself. Look now, then," he said merrily, holding up his hands. "No chains, no shackles, no more of that for me. And soon, no walls to hold me either. I've nothing to fear now, not here."

Lucas stared at him, disbelieving. Did the man court death? Was he addled? Or was this only another trap? Could Henry have guessed the unimaginable? Or perhaps only thought to trap him in some mad scheme involving Warbeck? He had to get the information he sought quickly and leave soon after that, he told himself. But before he could formulate the right question to test Perkin's sanity and purpose, Perkin spoke again, in amused tones.

"Why do they say you are so unreadable, I wonder, my Lucas? Come, don't take fright. I say only what I mean. I am safe enough here. Don't you see? That safety itself has proved my case to my jailers and . . . others. I live—more, I, as you say, thrive. And why? Think on it. It is because Henry *is* no fool. He dares not shed royal blood."

Perkin sat back proudly and smiled again. Lucas thought of all the blood Henry had already shed, royal or not, and all that he would not hesitate to spill in future, to ensure that heirs of his blood would retain the throne. Everyone knew that. This, then, was madness. There was no more for him to seek here. Whatever Perkin Warbeck was, or had been, made no matter. He was a madman now. And so, whatever the stresses that had brought out the hidden flaw, clearly not his brother. Richard had been sound, as had been all his line. No brother of his would succumb to insanity; it wasn't in the blood. It was Henry's line that produced the madmen, *his* royal uncle who had suffered from brainstorms and died lackwit. Lucas rose, prepared to leave, his unasked question answered.

He was as relieved as saddened. He'd lost an illusion, but gained an advantage. He'd tell Henry of the appearance of a plot straightaway, and then be done with his part in the destruction of the pretender. He'd no stomach to investigate it further. He didn't have to; his verification of it should be enough to end it. For if he knew, surely others would as well. Soon enough, then, Perkin would be gone. Then it would be his turn, at last, to try for the crown.

"There is only one thing I lack to ensure my every happiness," Perkin said in a softer voice. "I would wish my brother had been spared. It only lacks that to make victory complete. He should have been king, for he was truly kingly. I shall only do my best to try to be what he would have been. . . . Have you a brother, Lucas?"

"I'd one," Lucas said on a rueful smile, accepting, at last, that he'd lost his brother forever, and so burying him here, where he ought to have died, by admitting it to this madman. "He died of the smallpox, years ago."

"Ah. As did mine." Perkin sighed.

Lucas froze in place.

"You said," Lucas said carefully, "you said your brother died at the hands of a murderer, here, in the Tower."

"Did I?" Perkin asked slyly. "Did I? Or did I say I'd lost him at God's hand? I wonder, what did I say? Or what did they think I did? People believe what they wish, my Lucas, they believe what they want to, and a man who seeks to reclaim all that was taken from him by God and man says what people want to hear, does he not?"

"Your brother . . ." said Lucas as he sank down into his chair again and stared at Perkin.

But Perkin's mood had turned, or else he'd decided he'd said too much, Lucas thought, for he rose even as Lucas sat, and cocking his leonine head to the side, looked at his visitor with a bright and sparkling blue eye.

"You care for me, Lucas. So I've a treat for you. It's time for me to visit with my cousin Edward. Should you like to come? He's wary of strangers, but as I've such a warm feeling about you, he shouldn't take fright. He can sense things like that. Shy people and babes and dogs, and madmen too, they say, rely more on their senses than their wits . . ." Perkin mused, and then stopped, a faint frown beginning to crease the white skin between his wide, unblinking blue eyes, before he smiled again and said, "And after all, as you look like me, a little . . . did you know that? Katherine remarked it once, and 'tis true, I think, although you are so lean . . ."

"Edward?" Lucas asked, scarcely breathing, hardly daring to believe what he'd heard.

"Oh, aye, my cousin Edward of Warwick. He lives near to me here, poor lad. I've befriended him, and so go in to his rooms each day to solace him, for he's a melancholy lad, and won't step outside his door. He's unused to people. But then, consider—we're almost of an age, he and I, but he's been here for most of his life. Think on it! Over fifteen years here, in the same room—save for once, when Henry took him out to show the people of London that Lambert Simnel was a liar and a pretender, pretending to be him . . ."

Perkin frowned and shook his head slowly so the curled-under ends of his straight sheaf of golden hair swayed to cup the bottom of one cheek and then the other. "Ah, how dearly that pretender has cost me! No matter, when I'm king, I shall set him free. *I'll* have naught to fear from pretenders then, and Edward . . . ah, but Edward has told me he doesn't want his freedom. Think on that, Lucas! To grow so much inward in captivity that you've no wish to fly free again—I hear it's the way of certain caged birds . . . but a man? We shall see," he said gruffly, "when we are able, if we can't wean him from his shell. But come now, it's almost time for our afternoon repast. That's when he looks for me."

Perkin stepped to the door, head high, and such was his air of command that Lucas rose to follow, and only halted when he again noticed the slight shambling to Perkin's gait, and realized he'd halted at his door because it was locked to him. Perkin hit the door with the flat of his hand, and waited. A few moments later, the door opened slowly and the guard looked nervously to Lucas.

"I didn't come afore because I . . . Is he coming too? You know . . ." he whispered with a jerk of his head. "Is he?"

"Yes, Lucas Lovat will come with me. Don't worry, he's a friend," Perkin said as he walked through the doorway of his cell.

Lucas, his soft-soled boots making no sound at all on the hard stone floor, followed Perkin's shuffling strides along the corridor toward what he said would be the room of his "cousin" Edward. If it were indeed Edward, Earl of Warwick, his murdered Uncle George, Duke of Clarence's son, then Lucas knew him. If he was . . . There was a moment when he wondered if what he was doing was particularly wise, even though all of it, he began to understand, was folly. But he followed because Perkin had seduced him with his talk of his brother—no, he admitted, no man could seduce another man, or woman, unless the person was halfway lost before the courtship had begun; no, he followed because of his own curiosity.

No one had seen the unlucky earl except once in fifteen years. Yet few forgot him. After all, if there were truth to the line of succession, it should be Edward, Earl of Warwick, last surviving son of the Plantagenet line, who should be king—which was why one of Henry's first acts had been to imprison the ten-year-old, threat to his new throne. But he only locked him away. Trust Henry to keep the politically dead alive in a sort of half-life for his own reasons, Lucas thought: Lambert Simnel turning his roasts in his kitchens, Perkin Warbeck living side by side with a prisoner of the true blood, Edward, Earl of Warwick, in the dank recesses of the damned Tower. And he himself, Lucas wondered, pausing in his steps . . . Was this coincidence?

What if Edward should remember? He reassured himself on both counts because he so badly wanted to see what lay ahead; he could do nothing but what he was already doing, even if Henry had somehow guessed the incredible truth, and he doubted any man would recognize another he'd not seen since they'd both been boys.

He'd known Edward in those lost days—no, he thought, no, he hadn't, not really. They'd been a boisterous lot of children when they'd got together in those days, cousins, brothers, and their kin, and Edward had always been shy; a small, pale, quiet boy, fearful even then, when he'd nothing to fear but the braying laughter of his father. Fearful? Or simpleminded, as they now whispered that he was? He'd never thought it then. But then, he'd always been too preoccupied to care. Now it mattered very much. Lucas hurried after Perkin.

They paused outside a door near to a window slit. Perkin stood still and straight, without a word.

"Do we . . . ?" Lucas began as Perkin turned around, and then, as if remembering only that he was there, seemed to light up from within, and smiling, said, "We wait. Knocking or scratching will make no difference. He opens the door at the same time every day, and closes it until the next, if I am not here. They don't even bother to lock it anymore," he said on a grin, "since nothing would induce Edward to step out. We wait . . . Ah, cousin," he said as the door began to peel open. "Wait. I've a guest today. You may see him or not, as you will. But he is a friend. Lucas Lovat. Wait until you see him," he added heartily. "He looks very like me."

The door remained open only so far as to permit Perkin to look in. Lucas waited for what seemed like hours for the door to open to admit him, or to close on his toes, when a sound on the stair near him made him leap back into the shadows. A guard appeared on the top step of the long spiraling flight of stone stairs, and seeing the door open, whispered harshly, "Make haste. In or out. Don't stand in the hall all day. Here, your lordship, you want them or not?" he called out, low.

The door opened all the way.

By the time Lucas and Perkin had entered, the man who had admitted them had already turned his back and walked to the table in the center of the room. It was a larger room than Perkin's, although the adjoining one was smaller, and looked very like a wretched cell and only that, for it had room only for the thin cot that was within it. But the larger room was unlike any Lucas had seen in the Tower, being filled with books—more than he'd seen in some palaces, and all piled neatly within this one room, so many that it was apparent that this was a much larger room than it appeared, because all the leather-and-parchment volumes and sheafs had made an irregular inner wall all around the room's perimeter. There were boxes and parchments on the tabletop. The tall, painfully thin man who stood at the table held a pen in his hand. His hair was baby fine and fair, and his skin as white as an invalid's or cadaver's. But when he looked up, his eyes were alive, and palest blue.

He's only been stretched out; I wonder if it was the rack that did it, because nothing else about him has changed with age, Lucas thought, forcing back a rising laugh, or wail, for there was no doubt this man was his cousin Edward, to the life, or death of what that boy had been, so long ago.

"And how are you today, cousin?" Perkin asked in a slightly louder voice than usual.

Edward tilted his head to the side, as if listening to something unsaid.

"How long have you known this man Lucas Lovat?" he asked in a surprisingly clear and strong voice.

"Known him well? Since a year past, but we shared a toast or two abroad, long before. He's lived in Italy for many years. He trades his father's wool abroad. And who knows what else. He has Henry's ear. I wouldn't be at all surprised if he doesn't run his errands now and again," Perkin answered, smiling sidewise at Lucas, "but my lady trusts him, as do I. Don't worry, cousin, I said 'as do I.' "

Edward's head remained tilted to the side as he stood

in silence, looking at Lucas for a long moment. Then he nodded, and Perkin sighed.

"Do you read very much?" Edward asked Lucas.

No madness here, Lucas thought with relief, nor recognition either; the blue eyes were peering intently because they were obviously unfocused by shortsightedness.

"When I can find a new volume, I do," Lucas answered.

"I prefer old ones," Edward said, "but the problem is that I grow bored with them and then must take the risk of a new one, and then must wait until the new one becomes old enough to enjoy thoroughly. I don't like surprises," he added.

"Then it was kind of you to see me," Lucas said.

"No, I know you," Edward answered. "Do you like feathers?"

Lucas grew very still, and Perkin looked at him oddly.

"I am not mad, you know," Edward said. "I just don't have the gift of conversation. I feel I know you because of Richard—he's talked about you, yes, don't you remember, Richard? Well-a-day, you have. And I collect feathers. I scarce have room for birds here, do I? And it would be cruel to cage one when I can see so many from out of my window, and imagine so many more from their feathers. Here, look."

He raised the lid off the largest box on his table, and as Lucas drew near he could see it was filled with feathers. Hard black raven quills, of course, and not a few that had obviously been dropped from the tails of peacocks that strutted on the green here. But as he was no naturalist, Lucas could put no names to the dozens of other variously sized and colored curled and downy ones nestled in the box.

"Enough to make a bed, as Edgar, my night guard, always says, I know," Edward said, "and I have boxes more. I take the best and draw them over on paper, and label them and put them into notebooks. I have volumes of those, with notations of habits and habitations and flight patterns. I cull those things from books, and the observations of myself and others. These are what's left over. And still my collection grows, because they bring me new ones all the time. Some are very odd, and rare, from the menagerie, and elsewhere. I'll have something of merit to leave behind me," he said, nodding. "I want nothing else," he added abruptly as he looked up and met Lucas' eyes.

"Well-a-day," he went on, "betimes, I think mayhap Henry, or Richard here, or others, may wonder if I want to be king. Not I."

"It would be difficult to reign from this room, would it not? Cousin, cousin, one day soon you'll walk out of here with me and see the world, I vow it," Perkin said.

"No, no," Edward said, shrinking back. "It's time to leave. Please go."

"But you haven't met Lucas properly, and I've a thing or two to tell you today," Perkin said.

"I know him well," Edward answered, turning his back on them both, "as well as I know what you're going to say, for it's the same as yesterday. I pray you go."

Perkin left first, and when Lucas reached the door, Edward spoke again.

"You may come back sometime, Lucas, if you will," he said softly. "Only understand I don't want to go out. Whether it is to be Henry, or Richard, or you who gets to be anointed king, it has nothing to do with me. It's too late for me. Forget me. I was born at an inconvenient hour, and for all that it's unmanly of me, I only want to live. That is all. But," he whispered, "you may come back sometime, if you like."

"Poor lad," Perkin said expansively when they'd gone back to his rooms and the guard had appeared from out of the shadows to lock the door behind them again. "What's the point of living if you're afraid to live? Why should he cling to such a life? Ah, so many sorrows. Now, come, Lucas, what shall you do next?"

"I had thought to wait upon events," Lucas said casually.

"Indeed?" Perkin seemed amused.

"Indeed," Lucas said, not liking Perkin's secret good humor, or the half-smile he wore.

"Then you may wait a long while," Perkin said.

"Ah. So you do believe I do the odd 'errand for Henry,' as you said, do you? I wonder why you saw me at all, then, or is it only that you've so much company coming in and out of here that it makes no difference whom you admit?" Lucas asked, feeling curiously hurt, and then suddenly more alarmed at that than he was by anything else that had happened during this strange interview.

"Yes, many visit. They do come in and out, and we do have merry times, but try to uncover it before the appointed hour, and all evidence of it will vanish like mist, for I've friends, allies, and . . ." Perkin caught himself, and his strange intensity disappeared. "Come, come, you of all people must know I'd be a fool or a madman to trust you with all, just now," he said, clapping Lucas on the shoulder, suddenly warm and jovial once more. "I've plans, Lucas. Great plans. Things of wonder and import will be done, oh yes. But first I must learn to know you again, mustn't I?"

"I understand," Lucas said, smiling as well, though he did not. Surely a man with great plans wouldn't so much as mention them to a man he didn't wholly trust, and Perkin had no good reason as yet to trust him so completely. But he nodded as if in complete accord because he found it easier to agree than not in such cases, even if this whole interview had got him off-balance. He'd learned long before to swallow everything that he could at once, and digest it later, when it was safer to, very much like a snake or one of the birds his cousin studied would do. "I understand," he said. "Like Edward, you don't like surprises, and so must read me over several dozen times before you enjoy my company fully."

"I am not at all like my cousin Edward," Perkin said, his voice almost unrecognizable. That, Lucas realized, was because he was angry, and he'd never heard him so.

"I only meant that you were circumspect," Lucas said. "If I've offended, forgive me."

"You have not," Perkin said, sounding like himself again. He sighed and looked straight at Lucas with a sad smile that reached his heavy unblinking eyes. "It's only that I'm weary. I've done my time in Henry's underrooms here, and though I'm strong, and as well as any man could be, better than most, in truth—still there are times when I tire. The rack draws strength that needs must build back slowly. It takes as slowly too. . . . But that is past now. Long past. That was a long time ago. And will never be again. I shall burn the racks when I am king," he said, and Lucas nodded, disliking that which was in

Perkin's voice and eyes as much as he was growing wary
of his rapidly changing moods.

Lucas discovered himself moving toward the door, a
thing which shocked him badly. Because a wise spy never
left before he was dismissed. But he was as weary with
being a spy, he realized, as Perkin so obviously was with
being entertained by the rack.

"For now, my dear Lucas," Perkin said mildly, restored so completely in voice and manner to what he'd
been before he'd occupied the Tower that Lucas had
difficulty remembering the odd unease that had just gripped
him, "I must beg you to leave me. My chaplain commonly visits me at this hour, to see to the welfare of my
soul. If you wish, you can return. Not tomorrow, for I
fear I've other business then, and the guard on duty is
singularly humorless. But, say, in two days' time, at the
same time as today?"

"I'd like that," Lucas said as Perkin approached him.

He offered his hand, but stopped as he remembered
something that all his planning, and everything that had
gone amiss with it, had made him forget.

"Your lady," Lucas said. "I'll see her now that I'm
back at court. Have you a message for her?"

"Ah," Perkin said. His own hand paused as it was held
out, as though he were suddenly remembering something
too. "Yes," he said with the glowing, warming beatific
smile Lucas now remembered having missed, only because it had been so long since he'd seen it. "The usual:
that I hold her foremost in my heart and in my mind, if
you please."

And then, without offering it to Lucas, Perkin raised
his hand and struck the door with the flat of it, and a
moment later it swung open to let Lucas out.

He was walking down the stair when he saw a man in a
cassock gliding upward, and for a moment he almost
missed his step.

"Hello, brother, he's waiting," the guard said, and
then continued to lead Lucas downward.

Lucas tightened his muscles involuntarily, but as the
man came up out of the winding gloom of the stair and
Lucas pressed against the wall to make room for him to
pass as they came abreast, he saw that the visiting monk
was a fresh-faced man who didn't wear his cowl up, and

nothing about him remained in shadow, and nothing about him was familiar. So he took the last steps lightly and came out into the light of the afternoon to find the guard vanished, and all that he'd lately done receded into the background, like the interior of the dim Tower he was so rapidly putting behind him.

Lucas let out the breath he hadn't realized he still held as he took pleasure in the world he'd reentered. He stared about himself like a man leaving a sickbed after a long illness, delighting in the color and variety of life around him. Gaily dressed ladies and gentlemen walked the paths, the scarlet-clad guards glowed with their healthy, whole-some hues, even the townsmen's robes were so richly colored that the occasional black, brown, or gray garb of a laborer or monk seemed necessary to the whole pic-ture, to give it balance. Here was the lively sound of ongoing life, not just hushed conversation deadened and muted by layers of rock. The filtered gray light in the Tower rooms and corridors, the spectrally white face of the Earl of Warwick: now all of it seemed like a frail and fragile memory of something dimly seen in a bad dream that faded away with the dawn. Now, when he thought of Perkin again, Lucas saw the pensive, regal, and beautiful face he'd remembered in his night thoughts abroad, and it bore none of the small changes that he'd just seen.

But because he found the comfort he gained by forget-ting too dangerous, he looked back just once to see where he'd come from, to verify the reality he'd tried to bury. And saw, of course, what he'd seen in his mind's eye all along, as a tall figure—gray as mist even amidst all the brave colors of daylight—hooded, cowled, and humble, glided into the Tower he'd lately left.

"What is it? Is there anything amiss?" a soft, anxious voice asked, recalling him to himself and where he stood arrested.

She was alone this time, as she'd been that last night, but this time it was day, and there was time to study her, alone. He found he'd remembered every detail of her face correctly, even the fact that the sunlight glancing off her eyes turned them to light gold, except for the dark center of them, and the ring around that, wherein small stars and rods of deepest brown were clustered.

"How now? Are you employed by the Tower now, my

lady?" Lucas asked lightly, coolly, "to cheer the mournful visitor on his way? Last time I tarried here, I remember you asked me the same question, but then it was night and springtime. Do they not let you have time off in any season?"

She stiffened. After a blink her eyes glowed with rage.

"Last time," Megan spat at him, so angry at his cold smile and colder question that she fought back to save the visible part of her heart from his scorn, "at least my question sent you away for a year. Shall I be so fortunate now?"

"A year and too many days," he said on a tired smile, for really, he thought, he was exhausted now, "far too many. And it was never you who sent me away, lady. Rather, mayhap, it was the thought of you that hastened my return . . . in part," he added, careful not to give her false coin—he'd given her too much of that already. "Cry truce, my lady?" he asked.

"I know I don't deserve it, but I do need a friend," he explained, and paused, puzzled, surprised, and faintly disturbed because he'd spoken nothing but plain truth.

Before he could damn himself for it, or laugh or joke the words away, she'd answered, despite herself, as well.

"As do I," she said. "Truce, then, and peace."

14

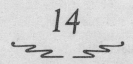

Matthew looked down at his own thick legs, clad in elegant black silk hose. Then he looked across the room again, to where Lucas Lovat was holding court.

"Even so," he said complacently, "I think it is too much. One black leg and one striped gold is very Italianate, but however much we admire them, I don't think it will do for England at all. No, no. Why, see how it exaggerates the one and diminishes the other? It lends an air of . . . imbalance, I'd say."

A week ago, so too would Megan have said, even if she didn't think it, even though she doubted Matthew would have heard her usual softly voiced agreement. But there was nothing unbalanced about the way that Lucas looked in his variously colored hose or the calf-high soft leather boots he had on over them, and neither did his hip-length dark gold velvet doublet with its slashed and puffed sleeves present a semblance of lack of proportion. Neither was it his clothes that called attention to his limbs or body. And that, Megan realized, was the thing that Matthew would never believe—or if he did, admit to.

Her realization of this was the only problem she found with Lucas' appearance, no matter what Matthew said of his fashion. But she'd misjudged her escort. Because it seemed that at least he'd heard her lack of response.

"How so? You don't agree?" he asked with mock astonishment, teasing her.

She smiled and ducked her head, knowing that with Matthew coyness would always answer where reason could not.

"Yes," Matthew said decisively, "unbalanced. It is that which takes the eye."

And his face, and his grace, and the sound of his laughter, Megan thought, which lure the eyes of every lady at court tonight, and those of all of their men, as well. How often do we see sunlight walking among us, after all? she thought, and said, "Yes, Matthew."

"He looks over here every so often," Matthew observed, and then offered her his arm. "Shall we, then?"

It was the last place she wanted to go. But as Matthew had already begun to stroll over to join the group of knights, ladies, and gentlemen of the court that had congregated near Lucas, Megan could scarcely snatch her hand off his arm. Instead, she ducked her head, plucked up a light handful of skirt to clear the way for her shoes, pinned a smile to her lips to disguise her heart, and went with him. There was no reason to refuse—or rather, no reason that Matthew should know, or any she'd allow herself to give in to.

Matthew was near to offering for her; he'd been hinting his way toward it for days now, because he wasn't the sort of man who'd relish committing himself to any cause that might cause him embarrassment. He'd less money than ambition, fewer graces than he knew, but he had a kind heart and came from a good old family. If he was never invited to Greenwich or Sheen, he was almost always in attendance at Westminster, and though he'd an uncle and two cousins in higher places, he couldn't be sure that his name or face was recognizable to the king. He could wed a younger girl, one from a powerful family as well. But Megan knew her own dowry would be as good and was well aware of her most valuable asset in Matthew's estimate: her tie to the king.

Matthew's problem was that the woman he'd decided he might marry had no father or brother to feel his way with, and so he was in the unusual position of having to find out whether he could have her by asking her that. It wasn't his way to ask a woman such a thing. Instead, he'd been insinuating and hinting to find out if she thought Henry would permit his suit before he offered it.

She'd been drifting toward encouraging him to ask Henry for her soon. That would be enough to accomplish it. Henry had no reason to withhold marriage from her;

she'd served him well, and so he'd said. What more was there for her now? Twenty now, she was no longer young, and getting nothing but older every day. She watched each day wear away as her lady grew more desperate, for time brought them both the promise of nothing but age and defeat. At least Maeve had kept Megan amused. She'd been rude, but lively, and a friend . . . before her betrayal. Because then, for all Megan realized that Maeve's falling into Lucas' open arms had been her nature, not her cruelty, still it had hurt, and she refused to believe that one friend would hurt another. Lucas had taken two illusions with him when he'd gone.

Meave had left soon after, to wed, but their friendship was over long before she'd gone. And if now and again Megan thought that Maeve had accepted a bad marriage too hastily, and had done it in a blurred, reckless manner that was very unlike herself, she blamed that on Maeve's own guilty conscience. The thought that her own rejection of Maeve had hurried the decision was too hurtful to contemplate. As was the thought that came to her now as she saw Lucas Lovat before her once again.

Because now she wondered if Maeve's decision was only a reasonable one, after all. Because it might only be that a woman could hope for nothing more after having once had, and then having lost this man. Which was precisely why, after she looked at Lucas, she glanced up to Matthew, and even knowing all his faults—*especially* knowing all of them, she thought—she believed herself lucky to have found him.

"And then the jester said, 'Marry, but I thought it was too dark for June!' " Lucas said, finishing the tale he was telling. The company around him laughed uproariously, for the jest was more than to do with a randy man and a sly woman, it was a clever story filled with innuendo and surprise, and none of them had heard it before.

Another man began a short tale to do with a monk's wife, but was hooted down, since everyone knew it and had heard it told much more cleverly. A knight asked the riddle to do with a lake, and much encouraged by the laughter when a gentleman called out the answer, a lady asked a rarer one about a rabbit, and as everyone groaned at the answer, Megan relaxed at last. She had a gentleman at her side and a smile on her face, and Lucas Lovat could see them both. This night was the embodiment of all her dreams of revenge in the nights since he had left. She looked very well too, she knew. Well, and she ought to, she thought, since she'd dressed so carefully for this moment.

She'd washed her hair in lemon so as to bring out hidden tints of red and gold in it, and, only lightly covered by a hood, it lay in careful long curls on her shoulders, and she had on her best gown. It was low enough at the breast to be fashionable, and just the fraction lower enough to be enticing. It was deep blue, with figures of blue and gold roses embroidered at the bodice and sleeves to liven it and catch the eye—like stars in a late-evening sky—and it had an underskirt of dawn rose that showed when she walked, as each step spread the panel at the front of her skirt. Matthew stood square and solid at her side, a guarantee to her future and a bulwark against her own folly. Now she could watch Lucas with a gentle, vaguely amused smile, appreciating his handsomeness as well as his wit openly, as though she were an old woman with her life behind her, her only chance for ruin safe in her mind.

Until Lucas looked at her consideringly, and then strolled to her side.

He bowed to Matthew, and Matthew acknowledged him with pleasure, for he knew he was a man of note, even if he wasn't exactly sure what it was he was noted for.

They exchanged polite insignificances. But after a few moments it was clear that Matthew was listening with only half an ear, his attention on the stretch for the riddles and jests being told. Dinner was done, the long tables had been cleared of foodstuffs, the musicians had stilled, the jesters and jugglers were at their own dinners in the kitchens now. The hour was late, the light in the vast dining hall emphasized that, for however many torches there were, they could only hint at the richness of the dark brocaded tapestries that hung upon the high walls, and the satins, velvets, and furs that graced the guests. But there were enough rushlights blazing to illuminate portions of the vast room, and their light struck golden glances from the intricate designs on the burnished walls, as well as from the ornaments on the ears and breasts and fingers of the richly dressed company.

The dining may have been done, but the evening had only just gotten under way. Cards and dice, backgammon and chess, all manner of amusement to while away the rest of the night awaited. Until the gaming began, the members of the court amused themselves with tales and riddles—the more ribald, the better, the more subtle, the most unusual of all. Invention was flagging in the group Megan, Matthew, and Lucas had joined, and after a tale to do with a dairy maid and a tinker, there was a brief, uneasy silence. Raucous laughter came from other clots of ladies and gentlemen around them, and it made their little group seem paltry because they were so still. Lucas filled the gap with a charming and provocative riddle that soon had the men roaring and slapping each other's backs at the deliciously double-edged and unexpected answer: a needle.

"Forgive me," Lucas said as Megan turned her blushing cheek aside, "but it was all the rage abroad . . ."

"Oh, no," she protested honestly, "it was very amusing, and so well told."

It was as hard to meet that amused and complete regard as it then was to try to tear her gaze away from his, and she felt Matthew shifting from foot to foot and then heard him clearing his throat to get her attention, but she went on, "And it was original too."

"Ah, but there's another I heard," Lucas confided to them both in a low voice, "on a similar theme, something to do with an eye . . . but alas! my wretched memory! I can't get it right, having heard it only once—"

"But I can!" Matthew cried eagerly. "I know it!"

And so does everyone else, Megan was about to groan, but even as she checked, thinking how to rephrase that politely, Matthew, seeing that he'd won everyone's attention, smugly announced that he'd a riddle:

A vessel I have
That is round like a pear,
Moist in the middle,
Surrounded with hair,
And often it happens
That water flows there.

The gentlemen guffawed. They always did. The ladies smiled and then quickly ducked their heads, as though they were shocked, as though they hadn't heard it a dozen dozen times before. And no one asked what the answer was, of course. So when Matthew looked to Megan to see her response, he was as vexed as confused to see nothing but the traces of a pettish frown on her averted face.

"Delightful!" Lucas said, so very much pleased that Matthew grinned again. Seeing that, Megan could have slapped Matthew for his innocence and confidence, the very things she'd liked best about him before . . . before Lucas had returned, she realized, hating him as much as Matthew now.

"Do you know any others?" Lucas asked charmingly.

He did—the same ones everyone else knew. By the time he was clearing his throat, ready to launch into his third one, Lucas took pity on Megan. Or else, she thought, her face burning with the humiliation of having to stand, pretending delight, listening to bawdy rhymes she'd not giggled at when she'd first heard them as a child, he spoke up because he was as bored with them as she was. For he interrupted Matthew before he could begin reciting another line.

"Ah, the play has begun. Hazard, I see. But I don't trust dice. I prefer holding hands with kings, and so enjoy the cards more. I expect they'll be playing Primero, Trump, and All Fours here tonight. But do they play Post and Pair, I wonder? We hear of little else in Italy. I've been away too long, and don't know how to go about it. You seem a man of parts and experience, Lorrilard, do you know the way of it?" he asked as the others in the group around them began to drift off to other diversions, since the gambling had indeed begun.

Matthew glowed with pleasure. He might have criticized Lucas Lovat's fashion, but that was his way with all things new and daring and never meant that he didn't admire them. He was as dazzled by Lovat as he saw most of the ladies were, and never imagined the fellow would single him out for company, much less advice. It was Megan, he thought, priding himself on his good taste again; she was as highly connected as lovely. It wouldn't do for him not to measure up to her now. Post and Pair, or Bone Ace, was a risky game, and so one he never played, but now he saw there was something he could do that Lovat could not, and was delighted.

The men playing Post and Pair made room for another player, and Lucas and Megan stood behind Matthew as he commenced his game. Matthew could hardly explain his actions without distracting the others, so he held his cards high enough for Lucas to see, and pointed to each one as he wagered on what he'd been dealt. It was a simple-enough game: each hand held only three cards, and the point of it was the wager, or bluff. It couldn't have taken Lucas, or any other onlooker, long to reason the rules out. But it wasn't called "the fools' game" for nothing, and so no one was surprised when Lucas didn't enter into the gaming, even after he'd time to see the way of it. Not even Matthew—since after a few hands he was lost to the onlookers and everything else except for his passion to recoup some of his losses.

"I fear the game is not for me, after all," Lucas sighed to Megan as he stepped away from the players so he could speak without distracting them. "I'm not a fellow who enjoys taking risks."

She followed, but there was no answering smile in her eyes.

"Pray acquit me of seducing him into the play," he said softly. "I'm not playing, you see, so it doesn't profit me. And how should I have known he was such a fiend for gaming? You might have said something," he chided her.

She hadn't known, but somehow, she was sure Lucas had. And she suspected him of playing another game. So she said nothing, but only looked at him with anger, the more so when she realized she was afraid to look at him without it. He had a way of making the crowded chamber seem empty of everyone else in it when he gazed at her, and looking at him reminded her of all the things she'd hoped she'd forgot. She glanced away, shaken.

"Forgive me," he said. "A poor jest. I didn't know either. But I did anticipate it. He seems a man who doesn't know when to give up. I do—unfortunately for me. That's no vice in him, you know. It's his greatest strength, I'd warrant. But he's not for you, Megan, never think it," he said suddenly. "You need a strength you can rest upon when you need it, not one that will always hang heavy over you."

"I need," she said through teeth clenched to ensure her lips from quivering, surprising herself as well as him, "constancy. I need trust. I need a friend as well as a lover. Which means I do not need betrayal. That is the strength I need."

Something in those light watchful eyes flickered before he allowed himself to wince theatrically.

"A redundancy. That's a strength you already have," he said, "within yourself. It may be," he said thoughtfully, "that it's giving you should be after, not getting. It could be that what you need is to offer that strength to someone else. Some worthy charity," he added, trying to lighten a moment that had, inexplicably, gotten out of control and become too dark for his purposes.

"Such as yourself?" she asked, trying to make her words sound incredulous and witty, instead of the forlorn query they became as they left her lips.

"Oh, no," he whispered, backing up a pace. "Not I. A *worthy* charity, I said."

"And Matthew is not worthy?" she asked angrily, expressing rage rather than the crushing shame and disappointment she felt.

"Not worthy of you," he said, as a lover might say something very different. "No, not of you, dearling."

She stared at him for only another heartbeat, and then turned away. Matthew was still engrossed in his game, her lady was at the other side of the room, and at any rate, it was difficult for Megan to see her through the mist that had suddenly come over her eyes. So she plucked up her skirt and walked away quickly, seeking the withdrawing room set aside for the ladies, pretending that was her pressing need, not her longing to stay as well as be away from him. She was halfway there before she allowed herself to know that it had been his hand on her arm that had tried to stay her, for all that it had been as cold as her own heart was.

He stood by himself until he heard the soft voice at his elbow.

"What is it you want of my little Megan, Lucas Lovat?" Lady Katherine asked.

"You repeat yourself, lady," Lucas answered abruptly,

before he remembered himself, and taking her hand, bowed over it as he spoke softly. "My pardon. It's your every right to ask, and I'm a churl to speak so. I'm unaccustomed to denial, you see. But don't worry, it appears that your little Megan is unassailable. I congratulate you."

"Congratulate her instead," Lady Katherine said. "And it may be that you'll have to ere long. Matthew Lorrilard is wellborn and well-to-do. You should see that I may be losing my little Megan to him soon enough."

"Should I?" he asked. "Pity, I don't. He doesn't deserve her."

"Matthew Lorrilard not worthy of her?" she murmured. "Possibly so. Do you know a man who is?"

Did she seriously expect him to make some sort of declaration, even if only one of evil intent? He smiled, shaking his head in denial, smiling the more to show her how ill she'd judged him.

"I didn't ask you for the name of one worthy of wedding her," she said carefully, with her own secretive smile in place, "only the name of one worthy . . . of her."

A year had changed her, he thought, but she was still lovely. Faint shadows stained the purity of skin beneath her lustrous blue eyes; her high cheekbones had more than shallows beneath them. Those marks of suffering only added human dimension to her beauty. But he'd remembered her as being soft and compliant in every word and gesture, only allowing those hard edges that made her truly beautiful to show through now and again when she couldn't help it. Or when, he suspected, as now, she wished to show her formidable intelligence for some other reason.

"Ah! I see," he exclaimed, as though at a revelation, and then fell silent and studied her closely. She didn't flinch. His light eyes, so reminiscent in their clarity, so different in their coldness from those of her lord, gazed at her gravely. What he thought was clear to read in his face, although he said not a word. She'd the grace to flush, but the determination not to look away. Yes, her steady gaze said, she'd pander for her purposes. Yes, her continued silence said, no sacrifice was too much for them.

"Ah," he said again, "you approve of me. My thanks," he said mockingly, "but how does that avail me? For all I know she loves you well, the lady isn't a puppet. That's precisely why I am . . . interested in her."

"No, she's not. But my word carries weight with her," Lady Katherine said. "My approval can gain you moments alone with her, at the very least. The very most, I leave to your experience and skill."

She didn't lower her eyes until she was done with what she had to say. And then she closed them so that he couldn't see more, and neither would she.

"Well, well," he said as if to himself, before he asked, as she knew he would, "And since even God above us doesn't give without asking in return—since he wants love and devotion, at the very least, in exchange for a favor—what is it that I can offer you, my lady, in return for such sweet words spoken into that sweet ear? And for those moments alone in order to say my own, in turn?"

"I would see my lord," she whispered fiercely, her eyes snapping open.

"Ah," he said with maddening calm, as if asking to see her husband in the Tower where he'd been locked away wasn't an enormous thing.

"I know others have seen him," she said in a hiss of a whisper, "but Henry refuses me time and again, and warns me now not to ask again. But it's been over a year now. I must see him. Dear God, I must."

"You address me thus? You must be overset to confuse me with God," Lucas replied easily. Before she could spin on her heel and stalk away from his mockery, he went on, "But it well may be that I can go where angels fear to tread. Once would be enough? One visit, and your word to keep it close, and your further word to bring nothing but yourself to the interview, and hasten away without argument when you are bidden to go?"

Her eyes gave her answer before she choked, "Aye, yes, my word on it."

"And for your part?" he asked slowly.

"All I can do on your behalf," she vowed. "And"—she gazed to where Matthew was frowning and sweating as he watched his coins dwindle—"all I can do against his."

"That," Lucas said on an easy smile, "will not be

necessary if you accomplish the first. I'll send word, when I can, when I know."

She nodded, then paused.

"You'd do all this—merely for an hour with a maid?" she asked.

"I've done more for less," he said, shrugging, hoping she'd be content with that. Because, he thought, he'd be getting far more than a chance to try a lovely lady's virtue once again. He'd be gaining Perkin's gratitude, Henry's amusement, and perhaps, what he wanted most of all: an answer for himself.

"Why not ask me to resurrect the dead whilst you are at it?" Henry asked.

But he was smiling.

"I can't see what harm lies in it," Lucas answered easily, and instantly regretted it.

"Oh, can you not?" Henry purred in a voice too pleased to be pleased. "Why, then, why should I wrestle with the problems of rule, when I have such as you to advise me so easily, I wonder?"

It was worse than Lucas had expected. It was a bad time to be summoned for the interview he'd requested, and he knew it, but a petitioner must take what he is offered whenever it is given. It was late in the night of an uncomfortable day, an hour after the last courtier had made his way to bed, and long after Henry's counselors had closed their eyes. It was an exhausted hour, the worst time for anything but nightmares and confession. But the king himself was still dressed, awake and restive, alone except for the dark-cowled monk beside him in the small, spare chamber Lucas had been admitted to.

Henry had been in a terrible mood all day. Lucas knew it must be even worse than it looked, since as a rule Henry was careful never to show his moods in public. But he'd frowned all afternoon, on commoners and lords alike; even the sight of his children at the hour of their audience with him had done little more than ease his abstraction for a few moments. He'd been silent during his dinner, and most unusual of all, had obviously been listening with only half an ear to the chorus who'd sung his supper in. The masques, games, and furnishings of luxury at his lavish court were only the necessary trappings of evident power to him, solely for others to see and admire, never for his own pleasure. Music was his one delight. But tonight he'd had no time for it. It was his own misfortune, Lucas thought, that he'd been spared the time for an audience with his sullen king now.

But if he ever showed Henry less than an unquenchable spirit, or more than a moment of hesitation, he might as well give up all his ambitions.

"Aye, in sooth, it's true I don't know all, I'm merely your humble servant, sire," Lucas said, with nothing of humility in his voice or stance. "It's only that I thought such a meeting might show more to an interested observer than no meeting at all. But, as you say, I haven't the wisdom of power," he concluded in a bored voice.

Henry looked at him narrowly and waved a hand to silence Brother Robert, or whatever hooded monk of the same size and importance to him as that friar was that stood beside him now was about to utter.

"What could she say, do you think?" he asked Lucas.

Lucas shrugged to hide his sudden elation. He'd won.

"Marry, I surely cannot say," he offered lightly, "but there's something afoot. Something all my gold can't buy a word about. Mayhap a misplaced word spoken in the first flush of such a gentle reunion between the lady and her Perkin might bare it?"

"Will you hide beneath their bed, then, and wait for him to wheeze it out whilst he's at his pleasure?" Henry asked with as much humor, which was to say, none.

But he'd been baited too often for that to hurt. Lucas only smiled seraphically.

"If you wish," he said, "but I'd thought to ensure a more chaste meeting. I believed you didn't want any more offspring from that treasonous union."

Henry was still for a moment. Then his eyes glittered, even in the gloom of the silent room. "You suggest I let a confessed traitor's wife in to visit him? A man I swore to keep from the sight of even the sun and moon?" he asked, as though incredulous.

"Your pardon, sire," Lucas said sweetly, "but I wouldn't hesitate to ask a maid for her favors once I knew they'd been given to three or four other fellows, however much she cried her chastity," and as the king's sallow face grew white about the lips, Lucas continued, as though he had no fear for his life or limbs, "I never used your seal to effect entry to the pretender's cell, exactly so that I might see if it were possible. It was, of course. Nor, however charming as I may be, do I doubt I was not the first to enter there. He's been visited by others—as I'm sure you know," he added with a pointed look to the silent monk at the side of Henry's chair.

"Mayhap," Henry said, "but never by his lady, and you know that too. Still, now you propose I look the other way whilst you whisk her in? Only just so you may discover if there is a plot afoot to free him? *You?* Sooth, Lovat, you rate yourself high, do you not?"

"Not I," Lucas said, "but I thought you did. God save you, sire, if you feel you can learn more from another, I've no objection."

"Or is it that you expect the lady to give you something more than her gratitude?" Henry asked in a hard voice.

"I don't fancy bedding saints," Lucas answered, his annoyance almost getting the upper hand. "I do have my vanity. I don't doubt I can make most women merry, but still and all, and pray forgive me, sire and gentle brother both, although I think I could make her sing a pretty tune if I'd a mind to, I don't fancy having someone else's name sung out in my ear at a crucial moment. Alas for my vanity."

"Alas, indeed," Henry said dryly. "It may one day be the death of you." Before Lucas could reflect on the truth of that, he went on, "But there is another woman, is there not?"

The walls, the floors, the very air had ears in this accursed court, Lucas thought, and answered immediately, "Of course. There always is, I find."

"Chaste, too, and lovely. You failed there once, I hear," Henry said.

"All the more reason to try again. Unless you've an objection?" Lucas asked, even as he immediately, if regretfully, decided to leave Megan Baswell untried. He'd never be able to have her now without picturing Henry's mocking half-smile floating in the air somewhere above them even as they rocked in the act of love.

"She is my ward . . ." Henry replied, thoughtful now.

He remained still, thinking deeply. And then he shocked Lucas as he'd seldom done.

"She's almost got young Lorrilard's name. For all he's a dolt, he's got more pride than sense, and if she gives him up for you even for a moment . . . I dislike leaving her with nothing," Henry mused. "Her father was a good man. No, I find I'd prefer giving her for life than for an idle hour. Do you want her for more than a night? She comes well-dowered."

Games, Lucas thought rapidly, sorting through plots and counterpurposes to find the true reason for Henry's generosity, as he answered from the shallows of his busy mind. "Marriage? Nay," he laughed. "Sooth, I'm an inconstant knave—at least so far as women are concerned."

"You're famous for your success with them. You grow no younger. For all the ones you've bedded, it's passing strange that you've never wedded. Do you want no heirs?" Henry asked with what might have been real curiosity.

"Marry, sire," Lucas said on a laugh, "many who know me swear my father never wedded either. As to that, why, he's some ideas of his own for my future. So as I want nothing permanent just yet—and it's the permanence of wedlock, like death, that discourages me from embracing it, however tempting it sometimes appears to be—if you want me to leave the little lady alone, consider it done. She shall be as chaste as she was before we met, on the day after I say farewell to her forever."

"No need to be so extravagantly noble," Henry said, as though bored now. "You'd not fit comfortably into a cassock, as does my good Brother Robert. No, you may do as you will there—although from all I hear of her, I don't expect you will. But to plead for a lady's right to visit her husband with no hope of a reward? I didn't look to see such charity in you."

"Nor I," Lucas admitted, "but I see gain there. The lady will cease to implore me, and you. I'll be reckoned a true friend to both her and her husband, and so it may be we'll each of us be able to discover something new."

Henry looked at his monk, and whatever he saw, or did not see, in the recesses of the dark cowl seemed to make up his mind for him.

"When do you take Lady Katherine for her audience?" he asked.

"Soon, if it please you," Lucas said briskly. "As you say, it would be best if you continued to look the other way and let me buy her way in. I will, by daylight. I need to see her reaction to him in clear light of day. He's not the same man he was, but I can't say why. Her face may tell me."

"He doesn't recant now," Henry said.

Glancing to the cowled brother at the king's side, Lucas didn't wonder why that hadn't been phrased as a question.

"No," Lucas said.

"He speaks with confidence of a future in the world again, does he not?" Henry said.

"Yes," Lucas said.

"Find out the rest," Henry said, and rose, waving his hand as though dismissing a servant.

I shall discover all, Lucas promised himself as he bowed himself out. It is what I will do then, sire, that you should have asked me.

"Very humble, our Lucas Lovat, is he not?" Henry asked the monk when Lucas had left them.

"Less faithful men may seem humbler," the monk replied.

"Morton and some of my other advisers, spiritual and not, don't trust him. You do. Is it that you trust in God so much that you fear no man, holy brother? Or is it that you are so holy you trust in all men?" Henry asked softly.

"I trust in God to show me the way to trust in men," Brother Robert replied calmly.

"You always have an answer," Henry said on a brusque laugh, "and so, for all that my other advisers know more of the world, still I listen to you—and I would that I were more like you."

"I would that I were holier, for you," the monk said sadly.

Henry smiled, a true smile, at last, if a weary one. "Do you?" he asked. "How could that be? Still, and for all, you've pledged yourself to me, haven't you? That says something for the hope of my eternal soul." He passed a hand over his face. "Tell me, Robert," he asked abruptly, "is it a sin to love too well?"

"It is never a sin to love God too well," Brother

Robert answered softly, "but I don't think you've asked that. Aye, too-intense love for mortal things, however innocent, can be sin, if by such loving God is forgotten—and in such consuming mortal love I have found God is often forgotten."

"Not all of us can love our unseen God as much as we do his creations," Henry said wryly. "Not even men of your order can, Robert. No, most of us risk God's love in order to serve our mortal ones, and hope he forgives us it, in time."

Henry fell silent, and the monk stood waiting, patient, listening with an intentness that was almost audible, knowing his king, and knowing that his own silence was an invitation for his king to speak again. After a long moment, Henry's voice came grudging, but clear.

"My Arthur is of an age to wed . . . *is* wedded—thrice—to Spanish Katherine. In name only. No children can be got by a paper union," Henry said, as though the words were being dragged forth, and they were, because for all he'd done and would do and must do, he'd been born a God-fearing man. "Paper, I've enough paper to cover over all of Westminster. I've another letter just this day, the same as the month before. Again Isabella and Ferdinand refuse to send her to us unless they're sure there's no danger here for her. Or him. They demand assurance that the throne is secure. And I cannot give it."

The king coughed, or it might have been that he laughed.

"No," Henry said then, as though the monk had spoken, or moved, or done more than stand as still as his own cast shadow, "it's not Perkin Warbeck, they're not fools enough to think more of him than I do. It is Warwick," he said in chagrin, "it is still Warwick. Imagine—they fear poor, witless Warwick. His blood—they fear his blood. And balls. For he's the true heir and carries the seed of kings, for all he wouldn't know how to sow it, but as they can't forget it, they fear no one else can. Warwick!" He shook his head. His hand went involuntarily to his breast, where he bore the latest message he'd received from another holy man, his archbishop and mentor, and it was, in its brief way, a sermon.

There were also jests in it; the old man was capable of

them when he was in a good enough mood. He'd been very merry when he'd penned this sermon.

"Yes. A good solution. Warwick's an innocent," the coded letter read when read right, "but whilst he lives, so too will Arthur be—or at least he will continue to sleep in an empty marriage bed. Warbeck yearns to be free, and is a fool. Mayhap even a dangerous one. Yes, then proceed. Now. The time is ripe. Let Warbeck be your Samson. In his blindness, he'll bring the Tower down, and everyone with him. Amen."

"Aye, the walls will come tumbling down," Henry muttered, as if to himself. "They must. There's no help for it. There are things that must be. There are things a king must do for himself and his house and his country. It's fair enough, fairer than warfare, for as you've told me often enough, Robert, as with most temptations, only those who fall from grace will be ill-served—they, and Warwick, of course."

He raised a narrow hand and looked away, although the only man in the room with him had neither moved nor spoken, "No, say nothing more, Robert," he commanded. "Let be. You know my mind in this."

"And Lovat?" was the only thing the monk did say after a long moment.

"Well-a-day," Henry said with a small sour smile, becoming animated again. "You were right. He does amuse me. It should be interesting to see if he can see all he thinks he can. If he can, then he can sidestep and scurry away in time, can't he? If he can't . . . ? Enough. It's late. For now," he said, rising, "I'll let the lady into the Tower. You'll be there?"

There was only a moment of silence.

Then, "As always," Brother Robert said, "as always."

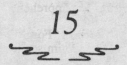

15

"You want me to see him," Megan repeated, incredulous. And then, when the surprise of that had worn off, she dared ask, afraid that she knew the answer, "You would that I were . . . compliant as well? But scarcely a year ago you advised me against him—for my own good, as well as yours, you said."

"There is compliant and then there is compliant," Lady Katherine snapped. "I do not bid you lie with him. Not that that would be the end of the world. He's fair enough to tempt a saint. Nothing remains the same as last year: where once I doubted him, now I've a certain need of him. Time changes all things—save you, mayhap," she said in annoyance. "As to that, you're yet a maiden, yet at your age scarcely a maid anymore, are you?"

Megan cast her gaze down.

"But I'm not rude to him, I . . . I am not unfriendly," she said softly.

"Such friendliness he can have from nuns!" Lady Katherine said, exasperated.

Megan's head came up with her eyes widened.

"God's wounds!" Lady Katherine whispered sharply, in a tone no male had every heard her utter, as she paced in agitation. "Don't you understand? You're old enough to have had a litter of your own by now, and I don't see you begging Henry to place you in a cloister! No matter. I will not argue virtue, your chastity is your own affair. I only say that it would please me if you were more than less-than-rude to Lovat. If you . . . encouraged him. It shouldn't be so difficult. He has charm and presence. Every other maid will envy you . . ."

She cast a glance to Megan from beneath her heavy

242

lashes: the girl was white-faced, her golden-brown eyes dilated with confusion and apprehension. Lady Katherine stifled an impatient groan.

"Ah!" she said instead. "Forgive me. I forget your condition, because I need him so. It may be that he can help me—us," she admitted, coming to stand before Megan, her spite as well as her confidence seemingly vanished, leaving her lovely face with only a lost look upon it. And so every word finally reached Megan's heart and not just her fear and pride.

"I'll try, indeed I will," Megan said at once, daring to take her mistress's icy hands in her own. "I'm old enough to know how to be pleasant without being . . . I am no Maeve, you know," she said in heartier accents, although she scarcely knew what she was, or what to do with this new request. "But," she added as Lady Katherine heaved a sigh, "what of Matthew?"

"What of him?" Lady Katherine demanded, her vexation on the rise again, before she remembered herself and moderated her voice, with effort. "Are you so lost in love with him you cannot see another man? I didn't think so," she said as Megan turned her head away. "God's grace, Megan, I speak of moments, not years. But if you think he needs to be reassured as to your constancy, I'll give you time to be alone with him and expect you'll be able to allay his fears with sweet words and kisses. All I need from you for Lovat are smiles and promises."

Megan's pale skin grew rosy, and Lady Katherine suppressed an urge to shake her. She was as annoyed as impatient with her lady-in-waiting's virginal protests. She wondered why an experienced rogue like Lovat would show preference for such a skittish wench, but accepted that he did; his eyes seldom left her when they were in the same room. So she took a minute inventory of Megan's attributes as she waited for her answer, since in the usual way of things she didn't notice other women's charms after a first glance showed herself to be superior. Good skin and hair, a pert form, and oddly attractive tilted eyes: a pretty-enough wench, but there were prettier, she decided with the dispassionate surety in her own standard of excellence that only a famous beauty could have.

To be sure, the girl had charm and wit—and innocence, of course, the thing that was so vexing to her now.

Perhaps it was that very innocence that lured Lovat. Such
a man had likely had his fill of every other feminine grace
but that one. And then she thought of what Lovat was,
and her heart softened a little toward Megan. For all his
graces, Lovat was nothing like her own lord, save in
looks, and Matthew Lorrilard, although a block, was safe
enough. After all, Megan had nothing but her virtue and
youth to buy her future with, and both of those ephem-
eral things would be gone soon enough, and likely one
even the sooner if she obeyed in the matter of pleasing
Lovat. That was why Lady Katherine held her temper
when Megan spoke again.

"Are you sure that Clarisse would not do as well, my
lady? It's not that she's a bawd, far from it, only that she
is always so accommodating in every respect. She's well-
liked by the gentlemen."

"If they notice her at all. It's not that she's a bawd,
she's a bore. Lovat doesn't even know of her existence,
though she stands in your tracks every day. No, no, it's
you he watches," Lady Katherine said, and taking Megan's
two hands tight, touching her on purpose for the first
time in their acquaintance, she added in a rapid whisper,
"And I do not trust her, Megan. For all her simplemind-
edness, she's too careful to be close when she has no
need to be. Do you understand? There are those who
whisper everything I say into Henry's ear.

"Not that I have anything to hide," she said distractedly,
dropping Megan's hands so she could pace again, and so
never seeing the guilt and fear that had sprung up on her
face, "but if it comes to pass that I do . . . No, no, it
cannot be anyone but you, Megan," she said, spinning
around in a flurry of her skirts, to face her again. A
woman who was so used to admiration that she only felt
its lack, she knew to a fraction how much this girl was
awed by her. Now she saw Megan's expression and read
it as fear of the task she'd been given. So she softened
her voice, and easy tears came into her eyes, as ever,
when she needed them. "I trust you," she said hoarsely.
"I pray you—it means much to me, and mayhap to my
lord as well. Can you not find it in your heart to give
Lucas Lovat some of your time and your smiles? As for
aught else—that is your own business," she said abruptly,
turning away again.

It was almost funny, Megan thought, to be so overset because she'd been commanded, coerced, and then begged to do what she most wanted, in her deepest heart, to do. But she'd common sense, and it reeled under all the new demands made upon it. And she'd this conscience to appease, and it ached from all the assaults made on it of late. She felt her spirit writhe under the demands of her three masters: the king, Lady Katherine, and her own honor. One she relied on for her continuance, one she admired with all her heart, and the last she needed so as to call her soul her own. All the king wanted was to know everything that she heard and saw and did. Her lady wanted her to encourage a man she wanted, but knew she should not. And for her soul, now she no longer knew where honor lay. Not in the sheets with Lucas Lovat, surely not. Nor in the king's deep games. Nor in Lady Katherine's machinations. But her lady was waiting for her answer. And so she gave the simplest one.

"I will do your will, my lady," she said meekly.

But there was a new light in her eyes when she followed her lady down the stair to greet the day.

"And here, this one's only a simple jay's. I've many of those. But this one is darker than the rest. Far so. They do say that London's grown so many new chimneys that the soot colors the very air now, although I see it clear enough here. But if the air become beshrouded, then would not the birds of the air change color too? I wonder about that. And so, see this box? Jay feathers, each one darker than the last . . . Have I found something important here?" the slight young man murmured with ill-suppressed excitement.

"It's my fondest wish . . . but mark you," he said, looking up and catching the expression on Lucas' face, "I don't rely on it. It's just that it may be, you see," he muttered, sorting through his box of feathers as though looking for something, clearly embarrassed, as though he saw how odd his enthusiasm must seem to Lucas, and yet by so doing convincing Lucas once again that he was sane, and saddening him the more for it.

"Yes, it's likely, though I hadn't thought on it. I would, had I known of your interest before this, since I've lately come from Italy, you know, and could've brought you some exotic specimens," Lucas said.

"Oh, no," the Earl of Warwick said quickly. "Thank you. But England is enough for me."

"Just as well. I confess I wouldn't know a jay from an eagle," Lucas said on a laugh.

"Nor would I, mayhap, in the sky. It's the feathers I know, you see," the earl said with sincerity.

But he said everything so, and it made his conversation odd and stilted, because grown men never took every word they said so seriously. It was that which gave him his air of childishness as much as the fact that he seldom spoke of what other men did. Not madness, no, nor feeblemindedness either, Lucas thought, but only what might be expected from a man who'd been locked away from the world since he'd been a boy, for the crime of being what he would be if he grew to manhood: a direct Plantagenet heir to the throne of England.

Thin, pale, attenuated, with downy thin pale hair on his cheeks and head, the earl, Lucas fancied, looked very like a weed struggling up from a shadowed chink of wall might, grown spindly and crooked from seeking distant light. In the past fifteen years, the majority of his life, he'd spoken only to his jailers, his confessors, and, of late, the man in the neighboring cell who claimed to be his long-lost cousin, Richard, Prince of York. And now he spoke to the man he knew as Lucas Lovat. And it may have been that he was the only one of them that didn't think the earl addled or dim.

There was a danger in this; Lucas knew it. But his life had always been lived in danger, and he didn't count this a large one. Sixteen years was a lifetime; he'd known his cousin when they'd met again only because he'd taken care to seek the boy in the man's face. For all he'd seen it immediately, it was like hearing the answer to a riddle before the clues were given, and then wondering why no one else could solve it at once when he heard it: easy enough—if done backwards.

The man did look like the boy grown, but Lucas doubted he'd have felt more than a fleeting sense of familiarity without a name to put to that altered face. It wasn't likely to work both ways; his cousin Edward had no such name to put to the test with him. His mind was not as other men's were, anyway. He wasn't a madman or a fool; his mind was not so much gone, as grown inward. Or so Lucas believed, and so he was patient with him as few others were.

Because even now, as ever, after only a few minutes in his company, Perkin was growing restive again. He paced the room, so distracted that he forgot to conceal the way his left leg dragged as he did.

"Cousin," Perkin said, "I dislike leaving you so soon, but I've other things to do now. I'll leave you my friend Lucas, if you will, for the rest of our hour today. Well, and it's already paid for—no sense in wasting expensive time. How say you, Edward? Have I leave to go, with your goodwill? Will you have Lucas in my stead?"

"Oh. Yes. He's welcome. But you . . . Do you think it wise?" the earl asked hesitantly.

"I do, lad," Perkin said, as though addressing one years his junior, although they were the same age. "Trust me, I do," he said, putting a hand on the earl's slight shoulder, encompassing almost the whole of it as he did.

Perkin seemed hale and whole and wholly regal next to Edward. He would have clapped any other man on the shoulder before he left, but that would have been as a blow to the earl, so he only squeezed the bony arch of shoulder beneath his hand and grinned before he made his way across the room to the great oak door. He struck it with the flat of his hand and nodded to Lucas.

"I'll see you anon, when the hour is up. Long Roger's in charge of the guard today, and while he's a merry fellow, he's a greedy one. He counts the hours to the last grain of sand, so as to be sure to get his money's worth next time. But remember, you've paid for another hour in my chamber after this. Till then, adieu," he said as the door opened and he stepped out.

It was silent when the door closed, so quiet Lucas wondered if the earl regretted his decision to be left alone with him. He'd visited a few times now with Perkin, but they'd never been alone before. The earl's eyes were open wide, and since they were so light-lashed they seemed lashless, they appeared wider as he stared at his guest. His unease communicated itself to Lucas, making him feel hulking, grotesquely healthy, and somehow clumsy, even to himself, the way he thought he might feel if alone in the company of nuns or at the deathbed of a child.

"He ought not to meet with them," Edward said. "He tried to bring them to see me, but I'd none of it. I am not very wise in the ways of the world, and he is. But I know my world better than anyone alive. He ought not to meet with men who come to court him and promise him escape and kingdoms. This is our kingdom now and forever, and he should know it. But he won't listen to me."

"Which men?" Lucas asked.

And received a sad-eyed stare as answer.

"Ah. Doubtless you are right—you are, as you say, the expert here," Lucas said, holding up two empty hands, as a captured man might do.

This time it was Edward who fixed him with a sad, sympathetic stare.

"You are welcome here," Edward said. "Never doubt it. I don't see those men that Richard does. Or anyone else from beyond. Except for my guards. Once, when they were in their cups, they thought it would be amusing to bring me a woman, a long time ago. She was nothing like the women I remembered. I wouldn't touch her. Even when they left us alone. Another time they brought me another one, out of sympathy, I think."

He turned his head, so large and vulnerable on that frail stalk of neck that it seemed to Lucas it was difficult for him to keep it uplifted. "I studied her," he said with a slight smile. "Only that. I was curious, nothing more. They never brought me another one. That's how I know they were watching. I think they were ashamed. They're not evil men, you see. Only bored, and sometimes sympathetic. I don't lust after the same things they do—or my cousin Richard does, or you do. I only wish to be let alone."

"And to be free?" Lucas asked softly.

The great blue eyes studied his, unblinking.

"Yes. But only to be *here* and free. It's my world. I have no courage, you see. Every night I worry if there's to be another tomorrow for me. Because I want there to be. It mayn't seem like much of a life to a man like yourself, but I'll do nothing to hasten the end of it. A man with gold may spend recklessly. A man who's never had a coin shivers before he spends the one he's given.

Or so they tell me. Don't pity me. I've never had your courage, and so I don't miss it. Shall we talk of eagles, or would you rather leave?"

The thing Lucas wanted to do was to ask why the earl suffered his presence, why he seemed to have accepted him from the first. But he didn't want to know the answer. He told himself it was because a self-professed coward was the last person in the world he'd wish to know his secret; he told himself it was because if Edward had guessed it, he'd have to be destroyed, or his own scheme abandoned. He assured himself it was wisdom to ignore the question, and wondered if cowardice was contagious as he asked, instead, "Is that what's in that box?"

Edward, Earl of Warwick, nodded, pleased. "Yes. Eagles. Come see," he said.

When the door opened and a harsh whisper called, "Hist! God save you, sirs, but time's up," Lucas blinked and straightened, remembering where he was again.

The earl had talked of birds, of pinion feathers and nestlings, wings and rudders and patterns of flight, until his voice had become only a background to Lucas' own thoughts. He'd left off watching the pale bony fingers sifting through the boxes of feathers long before, and left only a part of his mind alert for the sound of a true interrogatory note, which had never come, since the earl's frequent "you see's" were never meant as questions.

"Good-bye," Edward said then. "Come again, please do. It pleases me to see you."

"As you will, my lord," Lucas answered, avoiding the mild blue eyes lest he see some other sort of recognition there.

As he stepped out into the dim hallway, he vowed never to return, even as he knew he would if he stayed in London. He was so busily wondering what question it was that he could ask Perkin now that would give him the answer he needed in order to be free himself—so that he might flee this damned place today and then forever—that it took him another moment to realize someone else was coming up the stair and into the narrow stone hallway. And that slip on his part was so odd that he stopped in his tracks.

That was how they saw him as they rounded the curve in the hall: a tall, richly dressed, well-made man, gleam-

ing softly in the darkened light of the stone corridor, his
proud bright head uplifted in alarm, like a stag scenting
the chase from afar, frozen in his steps.

It was the right day and time, and it was only astonishing that he'd forgotten. That was why Lucas was as
delighted as he was outraged to see Megan Baswell trail-
ing behind the Lady Katherine, because it gave him
something other than himself to fear and rage about.

"God's blood, madam! What were you thinking? Did
you bring the whole of Henry's court here with you?" he
hissed through clenched teeth.

"Ask the guards, sirrah," Lady Katherine answered in
just as tight a voice. "Do you think it my decision? I'd
trust this girl with my life, but now I'm forced to. They'd
not admit me without a maid. Should I take that idiot
Clarisse instead?"

"Er, but what if she swooned, sir," the guard asked as
Lucas glared at him, "or said she was about to and sent
us for help? She's a lady—and then she'd be alone with
'im, seeing as 'ow 'e wouldn't leave her if she said she
was sick—and who's to know the truth of it? Eh? We was
talking on it t'other night and voted two was better'n
one, for our own safety. With two in the room," he
whispered, bending to Lucas, "it's not likely one'll get
with child, do you see? And what if she really does 'ave a
fit, or something like, what then? Only women knows
women, we say."

Megan's face was as white as her lady's, and there
were both fear and pleading in her silence as she paused,
the embodiment of the uninvited guest upon the doorstep.

"It's done," Lucas said. "Come, time will not wait."

The guard swung open the door, and Perkin's head
came up from studying the papers spread on the table
before him. He stood. He looked. Lady Katherine stood
as still as stone before she broke. She fled, in the first
gracelessness Lucas had seen of her, stumbling toward
Perkin, her arms before her groping wildly, until she
reached his open arms. And all he did was gather her up
and lower his cheek to hers as they embraced, rocking
back and forth soundlessly together.

" 'Ere," the guard whispered to Lucas, licking his lips
nervously as he watched them, "I'm locking you in with

them. Don't turn your eyes aside. Not for a minute. You paid for them meeting, not swiving. 'Ear?''

But even as the door closed behind the guard, the couple only held to each other. When, at last, the lady moved away a step, she put her hands to her husband's face and let them walk his features, making sure of them as her weeping eyes could not. And Perkin Warbeck closed his eyes and held one hand aside her head, as the other traced the line of her nose, her lips. When they at last let their lips touch, Megan was openly weeping, and when the kiss lengthened and Lucas cleared his throat, she turned upon him.

"Let them have this, at least!" she whispered savagely.

"Lady," he said tonelessly, "I requested it."

"My Katherine," Perkin murmured, as Megan looked away at last, as shamed at her envy as she was of her fascination at the look in Perkin's glowing eyes.

"Come, sit with me and talk with me," Perkin said as he drew his lady to a chair, and sat, with her in his arms. She curled up to him like a child, and Perkin looked up at last at the world outside his arms, at Lucas and Megan.

"We will just talk together," he said quietly, as his gaze held hard to Lucas'.

Lucas nodded, and turned his attention to Megan. She looked away from the couple sitting so close and speaking softly and murmurously, punctuating every other sentence with a kiss, or a touch, or a sigh. Dark and light, she thought, matched as night and day, each perfect and yet incomplete without the other, for now the Lady Katherine was as soft as a night's breeze, as Perkin Warbeck's own golden splendor was gentled by her presence. And then she looked to see Lucas Lovat watching her with his hard, bright, clear eyes, and she shuddered—both for what she felt at the way he gazed at her, and at how she saw they two were again the echoed opposites of the pair across the room—ill-matched and met in mistrust and latent base desire once again.

Those things that she and Lucas spoke about as they sought to pass the time were nothing to remember, because it seemed they both were shamed at what they had no part in, and both wished they were elsewhere then. It seemed he knew that just as well as she did, and so his voice was gentle and his words called her from her disquiet, and she answered light questions to do with little, and asked the same of him. And so they passed the most of their long hour—and Perkin and his lady's brief one—in charity with each other, grateful for each other, helping each other to avoid what was before their eyes as well as what was in the back of their minds.

Because this was no time for flirtation, no time to try to raise or satisfy quick passions, or to quip or cast out lures or fence and parry, they spoke of the safe and trivial business of living, and learned and relearned foolish things about each other that gave them more to talk about. It seemed he sang and played at the lute, and she at the guitar; he had a sister, she'd one too; he didn't care for the hunt so much as for the riding in it, she hardly ever rode but liked the look of it; they both enjoyed tournaments and riding at the ring—he the doing, she the watching. They both could read and write, and preferred springtime to summer, and loved the sea. But neither cared for turnips or whiting, or neat's tongue, for that matter. And they both of them had never felt such a longing as they did as they tried not to watch how the reunited couple whispered and touched each other. And neither knew if they ached more to know the same thing as that blessed couple did, or to be gone so that the couple could touch the more and they themselves know less.

Both were relieved as well as saddened when a guard swung the door wide and said urgently, "Time, time to be gone, your time is over, make haste to go."

This was the moment they'd all dreaded. But Lady Katherine was a lady even in her utmost distress. And Perkin was, as ever, noble.

She arose from her husband's lap and touched her fingers to the prominent ball of his chin.

"We will meet again in joy, my love," she said.

"Yes, yes, be sure, we will," he said as he rose and his lips skimmed her forehead.

I would shriek and curse, I think, Megan thought, watching them; they might even have to drag me off. And Lucas thought of the many ways he'd kill the guard if he were Perkin.

They took the stair in silence this time, the three of them that had so lately been four. But when they reached the light of day again, Lady Katherine took Lucas aside.

Megan stood a step apart, raising her face to the weak setting sun as though it was giving her renewed life.

"There are things I must speak to you about," Lady Katherine said, and as he raised one brow and looked down to her, she added quickly, "Not here and now. But there are things I've heard I can't like the sound of. He trusts too much," she whispered.

"Anytime you wish, I am at your bidding, here and now, or later at dinner, or afterward, or after that," Lucas said.

"Later, later. We're promised to Matthew Lorrilard now," Lady Katherine said hurriedly, speaking more loudly so as to include Megan again. "We're late. An hour past, in fact. My Clarisse is already with him, and they'll hear that Megan fell ill after luncheon. We met you then, and you assisted her, should they ask," she instructed him.

"Oh. Yes, of course, and was alarmed at how she cast up her meal all over my finest linen," Lucas agreed. "But don't fret, I'll forgive that, and loudly—so as to preserve your dainty vision in his eyes," he explained to Megan, erasing her quizzical smile, "since Lady Clarisse is formidable competition enough, and I wouldn't like to be the one to ruin all your chances."

But for all her frowns, Megan forgave him even as she turned up her nose and turned on her heel to leave him. Because it helped return things to normal, and on the whole, it was better to leave him with disdain than with what she'd been feeling toward him before he'd spoken.

The first chill of autumn was in the night air, and as no fire had been lighted as yet, the room was dank and cool. But Megan felt suffocated. His mouth was hot and his hands were damp and all his body was moist with excitement. She'd reason to know it and detest it. She'd thought he had a fair-enough form, but his expensive clothing and well-cut doublet had concealed much; pressed up against her as he was now, she couldn't help but feel the pressure of a rounded belly against hers, and it revolted her. As did the strong sweet odors of rose and musk that he always wore that rose from him, overlaid now with the sharp sour tang of his excitement. But she told herself it was the heat that made her ill, the heat foremost. Because the heat of that swollen belly and from that which rose below it now, as well as that from his searching hands and mouth, made her frantic to tear her lips from his and gulp in cool clean air. She wrenched away from Matthew, only to be pulled back into his arms; for all his softness, he had considerable strength.

But for all his evident passion, at least he remembered he was courting her and not bent on overpowering her. He knew he had to try to call her back to him, not force her, and so had to leave off kissing her to speak.

"No, no, no, little dearling," Matthew said on a series of gusty broken chuckles, his moist mouth sliding along the side of her averted face, one hand at her waist to hold her, the other at her breast. "Don't worry. I'll have a care. I'm in control, even if we are alone. But let's not waste these moments we've been given."

Given, yes. Just before they'd been about to take leave of him, Lady Katherine had pulled Clarisse from the room with her on the pretense of suddenly remembering that she'd left her favorite comb at Elizabeth Warren's apartments, where they'd stopped before. As Megan had begun to follow, her lady had insisted, "No, no, my sweet Megan, no need. It will take only a moment or two. You can come along with Matthew when you will. We'll be at the gate, where our footman always awaits us, after we recover the comb. It not, why, then, I trust Matthew to return you in good order in time for dinner."

A reward. It had been meant as a reward for her good work of the afternoon. When Matthew had first gathered her in his arms, Megan had thought it as such. Because she'd been filled with an inchoate longing for a human touch, for a loving hand, for the sense of another person holding her, treasuring her, all this afternoon. But not this. Not this frantic, sweaty clutching of Matthew's, not Matthew quivering as he touched her, pressing close so she could be as aroused as he was by his trembling body. Not these things Matthew did, no, not this Matthew—not Matthew at all, in truth.

She'd been touched by other men, kissed by others too. If she hadn't the freedom to lose her virginity, a maid had the right to touch and be touched in order to discover whose touch she was best pleased with. Or at least a maid in the service of a lady at court had that right, even if a well-brought-up girl of respectable family supposedly did not. But she'd never been impressed by any man's lovemaking but once. Nor had she ever known Matthew's intimate touch, or guessed that it would frighten her as much as that other's had, for opposite reasons. And it was only too bad that the memory of one man's devotion, lately seen, and of another man's lust, long since experienced, should add to the despair of this moment.

"Ah, but don't weep," Matthew said with a touch of pride, for after all, his lovemaking had never moved a woman to tears; he usually had to pay, and dearly, for so much as moans. "I'll stop."

He was a good man, Megan thought as he touched her eyes with his sleeve to dry them. And a kindly one, she thought as he touched his lips gently to her forehead. And she could not bear his touch, and wanted to claw off his smug smile when she saw it, and hated him as well as herself as she understood her own hopelessness.

They strolled to the gate like lovers. He delivered her to Lady Katherine with a bow and a flourish and sauntered back to his rooms to dress for dinner, feeling as though he'd had her thrice over, she'd made him feel that good about himself. But whereas he hummed as he dressed, and emptied half a bottle of rosewater over his head before he left his rooms to see her again, she went soundless to her corner of her own room. When she reached it she filled a basin with water and vinegar and scrubbed until her skin squeaked, and wept silently because she still could not get the smell of him off herself. Because she feared she'd taken it too far, encouraged him too much, and might yet have to marry him.

Was she the only one, Megan wondered as she sat at her dinner that same night, that saw the new relaxation evident in her lady's posture, and noted the new calculations that were taking place behind her eyes? She'd scarcely time to worry about it, because she passed more of her time trying to avoid Matthew's proprietary eye. He smiled and sent her little waggings of his head from where he sat at another table; he never left off looking over to her all evening. He winked once, and waggled his fingers another time, until she was sure everyone at court thought she'd passed the day in his arms. And as she had—at

least, the latter part of it—she lowered her gaze to her
untouched trencher and kept it there.

Tonight Henry's musicians sang of love. The minstrels
as well as the choruses of sweet-voiced boys chanted of
it. There was a short pageant presented on the subject,
between the fish and game, and when the kettledrums
sounded and the trumpets called attention to a new course
and a new entertainment served up with it, none other
than young Prince Arthur himself offered a song for his
father, and it had to do with love too. He'd a thin but
true voice, silver to a professional minstrel's gold, but it
was a sweet song he sang. He stood before the king and
queen and gave love to love, because his mother wore
one of her rare sad smiles and his father's pinched face
showed nothing but the astonished look of perfect love it
always bore when he gazed upon this, his firstborn, most
beloved son. By the time he'd done, and the spun-sugar
trenchers stuffed with dates and bright flowers and biscuits and candied fruits were borne in, the court was all
a-sigh, Matthew's eyes were moist with promise of his
undying love, and Megan had forgotten everything but
the need to escape.

As soon as the king had risen and the court was released to go where it would, Megan sprang up, and
murmuring something to her lady about her stomach,
was given leave, by an abstracted nod, to take her own
leave. She was the first up, and the first off, and so had
the opportunity to lose herself in the newly sprouted
forest of bodies and limbs created as the ladies and
gentlemen of the court arose from their dinners. There
was a turn in the corridor to the side of the dining hall,
and a short stair to the right of that that led to a corner,
and around that there was a shallow shadow in an alcove
where she stopped and rested her head against the cool
stone wall and waited for her heart to slow.

The sight of Perkin Warbeck in his captivity had shaken
her, as had her moments with Lucas Lovat's kindness,
and she'd not had time to assimilate it all when her
foolish, previously safe suitor, Matthew, had shown he
was no safe harbor, and his unexpected ardor had shaken
her once again. There were too many futures, her own
and others', to worry over now for her to comprehend it

all at once. The one thing she didn't want or need was to have to pretend anything else to anyone else tonight.

Which was why Megan's faint color vanished entirely when she finally crept from her secret corner in order to seek her bed, and heard her name spoken behind her, instead.

"Lady? Lady Megan Baswell?" the young page asked.

He'd seen her leave, because he'd watched for his chance all evening to deliver his message to her in private as he'd been bidden. Small and quick, he'd followed on her heels, close behind her since she'd left her table. He'd waited until it looked as if she could speak. He didn't know why she'd flown from the dining hall and hidden herself, and didn't particularly care; he was only intent on doing his errand and getting it right.

"Your confessor would see you, lady, this night, in the usual place, at the usual time. My lady," he said, and bowed, glad to have the business done so he could hurry to the kitchens to get his own dinner, at last.

The usual time would not be for hours, Megan thought, letting the thought of the time be her only one, since she couldn't bear to think of what she'd have to do when the time was ripe. She walked unseeing, heading toward her chamber, with the vague notion of lying down until her hour came around. Another voice stopped her.

"Are you all right? It's my turn to ask that, at last," Lucas said in a soft voice.

He'd followed. But not being so small, or so insignificant as a little page boy, he'd been stopped here and there, and once again, by various members of the company after he'd seen her hastening from shadow to shadow out of the light of the great hall. Then he'd lost her, now he'd found her again, and decided he'd been right to track her down. A dozen other women had offered him more tonight, as they did every night. But he wanted her. Because of what they'd shared today, he thought. Because of what they'd almost had once before, as well. Because of what he saw that dolt Matthew Lorrilard wanted—or had already had—of her. Because he'd been as shaken by the events of the day as she'd been, and needed a friend, but as usual, would settle for losing himself in a woman, and she was that woman. And because he was no more tranquil in his mind or safe in his own company than she was in her own tonight.

"I am well," she said.

But then she saw him. She shook her head.

Against all reason, but because now she acted on impulse, not reason, she came at once, unasked, into his arms. And simply lay there resting against the soft nap of his velvet-clad chest.

"I wish . . . I wish I could trust you," she murmured.

"Ah," he said, surprised into entire honesty, "so do I, lady, so do I."

She hadn't thought that the mere touch of his lips could banish the bad taste that had lingered on hers, or that their cool fire would soon be able to burn away the shame she'd felt, transmuting it to pure, devastating desire. But then, neither had he expected what he found on her mouth, or in her arms, or in her muted tears, and never suspected that her desperate innocence would shame him into tempering his desire to something too close to love to allow him to continue it.

"Now, why do we do this?" he asked her quizzically, drawing back to still his need, but holding her still, and touching a finger to one of her tears, to quieten his own heartbeat. "Why," he asked her and himself, with real wonder, "when we know very well we can't afford each other?"

"I cannot stay," she said, because that was all she could say now.

He smiled a slow sad smile.

"I know," he said, since that was all he could say to her, and released her.

The hour was the first of the new day. She'd crept from her room down long cold corridors to this small chamber, and there'd been a page to lead her silently all the way, as there always was when she was summoned thus to him.

Henry Tudor looked as weary as Megan felt when she came into the room, but he gave her leave to rise from her curtsy, and then asked her exactly what she'd been afraid he would.

There was little point in lying. There never was; in all likelihood he already knew all she had to report.

So Megan told him everything she could remember, everything that she thought he'd expect to hear from her.

"I see," Henry said at length. "And you heard nothing of what the pretender whispered to your lady while you waited for their audience to be over?"

"Nothing," she said.

"Or anything of future plans that Lady Katherine might have mentioned to Lucas Lovat when they'd left the Tower?"

"No, sire," she said.

"After that, what then?" he asked, studying her pale face.

But now, blurred with exhaustion and pulled too many ways to heed anything but her own heart, she stared into his eyes—or where she thought they were, since he sat half in shadow—and for the first time in her life, lied a little lie to him: her king, her sovereign lord and sole benefactor.

"Nothing, nothing of note," she said softly, lowering her eyes.

For what was a kiss to a king, after all? Or a foolish girl's realization of an impossible love?

And all unseen by her, his eyes narrowed. Because she was not good at his game, and he was a master of it, and now he knew that she'd lied about something.

16

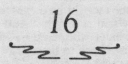

He was a dark, earnest young man in decent clothes; a sober fur-trimmed burgundy robe over dark hose, a neat flat black slouch hat atop his smooth long black hair, and a minimum of jewels at his chest. Although he was no member of the court, he was obviously a gentlemen, his long face serious and still, as if he'd long since learned that primary lesson of good breeding: control.

"I give you James Strangways," Lady Katherine said, her voice soft and gentle. "James, this is Lucas Lovat. He is . . . a friend of mine, and my lord's, as I've said."

Then she fell still, and lowered her lashes over her eyes, and Lucas was hard put not to smile at the transformation in her, for all he doubted she planned this complete subjugation of her personality whenever there was a new male in her orbit. It was a reflex, this guise of total docility when men were about; he'd seen it now and again in other women. But it was such second nature to the lady, he thought it might even be that she herself wasn't aware of the tiger's heart that beat behind that doe's breast of hers.

"Sir," James Strangways said as he bowed, and when he was done, he looked at Lucas with great dark burning eyes.

Another great heart hidden from the world, two of a kind, Lucas thought, and sighed.

"Lucas," Lady Katherine said softly, although they were alone on the wharf and the wind off the great river pulled their voices away even from each other, close as they stood, "James has a brother. He worries for him. Will you listen to what he has to say, I pray you?"

Yes, and when not in the presence of a strange gentleman, Lady Katherine would never say such a fatuous thing, Lucas thought wryly. Because they'd just met exactly where and when she'd specified in her message. He'd been standing on the Tower wharf, with a brisk autumn breeze discovering every gap in his seams and every chink in his cloak for the past ten minutes, waiting for her, after having sent Philip de Lacey hotfoot back to his rooms in search of the guard's daily ration of gold that he'd conveniently forgotten. And now she seriously asked if he'd listen to what her companion had to say. Still, she was so convincingly helpless that he swallowed a brusque retort.

"Speak, then, I pray you, sir," he said instead, but the words suited his sardonic expression so ill that it was a moment before Strangways, after a sidewise look to Lady Katherine, and an encouraging nod from her, did speak.

"I've a younger brother, sir," he said in a low, modulated voice filled with suppressed anxiety, "and I am concerned about him."

"Youth's a bother, but scarcely a crime," Lucas said negligently, in the hopes of pricking this tight gentleman into more speech. It was too chilly a morning to stand still and fence, far too brisk a day to pull words from him each by each, like posies from a meadow on a May morning.

Strangways had the wit to see Lucas' annoyance. He stared at him, and then took the leap of faith necessary to speak freely at last. He took in a deep breath and then spoke his mind, all at once.

"My brother Thomas is a dreamer," he said. "He loves lost causes. He has a fine sense of honor. This would be well if he were a historian or had been born in less-difficult times. But he's embroiled himself in something that has nothing but danger in it for him now. I don't mean that I'd wish him to be a coward," Strangways said, looking hard at Lucas, "understand that. In truth, had he been born a generation earlier, there'd be no doubt he'd be riding to battle beneath a lordly emblem, and I'd be proud of him. But the time for battles is done, the wars have ended. If a man wants victories now, he must win them in peace, or what passes for peace, at court."

Lucas nodded, watching the dark man closely as he

listened to him; this was no fool, this was a man he could respect.

"My brother," Strangways continued, "has come to believe in this good lady's husband's cause." He paused, being clever and cautious enough not to mention names even now, and when Lucas nodded again, he went on, "I've no quarrel with that, but as it turns out, I'd rather he passed his time wenching, gaming, and drinking, like other boys of his estate. In sooth, I believed that was what had been keeping him out late nights these last months, and accounted for the way he'd begun to slip and slide around me of late, trying to avoid my notice. We'd been close before—we're both bachelors, and live alone together in London, near St. Dunstan's, since our good parents died," he explained.

Lucas began to walk slowly along the wharfside, as much for the slight warmth that activity afforded him as for the look of it. A chance-met trio attracted less notice if they seemed to be strolling to some destination, even on such a lowering, windblown day as this. Strangways and Lady Katherine came with him, the lady between the two tall men, who leaned toward each other to speak over the top of her discreetly bowed head, though she missed not a word they said.

"He's been seeing the same men every day. He calls them friends, but some are far too old to have an interest in such an untried youth—that may have been what finally troubled me. That, and then, most definitely, this," he said, and passed a small object from the folds of his robe over to Lucas.

Lucas turned the bit of parchment in his gloved hands, as though expecting to see more than the ill-painted representation of the cross done in white and gold that was upon it.

"A youth with a religious bent—where's the harm in that?" Lucas asked.

"A religious man would carry a true cross, not oddly assorted scraps of parchment, each with the same picture on it, ready to disperse," Strangways said. "He has a dozen such in his inner pockets. And he is not religious. Though I had thought he was," he admitted, "for after I'd noted those scraps amidst a jumble of his clothes one night when he left the room where we'd been talking to

go outside to relieve himself, I saw what I took to be a
small Bible in the pocket of his discarded doublet. I
reached for it, but he saw me doing so as he came back
in, and snatched the doublet up and held it close as a
babe to his breast, and railed at me most violently, accus-
ing me of diverse nonsense to do with spying on him."

"But you were, were you not?" Lucas asked mildly.

Strangway's lean face grew red with more than the
brisk breeze that chafed at it as he said, "Not then, no.
Then it was only idle curiosity. After that, yes. Then I
was determined to see what it was that he defended from
me with such vigor. I love him well," he said as Lucas
looked at him.

"I'd a chance finally, not a week past, to look at his
'Bible,' " Strangways said with difficulty. "That night
he'd come to bed late. I think for the first time in many
months he'd acted his age, and had been drinking heavily, for he slept like the dead. I took his 'Bible' from his
pocket and carried it to my room to study it. Then I
replaced it. I dared not keep it, lest he know I'd found it.
It was no Bible, but only a little book of letters titled: 'A
B C—A Cross Row,' the sort a child at school would
have."

"And nothing more?" Lucas asked, but his voice was
deceptively idle, since his hand clenched hard around the
bit of parchment he still held.

"Oh, more," Strangways said in a voice of puzzled
sorrow. "There was a different symbol drawn in beneath
each letter, added later, I'm sure, for the book was one
of Caxton's or his ilk, and had been printed, not writ by
human hand. I didn't know what to make of it. I put it
back wondering if he'd fallen to the folly of some odd
fancy, such as unhealthy mysticism, because the only
other new thing in his room was another book: Dr.
Alcok's prognostications. That's the sort of thing he'd
have jested at a year ago. He puts no credence in such
science—he doesn't even have his future read in the stars
from time to time, as most men do. I couldn't understand
what sort of game he was at. You understand," he said,
half in apology, half in self-defense, "I'm not a man
given to light fancies. It troubled me only because it was
so childish, and yet he kept it so close."

"There's nothing childish about a code book kept by a

grown man," Lucas answered, "save for how ill it was
kept."

Something in Strangways' tense face relaxed and he
looked to Lucas with new hope.

"Yes. So I thought it might be. So I began to follow
him," he admitted, "myself, alone, to the neglect of my
own affairs. Not knowing what he'd got involved with,
but sure it was something dangerous because he was so
secret about it, I dared not trust another to it. I found
that he went divers places on different nights, but always
in the same company, and always to the same place every
Tuesday and Saturday afternoon. That was here, to the
Tower. To that one," he said, gesturing slightly with one
upraised shoulder to the place where Perkin was kept,
"where freemen are forbidden. But that is where I tracked
him to, and that is where he disappears within, for an
hour each time, I do swear it.

"The yeoman guard said I was mistaken when I asked,
and I dared not ask again. But sometimes as I waited to
see what I could, I'd see Lady Katherine lingering nearby.
I asked after her, and knowing who she was at last, and
seeing her evident sorrow, and knowing the cause of it, I
dared to speak to one of her attendants. She was told of
me, and then she deigned to speak to me, and I opened
my heart to her."

"Now, why would you do that?" Lucas asked quietly,
stopping to look hard at him.

Strangways lowered his eyes. "For my own selfish reasons, sir. And so I told her, at once. But think on it! If
my brother's acts were to do with Perkin Warbeck and
some secret cabal concerning him, I had to try to discover all, for his sake. He's a boy . . . well, he thinks as
one, for all he's a man. He has three-and-twenty sum-
mers to his name, but he's lived more in his fancies than
in this world. He was a sickly youth, and our mother—"

"Yes, yes," Lucas interrupted him, "but it's strange.
Why should you think the wife of Perkin Warbeck would
help you? Especially if it was indeed a plot concerning
her lord, and she known to love him entirely?" he asked,
too coldly for politeness, as his hand, beneath his cloak,
came to rest lightly on the pommel of the short sword at
his side. "I should think that would be like asking a

mother hen if she liked the taste of baked eggs, shouldn't you?"

"Yes," James Strangways admitted, gazing down to the top of Lady Katherine's hood, "and so, of course, I didn't ask anything like. I tried to deceive her. I admit it. I asked questions I thought were clever and roundabout. But she . . . she saw to the bottom of my heart at once," he said with a queer note of pride, "and I admitted all. I don't trust many men in this world," he said, raising his head so that Lucas could see the sincerity glittering in the depths of his dark eyes, "but I do trust this lady."

Well, and not so clever after all, Lucas thought on a suppressed sigh, since the lady would have your heart on a skewer if she thought one drop of its blood would ease her husband's thirst on a warm day. But insofar as he could trust any man, which was not so far as to ever endanger himself, he believed James Strangways. His tale had the half-finished, ill-conceived sound of something real. And Lady Katherine had brought him, and she'd do nothing to endanger her Perkin.

"I pray for my husband's release from his prison each day of my life," Lady Katherine said meekly, "but I would never counsel any man to seek it outside the law."

Strangways looked at her with pity and poorly masked adoration, and Lucas looked away so that he wouldn't gag. In, out, above, or below the law—if she'd thought she could effect Warbeck's release, she'd seek the means in the heart of hell itself. There was something else in this that had involved her, and something else again that made her turn to him now. She mightn't trust Lucas any more than he did her, but at least she knew that he didn't work toward her husband's downfall; however she knew that, he'd wager that she did.

"She said I must trust you, even though you're rumored to have the king's ear. I hesitated . . . Sir," Strangways said with decision, "I do trust you now, but if I find you've played me false . . . I'm not a knight or a man of the court, but I have funds, and my family still has some influence, and I vow I'll have vengeance if—"

"Yes, a good way to ask for my help, to threaten me," Lucas said to silence him, and then added abruptly, "Have done. Trust me, or leave me now. Ah, then," he said as he saw Strangways make up his mind and halt, abashed, "who are these men your brother meets with?"

"I know the names of several now," Strangways said eagerly. "There's Thomas Astewood, foremost. And Walter Bluett, and Edmund Carre, and John Fynche, John Audley, William Proude, and one Robert Longford . . . or Longfair, and others I haven't names for yet. But it's an odd collection of men for my brother to consort with, for some are gentlemen and some are tradesmen."

And some are king's men, and some are spies, Lucas thought, his mouth becoming dry at the mention of those he knew, now understanding why Lady Katherine would have none of the scheme from the moment she'd heard those names. Proude and Audley together? And Asterwood? This was very bad for Strangways' young brother, devastating for Warbeck, if it were true, and possibly even worse for himself.

"Don't follow them any longer," Lucas said at once. "There's danger for you as well as your brother if you do. Maintain a distance from them all—I do mean *all*—now."

He saw the stubborn set to Strangway's jaw and said angrily, "If a man is drowning in a hole in the ice, it does no good to stand at the edge of it and lend him a hand. Slow, subtle, and roundabout is the way to do it. And you've not the way of it. You've called for help; now you must trust in it. Let me nose around. Let me talk, and listen, and see. Go, now. It's not to my advantage to be seen with you here. I'll send for you if I discover anything you can do.

"But . . . Strangways," Lucas said, calling him back after he'd bowed and turned to leave them, "if you can, take your brother out of London. Now."

Lady Katherine watched Strangways' lean figure until it was out of sight. Only then did she speak again.

"It is that bad?" she asked.

"Is it?" he asked as answer.

"God's grace! I would not ask if I knew!" she said angrily. In her agitation, in her desire to protect her Perkin, her life, she became the grand lady she'd been before she'd married him, the lady who knew how to treat men who'd displeased her. Seeing her so pleased

Lucas. Because he didn't know what he distrusted more: her helplessness or her charm.

"If they seek to free him without the king's writ, it is madness," she said, "or else a trap for him. Only some few have ever escaped imprisonment here, and those, more legend than reality, I think. No. It cannot work, it cannot do anything but endanger him . . . can it?"

If nothing else convinced him of her honesty in this, that did.

"No, it cannot," he said, "not if even an innocent like James Strangways has discovered it, no."

"But my Richard . . . Lucas, he doesn't believe there's harm in it. Yes," she said, and there may have been real tears glinting in her eyes as she looked up to him, "he spoke of it to me. But with glee. With anticipation. He wouldn't hear my fears about it. He . . ." She paused to take a deep breath. "He is not the same man he was when he went into that terrible place," she admitted.

"No," he agreed, "he's not. So then it is up to us to protect him. And ourselves. Because, lady, he doesn't know what he does now."

"He is not mad!" she whispered harshly. "Only . . . changed. But time away from here, time outside this place, would change him back again, I know it would."

He fell silent, thinking of those things that might not change, as she said, in eerie countermeasure to his thoughts, "His arm . . . his leg—they . . . they will return to normal once again . . . with care, will they not? I didn't want to ask him. But I noted it and worry about it. He was so perfect, it may be that even heaven envied such perfection. . . . There's damage there, he cannot hide it from me, but I can hardly ask a physician's opinion, can I? These things, they will heal, will they not?"

"Oh, well-a-day, they may," he lied as he wondered now if anything about the pretender that had been so changed in his captivity could return to its previous shape again.

"For now, I think a trip out of London would do for you as well," he said as they walked back to where her two ladies were awaiting her, standing by the water gate, their cloaks and gowns billowing in the wind above their slender legs, like two colorful galleys about to set sail.

"These are delicate times. If the house falls," he said severely, "all beneath its roof will be crushed."

"I'll not leave him if I can help it," she insisted. "You will help us?" she asked.

"Yes," he said, because he was expected to.

But then she surprised him.

"Why?" she asked, and then frowned, knowing it was the wrong thing to ask, however much she wanted to know the answer.

But as he wouldn't know that himself until he knew the answer he sought of Perkin Warbeck, he only said what he knew she'd understand.

"For my own reasons, lady," he said.

And having been raised in a royal house, and knowing Henry's court as well, she was content—at least enough to let the matter lie.

"Megan, my child," Lady Katherine said when they came abreast of her two handmaidens, "I'm to my friend Mistress Robins for a visit and a concoction of her sweet herb liquor, since the wind bites so shrewdly. Clarisse shall come with me. You may join me later. I believe Lucas Lovat wants a word with you."

The lady and her one lady-in-waiting walked away, leaving Megan standing staring after them like a woman who sees her ship sinking as she clings to a spar in the sea.

"Ill-done of her," Lucas commented. "Or was it?" he asked, staring down at her with unreadable eyes. "Are you supposed to be my reward for a task done well, or a promissory note for a future one, I wonder? Come, lady, will you come with me to my bed now, or only to a few minutes in a shadow as a promise of what comes later if I continue to be good?"

She was beyond hurt, it seemed. She didn't fight. But her face was pale and her eyes were bleak.

He stood before her, tall, solid, and yet deceptively light, and with the light behind him she couldn't see his face. His hands were at his hips, so that his cloak flowed to form a dark wedge from his shoulders to his boot tops. He blocked the wind and the sun from her, and there was no way she could turn from him. Neither did she try.

"I've no part in this," she said wearily. "I've no idea

what she meant. I do not know, I'm not used to being currency."

But she might as well have shrieked "Help me!" because he saw it in her face and was ashamed.

He walked with her, slowly and silently, in Lady Katherine's wake, until they came to apartments where her friend Mistress Robins lived. Then he took Megan into the dim entryway, and took her into his arms, and held her close against himself for her warmth and for his apology, for only a moment before putting her aside with a deep sigh.

"It's as well," he breathed as he touched his lips to her forehead, "because I don't accept payment in such coin anyway."

At that moment, it was difficult to know which of them regretted it more.

They were alone, and yet Lucas couldn't communicate as he needed to with Perkin. It wasn't just because he doubted the security of anything said in this chamber. The walls looked thick enough, indeed, the windows were cut to a depth of a man's whole arm. Yet he knew it took only a chink in the stone of a wall for a man to listen and look through, and the walls everywhere in this compound were said to be catacombed with passageways, places where a carefully placed misplaced stone could make everything apparent to a hidden spy—and God knew, Lucas knew from very personal experience, Henry had enough of those. Still, a clever man could say and hear a great many things in plain sight that another man mightn't understand. But it was possible that he couldn't make himself understood to Perkin Warbeck any longer, however secret, dark, and private their meeting place was.

Because Perkin had changed and was altering more with every day.

"She frets about you. Your lady is deeply concerned," Lucas said more slowly than a moment before, because there was always the slim possibility that Perkin hadn't heard right the first time.

Perkin grew an indulgent smile to replace the faraway look he'd worn. "Such is Woman," he said sagely in his deep rich voice.

"She's rather more than that," Lucas insisted. "She's as clever as beautiful, which is to say a great deal. There are rumors that you meet with misguided men, and it disturbs her, as well it might. There's no escape from this place," he said, not bothering to lower his voice, since it was only plain truth he spoke.

"Truth cannot be hidden; it cries out from the very bowels of the earth to be heard," Perkin answered, his face aglow, his eyes brilliant with a light Lucas could not like.

"That's a sweet metaphor, and it well may be," Lucas said patiently, "but truth can't be drawn and quartered and have its head mounted on a pike, as can happen to the man who dares to speak it too loudly. It's not an easy ending," he went on in a bored monotone, because he dared not stress the words he spoke. "They hang the fellow to near-unconsciousness and then cut him down. When he's revived and opens his eyes in gratitude, they open his belly from his chest down, in one long knife stroke. Then they catch his guts as they tumble out, and toss them into a waiting fire, and if he is still aware enough to watch—and they do hope he is—he can see them burn before they quarter him into four rough parts like a roasted fowl, to show in all directions to the cheering throng. Sometimes they take his privy parts off separately, if they're in a sportive mood. And only then, as a reward for being so entertaining, he may have the pleasure of having his head lifted off, at long last. It's the approved end for traitors, not a seemly way to leave this earth, and never one a man would wish to treat his beloved to. Before God," Lucas whispered harshly, "if there's truth to these rumors, leave off, man! Henry's games are deep and cold, and no man who plays them with him can doubt the winning of them."

Now the tall golden gentleman did look disturbed. He placed a hand on Lucas' shoulder and said gravely, "Rest easy, my friend. No man can be sure of his ending, that's true, but although, yes, even kings have been called traitors in their time"—he smiled sadly—"such horrors are for common traitors, common men. There's honor among kings, at least. Should royalty come to grief, it only knows the clean chop of the ax upon its neck."

"He doesn't admit you're a king," Lucas said in frustration, running a hand through his hair as he paced away again. "If he decides to end your life, he'll never give you the honors of a king. He can't, and won't."

"Just so. If he ends my life, he as much as admits I am king," Perkin said with the same logic he'd used throughout the conversation. "Why murder a pretender? Lambert Simnel lives, does he not? To kill a pretender is to give him credence. Nay, he dares not acknowledge me, even by death. My shackles have been struck off long since, not my head." He chuckled. "Don't worry, my Lucas," he said, smiling again, smiling as he had all day.

"God knows why I do!" Lucas muttered to himself.

But that, of all the things Lucas had said this day, Perkin did hear and respond to.

"Because you have a bond with me, and you know it," Perkin said wisely.

Lucas froze. He tilted his head toward Perkin, and they stood so, two tall fair men, one wheaten-haired, lean, and tense, the other golden-haired, relaxed, even his outlines slightly blurred as if by too much good living, although it was confinement, not luxury, that had done it. But there was something else that echoed between them that wasn't in their faces, forms, or words. Or so, at least, Lucas thought in that moment.

"What? What is it?" he whispered, waiting.

Perkin laid a finger aside his nose and winked. And grinned, as Lucas' face paled.

"I . . . I speak to you as a brother might," Lucas said into the silence, at last, although it seemed his heart stopped beating after he said the words that had spilled from him, terrifying as much as easing his heart, but there was no response from Perkin, so he went on. "I've heard names. Some of these men are not your friends. Believe me."

"Oh, I do—believe you've heard that," Perkin answered slyly, "but just as some of those who seem to be my friends may not be, so also some of those who seem to be my enemies may be my friends. Things may not be as they seem, eh, Lucas, my friend?" he said, and smiled again. And for all his words were banal and foolish, yet still there was enough truth in them, and seemed to be such double meaning behind them, as well as in Perkin's voice and expression, that Lucas could only stare at him, hoping he'd say more.

Perkin smiled. He smiled too much these days, Lucas thought; it was as though he were feeding on some wonderful secret jest that bubbled up from time to time to light his eyes, even when he was at his most sincere. That sincerity itself was too much a parody of itself to be taken in earnest now. He was abstracted half the time he was spoken to, and the other half it seemed he listened too closely to words that weren't said. His dragging foot and dead arm emphasized the damage done to him, and the sudden glittering smile he sometimes wore was frightening to see. Whatever brief return to himself he'd had when Lady Katherine had visited with him was gone with her, and over when she'd left. There was no reason to believe him entirely sane now.

Yet, from time to time there was something in his voice and face that transcended sanity, to imprint itself on the heart of the man he spoke with. All his power, and it had been considerable, was condensed now, even as his world had been. Even though Lucas believed nothing about Perkin Warbeck now, and knew very well that God gave, even as he took, since madmen could look deeper into the human heart than other men could, he couldn't shake himself free of him—or of the absurd notion that somewhere in that majestic wreckage there was the heart of a prince, and so, the spirit of his lost brother. Especially when he was being deliberately cryptic, as now.

"Lucas, Lucas," Perkin said reproachfully, "believe in what you feel, not what you know, and you will be well."

"What do I know?" Lucas asked, and fell still, lest he ask the unaskable question.

Because for all he was seduced in Perkin's presence, for all that the weight of his secret was becoming more intolerable since he'd come back to the Tower and been forced to remember all he'd never forgotten, he'd been hunted for too many years to walk into the net now, whatever the bait. He'd the habit of secrecy long before he'd this urge to divulge what he'd never told another living soul. He'd never spoken the truth about himself aloud. Those few who knew him had always known him.

But still, as he looked into Perkin's considering eyes, he wondered . . .

"What is it, my Lucas?" Perkin asked gently.

If he'd said, "What is it, my Edward?", there would have been no holding back. As it was, Lucas took an involuntary step forward. But then, if he'd said "my Edward," it would have been the answer, not a question.

Lucas had no time to do more than think about how to phrase his answer as another question. Because the door swung open, and the gray shadow on the threshold was like the figure of Destiny himself, standing waiting for them both. Except he'd a Bible, not an hourglass and scythe, at the end of his long-sleeved arms, where a man would have hands.

"Brother Robert!" Perkin said with delight, recognizing the darkness beneath the cowl as easily as other men might know a face. "Well met! This is my friend Lucas Lovat. Have you met? I believe so. But I thought to look for you at a later hour. You come with the dusk most days, do you not?"

Lucas watched the hooded figure carefully. Henry knew he'd bought entry here, but was it supposed to be such a commonplace that his monk could be admitted while another was within Perkin's chamber, and there was no explanation or excuse given for it?

"I come from a death, and so I come early today," Brother Robert said in a clear, cool voice before he turned his cowl toward Lucas and then back to Perkin and chided him, "If your keepers have no care as to whom they give entry, you should have, my brother. I come to see to your soul, and God's word, not gold, is my key to your cell."

"And Lucas gives me word of the world. Now, where's harm in that?" Perkin asked jovially.

When the monk didn't answer, Lucas did.

"And the world calls me again. Good-bye, Master Warbeck, give you good day, brother," he said, and on a flourish and a bow he left by the door that the red-faced guard still held open.

When it had closed, he dropped a coin in the guard's callused hand, and when it remained outstretched, another. But after they struck the great oak door to the Earl of Warwick's adjoining cell, it opened only a fraction and the soft trembling voice within called out, "No, no, not today, come back tomorrow, perhaps, or the day after," before it fell still and the door snicked shut in their faces.

Lucas was pleased to be refused, because now he'd no reason to tarry. He visited Perkin so as to be sure there was no doubt about the impossibility of his claim. But he'd begun to visit with his cousin, the earl, for the same reason he supposed the monk gave Perkin for his visits: to give comfort. Because it seemed the earl enjoyed his company. And because since they'd met he couldn't forget the boy he'd been when they'd all been young, so long ago. If he'd neither scepter nor throne, Lucas thought ruefully as he walked back to where Philip de Lacey awaited him, still he'd some few responsibilities to family left. He knew that for a lie as he thought it, since he did derive a sort of pleasure from seeing his cousin, if only that of being with blood of his blood—as he assumed the earl did from seeing someone who neither scoffed at him nor urged him to freedom, treason, or terror.

But the queen was blood of his blood too, Lucas thought, and sister was closer than cousin—closer than mother or father's blood, being of both. And he felt nothing when he saw her, save for anger and pity and loss. Prince Arthur, the boy Prince Henry, and their sisters were blood to him too, and he felt only sick shame at his envy of them, and fear for their future if he should somehow, by some miracle, supplant them—as well as horror at how effectively their continued existence was killing off all his chances. And the proposed culmination of the match between Prince Arthur and Spain's princess, Katherine of Aragon—what would the marriage in life, and not just proxy, finally bring, if and when it came? His sister bred like a barn cat for Henry, and now her son was coming to the age when he could sow heirs too? Then how many more of his blood would be standing between him and his rightful throne? And when could he claim it? And how, if Perkin Warbeck still lived? Even if he was not his brother. . . .

Philip looked hurt because Lucas was curt with his questions about his health when they met again. He was more wounded when he was then ignored by a distracted and absentminded Lucas as they rode all the way back to Westminster.

Two notes awaited Lucas when he got back to his room. One was from his king and the other from his father. He read the one from his father first, and read it twice, to get the second message that was only for his eyes. Because for all it spoke of the harvest and the weather and his mother's health, for those who knew what letters to stress and which to ignore, it said only, again and again: Danger, Danger, Danger. And: Why do you tarry?

To try to discover if he is my brother, Lucas thought as answer, dropping to sit on the edge of his bed with his head in his hands, as he puzzled out the question over and again. His brother, Richard, was dead, long since, of the smallpox. Perkin Warbeck was a pretender and half-mad, if not entirely so, by now—as well as half-dead, and soon, no doubt, to be entirely so. And smooth-skinned as he was smooth-tongued. And so never his brother, Richard; Richard had died of the pox. He knew these things. And yet, and yet . . . What, after all, did he really know? They'd always lied to him, as he had done to all men, since that night he'd lost his brother—or the night they told him that he had.

He had to leave this place; that much he knew. He'd left many another, far better, in his lifetime. He'd actually stayed on in very few, anywhere, and seldom for very long. But now, suddenly, he didn't know how to go; he'd lost the art of leaving. After a long while, as the autumn afternoon began to darken, he plucked up the second letter and read it, and breathed a great sigh of relief, because now he knew how he could go. Because he had to. He was summoned, with the court, to the palace at Greenwich.

He was summoned to Henry's largest country home to celebrate the autumn, under guise of celebrating harvest home. To revel and frolic and sing and dance. To be entertained, and be entertaining in turn. To see pageant and plays and hear music and singing. To try knightly arts: to ride at the ring, to play at tournament and joust and melee. To have courtly and country pastimes: to sport with swords and cudgels, at football, archery, and wrestling; to hawk and hunt. To try some gentler arts as

well: to court and woo and make love or have sex—
whichever a man desired; to dine and drink and take
whatever pleasures a king's palace afforded. And most of
all and best of all, Lucas thought as he lay back on his
bed and closed his eyes in gratitude: to leave this place.

Her knees hurt. She usually didn't feel pain from the
cold stone beneath her when she was at prayer, but
they'd remained so for so long now that even the small
pillow beneath Megan's knees was no proof against the
unrelenting stone of the great cathedral's floor. Her lady
stayed in prayer, and so, then, must she. And it might
have been, she thought guiltily, that she felt the cold and
pain of it so acutely this time because her prayers did not
uplift her. They were too selfish for that.

Because this time she didn't pray so much for her lady
or her husband, Perkin, as for herself. And she couldn't
tell if her prayers were to be free of Lucas Lovat, or to
be with him, and she knew that hindered their being
granted as much as it had their being composed. More
than her legs were weary and more than her knees were
aching when at last she arose with her lady.

But God worked in mysterious ways; she never doubted
it. Because when they returned to her lady's chamber
and read the summons they'd been left, it seemed he'd
answered all her prayers at once and together, all at a
stroke. Because they were summoned to Greenwich for a
holiday. It was selfish to rejoice even as her mistress
blanched, thinking of the separation from the vicinity of
her beloved that she must endure.

But Megan couldn't help rejoicing. She was so grateful
that they were to be gone from this place now, she
couldn't help but send a silent prayer of thanks. Because,
she thought with profoundest gratitude, that meant they'd
be gone from all her own problems—gone and got
cleanly away, and just in time too.

17

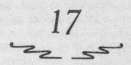

"They say that the new towers at Sheen are like those in Araby—such as my father saw when he went on pilgrimage, great rounded turrets with gilded vanes—there must be a half-dozen of them, they say," the well-dressed gentleman said with conviction.

"Nay, I've seen it with mine own eyes," another man in the circle of courtiers and knights protested, interrupting, "there are an even dozen already in place, and they do say there will be a dozen more . . . and windows! Such a quantity of windows there are! So many already in place that the sun will shine in every room from dawn to dusk, and they do say there will be even more put in, so that the wall paintings will be seen clear from day to night— and mayhap even by moonlight or starlight, there will be so many windows!"

No one of the assembled company of men that stood chatting in the great hall laughed at the rumor of such lavish use of glass. Because when it was done being rebuilt after the disastrous fire that had leveled it the year past at Christmastide, the splendor of Sheen, Henry's favorite palace, would be considerable—even under construction, it was already legendary.

The gentlemen guests stood on the bright painted floor of the great hall at Greenwich Palace, beneath a high gilded ceiling, surrounded by walls draped with rich and complex tapestries, beside a hearth that could hold a prize ox and his sire, and yet they spoke of nothing but the wonders of the palace that would be. But that was their way with all their pleasures; none was as profound as the one they had not yet experienced. That was the way of the ladies and gentlemen of all courts, from Florence to Paris to London, Lucas thought bemusedly: success led to excess, which bred more exotic longings. Only simplicity ensured satiety, or so it seemed, since a peasant seemed as pleased with this day's crust of bread as he was with yesterday's. But then, for all his travels, how could he be sure of that? Who knew what a peasant really thought? Not even the priests did, he suspected, since it was his experience that they only knew what they wanted men to think.

"I do hear," Philip de Lacy said eagerly, "that Henry often stays at the small manor at Hampton Court in spite of all inconvenience—for it's a cramped place fit only for the Knights Hospitalers who bide there—just so that he can be near to Sheen to watch how it rises from the ashes. He spends a fortune on it, and spares no expense for the look and luxury of it. Why, I hear the chapel alone will be a wondrous thing to see. When it's all done, it will be the greatest legacy he leaves to England, and he knows it. Or so they all do say," he added in a smaller voice, seeing Lucas' tilted grin.

"Be sure to add 'architectural' to that 'greatest legacy' bit," Lucas said softly, "if you want to keep a place to put your hat snug on your shoulders, lad. Kings don't tend to think in terms of brick and stone when they think of legacies for the future—unless they're of the ancient Egyptian sort—or so they do say," he said on a mocking smile. "No, it's the flimsier monuments of paper and ink and flesh and blood they're most concerned with. For all Henry loves Sheen, he'd burn it to the ground again in a moment if it would ensure Arthur's successful kingship in his time, and every law he puts his name to suits that purpose as well."

"You presume to know a great deal about kings, fellow!" a heavyset knight who'd overheard him said in badgering tones.

"Ah, tournament time, and the stallions are getting testy, are they?" Lucas said in an aside to Philip before he addressed the belligerent knight directly, saying more gently, "Put by your ax, my friend, I only speak in conjecture, the way you all do of Sheen. And as to that, why, I hear the courtyard there is to be of a size to make it possible to hold a grand melee without so much as an elbow or a fetlock being jostled by a neighbor as the knights ride in to set up side by side."

"Ah!" the knight said with pleasure. "There's happy news! The fields get too muddy for my taste. Give me a stone surface for combat. The courtyard here is well enough, but we were packed so close last year, I found it hard to hold my horse until the trumpets were blown— remember, John?" he asked another man.

"Not I!" the man he addressed said heartily. "I'm not fool enough for the melee: sitting your horse in a pack, packed in an enclosure with dozens of other fellows, with only your horse, banner, and cudgel to call your own, and then turning on your fellow knight when the trumpet sounds, to see who's still up when it sounds again? God's wounds, George! You and I are too long in the tooth for the melee—ah, but there was that widow you were trying to impress, wasn't there? Marry, there's better things to keep up to impress a wench, sir! Aye, a good thing you settled on Harry Bayne's daughter—another melee and we'd have been drinking at the side of your bier and not your wedding bed, I'd warrant," he said as the other men laughed and his friend's wind-roughened face turned a duller red.

"No, no," he went on, clapping his friend on the back to show he meant no insult, "the melee's got no art. All that indiscriminate pushing and shoving belongs in a marriage bed, not on a field of honor. No," he continued over renewed laughter, "I leave that to the young bucks. But the joust! Now, that's my meat. I've a new helmet this year," he said with a smirk, "the likes of which I'll warrant you've not seen. Straight from Flanders, and cost me a ducat or two. But the design! Forget about how finely chased it is—and it is—but that's not the half of it. Close it, and it fits like a clam shell, tight and true. Nothing can get through, but there's vents slim as fish gills at the side for air, and you can hear with it on too!"

"It sounds fair enough," his friend replied, all embarrassment forgotten, as he bragged, "But wait until you cast your eyes upon my new German helm! Flat as a pancake on the top, I vow it! And yet with an opening at the top to let in enough air to give you breath for a week. But nothing else aside from God's own gentle rain from heaven can get in up there—unless you meet up with a

giant knight on a ten-foot war-horse and he leans down
to spit on you!" He chuckled.

"Ha! For my money, there's nothing like good Greenwich armor, for all the foreign experiments. My helm has
hinges that slide smooth as silk, and I know many a
fellow with Italian fittings that catch when you most need
them to move easily, and then shriek like cats swiving
when they do," another knight proclaimed.

"There is nothing like an English heaume," another
knight agreed, as still others chimed in with claims about
the superiority of their own equipment. Soon the air was
filled with loud talk about greaves and cuisses, coudieres
and gauntlets, plain and ornamented paldrons and genou-
illieres, knee guards and neck pieces, breast- and backplates,
and a small contingent of men were arguing heatedly
about the relative merits of the new longer chain-mail
skirts that many knights now favored.

Lucas stepped away.

"They've grown more tedious—if possible," he whispered to Philip, "since Henry forbade them their own
private armies. Though, so far as I can see, their conversation is the most dangerous thing about them. They can
slay a man with their babble faster than with their lances.
I've heard them arguing for hours about the finest details
of joints and greaves, until my head ached as though
they'd assaulted me with their lances and not just their
tongues. God protect me from the talk of knights and
their armor! It's worse than the prattle of women about
their confinements," he said confidingly, "since at least
an observant fellow can glean some interesting tidbits
when the conversation gets down to particulars there.
Although," he said, smiling, "I will admit that sort of
talk gets more gory."

Philip's fair face flushed.

"Oh," Lucas said, remembering, honestly contrite, "how
does your lady wife?"

"Well, she does well—that is to say, passing fair. She
says. But her time is coming and I . . ." Philip paused,
and then said in a rush, "She's only had her sixteenth
birthday yesterweek, and my last wife never lived to give
me my heir."

"Don't worry, lad," Lucas said softly. "We all came
here down the same road, didn't we? Treat her gently,

feed her regularly, insist that you love her despite how she looks, and keep her from the quacks, and I'll warrant she'll do well enough to present you with a fine heir and live to horrify the other ladies with the talk of it for years to come. Come, come," he said more seriously. "There's risks to it, of course. As there are for any devoutly hoped-for joy. Just so. For the joys of it, I hear, outweigh the dangers, if the lady loves you well. And from your talk of her, I think she must. Then never fret. We get women with our children at our pleasure, and then leave them to deliver them to us at their discomfort and pain . . . that's true enough. But we didn't invent the process—few men are so cruel."

Philip looked at Lucas with horror, preventing himself from crossing himself only at the last moment, for his hand stopped as it rose to his forehead.

"Not blasphemy," Lucas said. "I always quarrel with him. Still, it's as well I don't live in Spain, eh? You're right, I'll stop. Both the getting of children and the philosophizing about it are things a man ought not to do in public, are they not?"

"Have you any children?" Philip asked, before he remembered it was not the sort of thing he should have asked, for though he sometimes considered Lucas a friend, the man was older, wiser, and both more dangerous and more noble than himself. And, too, he could scarcely call a man he was ordered to spy upon a friend, for all that Lucas Lovat's charm and easy ways so often made him both regret and forget that essential fact.

"I? Have a child? And I unmarried? How is that possible?" Lucas asked with such outsize astonishment that Philip had to laugh.

"No, no," Lucas went on to say more seriously, "none I know of. Bastards can be the very devil. My father, especially, disliked the idea of me lumbered with one, and as I value him, I'm careful . . . most careful in all sorts of ways," he said quietly, thoughtfully. "I've become adept at noting times and tides, and if I'm not sure of the phases of the moon—say, if it's a cloudy night, or a new or devious wench I'm at—why, then, I'm equally adroit at making myself leave just when it's generally considered the best moment to stay." He grimaced.

"And at that," Lucas mused, "I seldom stay in any one

place too long in other ways as well. So it may be that if I
do have one or two nameless innocents to my discredit,
I'd not know it anyway. And, too, given the sort of
woman I usually favor, if one whelped, it would be as
hard for her as it would be for me to know whose litter it
was. I am not terribly discriminate," he explained, and
for once there was more sadness than irony apparent in
his slight mocking smile, "or at least I did not use to be,"
he added as if to himself as he looked across the room—
as he'd done since he'd entered it—to where Megan
Baswell stood with her lady.

The entertainment was as lavish as the many courses
set before the company this gala night. Henry might be
famous for being frugal, but it was more of a jest than a
reality; at least, in the maintenance of his court it was. It
might well be that he winced as he paid out his gold, but
he knew only too well how much gilding suited a crown—
especially a disputed one. But his was not the face of a
generous man. He sat at his high table with the same
dour, ironic expression that he might wear at a trial, and
oversaw the festivities, watching his guests as though he
were counting their smiles as coin paid for the feast.

The courses were borne out by scarlet-and-gold-clad
yeomen of the guard, and presented with the flourish of
horns and the thunder of kettledrums. This night, not
only the king studied his food before he ate it. He waited
to dine until others could taste his food first, as usual, but
tonight his company paused too. Because whatever was
to be eaten this night had been dressed so as to be
praised for its beauty first.

Peacocks roasted and refeathered stood with fanned
tails in proud array, fowls dressed as fighting cocks seemed
to fight in their platters for the honor of being first
consumed by the company; there were miniature galleons
full of fresh-caught fish as lifeless yet lifelike as the tubs
of prawns goggling at the company with bulging black
boiled eyes; venison came with antlers rampant, geese
trailed dishes of sauced goslings in their wake, whole
lambs crouched on parslied platters as if they'd only
taken off their fleece because of the heat of the ovens
they'd lately come from, and pigs smiled through their

roasted apples, squinting glazed-eyed at the diners they were presented to.

Lucas ate sparingly, distracted, but not, it seemed, by the splendor of the feast.

"I don't care to be enticed by the semblance of life in the dead meat I am to eat," he answered absently to Lady Katherine's query about his flagging appetite.

But seeing her white shoulders leap at his words, he said more softly and with apology, "Forgive my churlishness, my lady. In truth, I'm as red-toothed as the rest of the company, it's only that I've never liked to make friends with my meal before I partake of it. It seems, somehow, ungrateful," he sighed, eyeing a smirking suckling pig with evident dismay, and so winning her laughter as the forgiveness he'd sought.

The other entertainments seemed to afford him more delight. He gave full attention to the fire-eaters and dancers, the singers and jugglers, the music of cittern and lute, virginal and flute; the performances of dancing bears and puppets, acrobats and minstrels and charlatans of every kind. And yet, through all, from the side of his light and lucent eyes, he missed nothing of the sight of Megan Baswell where she sat at the end of his table. Tonight she dined with her lady, if not by her. So it was not at all difficult for a man to catch sight of her while he appeared to be watching the entertainment. Although, God knew, he thought, she was spectacle enough in and of herself tonight—aside from the fact that she'd discovered him watching her, and so was passing the time in a charade of unconcern which pleased him the more because of how unsuccessful it was.

Each time she caught him gazing at her, she looked away. But as she couldn't help but peek every few minutes to see if he was still looking, she turned away often. And then back again. As the evening wore on, he was enchanted to find that laughter sat upon her lips as often as dismay had before she'd discovered the game they were playing. Tonight she was got up in a gown of rare design, made of rose silk and velvet brocade, spiced with gold in its intricate patternings. The long, wide, and full sleeves that drooped to the level of her knees were trimmed with rich black fur, as was the hem of the bell-shaped skirt. She wore a golden trinket at her breast, and the

gabled hood that framed her averted face was studded
with lesser jewels. The only fault he could find with her
costume was that her silken soft brown hair was hidden,
as were her eyes now, from his view.

"I entreated Henry to gift my ladies with new
gowns," Lady Katherine said, "and am most pleased
with the result. Isn't Clarisse lovely in her amber velvet?
Such a flattering color for her, don't you agree?"

He gave her a grin for answer to her jest.

"Indeed," he said, "but now, what sort of accessory is
that reddish hulk of a thing at my Lady Megan's elbow?
A new sort of handbag or purse? No, far too bulky for
that, but it never leaves her side."

Lady Katherine stared down the table at Megan's companion, the russet-clad Matthew Lorrilard.

"A purse? He'd prefer to be a girdle round her waist
or a chain at her breast, I think. But," she said simply, as
though there were nothing in her words but jest, "I see
your point and admire your taste. If you don't think he
complements my lady's new costume, why, then, I think
I can arrange to separate him from her this night."

Lucas paused. "Thank you, my lady," he said gently.
"No need to trouble yourself. I'll tend to it myself, it
being the sort of surgery I pride myself on performing."

It was a difficult thing said gracefully, and Lady Katherine's admiration was as clear as her relief.

"You look very well tonight yourself," she said. "Italian,
is that? It suits you," she commented, eyeing the richly
brocaded square-necked undershirt he wore beneath his
blue tunic, and then glancing away so he would understand it was not his bare smooth strong neck she was
studying.

There was no need for that; he knew she saw other
men only as gates to the one man she always held in her
mind's eye. So he only nodded, sipped at his cup, and
waited for the moment when dining would be done and
he'd be freed to pursue that which he beheld so clear
before him. Ordered to rest here, so far from London
that he could begin to forget it, he meant to make the
most of it. This respite was, after all, a holiday.

When dinner was done at long last, he excused himself
from Lady Katherine, arose, and made his way toward
the lady he'd been playing such amusing eye games with

all night, as well as all those more interesting games he'd played in his imagination with her since they'd met. She wasn't very far away, but he was stopped once by a question about France from a man of business, and then again by a query about nonsense from a lady of more nefarious business. By the time he'd dispatched them both, he found Megan already engaged in conversation, the portly Matthew effectively cut out of it, because her interest was entirely taken up by royalty. If it had been the king, Lucas would have waited, theatrically, until he was noticed, and then would have found an easy word, a timely jest, with which to cut in. But he hesitated when he saw it was worse than that, for him. For Megan was talking with a king's son: Prince Arthur.

And Arthur, as Lucas never forgot, was his nephew, his supplanter, his born enemy, and, because of nature's jest, a reminder of all that was lost and dearly beloved to him. The young prince had the look of his grandfather, Royal Edward, in his bright eyes and determined chin, and his skin was as pure and fair. But it wasn't that—sooth, Lucas thought, he'd be a melancholic if he despaired at every young man who resembled his profligate father. No, it was closer than that. Although there was that in the thinned line of Arthur's mouth and the gray of his eyes that hinted at his father, Henry Tudor—the young prince's grace and carriage, even the tilt of his head was as familiar to Lucas as the image that had gazed back at him from his own glass all those years ago. Yes, and Arthur was the exact age now that he himself had been when all that Arthur had now had been snatched away from him. Which was only one of the reasons why he'd never conversed with him before.

But tonight he was reckless, tonight he was trying to forget what lay back at the Tower in London, tonight all his concentration was focused on what lay before him here. Tonight he was on holiday.

The prince's alert eyes left Lady Megan's face and he colored slightly, alarmed and delighted, as Lucas neared her. She was not so distracted that she missed seeing the young prince's interest.

"Your royal highness," Megan said, "allow me to present Lucas Lovat. He is lately come from Italy, and France."

"Not so lately, surely," Arthur said in his clear light

voice. "I saw you at Westminster not long ago . . . and 'ere that, last year, right here at Greenwich too, did I not?"

"Ah, I see I must not play cards with you, your highness," Lucas answered, and noted from the slight flush on those beardless cheeks that the prince was pleased at the compliment. "It's true. But between those two times, I was abroad."

"You haven't the sort of face one forgets," Arthur said, and then, for fear that the elegant gentleman would think him flattering to some purpose other than conversation, added quickly, "I remember things, but it serves only my own amusement. I don't wager," he admitted, shrugging his slight shoulders. "I find no joy in it. They say that it's my father's blood in me," he added with a boyish grin, "because we're not famous for wasting our pennies, are we?"

"Ah, but your grandfather was noted for the opposite," Lucas said.

"On which side?" Arthur asked mischievously. "I think the Welshman in me holds sway—the game is never so much fun as the losing is painful. I become so angry—at myself—when I lose a wager that I think it best not to wager at all. No one likes to lose to a man who sulks. How much worse for them if it's their prince who sulks. They say there's an art to losing, and that it only takes years to acquire, but I'm thirteen, sir, and there are too many other fine arts I'd rather have the knack of . . ."

He looked at Megan, and then at Lucas, and for all he was a remarkably sophisticated youth, now he looked so uneasy he looked every month his age. Lucas wondered if his remark was the prelude to an advance to Megan—which would certainly be his Plantagenet grandfather's heritage asserting itself, and would complicate matters badly—when he spoke again, low and hastily.

"They also say that you're a master at tilting at the quintain, sir," Arthur said. "I hear you seldom lose. There's to be riding at the tilt in the tourney. I wondered if you'd mind showing me your way of it sometime before then. If you could, that is to say. I've no taste for the joust or the melee, though I do it, of course. I enjoy tennis, as my father does, and country games like football and a bit of wrestling—but I've an especial liking for the quintain, so I wondered . . ."

"Of course," Lucas said calmly. "It may be a case of your body's own wisdom that you prefer it. Slight fellows excel where their more beefy companions fail at it. It's not that you don't need strength, but it's a matter of timing and dexterity rather than brawn and perseverance. I find it as witty as chess and just as shrewd, although," he said ruefully, "if you make a wrong move with your knight on the board, you don't find yourself unhorsed and with a sore head. I'm honored, and will be pleased to show you what I know."

Arthur's thin face was alight, but the glow faded as Lucas added, "Ah . . . but if I could have but one boon in return?"

It was a measure of his training that Arthur didn't show his disappointment, but his lean face looked more like his father's in that moment, until Lucas spoke again.

"I heard that song you sang for your parents the last time I was here—the one to do with the girl in the green valley. I hadn't heard it before, or since. Do you think you might teach me the way of it? It wouldn't take long—I'm quick enough if you show me the fingering on the lute, and the words will fall to the tune if I hear them again."

"I wrote that one!" Arthur said with pleasure and shy delight. "I'd be pleased. But not tonight. Because I'm promised to my lords Rackham and Dover now. And not tomorrow, because I must practice for the tourney. But soon, I promise. Will you be at practice tomorrow morning?"

"Well-a-day," Lucas said thoughtfully, "I seldom practice at anything in public, it not being wise to show all your skill before the final test. But I think that if you'd like to see my method, it might be best to do it when there weren't so many other aspirants about. Mayhap about noon, while all the rest are readying for their afternoon meal?"

"Oh, yes!" Arthur said, and stood grinning, before he remembered again that he was awaited elsewhere. He took Megan's hand to show he had not quite forgotten her entirely, smiled at Lucas, and then left them both.

"*Not* like his grandfather Royal Edward," Lucas said,

shaking his head. "No, that fellow would never ignore a lovely lady."

"He's not like his father either," Megan said. "He's more a scholar, even now."

"Is that what Tudor and Plantagenet produce together? Hot blood and cold sense combine to create cool scholarship?" Lucas asked, watching the slight young prince disappear into a crowd of courtiers and willing cynicism into his voice and thoughts so as to dispel the disquieting sense of kinship he'd experienced with Arthur.

"There'd be nothing wrong with a scholar king," Megan said at once, "and at that . . ." She paused, her head tilted to one side. "We almost had one once before. Now I remember that other young prince—Edward, he was just such a studious youth. But that doesn't mean he would have been a weak king. From what I recall now, from when I was so young, he was as strong as he was comely, for all he was yet slight of body. My father used to say he'd the look of his father, as well as his joy of life, along with the calculating mind of his mother's Woodville relatives. There was much hope for him, even though he was known to be a prodigious scholar. Yes . . . and Arthur," she said musingly, her brown eyes unfocused as she looked past Lucas into some deeper past, "has the look of him, do you know?"

"Indeed?" Lucas asked, raising one brow. "I think not. The lad's slender, but no skeleton, and as Prince Edward is dead and buried this decade and more past, that's hardly a compliment. What if he heard you?"

"What if he did?" she asked, amazed.

"Well-a-day, to compare him to a dead prince, and one he has, through no fault of his own, supplanted, is hardly the way to his heart. You must leave off uncomfortable comparisons if you seek to please princes."

"I don't seek to please princes," she said, puzzled. "He's a nice boy for all he's a prince."

"Oh," Lucas said, at his most sanguine, "I thought you sought more—you were twinkling up at him enough . . . marry, you were starry-eyed and twittering like a caged bird being offered a bit of apple when I came upon you two."

"I don't like him in *that* way," she said angrily, entirely forgetting her previous subject, as he'd intended her to do. "He's just a boy."

"A boy? Indeed? He's married these five months. A proxy groom, I'll grant you, but over boyhood's threshold —man enough, I'd wager, to be one in fact if they'd let his Spanish Katherine come to his bed. And a comely youth, for all his sensitivity."

"Which you know nothing about," she said furiously, and prepared to march off.

He touched her sleeve.

"It may be," he said quietly, "my jealousy and not my wits speaking. I've nothing to offer you, you know. And so I see rivals in graybeards and boys, I see them everywhere about you."

She gazed up at him, her hands clenched beneath her long sleeves, because she couldn't understand why he claimed interest in her—nay, even more—and then insisted he could offer nothing more, as he had that time before, before he'd hurt her so. But she couldn't very well ask him about that.

"Why . . . why can't you offer more?" she blurted.

They stood still and stared at each other, each aware that they'd said the wrong thing, each wishing they could put it right and somehow save their dignity, if not their pride or hearts.

He reached out to touch the side of her upturned face with the tips of his fingers.

"I begin to wonder too," he said, and grew still before he said, "but I think it is to save you, as well as myself. No matter. We're here, Megan, and this is a holiday. You are my friend, you know, or at least I count you so, and I've not so many that I lose count often. Can we forget the 'whys' for a space? Tonight, will you dance with me if they play a coranto or a cinque pas? But not a volta, I'm far too old for such liveliness—still, I do get to lift you in my arms if I do, surely that's worth a creaking back. . . . Come, come, lady, it's a holiday. I promise, I'll leave off begging that you spend the night with me if you'll come talk, and dance, and pass the evening with me."

He paused, watching her closely.

She hesitated, and then put her hand on his sleeve.

"But only just for tonight, you understand," he said

gravely, and she laughed until he knew she was really laughing, and then he joined her.

They continued to laugh, when they weren't talking, or dancing, or seeking corners of the vast hall where they could escape Matthew's hot and envious eyes. And then they'd laugh again, the more because it was guilt that inspired it on her side, and awareness of his own danger that inspired his. When the evening was done and true night came on, and the Lady Katherine arose and made a show of preparing to leave, Lucas walked Megan to a darkened corner of the hall. Then, very unlike himself, or her own expectations, he only placed a light kiss on her forehead as farewell. And then, very unlike her intentions, she rose up on her toes to place a quick light kiss on his cool lips in return. Then, each wondering why it was that they'd surprised themselves as much as each other, they stared at each other in the flaring, hissing torchlight.

"Tomorrow too," he said at last.

"Yes," she answered, because she hadn't a thought for all the witty answers she had thought to say.

"In Italy . . ." Lucas began, and then stopped speaking, as he stopped walking in the garden. "Oh, Lord!" he sighed. "Will I grow to be one of those old bores who can talk of nothing but the travels he made when he was young? We'd a tutor that all the boys mocked behind his back. 'Old Jerusalem' we called him. Because he was always saying, 'When we entered Jerusalem . . .' He'd gone on pilgrimage and hadn't seemed to live beyond those glory years, although he did live on for decades more. Shall you call me 'Old Italy' one day, I wonder?"

"I *asked* you," she said, and prodded his arm with one finger.

He smiled at how daring she'd become since he'd left off trying to seduce her. He saw the way the sunlight turned her brown eyes to molten gold; how the blatant light of morning suited her as well as the inconstant moon and torchlight, and reminded himself that the truth of it was how easy she'd become with him since he'd told her he'd left off trying to seduce her. He smiled.

The first hints of a chill autumn had discouraged most of the flowers in the walled garden they strolled in, but there were enough hardy roses to give both color and scent to the morning as the sun warmed it. There were sanded paths and boxwood alleys to walk through, small mounts with dwarfed trees to walk around, stone statues of griffins and lions rampant to see, and at every turn, another sundial to remind them of time's swift passage. The garden was as fashionable a place as any in the palace, passing time in it was a courtly occupation, and many pairs of guests were also enjoying it this morning.

Couples strolled two by two, and now and again, by three, as some fashionable swain trailed a pair of ladies while strumming his lute and singing of his devotion. But most of the talk, if not about love or gossip of it, was about how much more ornate the knot gardens at Sheen would be when they were done, how many more dozens of roses Henry had planted there, and how altogether more satisfactory a garden it would eventually be. As if, Lucas thought, looking down to the glowing girl beside him, any of them could want anything more than he had now: a scented, sunny, private place in which to amuse oneself with a beautiful woman and mouth noble nonsense and chat about nothing, and pretend that winter would never come again.

He saw other ladies in the garden who'd already offered him more than laughter and conversation, but such was his mood since he'd come to Greenwich that he didn't know why a man would want more. Besides, he thought, he was sated. In London, as usual, there'd been impersonal couplings born of passing meetings. Or so, at least, he thought there'd been, and as it seemed the same, it was the same to him. Besides, she was charming and he wanted her. He wondered how far she would go to please her lady . . . or him. Besides, he thought . . . And then stopped thinking of it, and let himself enjoy the moment. It was, after all, a holiday.

Megan looked about the garden and felt as though she were a figure walking through a scene in a rich wall tapestry, and smiled to herself as she saw some of the other couples posturing, wondering how many others felt precisely the same. But none of the other ladies had such cause as she. She saw the other men in the garden and thought none of them so handsome as her escort, and knew any one of them would be better for her than he was. But she'd her orders, and she reveled in them—at least, here in the open light in this innocent place, she did. And everywhere else, as well, she admitted to herself. Because no one challenged her as much as he did, none of them saw her as such a separate person, not even Matthew. Especially not Matthew. Which was odd, because Matthew wanted her hand in marriage, and her body too, of course, but for babies. And Lucas wanted only her body for amusement for a little while. So why, then, she wondered, did he seem so interested in her mind, and occupy it so? No matter. For now, she'd enjoy it.

"I want to know more," Megan insisted. "It's not at all the same as your 'Old Jerusalem.' What would you call a lady who'd never left her own home and yet talked of it all the time, as so many of us do? 'Old Hearth'? 'Old Kitchen'?" she asked as he chuckled. "Huh," she sniffed, "be sure, if I'd traveled the world I'd never be still about it. Since I never shall, I want to hear more. Tell me," she demanded, walking on with him, "what you were saying about the way winter never comes to Florence."

"Oh, but it does," he answered, putting his hand over hers where it rested on his arm, "and does not—in a way. They love the summer sun so well that they've captured it forever, in their art, as well as in their wines. I thought to bring wine back with me, but forgot the art, like the sun, until I was without it again. That's what I miss the most, I think," he said. "You've never seen such paintings as they do. I'd never thought such things possible before I went there. Pictures of life so lifelike that I swear you expect the figures to move, the flowers to have scent—you can warm your hands on the glow of their painted suns. The colors, the subtlest tones of flesh . . . My artist friend Sandro, who makes a livelihood painting for the great houses of Italy—they compete with art, as we do with tourneys—I swear it's true"—he shook his head in amusement—"he painted me once, putting me in a scene in a crowd. It was, and was not, me. Or, at least, it was myself as I might be, I think, if they made a mistake and let me into heaven. I was too beautiful, it was absurd. I'm vain, but not blind." He smiled. "But still, it was recognizably me. I know this makes no sense, but they improve reality, even as they show it perfectly.

Here, look. It's a fine morning. But if they were to paint it, it would be finer. And such light! Perhaps it's because their light is gold, and ours is not . . . I cannot say.

"And the pagan things they paint! Gods and goddesses and mythical places, nor is it only paintings. They've statues of youths that you'd expect to step off their pedestals. I knew a lady in Florence who vowed she'd fallen in love with a young bronze David—and who could blame her? He was magnificent, and all he had on was his sword and helmet."

Megan thought of all the paintings she'd seen, in palaces, in churches, and the more common ones painted directly on the walls of most well-furnished homes. She wondered if he was jesting about the statues, since she'd never seen a representation of an unclothed man or woman. She stayed silent, considering it. She envisioned the suffering saints and the pious virgins she'd seen, as well as all the knights and ladies carved on their own caskets. None of them had seemed like life to her for a moment; the things within the paintings were flat, the statues were stiff; such was art, but despite the evidence of her eyes, she didn't doubt him.

"Why did you leave, then?" she said in a small hurt voice, and wondered why she should envy a country. Hearing herself, she was shamed at her transparent yearnings, and sorry she'd asked what she'd immediately thought. And then was not.

Because he looked down to her and there was more light in his eyes than in any painting she'd ever seen, as he said, "Because for all that it was beautiful, it was not my home. This is my home, this is my country, and I think it is time that I live or die here."

She saw the longing in his face, and heard it beneath each word, and wondered why a man would long for what he had.

He saw what she'd heard, and lifted her hand to his lips to distract her. Then he remembered what he'd forgotten, as they stood in that scented garden, and he was for the first time in a very long time astonished. Because for a brief time she'd done what no woman he could remember had ever done. She'd made him forget she was a woman, and how much he desired her, and he'd spoken to her from his heart. And that, as all new experiences were to a man who must plan and plot his every step, was exceedingly dangerous.

"How grave you look," she said. "What is it?"

Then she fell still, and lowered her gaze, astonished at how bold she'd become with him, how she'd reversed her emotions. Because when she thought of him, or glimpsed him from across a room, she was terrified each time anew by his poise and cold attractiveness. Yet when she walked and talked with him, as now, she felt as comfortable as if she were with an old friend, well met, in a land of strangers. And that, she knew, was dangerous nonsense.

"Nothing," he said truthfully. "It was nothing but my remembering how brief this is, our holiday."

18

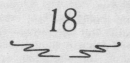

He sat his horse with such languorous ease, it was as if they were about to go for a canter across the green meadows, and not into any kind of competition. He wore no mail or armor, his long shining fair hair was his only helm, and the only emblem he bore was her own scarf tied about his upper arm. And yet Megan thought no knight on the field fairer than Lucas Lovat, none more confident, and rightly so, because she believed no other so sure of success.

But that was hardly a thing she could say with Prince Arthur so nearby, also waiting his turn to try for the tilt. Yet the young prince's smile told her he knew, as did her lady, as did almost anyone with eyes on this field, in this palace, in this world. Because she'd passed all her free hours with Lucas Lovat; they'd dined and strolled and laughed and danced together for all these past days. Even Matthew had given up his claim, and was passing his hours with the comeliest girls he could find to parade past her nose to show her how little he cared for her choice. And that choice was clear to see in her eyes as well as in the fluttering silken scarf Lucas wore on his sleeve, as token of where she'd placed her heart.

The astonishing thing of it was that he hadn't as yet asked for more, for all his teasing talk. For all, Megan thought as she watched him salute her with a grin as he brought his horse up to the line, that she began to realize that she'd as much as promised, without words, to give him anything he asked, whatever the cost. And for all that she could ill afford what he might ask, and knew it all too well, these last days and nights had been so golden and perfect that she'd not even had the time to take

fright at how she'd surely have to pay for them. Because
whatever else she was, she was scrupulously honest and
not in the habit of being in debt, even if that ultimate
payment might bankrupt her future. This didn't trouble
her so much as she knew it should, because this was no
time for accounting; this was time for tournament and
games.

The quintain was set up far down at the end of a long
grassy alley. It was a life-size wooden figure of a fiercely
scowling knight, painted in full regalia, and with a shield
bearing a nonsensical device. The knight was mounted on
one end of a crossbar on a pivot, and held a blunted
sword. If the onrushing rider did not hit him at the exact
right spot—at the tip of the long nose he looked down—
the knight would swivel about immediately and smite the
rider on the back with his sword, toppling him from his
horse, at the least. Today, as all the participants noted,
groaning, Sir Knight had a double threat: even if he were
struck true, there was a bag of flour at the other end of
the bar, and if the rider didn't get away swiftly enough,
he'd get the flour bag at the back of his neck as a
farewell.

"At least," a knight near Megan and Lady Katherine
whispered, "it's a bag of flour, not sand. But if Arthur
weren't riding today . . ."

Of course Henry wouldn't risk his son's life for a
sporting jest, but the sack of flour was in itself a heavy
jest, Megan thought nervously.

"God's teeth!" Lady Katherine hissed, seeing Megan's
pallor as she eyed the bulging sack of flour, "Lovat's no
knight in the joust or melee. All he risks is a sore head,
not a lost one. Smile for the man, dolt."

The retort that sprang to Megan's lips was bitten back—
not because she realized she couldn't be saucy to her
lady, but because she suddenly remembered that her lady
would be grateful if her Perkin could risk his life and
limbs anywhere in the cool clean sunshine now.

Megan smiled, and as so often happens when the semblance of pleasure is put on, her heart eased and she
relaxed. But the fate of the first rider chased the color
from her cheeks again.

The muscular youth on his strapping black stallion had
been as anxious as his high-stepping mount to begin. He

was clad in yellow and white and festooned with ribbons, and carried a shield with a bird of prey emblazoned on it. He'd his lance tucked beneath his right arm, and when the signal was given, he tore down the green alley with a bloodcurdling cry. His lance pointed true and struck hard— and faster than Megan's eye could register it, the wooden knight spun like a top and in a second it was the stallion alone that was pounding away, spurred on by the bag of flour that swung over him next, as he ran. And the boy flew over his horse's ears and spun to the ground, where he rolled like a gaily colored log, until he came to a stop to lie flat on his back as though dead.

But all the men were laughing, and when they'd raised up the boy and his eyes opened, he shook his head again and again and his first words were his vow to try it again.

The second rider, with the arms of Harbord on his shield, struck hard and was smitten just as hard in return. Young Salisbury struck true and was then fetched such a blow on the back of the neck from the bag of flour as he tried to escape that there was blood spilling from his mouth as his head hit the ground. But the crowd of men come to raise him up soon saw that it was nothing but that he'd bitten through his lip in the fall, and they bore him away, cursing as much as he was bleeding.

Thomas Dalzell was laid flat by the flour, his father by the knight. John of Dorset hit the knight and made a good getaway, but overbalanced so that he dropped his lance and very nearly himself from the saddle as he did it. The barons Downshire, Alban, and Austell were felled by the knight. The Earl of Carnwell was struck insensible for so long by the flour that an argument ensued as to whether to lighten the sack before the prince rode through, which resulted in the prince growing so angry that the subject was dropped, though it was noted that a youth was sent running downfield to the king, where he was watching men at the bow.

The knight made short work of Baron Kilworth and his friend John Stamp, and then it was Lucas' turn.

It was done so fast, and done so sweetly, that the only way it could be seen was by replaying it in the mind's eye when it was done.

A waiting knight tossed Lucas his shield just before he was given his mark, and he carried it as easily as though he'd held it all the while. He held his lance negligently, and kneed his horse and raced down the green alley, and swung up the lance and smote the knight, and then swung himself to the side and down as if he were riding the side of the horse and not its back, and cantered off easily as the sack of flour kept swinging round and round as though searching for the rogue that had got away so cleanly. It was all done with ease and seeming effortlessness, and the grace of it made it a pretty thing to see. Lucas came riding back, and tossed his shield back to the generous knight who'd lent it, and his eyes were filled with laughter and light, and the first thing they did was to seek Megan, and he smiled, aglow with the race and the day and the light. Then he saw Prince Arthur readying himself, and as he rode by he whispered a word and Arthur nodded and grinned, and relaxed his grip on his lance until his knuckles no longer showed white.

If the prince was then not as fluid and astonishing in his run and lunge and flight, he was, at least, as successful as Lucas had been. It was true he almost overbalanced as he fled, and truer that he was flushed and shaken when he was done, rather than coolly glowing, but by the time he rode back to Lucas, he was so excited that he rode past his father without seeing him. He kneed his horse to Lucas' side and clapped his arm about his shoulders and cried his thanks even as his face almost split from his smile of relief and astonished delight.

"Smooth as silk, as you promised," Arthur shouted. "I floated. I bore down on his nose, and then bore myself down to the left, riding ribs instead of back. By God's body, Lucas, you were right! Oh, Lord! What a feeling!"

The sun glanced down on them, the prince and his tilting master: the one fair, white-skinned, and broad at the shoulder, the other slighter, darker-haired, and more slender, but in that moment they bore matching smiles of pleasure, and it seemed that they were matched in more than pleasure. It might have been that they both had long, straight bobbed hair and fine, almost delicate features, for all they were manly ones. It could have been that side by side in good humor, there was an echoing note that could be felt as well as seen; they were almost as brothers in that moment.

In that moment Megan saw Lucas as he'd never been,

but seemed to be made to be: relaxed and gallant and free of whatever dark thoughts they were that usually twisted his smile and his humor and cramped his spirit. Lady Katherine caught her breath in that moment, and it was as if she saw her own princely husband again, as he was in his glory days—she saw him that clearly in Lucas' smiling, gentled face. And Henry Tudor stood and watched and saw his son in his triumph, rejoicing with his new teacher, and he celebrated that glowing youth, as ever; even as he frowned, worrying for him.

They stayed at the quintain until long past noon. Arthur was tumbled for his vanity once, and again for his overanxiousness, and only quit the field when he'd achieved a clean stroke and retreat again as smoothly and graciously as Lucas did each time he tried it. Then Arthur went to be armored for the joust, and Lucas took Megan, with her lady's permission, to witness it.

After they'd taken seats in the full weak autumn sunlight, he sat back beside her to watch knight meet knight in crashes of steel. His arm seemed to rest on the chair rim behind her shoulder and his hand grazed the side of her neck lightly as thistledown, so heavily that she could feel nothing else but his long fingers as they toyed with the nape of her neck beneath her gabled hood—nothing else, not the dilute sun or the cool breeze or the weight of the speculative stares they were receiving. He bore the scent of horse, as well as his own exertion, and the spiced scent he always wore was overlaid with the sharp ripening odor of hay and autumn grasses. She breathed him in and tried to stare at anything else but him unless she had to, such as when an amusing thing happened. When fat Sir Lindsey met old Sir Beaumont and they both missed their mark, rushing past each other to skewer air, she'd only to look to him to see him looking to her to share her suppressed laughter. And when Prince Arthur rode out and stayed on his horse, even when given a smart stroke by his challenger, they exchanged similar smug glances, although she saw his fade as he looked after the young prince.

"Didn't you think he did well?" she asked.

"Oh. Aye," he answered. "It's only that I don't know why I'm so mightily pleased for him."

"He *is* your prince," she said, on a laugh.

"Oh. Aye," he said, and smiled his half-smile for the first time that day.

"How paltry you must think me," he said when the afternoon drew to an end and they arose, because there were no more knights on the field for its fading light to glint upon. "No armor. No mail. No glorious jousts for me to ride your favor into. Only the quintain to impress you, and that a thing for bumpkins and country boys."

"And princes," she reminded him.

"Yes, just so," he said, but he was no longer smiling. Until he looked up from his thoughts and out at the world, and her face again.

"My frown chased your smile," he said wonderingly, touching the tip of her nose with one finger.

"Of course," she answered.

And then she could not tell if he laughed or sighed at her.

But they laughed enough at the dinner table, so much so that they even got the Lady Katherine to join them. Lucas' jests were so witty that even the dark lady relented and clapped her ringed hands together at the cleverness of his retorts. She only stopped as all the hall grew still when Prince Arthur took up his song, and then summoned Lucas to his side, and they sang it together, for a reprise. Their voices complemented each other, or so it seemed, though it might have been that Lucas was so adept at harmony he could follow that clear young voice and enhance it, until they sounded like two tenor-calling birds singing apace. In the flaring torchlight their shadows entwined, and as they sang of lost love, the queen looked up at what was before her as well as what was behind her, for once. As she watched them, her lips fell open and her face bore a look of such tender hope and yearning that her husband, Henry Tudor, at her side, reached out one bejeweled hand and almost covered hers with it before he remembered where he was and what he was, and what he was to her. Then he turned and watched his second-most-beloved sight, his son Arthur. He gave them both applause when he was done, though his eyes never left Lucas Lovat, even as he did.

When the singing was done, and the dancing begun, Lucas took Megan's hand as though to lead her into the circle. Instead, he led her beyond it, and past it, and off into the dark at the perimeter of the hall, and then beyond that, on behind the back of a yeoman guard to a darkened niche in a corner of a corridor. She came into his arms without his asking, and gave him her lips without a thought, and the only thing he had to say was to ask her to open her mouth against his, and his words were encompassed by her mouth before they were done being said. It was a long and searching kiss, and he found what he'd sowed all these past days and nights in it—and more that he hadn't expected.

He'd forgotten the taste of innocence, for all that the hot tang of desire was better than he'd remembered it ever having been before. Her body strove against his, and her high hard-tipped breasts fitted into his palms and she turned her neck from side to side for his kisses, before, as jealous as she was fearful of the demands her breasts were making of his mouth, she turned her lips back for more. Because she tasted nothing but sweetness in his mouth and felt nothing but excitement at his hands, despite all she knew and had warned herself about.

It was he who stopped; he who stepped back a pace even as she became aware that his body had grown a new insistent pulsing part that pressed hard against her belly, and before she could decide if she was frightened or excited by it, it was he who spoke first, at last.

"No need to tell you how I want you, is there?" he murmured on a shaken laugh. "But I want more than your need in return. And I find I must have it in words, not just embraces," he said ruefully. When she could only look up at him, perplexed, he said gently, running his hand lightly along her collarbone, as though he could feel traces of the kisses he'd left there, "What I'd take from you cannot be restored, Megan."

She looked away, as though she could avoid the reality that was closing in upon her and staining the night. "I could, but I won't settle for less," he said on a sigh, "because with all my best intentions, you move me very much, and I cannot promise what I'm not sure I can—or in this case—cannot"—he gave a broken chuckle—"do. Still, there's Matthew to be considered. Or if not he, then another very like him someday. I must be sure you are sure, since, as you've said so many times before, and rightly so, that's the only needful portion you can bring

to your wedding that you can call your own—one even
Henry can't give you—and you've saved it for your marriage night. I won't take it unless I'm offered it. I've a
conscience, I think," he said wonderingly.

"No hurry to answer, don't worry," he said when she
remained silent. Refusing to look at her face, but placing
a light kiss on her forehead instead, he added, drawing
her near again, "We've time. This time, we've time."

She spoke at last, and he felt the tremor in her voice
where it began in her heart, and even so, didn't move his
hand from her breast until she wrenched away and left
him standing alone in the dark.

"A conscience, but no heart, sir," she managed to say
as she did.

He was more shaken than he'd expected to be. It
seemed an effort to mount the twisting stone stairs to his
room. It was true he hadn't known thwarted physical
desire since he'd come to manhood, but although Lucas
was able to attribute various aches as well as the hollow-
ness of his legs to that, he knew that it was his own
confusion that was affecting him just as acutely. He'd
given up what he'd earned just before he was about to
take it. And to the best of his knowledge—which wasn't
much, as he'd never done such a thing before—it was
because he'd not been able to forget who she was as he
was preparing to enjoy what she was.

He supposed he'd thought he was being generous; he'd
won, but she hadn't realized it yet. She'd obviously not
known what the next logical steps they were about to
take were. And they were, for her, considerably long
ones. Well-a-day, he thought bitterly, that was what came
of dealing with innocents. He'd pulled away, trying to
delay the urge to take her immediately, also believing he
was doing it for the art of it and for their eventual mutual
pleasure. He'd not known until he'd heard himself speaking that he hadn't wanted to hurt her even more than
he'd wanted to have her, and that was a considerable
wanting—he was still trembling with interrupted and
unchanneled desire. So he was less than acutely aware
when he entered his chamber.

But he'd been living in the shadows too long not to see
a movement in them, and his hand was at his hip as soon

as the man turned in the dim light of the one rushlight in the small chamber.

"Father!" Lucas cried gladly, thrusting his dagger back into its sheath as he came into the light and held out his arms to embrace the man.

But Sir Charles only gave him a bleak and encompassing look, up and down his frame, and stood still, neither returning nor permitting the gesture.

"Ah," Lucas said, dropping his hands, and then his troubled frown froze and his face grew ashen. "Mother?" he asked at once, with dread.

"Nay, nay, she's well," Sir Charles said, some sympathy in his voice before he said more gruffly, "as she would not be, by God's faith, if she were here, and saw you, as I did."

"Saw me . . . what?" Lucas said, now calm, now cold, now edging toward the truth as though he were disinterested in it, as he so often did with strangers.

"Saw you capering in the hall like some penny-a-piece minstrel with the young *prince*," Sir Charles spat in a fierce undervoice, "after I'd concealed myself and watched you all the day—I saw you riding to the quintain with him, and then hugging like lovers after—aye, and saw you making love standing up against a wall in a corridor just now, like a homeless knight with a serving maid, and she a girl of family and honor. God's wounds! Where are your wits? In your breeches? Or your head? Aye, and if they are in your codpiece, keep them there—since at least if they bide low, you may keep them, for you're sure to lose your head if you keep up this way."

But now Lucas lounged against a table, his eyes glittering in the flickering light, and now his voice was calm and clear and chill, and Sir Charles looked up, his face stricken at the familiar sound of it.

"Aye, marry, a sweet hello," Lucas drawled. "Why don't you simply have at me with a broadsword and be done? These words are only tickles from Italian knives—stilettos—cruel sharp sly cuts that bleed a man lamentably slow. I thought you more charitable, sir. You bid me not to sing, not to sport, not to take a little ease with a lady—and before God, sir, it was pitiful little ease I had of her, since I gave her up to what is left of my conscience before I left her. And at that, I wonder if I wounded her more than if I'd taken her maidenhead, because I robbed her of a more precious thing—her trust," he mused, before he said with suppressed rage, "God save you, sir, what would you have of me? It's a holiday. I thought to play for a while. Beg pardon if I forgot my holy mission for a time, and sought to sport, to feel a maiden's warm breast instead of cold regret for my brief hour. Grant me your pardon," he said, inclining his head before he bent into a great mock bow.

Sir Charles shook his head as though to clear it and then his eyes widened until their whites were seen even in the meager light. He spoke low and fervently, in a rush of words. "Before God, your majesty, forgive me! I forgot, I forgot," he said, hitting the side of his head with a clenched fist. "I think of you as the son I lost, even as I know you the king I lost, ahh . . ." he said, grieving against Lucas' shoulder after he lost the brief struggle to drop to his knees and was instead borne up by the younger man and held fast in his arms.

"Hush, Father," Lucas said over and again, as though he held a child and not a trembling old man, and he thought fleetingly of how he comforted so many he loved and wounded this night as he said, stroking the sparse hair beneath his hand, "Hush, hush, for your sake, my dear sir, as well as for mine own, I pray you. The insult never hurt me half so much as your tears do," and realized that too was again true.

"That I should speak so—to you . . ." the old man finally said, drawing away, turning his head so that his face could not be seen. He ran a finger beneath his nose, and said in more normal tones, "Forgive me."

"For such heinous crimes as love and loyalty and concern for my wretched hide? You ask a great deal," Lucas said, smiling, "but come, why such heat in any event? I rode to the quintain because I do it well and enjoy it. I sang for Arthur because I loved the song . . ."

"Ah," Sir Charles muttered, abashed, "I thought the quintain was too much a rude, country sport for you."

"Arthur seeks to excel at it," Lucas said.

"Aye, there . . . there, that!" the older man said, wagging a finger. "The two of you face-to-face and side-by-side, singing together! I thought my old heart would give out. You looked peas in a pod, anyone could see it."

"Anyone who knew the truth, and was looking for it, and anyone who'd believe it. Precious few that would be—ask any of the ill-fated pretenders. No, I've been deemed dead for over a decade. It'll be difficult enough if ever the time comes to deny it," Lucas said. "It's only the thief with the coin in his pocket who thinks he's being watched. Come, sir, given my father, my face is as common at this court as his once was in every bedchamber here. As for the maid—there you've the right of it: I oughtn't to tarry with virtuous maidens. But I don't remember your being so pious with me. Marry, you're faithful as the sun to the sky with your lady, but you've never raked me for my morals before. Have I grown that bad, I wonder?"

"Nay, your morals are too good, my Lucas," Sir Charles said emphatically, the "my Lucas" that he substituted for the "your majesty" so that it would not be on his lips as it was always on his mind, showing Lucas how overset he still was, "it's because she *is* a virtuous, wellborn maiden— though she certainly wasn't acting one when I came upon you—that you ought to let her be. You can't involve yourself with such; such wenches are for wedding, and she's not high enough for you for that. You've got to leave yourself free for a princess. Spanish Katherine is ripe. You can't tie yourself up with a houseless lady-in-waiting, however well-bred."

"Katherine," Lucas said softly, "is wedded to Arthur this five-month."

"Proxy, proxy," Sir Charles growled, his words sounding like "poxy, poxy" as he started to pace the floor. "There's many a slip 'twixt the cup and the lip. Isabella and Ferdinand are no fools. They keep the bride, do they not? Though Henry petitions for her every week. It's because they don't want their best pawn to end up like poor Scots Katherine, wasted on a pretender and left to exile and ignominy. Everyone knows it's because of their fear of more legal heirs to Henry's stolen crown. Aye, even now. It's Warwick, of course, the poor addled lad in the Tower—he's got the true blood, and they know it, for all they say it's because of all the other pretenders. So now's a good time to stay free and ready."

"Ready?" Lucas breathed. "For what? Father," he said, bitterness making him speak, slow anger shaping

the words, and frustration making them the truth, at last,
"I have been ready for sixteen years. I've felt the weight
of that crown they pulled me from my bed to place upon
my head that night at Ludlow for sixteen years now.
Sixteen. Each year of them that passes, I become one of
the fewer to know or care that it was ever there. I, as
much as you, have tried to forget that.

"Father," Lucas said gently, coming to stand by the
old man, and trying to look into his averted face, "I am
tired. I wait, like an abandoned bride, foolish and forlorn, for a groom who will never come to me. I was, as
my poor addled cousin Warwick said of himself, born at
an inconvenient hour. And it grows later. Too late to do
anything about any longer. Henry's strong, and grows
stronger. As one of his many, many spies, let me tell you
he has bound this land of ours up in invisible coils. It is
not at all bad—for England. It is the death of illusion as
well as ambition, for me. Behind Henry, there is Arthur.
Behind him, his own get will come soon enough, and if
they tarry, there are still young Henry and all the princesses. My sister is yet young. How many more princes
shall she spawn for him for me to envy and combat? I
would have to hack a long and bloody swath to the
throne even now."

Sir Charles wheeled about, his eyes blazing.

"And are you not man enough for that?" he whispered
in a furious undervoice, "man enough to be the king you
were born to be?"

"Am I monster enough?" Lucas asked wearily. "Even
if I were, it would be to no avail. Father, here's truth.
Hear me. I was born to no purpose. I was raised to a lost
cause. No, look at me, and see truth. I'm a man grown. I
have no friends, because I could never afford them; no
enemies, because I could never let them know who I was
or what I stood for; no wife, nor true love either, and no
children, because a king must make an advantageous
match. I have lived alone all my life, waiting for a time
that will come no more. A king? I am scarcely a man at
all.

"Only now and again do I dare see it myself. Had I
been a year older when my father died—I was a preco-
cious lad, strong for my age, I could have held it together, were I but a year more then. I could have withstood

my uncle, with but a year more in my hands. When Henry came, he was an exiled, fatherless boy too. I'd the right, and the blood, but he'd the one thing I'd not—more years on earth. Do you think I haven't passed my life thinking it? Had my brother lived . . . and at that, what if he has?" he murmured, passing his hand over his eyes. "Aye, even if Henry were weaker even now, but he's clever, clever . . .

"Father," he said with a raw note in his voice Sir Charles had not heard before, not even that first night he'd come to him as son, "Buckingham's gone, Throckmorton, Wainright, Hastings, Lincoln, Fitzgerald, Lovell, North, Brampton, and more, more. All of our friends—gone or lost or strayed or stolen; our allies grow old, our enemies multiply, all unknowing. Even our staunchest friends—John Argentine speaks with me, but avoids me when he can—he's no deserter, but a wise physician knows when to abandon the dead . . . whether it's a man or his cause. Father, it's over. I was born at the wrong hour, and we can't turn back time."

There was silence in the room. Sir Charles picked up one hand and put it down again.

"But, lad," he eventually whispered, "these are yet turbulent times. The door hasn't closed yet. Henry is not immortal. Nor are his kin. However many we've lost, enough still remember the white rose to cultivate it—see how even crass impostors can raise armies? As you've waited this long . . . a little longer? A little longer surely cannot hurt? As you say, sometimes it is only a matter of years."

His wrinkled face was drawn and anxious, his thick body surely more shrunken now than it had been a month past. Lucas wondered. He was pleading for more than a little longer, Lucas knew, more than a year; he was pleading for his purpose in life. And he'd so much less of it left to him than Lucas had of his.

"Forgive me," Lucas said. "I have this . . . spleen to vent from time to time. And the lady refused me, marry, I'm not used to hearing 'no,' any more than my poor body is, I think. It was a passing distemper. Forget it. I'm yours . . . I am well again. Forgive me."

"*Just* like your father," Sir Charles said on a sigh, with a dawning smile that lightened his face and lifted years from it. "He'd just such a temper too—soft as a poet's when the mood was upon him, for all his valor. And never a man to gladly bear a 'no' from a maid either.

"Now, then," he said, rubbing his hands together, "come see what I've brought you. It's all very well to excel at the quintain, but as my son, you must expect them to expect more. Here, I know you've no time to be fitted for mail, but here's your helm, remember it? It did when you were younger, before you left us, and once a man's got his growth, his head remains the same."

"On the outside," Lucas said, and his father laughed, and rummaging through a pile of objects in the trunk he'd brought, said, "Here's my own new chain shirt, the shoulders will do—I've the figure of a troll, or so your mother always said, but what I took up in the belly, you'll need in the length, so 'twill even out, 'twill do. We'll piece this and that for the rest, and Saraband's the sweetest horse in the land. It would do me good to see you joust as a king . . . as my son should," he corrected himself quickly.

Lucas held the heavy linked-mail shirt up to the intermittent light. "I'm no true knight," he said quietly.

"God's teeth!" Sir Charles choked, and spat, and then said harshly, "You're the highest knight in all the land, did they but know it . . . but what you say is true—or must be, to their eyes. Still, you're my son, and it will be only the melee, which is more spectacle than sport, and no danger to a man like you. It would do my heart good to see you as you should be seen."

"Then it will do," Lucas said simply. "I'd some practice in Italy, now and again, with my princely friends. It's as well it's not single combat—I'm not mad enough to try the joust with another man's horse, however fine: a man and his horse must be one or they are nothing at all at it. But I'd be pleased to try to do you proud."

"Try?" Sir Charles asked. "Ha! The sight of you will feed my spirit, and your own, I think, my vallant lad. Here—here is your shield. And I've thought of a motto for us. *'Non Generant Aquilae Columbus,'* " he intoned proudly.

" 'Eagles do not bring forth doves,' " Lucas translated as he traced patterns on the shield with one finger. "You're right. It's perfect." He wore a small sad smile. "Yes. Perfect," he said.

"I can't see the glory of it," Megan said nervously, whispering to Clarisse, "for all I've seen it before."

The aspirant knights and gentlemen and boys and men who'd volunteered for the melee sat their mounts, awaiting the sound of the trumpet. They clustered in a welter of shifting, prancing, dancing, richly draped and armored horses, standing flank by flank and nose to tail, crammed in a space too small to maneuver in. The bright banners atop the riders' tall straight lances fluttered in the wind high above them, and were the only free thing about them.

"It is a courtly art," Clarisse said, "and a proud honor. Matthew wears my favor," she added sweetly.

But from where she sat with the ladies, Megan couldn't make out her former suitor, or any other individual combatant in the crowd, nor did she try. Her eyes were too busily trying to keep track of the figure of the knight with the blue-and-gold shield, the one astride the chestnut horse with the blue-and-gold fittings, the one who still wore her scarf on his sleeve: the one who, despite all he'd done and all she'd so shamelessly wanted him to do, still held her heart in his hand just as surely as he did the blunted lance he bore.

"It's as foolish as putting a crowd of boys in a room with clubs and promising the winner a sweet when it's done," Megan insisted anxiously. "I see nothing of honor or valor in it. Only pride."

"Which is what men are all about. Hush, foolish girl," Lady Katherine said, "and smile, or you'll be thought an unnatural girl, and where will that leave me? Be grateful all he risks is a sore head."

But when the horn sounded and the thrashing began, with the crowd of armored men turning on each other, roiling about, their horses screaming and rearing as cudgels and lances came down hard on helms and arms and gauntlets, and even the pennants above them were set to dipping and reeling as their bearers below were stunned or felled, Megan feared there was more at risk than a bruised head for most of the men. She tried to keep sight of Lucas, and now and again could catch a glimpse of him steering out of a pileup of horses, ducking under and away from a

slashing blow, avoiding harm, even as he inflicted none.
Clarisse clapped her hands together and glowed as at an
annunciation when she saw Matthew. She crowed, and
tugged at Megan's sleeve when she saw the portly knight in
bronzed armor send a blow to set a youth down reeling,
clutching his saddle to keep upright.

The final trumpet could not come too soon for Megan,
and she let out all of her breath when she heard it. Only
then did she send a stunning smile to Lucas, she was so
relieved to see him still sitting upright as he tugged at his
helm to free himself of it and she caught sight of his face
as he shook his glowing hair free. He looked to her, so
she knew he'd known where she was all along, and smiled
back. And then Matthew edged up beside him and felled
him with one blow, and bent low, to aim and deliver
another to wherever he lay now, beneath the horses'
hooves.

"Pride," the voice whispered when Lucas opened his
eyes.

"Foolish, pointless, useless old man's pride," Sir Charles
said brokenly as Lucas' eyes focused upon him at his
bedside.

"Oh. It's you, sir. For a moment," Lucas said, wincing
as he tried to raise his head, and so lowering it again, "I
thought it was the recording angel, beginning to read off
my sins. I was waiting for 'Lust' and 'Avarice'—why are
you weeping? Have I lost something other than my senses
for a few hours?" he asked suddenly, surreptitiously testing his legs and arms, remembering knights who'd left
combat whole, but with backs broken so they'd lost all
movement, wondering if he'd lost more than he knew.

"Oh, thanks be to God, Christ be praised," Sir Charles
said, slipping to his knees by the bed and taking Lucas'
hand. "I'll endow a monastery, as I promised—a nunnery
too. Praise God. A day, my boy, not a few hours, we lost
you for a day and a night into morning. That villain, that
dastard, that bawdy lobcock whoreson, he laid you low
after the trump had sounded. After! And you with your
head uncovered. Then, holy and meek, he crawls to
Henry for forgiveness and gets it! He heard no trumpet
in the heat of it, he vows."

"Who?" Lucas asked, eyes widened.

"One Matthew Lorrilard. And he goes unpunished. Unpunished! Dunned from court by scorn, but not fury! Henry must know, he knows!" Sir Charles whispered fiercely, his red-rimmed eyes wild as he gazed into Lucas'.

"Henry knows he's an idiot," Lucas said, relaxing, patting the two hands that gripped his one, and wincing again at the pain that shot up his arm as he did. "If Henry wanted me dead, he's cleverer and surer methods than that, trust me. Matthew, was it? He fancied himself my lady Megan's lover until I came along. That's all it was."

Sir Charles's gnarled hands stopped shaking.

"Ah, well-a-day," he said, rising, stiff-legged. "How do you feel now? The leech said it would take a day to unscramble your wits, and so it has. You've a bit of pelt missing on the side of your head, to the back—no, don't touch it, of course it hurts, he's sewed up the worst. You can't breathe deep because we've bound up your ribs, there's a few broken, and with that white hide of yours," he said too gruffly to deceive Lucas as to the pain he felt, "it's already turned blue as a druid's arse there, but 'twill fade."

"I've had worse," Lucas said truthfully, lying back on his pillow.

"No more," Sir Charles said, standing over the long form that still lay motionless on the bed; looking down, as he'd done for a day and a night, at that twice-familiar face, at what had seemed to be a twice-watched death-watch, as Lucas had lain drowned in soundest sleep.

When Lucas looked up at him, his dark gold brows knit in perplexity, Sir Charles went on, "I've had a day and a night to think, and to pray for the wisdom I owed you—wisdom I lacked. It was my pride that got you these wounds, but as you say, you've had worse. You'll have worse if I don't face the truth you already have. It's too late. It is," he said, tears overflowing his closed eyes. "No . . . no, don't speak now. It's my turn. I told myself I kept your dream alive for your father's sake—as I was his man, I was yours. But I kept your mission alive as I tried to keep my youth and dreams alive. There was no sense to it. It has become like an engine that starts of itself and cannot stop, like the one they say keeps the sea salt.

"You had regrets, you said?" Sir Charles laughed.
"You, who are blameless? We feared to act when you
were old enough. We hesitated; we planned and plotted
and yet were afraid to put it to the touch. Another day,
we said, another hour. And then some damned pretender
acted, and ruined it for you, for us. For years. As it
turned out, forever. Aye, for then there was another
pretender to your crown. How can any man claim to be
the true heir when so many were false? And Henry so
strong and getting stronger, mayhap even because of the
false kings he dealt with so firmly? You came home, we
sent you off again and again; each time, there were fewer
of us to see you off. Not time, not time, we said each
time. It was never the right time. That, at least, was true.
But we should have given you back your life when we
realized we couldn't restore your name, your rightful
place.

"I do not say give up forever," Sir Charles said with a
touch of spirit, straightening his back. "Life is very strange.
But I do say—and as I say it, so shall those few who
remain in this with us say it, I promise you—it is time for
you to live as Lucas, if never as Edward again. I love
you. Although I honor myself beyond my rewards by
saying so: you are my son, you have everything I own. It
is not what you might have had, but it is not nothing.
Give up our failed quest, take up another. Take your
virtuous lady to wive—or another, as you choose, you've
earned that right. Breed sons and daughters aplenty, and
tell them their heritage so that if someday they're needed,
there will be quivers full of them to claim their rightful
kingdom. And forgive me, your majesty, my liege lord,
my son, forgive me."

Lucas was too tired to argue. When Sir Charles left
him at last, Lucas was too confused to even argue with
himself. He could talk the old man round again, he
thought. He couldn't, he realized. He didn't know if he
should, if he could. It was almost unthinkable to finally
give up the dream of what had been the reality, even if
he'd been thinking it increasingly of late. He'd been king
once, if only for a matter of weeks. But he doubted he
would ever be again, at any cost, and the cost might be
too high for him to pay now. He was very weary.

And it just might be that surviving to bring his father's

grandchildren into the world was a better monument to his house than dying foolishly for what could never be.

But he was so used to secrecy and stealth, and hopeless dreams fed by fury and despair, that it was hard to accept that he might at last be free of the crushing burden of who he was. There was a stillness to it he could not trust, much less believe. So he was doubly glad, if that were possible, when he saw he had company—and company he wanted above all others. The door opened and he saw her face peek in. He closed his eyes at once.

"Yes, yes, go in," Sir Charles's voice urged Megan. "He woke, just before. He needs a soft hand on his forehead."

That was what he got, after a few long moments. At first he could only scent the roses on her skin, heated by her nervousness, as she stood nearby, obviously only looking at him. Then he felt her small, cool trembling hand on his brow. She jumped when his hand snaked out and caught hers, and his bright light eyes smiled up into hers as he drew her down beside him.

"Shh, don't struggle," he said. "This is a form of rigor, my muscles are tightening, I am in my death throes, ah," he breathed, finally taking his lips from hers, "perhaps not. How good it is to kiss in the sunlight. No, stay. Stay with me. I mean," he said, as she sat, irresolute, as he stroked her hair, "stay with me. Truly, this time. I think that blow knocked some sense into my head. I found life is not so expensive as I'd thought. It can be lost so cheaply. And though I find that what I want and need is beyond price, even a king's ransom . . ."—he chuckled to himself before he stared at her disbelieving face again— "still, poor thing that I am—that I have proved I am so many times to you—I think . . . that is to say, I hope, I can afford it now. Will you stay with me, Megan? Honorably, and forever—or for however long God grants to us?"

But she'd never left him, she thought, looking into those clear eyes she had never thought to see opened to sight again. During those long hours she'd kept vigil with him, watching Lucas' pillow for any hint of color beyond the sunlight of his hair there, praying for a word from his pale lips, Sir Charles had hinted that Lucas was not as he seemed, that nothing was as it appeared to be. This was true. The thought of his death had made her begin to think that there were more important things to a maid than her purity, and that honor as she knew it and virtue as she practiced it had little to do with life as she had to live it. Now he seemed to offer so much more—everything she'd ever wanted. She couldn't encompass the wonder of it and was afraid to voice it lest it be proved a mistake, another result of that blow to his head.

As she could not, she didn't answer. But she held on to his hand and sat up on his bed, and let him lay his head against her, so that he might hear her reply in the accelerated beat of her heart.

"Ah," he said, hearing that, and more, "sympathy wins where lust, anger, pleading, and coercion did not. Had I known this, I'd have half-killed myself weeks ago."

They sat still. He closed his eyes and saw a sweet green peace stretching endless before him, where before there had been nothing but an anxious jumble of design, or at best, the hope of hope. Her breast was soft beneath his cheek, but not at all maternal, and he smiled to himself to find desire mating with contentment. He wondered if it would always be so, and hoped he lived on long enough to test it a thousand ways. He wasn't sure if he deserved this. His heart filled as he wondered how it was that he could feel such joy with so little: merely life, and a maid who pleased him in his arms. This new life, he amended his thought, and this one maid with her wit and honor and humor, who had touched him as no woman he'd held much closer had in all the years of his exile. Which had been all of his life. He raised his head and turned his body, despite the pain, so he could bring her mouth beneath his on his pillow, to discover, he told himself, that since he felt so much with so little, how much more he would feel with more.

But then the door flew open. He released Megan, even as she drew back from him, and they both stared at the apparition in the doorway. Lady Katherine stood before them, hands trembling so that the parchment she held fluttered like the pennants he'd glimpsed as he'd fallen the last time he'd been stunned.

"Deceived!" she cried, and as Megan opened her lips to assure her that Lucas had declared something other than his lust for her, and Lucas began to speak in truth, of his honor and his plans for Megan, she cried out again. They saw she never saw them at all. Her hair was tangled, her face was white, she was as an avenging fury or a mad thing as she clasped her hands hard round herself and keened.

"Deceived! While we were gone," she wailed. "It was done in the dark when we left him. That devil seeks to destroy my prince, my Richard, my Perkin. Ah, me. They've arrested Strangways' young brother and all his friends, and more. In chains, in the Tower—they've put him back in chains again. He's to be tried. Warwick's to be tried, they're all to be tried, and then hanged for treason. While we laughed and danced, we were deceived. As you love him, as you love me, as you love justice, do not let them do this," she cried.

Lucas closed his eyes before he opened them to reality again. It had been too sweet. He ought to have known. It was, then, after all, as it may have always been, too late.

19

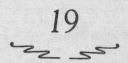

October, the time of fruit and late flowering and leaf-fall, was done. Now it was November, and well into that black month of blood and bonfires: for it was Martinmas, the festival of winter's beginning, of slaughter and fresh meat. With the sweet grasses turning gray, and winter's hand already upon the throat of autumn, those sheep, cattle, fowl, and swine that could not be fed through the winter had to be sacrificed so that the farmer could live through it. It was a time for making black puddings, and for curing, salting, and preserving. In a world where nothing could be wasted, it was, of course, a time for feasting, as well as death.

Henry's yeomen of the guard ate flesh every day, it was said. Good red beef as well as mutton, to go with their ale. But no man lives by food alone, and some men never have enough of anything, and so Lucas rode to the Tower with a heavy purse, and so that he might empty it, emptied his heart and mind of everything but his errand.

"Wait here, please," he told Philip. "God's blood, man, don't frown. Try to understand. If it was difficult to get in to see Warbeck before, now it will be almost impossible."

"Then why attempt it?" Philip asked as they sat their horses and looked over the bridge to the Tower.

"I said 'almost' impossible," Lucas answered absently, watching the wind send a dry oak leaf skittering across the wooden bridge, dragging one sere edge like a finger-nail, scraping so sharply they could hear it from where they sat.

"It is also possibly insanity," Philip said so casually it took a moment for Lucas to understand what he'd said and sit up sharply in his saddle to look at him.

"They've already arrested a dozen conspirators, with such a fine net cast so wide there'll be innocents as well as miscreants caught up in it when they're done hauling it in," Philip went on to explain, just as Sir Charles himself had done—albeit not so loudly, at such length, or with any of the passion that old gentleman had shown on the subject before Lucas had left for London.

"But you're here, and you know I am innocent—of that, at least," Lucas said at length, eyeing Philip as he at last voiced the thing Philip likely knew he knew, but that neither had ever put into words.

Philip flushed. But bit his lip and said, "Yes. I do. But I am not much, you know. I follow and report, it's what I've done from the first. But I'm only a messenger jumped up to a very bad informant. My wretched complexion deceives me. I think it was flattery to you that Henry set me on your traces from the first: a jest, a warning, nothing serious. No one ever has taken me seriously. Which is as well, since I'm no more easy in my mind about what I do than I am good at it."

Lucas watched him with a wide, unblinking stare. And then he smiled. The candid, penitent admission only convinced him that Philip was likely far better at what he did than he'd suspected he was. But his warning was also flattering; for whatever other reasons it had been given, it showed that someone, at least, cared if he put his neck into a noose. Whether it was Philip himself, or his master, Henry, where there was care expressed for a man's folly, there was love somewhere, and so always an exit left open for him to try to discover if he had to. So God himself had ordered the universe, so that the sinner could repent even at the last breath. And so earthly kings showed their own partiality. Or had done in the past, and in any case, there was no turning back now.

"It's to be hoped I'm not found strangled in the net before the hangman can get me," Lucas said. "I'd not like to deprive the crowd of their moment, for all I've amazingly little interest in seeing the color and length of my own intestines. But I've a duty to a lady, and so must have conversation with Warbeck before the hangman does."

"He's only to be put on trial—" Philip began.

"Yes. The way the capon is only put in the pot to see if

it is a good fit," Lucas answered, "a man in the Tower for treason who is put on trial again for treason is a dead man before his judge so much as hears his first word. In this case, even if he's innocent as an angel, they'll clip his wings before they open his gullet for him. They say he conspired with the Earl of Warwick to escape, and they need the Earl of Warwick to be very much dead, thank you, before Arthur and his unclaimed bride, Katherine of Aragon, get much older."

This time Philip's silence and subsequent blush sent a chill down Lucas' back, because, it seemed, he'd this childish hope he'd been speaking nonsense.

"At any event, I have to speak to Warbeck," he repeated sadly, "if only so that I can bring word to his lady that I did, and then lie to her about his being in spirits and hopes and health, and whatever else it is that a wife who is soon going to hear that her husband must die would want to know."

Which was only half a truth, because Lucas knew he needed to hear the very same things—as well as to convince himself, now, before the end came, that this was not his own brother meeting his end at last. If it had been an intolerable thought before, how much more so now, when he'd found a new reason for his own continuance: not just because he must survive, but because for the first time, he wanted to. Not just so that he could be a king, but so that he could become a complete and fulfilled man, at last. Now that he'd readmitted love and rejoiced in it, that very joy had made him acutely aware of how soon the sun came up, and how swiftly went down again. She had but to sneeze for him to picture her gone; he of all men knew how quickly it could happen. If his guilt for his life had been acute before, how much more so it would be by contrast now. How could he leave Perkin to the darkness of his tomb even as he longed for the darkness of his own wedding bed? If, Lucas thought again, *if* Perkin was indeed his brother, and not just, as Sir Charles insisted, another of the false or deluded men who'd ensured that he himself might never be king.

And Warwick? Ah, but Lucas had lost cousins before, and closer ones, and in truth, it seemed Warwick had been lost long ago, though he still breathed.

"They won't let you in," Philip said again. "They'll

only report that you tried. The ones who let you in before are themselves in chains now."

It had the ring of accuracy, and who should know better? Lucas thought.

"Let them. He'd wonder, your master and mine, if I didn't try," Lucas answered, urging his horse forward, "and I've still a chance. Death's shadow doesn't make men blind, or less greedy; they can see profit beyond the grave. Why put coins on a dead man's eyes? For symmetry? To keep him down?" He laughed. "Even death's own boatman takes gold for passage, or so the Greeks said."

He didn't know if Philip heard the truth in his words, since the wind took them away as he rode down the hill to the bridge to the Tower.

There were some different faces at the bridge gate, and many of them were turned to him, memorizing everything about him, from the top of his flat black hat to the tips of his soft leather boots. He was tempted to fling open his cape like a man on a street corner attempting to terrify ladies, so that they could take an inventory of his body as well as his face—and amused himself by the thought that he was wearing too much for that, even as he realized his humor was half-terror and took control of himself as he tethered his horse and walked on.

"Long Roger's in a cell beneath the cell beneath the basement, for doing just as you ask me to do, good sir," the first guard Lucas approached, a fresh-faced young lad, said with censure. His tone made Lucas feel some true twinge of guilt for attempting the young fellow's honor, his position, and so mayhap his young life as well, because of his request.

But then he felt both better and worse about it, as the young fellow went on.

"Now, nowadays, many's the gentlemen wants to see the villains," the guard said indulgently, "so they can gossip about them and amuse all their noble friends, not meaning no other harm. And God bless you, sir, I can see you're just such a fellow. So I'll take your coin to keep my mouth closed about your visit, I will, but not to let you in, and believe me, you'll thank me for it some-day, good sir, thank you kindly," he said as his hand disappeared into his scarlet tunic and came back empty so that he could touch his hat to the man whose coins he'd just swallowed up.

"Long Roger and John Williams, and who knows what others will be named?" another guard, whose face Lucas remembered, and whose hand had once taken gold and then the key to open Perkin's door, finally whispered to him after enough gold had weighed down his hand to loosen his tongue. They stood in a dark shadow of a darker room at the Tower at the side of the water gate.

"Poor lads, did they not share their gold around enough?" Lucas asked.

"Ah, 'tis never that," the guard spat, before he said quickly, " 'Tis fate. It were needful to have a name or two, a few to dangle afore the crowd, they could just as easily have been picked from a hat . . . not that I'm saying 'twere," he said nervously, sidling toward the closed door, "but may've been, and were the only fair way. But ain't a man who'd let you in to see the poor bastards till after they're gutted now—excepting if you was a priest. They fair infest the place now. Ask them, ask Gawd hisself to let you in, but don't ask me no more, for no more money, understand?"

"Understood," Lucas said, understanding even more. There was no sense tempting the poor fellow to self-murder, and no one else here left to ask, and no one to let him in. And so he told Lady Katherine when he met her where she stood trembling in the cold, waiting for him by the dockside.

"I cannot see my own brother," James Strangways said bitterly, "until the trial, they say. What trial? He's convicted where he stands. If only I could get word to him, so as to find out if there is anything I can say or do—"

"We shall not give up!" Lady Katherine said defiantly, although the fierce words coming from her black-draped and slight shaking frame made her appear as hopeless and gentle as she always wished to seem before all men. And so she may really have been today, because the lady swayed, and Megan slipped an arm around her to uphold her, and was not shaken off as she ordinarily would have been.

Megan said nothing, only looked at Lucas with her wide, tilted, beseeching eyes, as though, as with all young women lately given over to great love, she truly believed that her man could do anything, and would, to right matters in a wrong world. But then, they all three looked to him that way now.

"There's an order of precedence of whom to appeal to in such cases, and hopeless causes," he said on a sigh. "There are the king, the pope, and God. Let us try the highest in England first: the king."

Henry summoned them before they could petition him.

And having done so, Lucas saw, had also then staged their audience as well and as carefully as a guild's pageant on its saint's day. All we lack are wheels and a drunken crowd, Lucas thought as he dropped into his bow, for we've costume and stagecraft and all the characters at hand: Guilt and Folly, Sin and Cruelty, not to mention God on his cart, all here and at the ready. Everything, he thought, save from Truth, which, after all, has no part in such instructive morality plays.

"This," Henry said, shaking his head as he gazed at his audience, "is a sad thing, a sad, sad thing."

Everything save for Truth and a well-writ script to work from, Lucas thought, to stave off the feeling of horror that grew in his heart.

It was a crowded room at Westminster Palace; this was an official audience, no personal word could be spoken; if ever men dared to write down a word of Henry's dealings, they would be written here today. Henry Tudor sat with his queen at his side, and his elder son at his feet, and his younger one watching round-eyed from behind his mother's chair. His counselors stood in a row behind him, frowning, heavy with the robes of their offices and the weight of being unable to speak. There were courtiers here to the side, and clerics there in the press of men, and not a few men of means and title interspersed. And the shadow of a particular dark monk was cast upon all of them as he stood between them and the king and gazed from unseen eyes beneath his cowl on those who knelt before him.

Lucas upheld Lady Katherine; Megan and Clarisse stood a little to the side of them. James Strangways and other relatives of other named conspirators stood somewhere behind, somewhere in the teeming crowd, looking on.

"Lady, ah, lady," Henry sighed, still shaking his head

back and forth, from side to side, dire and slow, like an
adder sighting an unwary tidbit, Lucas thought, as he
seemed to seek words to speak.

"What shall I say?" Henry said. "I grieve for you and
with you. All England does, lady. This is a terrible thing,
a poor payment for trust, a sad disappointment. Ah,
lady, how sad to see the White Rose of Scotland brought
so low. Our hand is offered to you in sympathy and
friendship, our favor is with you still, but this is a sad
thing, a sad, sad thing."

Henry's narrow face was sallow in the muted light; a
man who knew all the uses of drama, he took care to
always sit in the shadows, leaving the sun for his queen
and his children and those whose complexions drank up
and then rewarded the bright daylight with a reflected
glow. His crown and his robes gleamed with dark jewels,
and only occasional turnings of his eyes showed the light.
Those eyes remained fixed on Lady Katherine: white and
dark and lovely Lady Katherine, where she bent before
him. There was that in the king's gaze that made Lucas
wonder, not for the first time, at all the reasons for
Henry's clemency toward her. Not that he'd ever done
more than gaze at her as he would at any of the lovely
things he never touched but seemed to know to admire.
If he had, Lucas was sure he'd have known of it; the lady
would've been swift to use it to her advantage.

No, and that might have explained it. Henry knew that
too; he was too clever to give any part of his body or
heart anywhere it could be held hostage. Or was he?
Lucas wondered when he saw Henry's expression before
he could change it as he looked toward his queen as she
stirred and rose, and crossed the small space that separated them, and took Lady Katherine into her arms.

The White Rose of the Plantagenets held the White
Rose of Scotland in her arms; the fair lady comforted the
dark, beauty against beauty, both at the mercy of one
man; the hostage queen and the hostage lady. Lucas, a
keen student of irony, watched them in each other's
arms: the one who grieved because she believed she was
going to be made the widow of the rightful king, this
queen's brother—and the other, an orphaned queen, who
walked through life as though still dreaming of it, and
whom no one but her children knew. And one of them,

Lucas thought, watching them as coolly and with as much suppressed emotion as Henry did, was his own sister, and the other, mayhap his sister-in-law.

He wondered what had shaken Elizabeth from her dreamy state; had Lady Katherine's tears recalled her own? Or was it possible she too believed Perkin Warbeck was her brother, about to be twice-murdered, so that her own son could be king? For all he'd suffered in his life, not for anything would Lucas have been his sister. Pale, lovely, and lost, she looked no more sorrowful now, in her sympathy, than she did each hour of her life, or at least those hours when her children weren't with her. He stood a handbreadth from her as she cradled Lady Katherine in her arms, so close he could detect her faint scent of amber and love-in-a-mist, and remembered it as having also been his mother's favorite.

Knowing sanctuary when she'd achieved it, Lady Katherine raised her tearstained face and spoke to the king from the depths of his queen's arms.

"None of this is proved, majesty. None of it. My Perkin has done nothing amiss. There are those who plot against him, those who will never forgive him, although all he's done is forgot and renounced by him—so he confessed, and so I vow it. He is innocent in this, I know it."

"I would he was," Henry answered, putting his hand on Arthur's shoulder as Arthur leaned forward to speak, or to question. "But here . . . how can I ignore this?"

He held out a sheaf of closely written parchments that crackled in his hands as he shook them at her, as though they could not wait to whisper the accusations written there.

"There were messages sent from the Tower and taken into it," Henry said. "Secret signals and signs: coded books and bits of cloth, bits of jewelry, ducats and gloves and spice boxes given, letters and badges and parchments and other tokens sent forth. It spread far and went deep: agents who were haberdashers, drapers, and clerks, yeomen and gentlemen of my own court, God forgive them. And some of noble blood—it is a sad, sad thing.

"Here," Henry went on, brandishing the papers. "It is all of it writ here, and we shall hear all of it at the trial, at the Guildhall, before the feast of St. Clement, before juries of sound and sane Englishmen. But here"—he pulled the papers back and scanned them—"here, names and places: second of August last," he read, "one Thomas Pounte and one William Basset, William Proude and Edward Dyxson, Thomas Asterwood and Thomas Ody— these men are heard to speak of a ship to take the Earl of Warwick from the Tower in London to the sea!"

The crowd in the room stirred, and Henry raised a shaking hand and read on. "Hear: here, twenty-fifth of August last: Thomas Ward, Dr. Alcok, and others—they speak of prophecies that the earl will become King of England! And here," he went on feverishly, "even so long ago as February last, Robert Cleymond and this same Asterwood were heard saying that 'the bear will shortly beat his chains within the city of London'! The Bear is Warwick's device, and so as to make doubly sure of what they meant, they cried 'A Warwick. A Warwick!' "

The room was murmurous with shock, but Lady Katherine raised her bowed head from the queen's breast and held herself up and away from her, so her words could be heard.

"This is all Warwick, I hear all Warwick, and know not of him. What of my Perkin?"

"Ah," Henry said sadly, "he may have once repented, but the Earl of Warwick's a clever and forceful man. They'd adjoining cells. Over the weeks, Warwick made himself a hole between their chambers through which he whispered sedition to your Perkin. It is my fault—that," he said, aside, to Prince Arthur. "I didn't think to put them in different towers. I didn't think to place them in rank dungeons. And so, how was I served? Freedom, whispered in the night to a prisoner, is heady stuff. How much more so must have been the talk of revenge, power, and kingship?

"Here," he intoned sadly, "it is here, all of it—slow poison does work, see here: twenty-fifth August, Asterwood sent tokens to Cleymond and John Watson and others on behalf of Peter Warbeck, so as to set him up as king. And here, Walter Bluet, John Audley, Asterwood, Cleymond, Roger Ray, Thomas Strangways, and others— others—too many others to read them all out now, all conspiring to make Peter Warbeck king."

He sighed and put the papers down and raised his

hands in a gesture of despair. "Warwick and Warbeck. They plotted to overthrow us, to set up themselves as kings. It is a sad, sad thing."

There was much mumbling of agreement in the room now, but Lady Katherine was as sharp of ear as of wit, and had found the discrepancy, and bit down hard on it. She stood apart from the queen, her eyes as wet and glittering and hard as her voice as she cried out, "Kings? How is this, 'kings'? What is this of 'kings'? They sought to overthrow your majesty and set themselves up as 'kings'? But England has only one throne—even a traitor knows this. How say you *kings?*"

Henry had the grace to flush, though it showed only as a darker shadow passing over his face.

"Some held for Warwick, 'tis true, some for your husband," he said quickly, with a trace of anger, quickly transmuted to sweet reason as he spoke to her with the outsize patience he might show to a child, "some for both. It matters not if they began in league with each other as Warwick and your husband did. I make no doubt one would have overwhelmed the other ere long. It is always so with such men. As my poor queen knows, for it was her own Uncle Richard who renounced and then most foully murdered her own brothers: Edward of Wales, and Richard of York, the true heirs to the throne—as your husband well knew and tried to use to his own purpose, if you'll remember—and all so that he could seize the crown. Yet, even so, there were good men then who believed his villainous claim. Good men led astray by arrant villainy. But if the devil were not glib, would not heaven be more crowded and a happier day already at hand? Nay, good men can be led astray, and so then how much more easily weak and flawed men? I have always taken that into account."

The crowd muttered its agreement, remembering the tragedy of the princes, as well as Henry's victory over Richard's supporters, and his clemency to some. After a moment Henry spoke on to Lady Katherine, and they fell silent to hear him.

"If good men can be so misled, how much easier to deceive one of your trusting, gentle sex, my lady," Henry said sadly. "You have been deceived. You saw your own nobility in a lesser being, my child. So it often is with women," Henry went on, now as much to her as to Prince Arthur, who was leaning in, following close on every word. "They reason with their emotions. Just so. Their tender hearts and frailty of nature make them easy prey for heartless men—conscienceless men—which is why we must protect them," he said ruefully to Arthur, and to the men of the court.

And that one hard-held truth obscured the other the lady had challenged, and the gentlemen nodded, whispering together until the room hissed with the sough of their sighs.

Oh, very clever, Lucas thought, actually smiling now as he gazed at Henry and then back to his sister, where she stood watching, her usual unreadable expression on her lovely face. And then the queen turned to him and looked at him with that same sweetly sad, all-knowing, unknowing gaze. Light eyes studied light. They stood so near: Lucas, taper tall and lean, and glowing with that unquenchable light that seemed to surround him, and she, fair and blond and fragile for all the womanliness of her. This close, at last he saw the ghost of the merry, cosseted child in the slight sad smile of the woman, and that, unexpectedly, caught at his heart. He began to step forward, only stopping when he realized he could come no closer, and even if he could, could never speak to her as he did now, silently, from his heart.

Ah, sister, sister, Lucas thought, so near to her that if he could whisper the words only so loud as his pulse raced, she'd have heard him clearly. Sister, have you ever known what you've done, lying with this man, your husband, your captor, your self-made king, Henry? Have you slept all this while as you've taken his seed and brought forth his children, marked with his dark stamp on their fair brows? They were sown in you with the force of two hopeless desires—for the uncontested crown, and for your love—to drive them deep into your womb. You're the receptacle of his dreams; are you anything else? Or was it that, like your brother, there was only this need for the heart to go on beating, this stubborn refusal to lie down and die when the heart was dead? If Perkin is our brother, will you know regret? Is it why you console his soon-to-be-widow now? Or is it me you know, and fear for, or is it only that you fear the knowing?

His bright light gaze searched hers, and it seemed she inclined her head, as if trying to understand a word she'd only half-heard. But that might have been the light changing, as the dark-cowled monk moved between the light and the king who watched them so narrowly, as he bent to whisper a word to him.

"Just so," Henry said. "You're right, good brother. This is no place for a trial."

"No, only for judgment!" Lady Katherine cried, and Lucas was shocked to hear her say what he'd thought, as she raged, her tears real, if her softened voice was not. "May I not see him, majesty? May I not see him?"

"No, no, no," Henry said, rising and placing his hand on her head as she knelt before him. "For your own sake, my child. That would not be fair to you. As we care for you, we must protect you. See to your lady," he said to Megan and Clarisse as he took his own lady's hand and drew her from the room with him, and all the company dropped to their knees as the royal presence passed among them.

"Sire!" a clear, cool voice called, and Henry stopped in his paces, looking back, even as his son Arthur was doing.

"An' it please you, majesty," Lucas Lovat said, "if the lady cannot see the pretender, mayhap another can see him for her?"

"Well-thought, Lovat," Henry said, nodding. "Brother Robert sees to the souls of all men, and frequents the Tower for their comfort too. He shall bear a message for you, lady, if you choose."

He'd begun his slow exit from the room when the voice rang out again, this time with, incredibly enough, laughter in it. "Ah, but, majesty, how can a monk say what a lady would say to her beloved husband? Especially if that husband's known to have a way with a lady? Marry, sire, would you turn your grayfriar red?"

The truth as well as the impudence of it overcame the astonishment at his presumption, and the crowd's gasps gave way to snickers and titters.

"Now, I, sire," Lovat went on, with that in his flexible voice which made what he said not so much presumption as sweet jest, "have no such sensibilities—alas. And as I serve you, I also call the lady friend. May I not go where holy brothers fear to tread?"

The unrestrained laughter of the crowd and the merriment in Prince Arthur's eyes would have made any answer of Henry's but "yes" a graceless one.

"Very well, then, Lovat," Henry said on a chuckle, "we shall never accuse you of holiness, so, aye, go to, and go from, and God save your soul, lad." He raised a hand as if in capitulation as the crowd laughed with him. But the humor in Henry's voice was not in his eyes as he left.

"Thank you," Lady Katherine whispered to Lucas fiercely as she leaned on Clarisse's arm and released her grip on Megan's. "We will speak later. Go with him, girl, and set a time."

"That was a brave thing," Megan said softly as she walked down a long corridor with Lucas.

"No," Lucas said, "doing what you have to do is never brave. Not doing it is cowardly, that's true, but doing it is not so much bravery as neccessity. I have to see him for my own purposes," he said, and fell silent, shocked at his honesty.

"Lucas," Megan said, "I know that there is much I don't know . . ."

She paused, and they stopped in the shadow of a pillar in a high-vaulted stone hall, and he saw that all the gray weight of the place couldn't pull the color from her rose-hued gown, or from her cheeks.

"I don't know how I can bear to see him die," she said in a soft rushed undervoice, "or see her suffer when he does," she added, bowing her head until he had to look at the top of her hood and not her vulnerable face, as with great daring for her, she placed one hand on his chest, "but in truth, I know I could not bear to see you hurt. So many have been charged, there is such suspicion everywhere now, the more so with anyone who has anything to do with Perkin . . . There's danger in this, and danger beyond that which I can see, though I am only a mere woman." There was sorrow in her small chuckle as she said that.

"I'm not Henry. No. I believe women can be fully as foolish as men," he said, lifting her chin with one gloved hand, so that she could see the truth in his eyes, "and just as dangerous—no, more so, because I don't know how to protect myself against this feeling I have for you, and I fear it more than any man I ever met."

She gave him her lips as an answer, and he found questions he could easily answer there. And so when they drew apart, she'd no more to say, because she realized he'd answered none of the ones that mattered most, and raised far more she couldn't know the answers to as yet.

"How simple you must find me," she said sadly. "You have only to kiss me to set all my doubts flying."

"I have only to step away to send them flying home again," he said ruefully.

"You know what I mean," she said more sharply. "You have had so many women."

"Yes, well-a-day, that makes me an expert on them, doesn't it? I know how to touch women," he said, his eyes glittering in the gray light, "and how to take their bodies—it's considered a great sport in many lands I've lived in, an art in others. That's true. But I don't know how to love them very well, nor have I tried. No more than I know how to love my fellowman—and apart from what our king believes, I don't think the two disciplines are that very different, aside from the bodily part of it. Although that part is one I don't ever wish to put aside," he said, smiling again.

But she did not.

"You said . . . some things . . . at Greenwich . . ." she stammered, then closed her eyes. "God's grace, Lucas," she said in a rush, "I've no brother or father to speak for me, and I'd thought . . . you said . . . What is it you would of me, Lucas?"

"I spoke of permanence," he said quietly, "and I did mean it. But now . . . things are in flux now, things are at stake, as you say, there is danger . . . I can't speak of the future beyond tomorrow just now, and even that may be presumptuous. But neither do I take back a word I said. Know this, my Megan: my behavior toward you will be as courtly and decent as if you'd two fathers and a legion of burly, bad-tempered brothers to defend you. Which is to say that I still speak of permanence, and will further, when I can. Until then, although I burn when I touch you, that is all I will do with you. My training will stand me in good stead, at least with that," he said ruefully, "so be easy in my arms as in my company, trust that I'll do nothing permanent to you—you've my solemn vow as to that . . . And nothing temporary with any other female either. Come, what else can I promise? Tell me, and I'll try."

"You're in danger," she said in a small voice.

"And so? I always have been," he answered. "I'm good at it. Don't worry for me, it will do me no good, and can only make you less easy with me. Which will do me harm. It is that easeful conversation, the gracious giving of your company, the lack of arch and coy games that cause men to think of women as Henry does of them, that I love so well in you. Your sincerity and honesty are what I need most now. They are what first and always draw me to you."

There was no more to be got from him on the subject of his welfare now; he'd closed the matter firmly, and she was wise enough to know it.

"Faith. My honesty and sincerity," she said on a sigh. "I knew it couldn't be my looks."

"Naturally not," he agreed, straight-faced, and waited to see her look of reproach before he kissed it away, before he put her away from him again with a regretful sigh.

They strolled on out of the shadow, and nodded to passersby, and talked of many different little things they were not thinking of.

"Tell your lady to prepare her message," Lucas said when he finally left her at her chamber door. "I'll see Perkin tomorrow, if I can. The next day, failing that. I can do nothing but visit with him, when I visit. But there will be other things I'll try," he said, passing his hand over his eyes. "I don't think he can wriggle loose from this net, no, too much is at stake, and he was in the wrong place at the right time, but a man must try. . . . But, Megan," he said suddenly, gripping her hand, "remember. If I ever fail you, it will be because I have failed myself, and for no other reason. None other, believe me."

She nodded, and he seemed assured. Then she watched him go away down the long corridor until the shadows ate his shadow and the vision of him winked out.

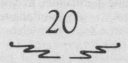

20

"Wait!"

Lucas paused on the top stair, and the guard, who'd gone before him, stopped as well and looked back curiously.

"I'd like to go there first," Lucas said, gesturing to the Earl of Warwick's closed door.

"No, no, sir, that's not where you want to go," the guard said, moving on. "That there is the Earl of Warwick's chamber. You want to see the pretender—he's down along here."

"I know," Lucas said, "but I wish to see the earl first."

The guard ran his hand over his mouth and gazed at Lucas. He was a clever fellow; all the guards round this tower were these days—all the guards in all the Tower were now, now that some of their own number were to meet the same fate as the traitors and villains that they'd guarded so casually were to suffer.

"Your papers say 'Warbeck,' sir," the guard finally said proudly, showing he could read, and had read, them, "not 'Warwick.' Sorry."

"My papers also say 'free and safe passage' within these walls," Lucas said imperturbably, with all the ease of a man born to rule. "Come, man, use your head," he said, allowing a touch of annoyance into his voice. It wasn't bluster, nor was it wheedling, because he knew that only an unsure man loses his temper, and only a beggar pleads. Most of all, he knew that whenever there was doubt, a civil servant would always rule for anything resembling official command.

"I've the king's seal and limited time, man," Lucas said, "and of course, an army at my back. God's teeth!

Am I so formidable you think I can overpower you all and spirit the fellow out? Here's a ducat for your trouble and another for your conscience. Now, let's to it, eh?''

"The last man who took gold when he shouldn't have done is in chains now," the guard said nervously, his eyes never leaving the dulcet gleam of the coins in Lucas' hand.

"What? Is he the last man on earth, then? Be sensible, the trap's sprung, the game is up, and moreover, Henry knows I'm here," Lucas said impatiently.

It was the familiar "Henry" that finally did it. The coins exchanged hands, the key was chosen and turned, and Lucas was ushered into the cell. After a whispered "half the hour—no more," the door was promptly closed behind him so the guard could at least say, if asked, that it had been another who'd let him in. Lucas' smile slipped when he saw that he'd been let into the wrong cell, for the earl must have been moved from this one.

It was larger and darker than the earl's room had been. And emptier. There was no clutter; there were no boxes and no books. Only bare stone walls and floors and a table and a chair. A few torches flickering, and one unmoving shadow against the wall. It spoke.

"Lucas Lovat," the Earl of Warwick said softly. "Hello again."

He was chained to the wall, and his head rested against it, the gray stone making that large head with its down of fair hair seem baby-fine and fragile. Someone had left a chair against the wall, but the earl sat on the floor, his thin wrists in chains so slack they hung down between his knees, as were his ankles in fetters, these fastened to the floor. It was as absurd as chaining up a crane fly, and it seemed the lanky earl couldn't so much as stir feebly in his present state.

"Oh, by God," Lucas said, dropping to a knee before him and hefting the weight of the chain in his hand as though he could lift it from the man by doing so, "why have they done this?"

"Because they say I'm a traitor and tried to escape," the earl said. "They don't bother me very much," he went on, lifting his fingers to indicate the chains on his arms. "I don't feel the weight because I stay still, and I don't mind that because I never moved around a great deal before. But when they took the boxes, I confess I was afraid. For my collections. But Brother Robert has them secure, he says, and comes every morning with a box so that I can go on identifying them so that there'll be not one left unknown when I die. They're going to kill me, you know," he said sadly. "They've gotten around to it at last. I don't know how I'm going to be able to do it," he said. "Here I am, all of . . . what is it now? . . . four-and-twenty—and I'm afraid I'll not be able to do it. My father would be ashamed of me."

"All men fear death," Lucas said, not knowing what else to say, wondering from the calm voice the earl used if he were entirely, blessedly, mad now.

"Oh, death," the earl said. "No, that's not it. I've been afraid of death for so long I know how to fear it very well. I've imagined the bite of the ax on my neck for so many years I think it will feel like they've done it before when they do it, even if it takes two or three cuts, because I've done that too, in the nights, in my mind, in all the years I've been here. I don't *like* it," he said, putting his head to the side to stare at Lucas. "Only a madman would. But I know it, and so I'm not exactly afraid of it. I hate it, to be sure. But it doesn't precisely frighten me. No, no, it's the going out-of-doors so they can do it, you see. And so they can try me. That means twice, twice over. Four times."

The blue eyes gazed steadily into Lucas' as the earl explained patiently, "Two comings and two goings. Out there." The thin fingers twitched as they tried to indicate the small window; the fetters did not so much as tremble. "I don't think I can bear that. I've been away from here only once, that time that Henry took me through London to Westminster, and back again, when he wanted to show everyone I was still alive, and that the pretender, Lambert Simnel, could never be me. But they never told me why I was leaving, and so I thought it was to take me to the block, you see. I rode through London with the crowds shouting, and Henry never said a word that I remember. When we came to the Abbey to pray, I thought it was for my eternal soul. Then we rode back here, in state, and I thought: Now, now it's the block. I pissed myself," Edward said very softly.

"And then they brought me back here, and I thought

they were so angry with me that they refused to take my head. Then I thought they wanted me to change my clothes so I could die like a man. But they didn't come back, and afterward, a priest told me what it had all been for. Well-a-day, I was only a boy then. Twelve. But too old to disgrace myself so. Much too old now. I don't pretend to be brave, but I'd like to be calm and dignified when I leave here. So you see, I don't fear the ax so much as wet breeches." He smiled to show it was a jest, but the pale lips trembled. "My father would be so ashamed of me."

All Lucas could remember of George, Duke of Clarence, was his braying laughter. But he felt such a surge of pity and love for this, his strange, childlike, yet oddly valiant cousin, that he couldn't speak for a moment. It seemed that when he least needed them, all the emotions he'd denied for so long were closing in on him. Having admitted love, he felt its attendant graces, pity and charity, crowding in as well. In that moment he felt as he had once when learning to swim, as he'd cried out for air and bubbled all the way down to the bottom of the sea before strong hands had borne him up again. Yet for all he felt he was drowning again, he knew he had to try to be such hands for his cousin now. Lies would not do. Hope could be offered, but later. Edward, Earl of Warwick, needed something better and rarer now; something like truth.

"Outside is only like inside, without a roof," he said. And was delighted to see Edward's singularly sweet smile.

"But I'm used to ceilings," Edward explained. "Things I'm used to I can endure. It is the new that frightens me."

"It isn't new to you. You know the birds, and their element, air. Who better than you can understand the sky? Other men gaze upward and see a world without end, and may be afraid. They may feel naked and unprotected. But not you, for you know the limits of the sky: how far up a bird can fly, how long and how far. For you know even the ether has its boundaries, although they're invisible to most men's eyes. Looking up, you can see just exactly how high the hawk can go—higher than even the damned ravens here, am I not right?"

"That is so," Edward said, his eyes widening as he listened. "Yes, just so, much higher, for they are birds of prey with far-vision, and their wings are made for soaring, tipped with lateral feathers that can open like fans against the wind, so they can lie on its currents and wait and watch the world beneath them. Very high, yes, very high," he said with animation.

"But not so high as the moon," Lucas said, "for each creature on earth has its paths, from the seas to the skies, and all are marked out as if by invisible lines, so that for all that the sky seems boundless, it has its margins laid as surely as if they were made of stone, as this ceiling above us does. Because the sky is only the ceiling of our little world, as this one is of this tiny chamber; nothing in God's earth or above it is limitless, save for his heaven, is that not so? And so it follows that a man in the open who knows the sky's limits is a man with a snug roof over his head, does it not?"

"Just so, yes, that is so," Edward breathed in a wondering tone, and lay still, his eyes still wide but now empty, as though he looked inward.

"Ah!" Edward cried out then. "Please, come closer, there is this . . . prickling in my fingers that comes after numbness. Brother Robert was so kind as to loosen the chains from the wall so they could lie in my lap, but I do think it would be better if I could raise them, and my arms, for a space, but I cannot. If you . . . The chair . . . For a while, at least, I pray you?"

Lucas bent and raised the slight body to the chair. The skin at his nape crept, for it seemed the body he held weighed less than the iron that weighed it down, and the man's bones were as fragile as a child's, or a bird's, beneath his hands as he helped sit him in the chair. It was as he was bending close to be sure the earl was comfortable that he heard as well as felt the faint breath at his neck, by his ear, and there was laughter as well as breathlessness at the unfamiliar exertion in the earl's soft voice.

"Thank you, Cousin Edward," the Earl of Warwick said.

Lucas drew back.

"Not too far," Edward, Earl of Warwick, said in that same low voice. "Here, as though you were tending to my chains. Yes, bend to me, here. They're so foolish," he confided, "to think I don't know every stone in these walls, every breach in them. I know better than those who made them years ago, I know every sound here, and how far exactly each sound carries and what makes it. This is my home and I know it better than any spy who slides through its walls. Rats slither and chirp, and beetles bang in the night—they do, though you wouldn't think such small things could—and the birds scratch like mice at the walls, but they rustle louder, and men sound like nothing else at all. There's a corridor there, behind you, and a peephole as well, in that wall, and one the size of a pin, to the left of the door; but an eye to a pinhole can see a whole room, and above me is the one they say I made to Perkin's cell, but they made it only last summer, to purify the air, they said. They are sly, but not clever. Don't worry—just here they can't hear us, cousin.

"Yes, I know you, that's why I spoke to you," Edward said, when Lucas still didn't answer. "I'd not confess my fear to anyone less, though I speak to Brother Robert about it, but he is more than any man of us is. But I remembered you as such a brave boy, and knew you'd help me if you could, and so you did. It will help me to think of the wide world as just another room, and so I shall. Thank you."

Lucas was as cold and still as the stone he rested his hand upon as he looked down to Edward. "You knew me from the first?" he asked slowly.

"Oh, yes," Edward said, "at once. I saw the boy become a man. But I don't take pride in that. It's no talent, I think. Only that I've not seen so many men since I saw you as a boy. My eyes haven't become blunted on so many faces as most men's have been, and so I remember the little I've seen very well."

"Did you tell . . . anyone?" Lucas asked, glad of a reason to lean against the solid wall now, for he thought he'd lost the use of all of his body save his busily working mind.

"Oh, no! Nor would I ever. Never. You were born to be free. I was only glad to see that you'd escaped from here, and sorry to see you return, even though it comforted me to know you'd lived on. Nor did I even tell you, for I thought you'd soon go again. But now I must, so as to warn you away. It's not safe for you here, Edward, in faith, it is not," he admonished him.

"I came back," Lucas said quietly, "to find out about

Perkin—Richard. . . ." He grew very still; his eyes flew wide, realizing that here, at last, he'd have his answer. He took a breath before he asked, "Edward, tell me, I pray you, cousin, if you've any love for me, is he . . . is he Richard?"

"Oh. He believes he is, he truly does," Edward said, "but I don't know. It was you I admired when we were young, and you I watched all the time. He looks very like, and he well may be. But, take care," Edward said, his thin fingers catching at Lucas' arm and his blue eyes huge with worry, "for whoever he is, he is mad now, I think. They say it is blood that will tell, but I think this place can do it too. Mayhap there is madness in all men's blood, and it takes special dark places to bring it out in them. This is such a place. And his injuries were severe. Take care with him, cousin, he is not himself, whoever that may be."

Lucas brought his hand around the cool thin fingers and pressed them hard. "I am here to bring freedom, if I can. I am here to free you too, cousin, if I can, believe me."

Edward stared at their entwined hands, and Lucas could feel the slight pressure that told him his cousin was trying to draw away. Lucas unclenched his hand and set Edward's free.

"I'm sorry if I hurt you," he began to say, but Edward interrupted, wonderingly, staring at his own hand. "Oh, no, no. It wasn't that. I am just unused to being touched. Even Brother Robert does not touch me. It's a strange feeling, is it not? I can't say if it's pleasant or not, it's too unusual. When I was young it was delightful, I remember, but now, after all these years, it's decidedly odd. I cannot say . . . But, no, Edward," he said sadly, gazing back to him, "I can't be free anymore. Not in the way you mean. Were you made my king again, cousin, still I could not be; all I'd ask of you is to let me stay here, as I am. But I would like that," he said more eagerly, as though trying to console Lucas.

But Lucas found he could not speak.

"Don't worry for me," Edward said anxiously from where he sat beneath Lucas, as Lucas turned his head into his clenched fist on the wall. "Ah," Edward said then, gazing up at the shadows above him, for his eyes

were attuned, as few men's were, to the stony shadows of
his cell, "thank you for that as well. It's comforting to
know that brave men can weep, as well as such as I am.
But, I pray you, no more," he said in an urgent whisper,
"for someone comes now."

Lucas heard nothing, but was so appalled that he'd lost
control that he contained himself immediately. He squared
his shoulders, waiting to hear the beginnings of sound
that had alerted Edward. But then Edward began speaking again.

"I find that few birds are so handsome as the common
rook," he said in his usual dry tones, "but men never
value the commonplace, however beautiful, do they?
Rooks are sleek and blue-black, with soft black down at
their breasts, and tails of iridescent black, more subtle
than a peacock and much more elegant than, say, the
lark. But then, the lark sings, but I've never heard one, I
only judge by appearances, you see . . . Ah, Brother
Robert, do come in, come see, I've company."

With a sound like a hiss, Lucas drew his silken sleeve
back from the wall and spun around to face the cowled
monk, who came in silently through the slightly open
door.

"I'll leave you now, my lord," Lucas said first; then,
turning on the monk, he said coldly, "I've come to see
Perkin, as you know. But I knew the earl from before,
from less strict days," he added on a bitter smile. "Is it
entirely necessary that he be chained up like a dog? He's
a dangerous rogue, to be sure, but surely sealing his door
would suffice?"

"He is chained up like an enemy to the king, and one
whom he fears," Brother Robert said in his clear calm
voice. "It is not necessary, it is only tradition, and in this,
the king acts with all ceremony. I try to alter that daily,
as I also come with fresh linen to wrap his wrists and
ankles against his iron bonds every day, and do all else
that I can to ease his discomfort. I shall not let him be
hurt."

And will you wrap linen about his neck so that the ax
doesn't bite so hard the day you walk with him to the
block? Lucas thought, but would not say it, not with the
earl's clear gaze upon them both.

"I come here to give comfort, as I try to do for the

king himself, as I would for any man in need of it. I am
not Edward's enemy, Lucas Lovat, nor yours, nor any
man's, believe me," the monk said softly.

"And why should I not, brother?" Lucas asked mockingly as he strode to the door, where the guard stood
watching, and then left with him.

His anger had scarcely time to cool before the guard,
fumbling with the key, opened Perkin's door.

"Here you be . . . Master Perkin, a guest for you!" the
guard called out as he ushered Lucas in, and then left,
closing the door behind him.

This time there'd been no tentative tap on the door to
ensure Perkin's privacy; this time Lucas had been fore-
warned by the sight of Edward in his chains. But nothing
had prepared him for the sight of Perkin Warbeck.

He stood tall and proud against the wall, as though
modeling his chains for an artist. His obstinate, pugnacious chin was up, his silken hair was bright against the
stones, and his eyes glittered like bits of sea glass as he
stared at Lucas. He was dressed in amber velvet, robust-
looking and unscarred, seeming even more regal in his
captivity than he'd been at his limited freedom in Henry's
royal court. For all that he seemed undefeated by his
condition, there was something badly wrong with him,
and although Lucas could not see it, he could almost feel
it in the air as he entered the room.

"Lucas!" Perkin boomed as he saw his visitor. "Well-
met! Come, man, have a seat. God's cross! If I'd the use
of my hands," he said, flexing his big hands against the
iron that encompassed them and held them to the wall at
his side, "I'd bring you a chair."

"It is hardly meet that I should sit while you stand,"
Lucas said, attempting a light note, and yet he started
when Perkin chuckled.

"Ah, well-a-day, but a king can scarcely stand on ceremony when he is also forced to stand against a wall, can
he? But I lie. Brother Robert provided me that chair. I
simply do not choose to sit now."

For a man in chains, even such a limited choice was a
large one, and Lucas respected that Perkin had made it a
choice. He also admired the way that Perkin stood, so
that both of his shoulders were equal, for now, up close,
he could see that the damage to the one of them had

increased, and every so often it would slump before
Perkin realized it and shored himself up straight again. Yet
it was not that which so disquieted Lucas. It was Perkin's
eyes. They were held too wide for a man whose eyes had
always had a slumberous cast; they were too bright with
excitement for a man pent alone in a cell; they reflected
too much and took in too little. Lucas had long since
learned how to disguise his emotions so that his eyes
became only flat mirrors of the world he plotted against
when he wished them to appear so—but these bright blue
eyes of Perkin's were sheerest glass, windows on some
infernally busy, gleaming, unknowable interior scene he
alone was seeing.

Lucas Lovat, born Edward, Prince of Wales, was, as
his cousin Edward, Earl of Warwick, had said, a very
brave man. But he nevertheless knew a sort of terror as
he gazed at Perkin Warbeck, and realized that whatever
his mission here had been, he was too late.

"Come, come, friend," Perkin said merrily. "What
news of my kingdom? Of my lady? My daughter? Come,
are you mute?"

"Your lady is well, and sends all her heart, as always.
Your little Margaret flourishes too," Lucas said.

"And what of my kingdom?" Perkin asked.

"It is ruled by Henry Tudor," Lucas said, and watched
to see what Perkin's answer would be.

He was startled anew when it came. For Perkin's lips
curled into a very human, weary grin, and he said softly,
"Ah! Marry, but I'd hoped you'd bring better news—that
of a plague or a sudden stroke of ill luck that would pluck
that usurper from the throne. May as well pray for a
great tidal wave or a holocaust, eh? Tell me, my friend,
is there any hope for us, do you think?"

"There are always hopes," Lucas said. He turned his
head with elaborate languor so that he was looking pointedly in the direction of the spyhole in the wall between
this and Warwick's cell, even as he seemed to be only
brushing a bit of feather off the velvet nap of his shoulder. "Life brings new hope with each dawn."

"Ah, don't fret about those who lurk in the shadows,
my friend, they'll try to have my head on the block even
if I'm discreet as a mouse," Perkin said, laughing heartily
now, "so let them listen at walls, at crooks and chinks

and secret passages, let them scurry and flurry and hurry and listen. Mayhap they'll learn something of royalty if they do."

Lucas didn't like the sound of the singsong rhymes. He frowned as he tried to see what this was before him—more cleverness, or certain madness—and said, "Aye, marry, but even kings show caution from time to time, do they not?"

"Oh, yes, 'tis so. As you, especially, should know," Perkin said, laughing, suffused with some inner mirth.

Lucas stood stiffly, catching his breath, wondering how to say what he had to say, and knowing he must not. It could have been a random jest, a madman's guess, or merely a reference to his relationship to Henry. Or it could have been his brother, sorely used, knowing who he was, and trying, at last, to reach him to tell him that he knew.

"What should I know?" Lucas asked, although he knew he should not.

Perkin cocked his head and looked at Lucas sidewise.

"Clever, clever fellow," he said softly, "surely I should not say?"

An Italian nobleman with a speck of Romany blood had once told Lucas, when they were drinking hard together, that fortune-tellers take their fortunes from men's eyes, and not their hands or cards or cups. So Lucas willed himself to serenity and a steady silence.

That was a thing Perkin seemed unable to bear now. He veered from the subject and spoke out angrily again.

"They seek to destroy me. By so doing, they declare me king as surely as my blood does," Perkin said. "How is it that they forget this?"

"It's said," Lucas reported honestly, "that the Earl of Warwick's their true prey. As documented Plantagenet heir to the throne, he's dangerous, if only because he could be a rallying point in future for Henry's—or his son's—enemies. Or so, at least, Ferdinand and Isabella think, and so it's a Spanish hand on the writ of treason, and not just an English one."

"They lie!" Perkin cried. "They don't attempt to sacrifice the turnspit Simnel, do they? Or"—he lowered his voice and looked at Lucas—"any others they distrust. God's wounds! It can't be poor simple Warwick they fear—he'd be too easy to dupe, don't you see?"

"No," Lucas said, "I do not, because he was not duped." And because he couldn't ask the question closest to his heart, Lucas asked another that might lead him to it. "They laid this trap, yes. But why did you walk into it? Whatever the music, there can be no dance without the dancers. The others couldn't have gone on without you. Warwick? He'd never have countenanced it. They could have fabricated the whole of it—but I wonder if even Henry would have dared be so bold. But meetings and plots, trinkets, papers and tokens given and received . . . why did you have any part of it?"

"Ah," Perkin said, eyes glowing, "there it is. There you have it. Warwick could not, indeed. But I could and can lead England, and they knew it."

Had his trials turned Perkin's wits, Lucas wondered, or had he been flattered into folly? Was he still flattered, even now as he stood in the shadows of the gibbet? Lucas sought to reach the man he'd known, or had never known. "Did you never think of your lady?" he asked gently. "Your child, your obligation to them?"

"My obligation is to fulfill my destiny—to be king. My lady knows that, has always known it, and never doubted or hindered me," Perkin said proudly. "She was born to be queen, and knows it. That's why she took my hand, and holds it still. Would she have loved me were I less, or had I given up my quest? No more than I'd love myself."

Lucas felt a flicker of disquiet at the possible truth of that as Perkin went on in a feverish voice, straining forward against his chains, "And so you must help me. For my sweet Katherine's sake, for England's sake, for Christ's sake, for God's sake, for truth and honor's sake," and as Lucas turned his head aside, he added, "Aye, and for your own sake, as you well know. Don't abandon me. How can you, knowing what you know?"

Lucas stared at him—no more free to leave than the man who spoke to him.

"You know this place," Perkin said softly. "You know the fear that breeds within its walls, as well as the rush of joy that comes when you leave it—how can you leave me to it, and death? Think. Will you ever rest easy again if you do? Save yourself and me. Speak for me, act for me, be for me as you once were. Help me again. I must leave here. Lead me to freedom—I will follow."

"But he is only a man," Brother Robert said as he entered the cell, "and for all his love, cannot melt chains, or the hearts of kings. Leave that to God, my brother, and leave this man to his own duty, which he has sworn to his king."

"And if I am that king?" Perkin asked, glaring at the monk.

"You'd best go now," Brother Robert said, although he didn't look at Lucas as he approached the chained man with something he picked up from the table.

But Perkin turned his head away from the cup that was offered him. "I don't understand. How can you leave me?" he cried after Lucas as he went to the door.

And for all that Philip gossiped and chattered all the way back to Westminster, and a newly shrill wind blew the last dead leaves in flurries about them, and the cries of London were loud with commerce, still Lucas heard only Perkin's words as they echoed again and again in his mind.

He washed, he dressed with care, he combed his hair and placed his flat black hat over it, and selected one jewel on a gold chain to wear about his neck, and for all the time and trouble he took with his appearance, Lucas saw nothing but Perkin's face and figure before him as he readied himself for the evening.

He was expected. The moment he set his hand on the door, it opened to him. The lady herself immediately stepped out on the threshold, as though she couldn't wait the requisite seconds it might take for him to enter the room.

"He sends his love to you and the little one, as well as his desire for you to be easy in your mind," Lucas told the Lady Katherine, to spare her the trouble of asking.

"How does he look?" she asked eagerly, staring at him intently, as though she thought if she looked hard enough she might still see the reflection of her husband there on the surface of his eyes. "Is he well? Is he sound?"

"He looks amazingly well, and he is sound in all but . . . his expectations," Lucas said, and the brief panic in the lady's expression vanished. "He frets, of course, for the day of the trial, but is readying himself for that."

She nodded, and then smiled at last. Then she beckoned Lucas into her chamber, and as he followed her, she said on a gratified sigh, "It is as you said, Brother Robert. Pray forgive me for doubting you."

Lucas' head snapped up. The damned ubiquitous monk! Were there no others in Westminster? he wondered. London's streets were aflow with the comings and goings of holy friars, and yet again, this monk of Henry's! He stared at the cowled figure in the center of the room and involuntarily shuddered; Megan was at one side, Clarisse on the other, and the tall form between them was draped in gray robes that flowed to the floor. Their bright faces and garments were separated by a shadow.

"I'd speak to the good brother awhile longer. Clarisse, you've that errand to perform, and you, Megan, may take Lucas to our table. I'll be along presently," Lady Katherine said.

"How often does he come to your lady?" Lucas demanded the moment they were alone in the corridor.

"Now and again he hears her doubts and calms her fears. He sees Perkin quite often," Megan explained, her face grown grave and fearful.

He touched her cheek and nodded. His finger strayed, seeking to smooth the line that had appeared between her downturned brows. "Aye, you do well to fear him— he's not all he seems, I fear," he said.

"No, no one here is," she agreed, and catching his hand, said, "but that isn't what I fear. What is it that alarms you, Lucas?"

"Only he," he said. "He troubles me."

"But he should not," she said. "Of all of us, he's the most innocent. He only seeks to help us . . . Ah, I see—you think it's because he attends the king . . . but so do we all, and Brother Robert *is* a holy man. I think he sees little difference between the souls of any man or woman, king or no. That's why the king values him, even as we do, even though sometimes what he says angers Henry. I know he pleads for Perkin now—"

"Do you?" Lucas asked harshly. "Do you really? How so? Because he says so? And who is he? Brother Robert. And what is that? Have you ever seen him without his cowl? Why, then, he could be any man, could he not?"

"No," she said, angered. "I am not a fool. I know his

figure . . . his voice. His voice," she said with conviction, "is clear and distinct, as his face is not. But he covers it over so that he can be nothing to any man or woman but a conduit to God."

"Oh, yes," Lucas said, "a faceless man in the service of God. Aye. I've seen such faceless men in my travels. And do you know, some of them nevertheless have lips that tell men's secrets to kings, and not just God. And some have fingers that take coins from men's purses and slip them into their own, and not just the church's. And some have bodies beneath those anonymous robes, male bodies that beget babes on trusting girls, and there is nothing immaculate about their conceptions." He took her chin hard in his hand and glowered at her. "If you are fool enough to trust, at least trust men you can see, and saints who have no corporal bodies, for men are vile, and you must be able to watch them, and saints have no concerns of the body, and I've never met one."

Even as he loosed her chin from his hard hold, he knew it wasn't that which had put the tears in her eyes. He caught her up and held her tightly against himself, and brushed aside her gabled hood so that he could feel the cool weight of her scented hair against his lips as he rocked her, as though she were a child, or he was.

"Forgive me, forgive me," he whispered. "I've looked on hell today and see evil everywhere now. I'm not a man who has a great deal of trust in anyone, but I'd no right to make you feel the weight of my distrust. No, not you, never you," he said, and held her close, and sighed, and then took her lips.

But he kissed her for only a little while, because for all it gave him pleasure, he didn't want to change this moment to another that would bring them to a moment of decision. He discovered it was enough to hold her and feel at peace with her, despite the desire for her, or perhaps even because of the companionship of their mutual denied desire.

"Am I forgiven?" he finally murmured, and his breath stopped when she didn't answer at once. Nor did it regain its normal pace until she stirred in his arms and nodded, and finally whispered, "Yes, yes, of course."

"Now, then," he said, with resolution, putting her from him and helping her to set her hood right again, "down to dine, and to watch the jesters and dancing bears, and behave as if there were nothing more important in the world than our entertainment and our dinner. In truth, is there?" he asked, and laughed, and, jesting, took her down the long and twisted stair as though there were not.

He was so merry throughout the service of the meal that those nearby him could not eat without dropping bits and pieces of their dinner on the table, or on themselves, their hands and mouths shook so with their mirth. Lady Katherine looked bright and brave, as did they all, and only the jesters, annoyed to find their own offerings ignored, looked upon them with displeasure.

He was so merry, and their laughter came so easily, that anyone would think he'd no time to note the lost and despairing look that came into the ladies' eyes when he was not setting them aroar. The Lady Katherine's sudden bouts of despair he could understand. The Lady Megan's he could not. But he'd dined with princesses who poisoned their rings before dinner as other women would polish their nails, and he'd sat with princes who'd fondled their dirks and planned where to sink them in their guests as other hosts might prefigure carving roasts for their guests in their minds. So he knew how to laugh as he worried, and how to jest as he wondered at how to discover the truth. And decided, at length, that there was only one way to do it, if he were ever to trust her entirely. And that he wanted to.

He waited until a small hour, until their dinner was done and the games were almost all played, and her lady had taken herself off to her bed, allowing, as ever, Megan her moment with her gallant in the corridor. Then he forestalled Megan with a touch on her sleeve. She lifted her lips to his. He put one long finger over them, not his own lips.

"Tell me," he said instead, "have you been seeing Brother Robert? Giving him anything, from confession to confidences?"

Then he lifted his finger.

She sighed.

"I've talked to him when my heart's been full, but of nothing I wouldn't tell any good friend. I consider him

one. But if you do not, I will not, and there's an end to
it. For you mean more to me than he."

She gave him her lips again. This time, he took them.
But when they drew apart, her eyes were still troubled,
and that troubled him. Still, he thought, after he'd kissed
her hand and bidden her good night, leaving her leaning
against the door to the chamber she shared with Clarisse,
it was better to worry over whatever fears she hadn't
shared with him than to face what he'd been staving off
all day and knew he must finally face later tonight.

She watched him go down the long corridor, from
torchlight to torchlight, his soft boots not leaving so
much as a whisper of sound to follow him out of sight.
And she knew she had lied, and knew that she must, and
knew that she couldn't anymore, just as she'd known and
thought all night. If she were to do anything, she must do
it now, before her fears cautioned her to safe and selfish
silence again, as always. If she was to leave him, and save
herself by so doing, she must be angry with him, and how
could she be angry with him for not being honest with
her if she weren't honest with him herself? Yes, and if
she were never to leave him, as she wished she never
would, she needed his trust as much as anything else
about him. And besides, she thought, watching him re-
cede in the dark, she was weary with waiting and watching as she'd done all her life. So before she could reason
herself back to sanity, she cast herself off from the door
and flew down the hall behind him.

Her soft slippers made no more noise than a moth's
wings might, but he was a man trained to hear shadows
shifting, and he turned round before he reached the stair
and opened his arms for her as she fell into them.

"Ah . . . but I tell the king everything," she blurted.

And then, having said it, she let herself weep into his
soft linen shirt. "I do, and have done, it is why I am
here," she said, raging at herself as her fists weakly
struck the truth home on his chest. "He summons me,
and I tell him. Brother Robert's often there with him. I
didn't lie so much as avoid the truth, for I don't
confess to Brother Robert, but to the king, and Brother
Robert hears. Forgive me," she said, and only then allowed herself the last brief luxury of feeling his hand cup
the back of her head while the other held her close. For

surely he couldn't want her any longer. But now, who would, now that she'd betrayed the king? she thought, and knew her folly even as she reveled in it.

"I knew," he eventually said as she shivered in the aftermath of tears, "or at least I thought as much, since, as I said, I trust no one. But now I have to trust you, don't I?" he asked wonderingly. "What have you done to me, Megan?"

"I thought you'd be glad," she said when she raised her head and he cupped it in his two hands and looked down at her.

"Glad to be rid of you? Or to have you? Which did you really want? I think you don't know how to trust any more than I do," he said quietly, "because trust's a burden, isn't it? Marry, I suspect that's why it takes two to carry it. But it's a precious weight. Thank you.

"Now what?" he asked after they'd kissed. "Shall you tell Henry of this?"

"No," she said, "but I'm not a very good liar. I believe that's why he believes me."

So many liars confessed how badly they lied to him today, he sighed. But this one, he believed.

"Then don't lie," he said firmly. "Leave that to me. I'm very good at it. Don't worry. He may not summon you so soon. If he does, I may have already spoken to him. And it may be that I'll have already taken you away with me before he does. I am taking you away with me, you know that?" he asked.

She nodded. He walked her back to her chamber door, and only then spoke again, and then he was laughing.

"Marry, there's trust!" he said as merrily as if he were still at the table. "She nods, and agrees, without saying a word that she's wondering. In wedlock, idiot mine," he said, smiling. "I'm taking you in wedlock when I take you away. Now, to sleep."

He left her, at last, and sauntered back to his room, humming a light tune to himself all the way, as if he'd not a dread appointment of his own to keep. It wasn't until he'd undressed and laid himself down on his bed that he let her bright image fade, and set aside the warm glow of her trust, and kept his appointed vigil with himself at last.

He'd told her the truth, but that truth was conditional,

marked by a small word here, marred by another there.

"It *may be* that I'll have taken you away before he does."

"I'm taking you in wedlock *when* I take you away."

All true, but the choice of a word made it all provisional, because so much as he wanted to do all he'd said, his life was not his own. How telling a mere word could be, he thought, hoping she'd not realize it, wishing he could remember such small words with less accuracy.

They'd been walking down that damned stone stair in the Tower, those years ago, and he could feel his brother Richard's small hot hand in his as he led him down in the wake of their mysterious saviors into the darkness. They went down as that other pair of wondering boys was straggling up, and he'd paused and Richard had whispered fiercely, "Hurry. We must leave here. Lead on—I'll follow."

But Perkin had said, "Lead me to freedom—I will follow."

Perkin had been in extremis. And many years had passed. And how many men had the memory he himself had? A simple coincidence? Or a true remembrance? Too close to know, too far to ignore.

"Lead on—I'll follow." "Lead me to freedom—I will follow."

A simple refrain, really, a little ditty I picked up in my travels, Lucas thought bitterly when he finally sat up in the small hours of the night, with the words still reeling in his head, over and again.

"I'm taking you in wedlock when I take you away" was a much better lyric, certainly, he thought. But then, he'd always preferred songs of love to dirges.

Then he held his heavy head in his hands and let his hair swing forward so that it obscured even the night. He thought of his love and thought of his brother and wanted one as much as the other, and knew that in the end, in all honor, he'd likely have to let one go off alone into the night in order to have the other.

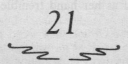

21

"It is a lie!" she cried, struggling in Lucas' arms, and he
held her back, using more force than he ordinarily would
with a woman, but then, Lady Katherine's panic had
made her extraordinarily strong. But it was words that
quieted her, in the end.

"If you cry out, if you protest, if they proclaim Perkin
was a black toad by night and a white mare by day and
you so much as whisper that he wasn't and they hear you,
you will have disgraced him, and yourself, and will do
neither of you any good," Lucas told her.

She grew still.

"If you cannot bear lies, do not go to courts of law,"
he said harshly. "Courtrooms spawn lies, truth has no
home there, and your calling out of so much as God's
own gospel truth would only make it seem like more lies.
Do you see? The trial will be done before it's acted out,
in any case. It will be decided long before it's heard, as
always. Or long after, by a miracle, or gold, or divine
coercion of some other sort. We'll work behind the court,
around it, and beyond it, as clever men must always do.
If you insist on going today, remember there'll be no
justice there, expect none, and if you wish to survive it,
don't listen."

"I must go," she said dully. "They won't let me see
him. How else can I see him and let him see me?"

There was truth in that. He loosed his grip on her and
let Megan take her into her arms. Brother Robert nodded, or at least his cowl rose and fell.

"I've a dram for you to drink," the monk said. "It
tastes of mint and will cool your temper and your
passions."

"Will you give such to my Perkin? Pray do not! He needs his wits about him," Lady Katherine cried, agitated again, even as her hand trembled on the cup the monk handed her.

"He needs nothing from me today," the monk assured her, and waited for her to drain the cup before he nodded again, and then left them to prepare the lady in other ways for her day of trial.

The Guildhall was crowded this Monday before the feast of St. Clement the Pope, the fourteenth of November in the fifteenth year of Henry Tudor's reign. There were twenty-four sworn jurors on the grand jury, and over three dozen unsworn alternates called before the special commission headed up by Nicholas Alwyn, the mayor of London, and eighteen other honored knights and gentlemen. There were over a dozen traitors to be charged. And hundreds of persons crowding in to see it, for it was a tale of treason and cunning, noble blood and disputed blood, and an aborted regicide to be told.

But it wasn't as Megan had expected it to be. Brother Robert might have spared his potion for another day, she thought, since even if Lady Katherine had been in her highest state of nerves, once it had begun, she'd have known it was nothing but an act of theater—high drama and not judgment—that was put before the world this day.

The prisoners came in chains, and were the most avidly watched; that much was so. All of them—from the yeoman guards to the gentlemen, the lost-looking youths and scholarly old men, the imperiously beautiful Perkin Warbeck, as well as the shy, confused Earl of Warwick, who stood blinking in the light, craning his long neck as if to study the high ceiling above his bobbing head—were as much on display as on trial. They stood in their fetters and heard the many charges read out to them by heralds whose mellifluous voices carried through all the hall and to every ear in the crowd. And that was to be the sum of their public trial today, or any other day.

For it transpired that the indictments had all been given and the testimony all taken, and the inquisitions all done previously, long before this day, and done in private. This was so as not to confuse the issues and intimi-

date the witnesses, delay justice or appeal to the baser
instincts of the crowd. Or so the heralds proclaimed. And
in truth, there were so many witnesses, and accusations
to make as well as to affirm, that if it had been per-
formed before them all now as it had already been done
in private, it would have taken from the Monday before
the feast of St. Clement to the Monday after, in order for
it all to be heard.

As it was, only bits and pieces of pertinent information
remained with those most interested, because there were
so many accusations and so much evidence to be read
out, one example after the other, that it became impossible to follow it all closely. All of it was exactly as it had
been written in those papers King Henry had held in his
hands that day he'd first told Lady Katherine about it,
even as he held them so today.

The words ran together even as they rang out.

". . . who with other traitors in confederacy with
Peter Warbeck of Tournay, born under the obedience of
the Archduke of Austria and Burgundy, conspired the
death of the king," a herald read out in the first indictment, "and for that treasonable purpose, the said Dyxson
and Carre met together on twelfth July at London at the
parish of St. Mary Wolnoth in Longburn Ward, and
Dyxson showed Carre that he and other traitors would
snatch Warbeck and the Earl of Warwick out of the
Tower of London and set them at large . . ."

During that indictment, Megan heard Lady Katherine
gasp only once, at first, when it was read that Thomas
Asterwood and William Loude had confessed to ducats
changing hands, although there was much more testimony following about ships being readied, allegiances
sworn and solemn vows taken. But by then she'd grown
still, and kept to that silence. The testimonies that followed in other indictments—to do with tokens and signs,
books and bits of painted parchments, gifts exchanged
and bribes given and taken, elaborate plans for escape
and deeper plots for what would occur after those
escapes—were read out and gasped over by the crowd,
which eventually grew more restive than shocked by the
repetitive nature of the deadening weight of the evidence
of treason as the hours wore on.

Some of the accused stood with heads down, the older

ones the more so as the hours fled, because of the weight of their chains as much as their crimes. Some of them shuffled their feet from time to time, causing their fetters to clank in eerie counterpoint to the charges being read out against them. Some looked frightened, some reconciled, and some seemed drugged by shame or sorrow.

But Perkin Warbeck stood upright, legs apart, wearing his chains as though they were light and noble as ermine, and his handsome face bore a faint polite and bored smile. Every eye in the crowd was on him at one time or another, but he never looked once at anyone, not even to where his wife sat drinking in the sight of him as a novitiate might watch a priest at a high mass. No, he looked into the distance, as though he saw a better thing there. And Edward, Earl of Warwick, after a time stopped goggling at the ceiling, even as he seemed to stop listening to the charges being read, and instead watched the sea of faces before him with all the wonder and candor of the overgrown child he appeared to be.

When the indictments were finally done with being read out, and the time came for the accused to plead to them, their cracked and small voices began to plead guilty or simply beg the mercy of their countrymen and king. The silence in the room was profound by the time the question was put to Perkin Warbeck.

And that same silence, and a smile, were his only answer. There was a thrill and a low buzz of awed conversation from the crowd to be heard in the vast chamber when he was asked again—only to answer the same way. But when he was passed over, and the question was put to the Earl of Warwick, that slight young nobleman looked up, astonished, and said, "What? Pray, what? What is it that I am supposed to say now?"

"Ah, poor soul," one woman was heard to say in the crowd. "Don't know 'is arse from 'is ear," another voice commented, and so the crowd began to murmur to itself about innocents and shames. But they were silenced by the king.

"Enough," Henry said, rising and putting his hand on Prince Arthur's shoulder. "My heart cracks to hear such villainy. No more now. Give them time to look into their hearts and souls. We shall reconvene on Friday, after the feast of St. Clement, and hear the rest of them out then, before we pass sentence."

"But . . . but what is the verdict?" Megan asked, confused, turning to Lucas as they all arose and bowed low so that the king could take his leave of them.

"Why, guilty, of course," Lucas said softly, putting his arm about her to comfort her, "from the first, and on all charges. The juries found them all true bills, didn't you hear?"

The summons came after dinner, when all the court had gone to their beds. Since the hearings at the Guildhall, they retired early or went to quiet pursuits; there was no merrymaking, with treason and treachery hanging so heavily on everyone's mind. Of course, the festivities would begin on the day of the executions, or so everyone said, but until then there were a brooding silence and a certain respectful sorrow shown in the halls of Westminster Palace.

Lady Katherine had gone to her bed early again, with the help of Brother Robert's possets. When she did, she slept soundly. She did not beg for her husband's life, nor did she seek an audience with Henry again; rather she bore herself bravely, like a grieving queen, and excited everyone's admiration, except that of her handmaiden Megan.

I'd screech, I'd scream, I'd set fire to the palace, I'd wreack havoc in some way, she vowed to herself, if I were she.

But she wasn't, and so she could only grieve silently, and hope to see Lucas and share her misery with him. But in the days since the trial he hadn't come to her, and when she did see him, it seemed he eyed Lady Katherine without sympathy, and herself with detachment, and was himself drawn and distant. He'd a kind smile for Megan when he noticed her, but was always distracted, and soon gone again on some other mysterious errand to do with the fate of Perkin Warbeck—or so, at least, he said he was. And so when Megan was summoned to the king's presence, she was singularly unprepared. But nevertheless she went immediately, knowing that a summons from the king was like one from Death himself, and whatever her state of grace at the time the call came, she had to go.

This night the king had his son Arthur, as well as Brother Robert, in his chamber with him when Megan was admitted. She rose from her curtsy and tried to contain her fear. Lucas had said not to lie, but every impulse told her that she must.

"Ah, Megan. And what have you to tell us tonight?" Henry Tudor asked.

"Nothing, sire," she said.

"Talk to me of Lucas Lovat, then."

She looked at her king with horror. He chuckled.

"Nothing, eh? Surely not. That color in your cheeks tells me that you've either passed the night sitting by the fire or have something to tell that a maiden cannot. Or should not. Beware, child," he said, shaking a thin finger at her, "Lovat's handsome and witty, but he's a notorious seducer and a clever one. But I don't ask about personal matters. Only matters of state. Come, speak up. You haven't lived in a shell these past days. Is there nothing to tell me—even if only of what Lovat says of these trials?"

For all she longed to speak up and not be reckoned a fool, she knew that one word would follow another, and had vowed to herself not to so much as mention Lucas again in Henry's presence. There was a hunger for blood abroad, and she knew it, and Lucas was several things she did not know, and she knew that too, and so, however demeaning to be thought an idiot, she'd rather that than be tricked into being a traitor to him.

"I don't know what you mean, sire," she said softly, gazing down at her hands. "We all speak of Perkin Warbeck. My lady said—"

"I didn't ask about your lady, I asked about Lucas Lovat," Henry said.

She felt her gown grow damp at the back and underarms, and suddenly realized that sometimes it took more courage to cower and seem afraid than it did to strike out as she yearned to do. She bit her lip and stammered, "Ah, but . . . marry, but what can I say? I remember nothing out of the ordinary . . ."

"Foolish maid," Henry said sadly. "Whatever he's had of you, or plans to have, he's not asked me for your hand, you know. Such, such is the frailty of women," he commented to Arthur. "Go, then," Henry said on a sigh.

"I know you've seen him repeatedly, and doubt you've heard nothing in all those hours, and so know your usefulness to me is over, however it turns out. I hope you've not pinned your hopes on a bird of passage. Ah," he added as the monk stirred at his side, "fear not, I sheltered you for your parents' sake, and shall continue to do so, so long as you've need of us."

She hurried from the room, stopping to stare when she saw who waited to enter after her.

"Lucas!" she whispered, but he put up his hand to stop her.

"We'll speak later," he said. "Don't worry."

But he was whiter than she'd ever seen him, and his smile was brittle, and she stood and looked after him until the guards at the door he'd gone through stared hard at her. Then she noticed one of them had a smile no guard had ever dared aim at her before, and she picked up the hem of her skirt and fled.

"Lovat," Henry said pleasantly as Lucas bowed, "we were just speaking of you."

"Indeed, sire," Lucas said. "I hope only good things."

"She is my creature," Henry said, watching him closely, "and always has been."

Lucas looked at Henry with mild inquiry. Though his eyes were shadowed beneath with faint blue smudges, they did not so much as flicker, and though his face was pale, nothing in it changed at his king's words.

"Ah," Henry said, sitting back, visibly disappointed, "you knew. Sooth, Lovat, is there a maid in England who is proof against you? There, brother, before you, is what you ought to preach against if you want to ensure chastity in England. Mark him well, Arthur, if you need to know the finer points of wooing. What is it you wished to see me about?" he asked suddenly, now regarding Lucas without a semblance of a smile.

"I wanted to speak of Perkin Warbeck," Lucas said calmly, "and of the sentence to be handed down."

"Which is none of your business," Henry snapped, "although I see you've attempted to make it so. You've been busy on his behalf, haven't you? You've visited Alwyn, Rede, Danvers, Lord Talbot, and Lord Sheffeld. And have more on the horizon. I'm surprised at you. You know they're all mine. Let them be. Warbeck's to

die. He's a traitor. Let him be. Leave him to me, and his
God's mercy, and be done with it. What concern is it of
yours?"

"I serve the Lady Katherine—"

"Ah! Yes, that's a task I charged you with, if you'll
remember. Have you been so long in the lady's company
that you've forgotten why you were there? Are you telling us that a worm in place too long in an apple begins to
believe that it was once a blossom too? Don't confuse
your pose with your reality, Lovat. I'm no silly maid, to
lie down and spread myself for your lies. I know you for
what you are."

Lucas' head came up, he grew deathly still, and his
light eyes glittered, but he said nothing.

"Be gone," Henry said. "Leave Warbeck to me, and
be pleased I don't take your recent work and this request
as proof of your complicity with him."

"If I might see him once more, before . . ." Lucas
said stiffly.

"You will see him once more, at the Guildhall, and
then again at Tyburn, where he will be drawn forth, and
hanged, and quartered, as befits his sins. If you wish to
see his several parts after, you've my permission. But no
more before that," Henry said, spacing his words with
harsh precision. "You may go now."

There was silence when Lucas had left. Henry looked
into his son's eyes, and looked away, before he spoke
again.

"It needs must sometimes that you try a man to his
limit," he explained, "to see if there's anything else you
have not seen in him. Yes. He's a good man at his tasks,
and a faithful one. But I have a care for you, my son, and
would try an angel to be sure of it before I'd let it remain
in your service. Brother, tell the lad that even saints are
tried by God," he said with a forced laugh. "Don't you
see?" he asked Arthur in a tone few of his subjects had
ever heard, when there was no answering laughter, as his
eyes worriedly sought his answer in the wide, beautiful
eyes, so like his mother's in all but hue, of this, his most
beloved son.

"I see," Arthur said softly, "but I trusted him from the
first. And disliked to see him brought low."

"Oh. By my faith!" Henry said, relieved. "He could

have been brought much, much lower, and well he knows it. Don't fret. I know such men as he. Neither be deceived; he has a dozen faces. I'll warrant he's got a happier one on now than the one he showed to us, and is already on his way to warm and welcoming arms in a snug bed, and laughing over this even now."

He was certainly too old to cry, and didn't consider that a possibility, and so was devastated that he felt the need. Lucas paced the narrow halls of the castle, soft-footed and restless, causing the guards' eyes to follow him as they stood motionless at their several posts, as he passed by them in his wanderings. Such was his preoccupation that he never cared if they noticed his agitation.

So Perkin would die, and painfully, and soon. What of it? He'd been a fool, and a careless one, and so twice a fool. Forgetting treason, a man who was so monumentally foolish could not expect, and did not deserve, to survive these days. Only a fool would mourn him. So the Lady Katherine would be a widow very soon. What of it? She was no fool. Perkin himself knew that his attraction to her had been his pose of princeliness, and she was the sort of martyr who'd be happier with the image of a wronged and dead prince as husband than with the body of a live and common mortal fool in her bed.

But each time Lucas turned toward his own small chamber, he heard the words, and then he'd turn and go up a long stair or down another, and tried to go on walking until he heard the words no more, although they kept time with his feet even as he fled them: "Lead on—I'll follow," "Lead me to freedom—I will follow."

His brother had died of the smallpox. He'd seen the terrible oozing lesions. He'd seen the small, still body. With his own two eyes he'd seen these things. But those same two eyes had seen two other boys go up as they'd gone down, to be left to be slain in their stead. Bodies were got cheaply enough. And made even more cheaply: how long, after all, would it take to kill Perkin, even as elaborately as treason required? When had they ever told him the truth? If it was as often as he himself had told it, it was rarer still.

"Lead me to freedom—I will follow." But he was leaving Perkin to death. "Lead on—I'll follow." He could still feel that small hot, damp hand in his. The hair, the eyes, the chin, so much was as it might be. Could he be leaving his brother to die again?

He was not in the habit of confidences, and so never thought to seek anyone to receive his now. He had been alone for all these years since he'd let go of his brother's hand, no matter how often he'd shared his body since. And now he felt the pressure of all those years bearing down upon him as though he were expected to birth some new thing to ease them. The tall, slender, fair-haired man roamed the castle's corridors like the ghost of some ancient, unsatisfied death as he wondered what he could do, what he should do, what he must not do, and couldn't decide what it was that life required of him now that he'd been stripped of his lifelong goal.

But even men such as Lucas Lovat grow bodily weary. At length he looked at his surroundings, and turned and sought his own chamber, so that his body might rest.

He'd been trained to react to every surprise, and so his dirk was in his hand even as he dropped to his knees. But that slight stir in the air was enough to wake her, for she hadn't been precisely sleeping, she'd been sitting at his door so long that she'd fallen into some deep and night-induced trance. Megan blinked and looked at him.

"For the love of Christ! What are you doing here?" Lucas hissed. His hand shook as he put away the knife, belatedly realizing how close he'd come to using it before his eyes could register who this visitor crouched in a small huddle on his doorsill was.

"I was waiting for you," she said. "How could I rest? What did he want of you? What did he say? I said nothing, and even so, he knew I'd betrayed his trust. What did he do?" she asked, clutching at his arms and struggling up to her feet as he rose with her.

It took a moment for him to realize she was talking about Henry.

"Nothing," he answered. "He was only testing me again."

"Oh, before God, Lucas," she said, resting her forehead against his chest, "I cannot bear this. I cannot."

"But you must," he said.

That was neither the answer she expected nor the one she wanted to hear from him. She looked up at what she could see of his face in the night.

"What did you say to Henry?" he asked, his voice careful and calm as his hands as they lay still on her back.

"Nothing, but it was that nothing that displeased him. He said I wasn't of any use to him any longer, but he seemed more sorry than angry with me, and promised to continue to keep me on here, so long as I needed. He . . ." she paused. "He warned me against you," she said softly. "That's why I was worried for you."

"For me?" Lucas smiled; she could see his teeth, white in the darkness, before his mood veered. "He meant for you to worry for yourself," he said abruptly, "and he was right."

"Why? Oh, Lucas, he's not going to punish you for visiting Perkin in the Tower, is he?" she asked, horrified, her voice rising with her fear.

He made a sound of exasperation, looked up and then down as far into the darkness of the corridor as he could before he drew her into the room with him and closed the door behind them.

His room was lit by a flaring rushlight. It was a simple chamber, having bed, table, chair, and wardrobe chest. His own bags and a small trunk were the only signs of his possession, but she'd have known the room as his by the slight scent of him that lingered here: the blend of citrus and spice that she always marked as his especial presence. It brought back a sudden memory of that long-ago time when Maeve had come back to her bed in the dawn so saturated with his scent it had been as if he were still there with her as he'd been all night. That remembrance of betrayal made her forget mere treason. She didn't want to be alone with him now, but there was nowhere else she wanted to be; it was that which robbed her of speech and made her eyes grow dark and wide.

For once, he misunderstood. But then, these days were addling his wits, and he saw nothing as clearly as he used to do. He let go of her hand and stepped back.

"Listen," he said quickly. "You're safe enough with me. I've only brought you here so no one can hear us—though who knows if this place isn't riddled with holes, and its walls crawling with spies too? But, before God," he said wearily, "a man cannot live with constant fear, even if it is prudent. I've been places where every mouthful could have been my last, but ate my dinner nonetheless. It's foolish to give up eating for fear of it, since starving will kill you as surely as poisoning will. At least, I think it's safer to talk here, and so we must believe it is.

"I'm in no more danger now than I was before. But it may be that being seen with me will put you in some danger, so you mustn't seek me out again for a while, and," he added more gently, "you must try to understand why I'll avoid you for a time, as well."

"If you're not in danger, why should your company put me in danger?" she asked.

"Faith!" he said angrily, turning from her. "Can you not take my word? Henry's mind works oddly. If he suspects me, you must stay away from me."

"But you say you aren't in danger. That makes no sense," she said, and as he knew it didn't, he was as alarmed as annoyed at how his exhaustion was coupling with his desire to keep her near, and so was making his wits slow and his words clumsy. He grasped her arm to lead her out so that she couldn't confuse him anymore.

"Life doesn't make sense, my Megan, but we live it anyway," he said through gritted teeth. "Have faith, do as I say, for God's sake, please."

It was the exhaustion in his voice, it was the way he spoke her name; it was the way she turned her face to him, it was the way she'd begun to weep. But she didn't cast herself upon his chest, and he didn't pull her close, and yet somehow they were in each other's arms. What began as a need to touch for comfort became an embrace, the embrace led to a kiss, and then another, and then a search for something more.

She knew, almost at once, as his hand came from caressing her throat to tentatively touch her breast, that this time it would be much more. It had already gone far beyond the games she'd played with him and men like Matthew, if only because it had begun as far more. It wasn't so much that his touch was wonderful to feel, or that his mouth was taking her wits as well as her breath away as it forced hers open with gentle relentless persistence. It was that she knew, even now, in this simple prefiguring, that she wouldn't be leaving him tonight until she'd left all her future here with him.

It was more than his skill, or her desire to experience

it; it had to be: she'd been trained up since birth to ignore pleasure because of her realities. It was that even in her confusion she sensed his real need of more than she'd ever given him. Because he seemed lost in her now. It began simply and was rushing onward. He held her close, his mouth as urgent as his body as it strained against hers; he was concentrating on her so intently he couldn't have heard anything but her sighs, or seen anything in the room but the white breast he was baring with shaking hands as he urged her gown down. And Lucas Lovat's hands never shook, he never forgot himself because he was, or had been, all skill, all confidence, all surety, since the day she'd met him.

So it really was not desire or duty or love or anything she'd ever expected to feel that decided her. Because for all her answering passion, that passion was composed of fierce sympathy as much as love; she didn't know physical passion enough to act on it. It wasn't the way she'd anticipated losing her virginity, yet whatever it entailed, she knew what must be. He needed something of her and it happened to be the only thing she had to give.

But it went against everything she held to be holy, against all common sense and hope of survival. It wasn't her wedding night; he was a spy, and possibly a traitor; if he were not to be hanged, he might just as easily walk away from her without a backward look when he was done with her; there was no guarantee in any of this; she'd never done anything so foolish or sinful.

But cool, clever, world-weary Lucas burned in her arms. His heart was racing against hers, his bright hair was soft against her neck now, his body was taut and dry and hot, and he trembled. And so she decided it was the right thing, because Lucas Lovat was in terrible pain, and she, most luckily and magically, seemed to have it within her power to ease him, if only for an hour.

He knew her decision when she made it. If she'd refused, he'd have understood and not insisted; that wasn't his way. But he didn't know if he could have borne it. Although he would have, of course, as he'd borne all that had gone before to bring him to this extremity. As it was, he felt her mouth and body relax against his. There was no need for words then. He drew back from her only once, to take her hand and lead her to his bed. They didn't have to part in order to uncover themselves either, because he knew how to free her even as he kissed and caressed her, and how to shrug himself out of his clothing at the same time, making disrobing a part of what he was doing. No matter how moved he was, he was, after all, expert at this; this was one of his chiefest skills.

She was warm and flushed from her recent state of near-sleep as well as her excitement, warm and sweetly damp as a sleeping child, or a puppy's belly, or other homey comfortable things that confused him by coming to his mind, because they had less to do with lust than warmth. And he'd never found himself in such need of warmth as he found in her arms. But it was definitely lust that drew him on to less-innocent pleasures.

She was shy beneath his gaze as she hadn't been beneath his touch, but he needed the look of her. He needed to know exactly who she was as well as what she was tonight. And she was all he'd wanted—sweet and supple and beautifully shaped, as he'd thought she must be—and yet even as he noted that, he took time to try to comfort her before he comforted himself with her. His lips smoothed the cruel lines left imprinted on her ribs from her tightly fitted gown even before he found more delicious things to taste. Her breasts were high and firm and tipped with fire to his hands and lips. Her waist was narrow, her hips smoothly rounded; the shadowed and cupped valley of her sex was covered from his eyes only by his hand, because for all he wanted to take the time to study what lay before him, he found he could not bear not to touch her.

She'd always seen his body clear beneath the taut skin of his velvet and satin clothes, but it was even more fascinating, frightening, and powerful clad only in rush-light and a slight golden haze of fine, downy hair. And then there was that other thing that she'd known of by hearing so much talk, although nothing could have prepared her for the sight of it. She was astonished that such a secret part could be such a large part, and shocked herself by finding it beautiful, even as he was; nothing about him put her off, except for her omnipresent fear of the future. For unlike him, she hadn't the knowledge of the joy to come to make her forget, even temporarily, the onrushing future that would come after.

He didn't use any of the easy words he usually did when at such pastimes. This was no pastime to him. He was carried away by a need that transcended the desire he'd thought the most important part of sexual union. He'd had courtesans and experienced women; many women who'd known the game as well as he, and some better, and yet never felt anything like the sheer need of this. It carried him past words; he felt he must reach her somewhere beyond words.

He spoke only once.

He held himself away from her on straight arms and looked down at her. His long pale hair made a frame for their faces as it swung over hers.

"Are you sure?" he asked.

She nodded. He needed more. She reached up to him and kissed him. He would not bend to her.

"Yes," she finally said.

He didn't know. That was the only thing to make her sad, despite the first sharp pain of it. He couldn't know the welter of emotions she felt as he strained to her: the absolute joy of being so close to him at last, the beginnings of joy as well as fear and hurt as he entered her entirely, the doubt that she'd be good enough to please him even now, the terror that by doing this, she'd be losing him.

But he knew. He'd known from the moment she'd taken his first kiss. He'd known exactly what it was she was giving, how much he was taking—to the smallest fraction of her fear and commitment, he knew. That was what made it different from any other time, despite how many other times there'd been for him. Because he couldn't remember ever having been trusted before, or having it be so important that he was. That was what made him rejoice at her allowing him complete entry, and what made him cry out her name when the end came; because he never for a second forgot who she was and what she was giving him, despite the blind force of the urge to possess her, and the incredible relief when he did. That was what gave him the solace that went beyond the familiar rush of ecstasy that usually staved off despair.

And that was what made him hold her close after, and knowing her confusion, pain, and growing fear, and aching himself for it, yet still made him regret only the end of it.

He touched his lips to her hair.

She lay still, stiffening in his arms rather than relaxing, and not only because she'd not had the release he'd had. He knew that very well too.

"Not wondrous for you the first time," he murmured, "no, not fair. But it was so for me, and will be for you, you'll see. It's taking, not just giving, that brings the pleasure. I know, you see," he said softly, "and yet I'm glad of it. It may have been charity, but I was in need. Thank you, Megan."

He grew as still as she was. And sighed. There was another compulsion growing within him. He surrendered to it, at last, against his will, as he'd done with everything that had to do with her tonight. He gave her that part of himself which was as integral to his concept of himself as her virginity had been to her.

"I'll never leave you, of my own choice," he said softly. "I love you, you know."

And lay silent, wondering, because he'd never said that to a woman before, or thought it.

The room was dark. He thought his passion had cooled, but as she turned into his arms again, he found it had not. But since the one wall had been breached, it was as if the whole of his defense crumbled. Now that he'd laid himself open to her, he wished to make his whole self, not just his heart, hostage. This trust, he thought, was a dangerous thing; no wonder he'd been spare with it before. It seemed he was being swept forward by irresistible forces tonight. There was more he had to say. Although he knew very well it might be the end of him, he had to say it.

"My name . . ." he said into her ear, so that even if Henry and his six counselors were in the wall behind his bed, they couldn't have heard it, but he said it into her ear, so that if she chose to speak it to Henry later, he couldn't help it,

"My name is not Lucas Lovat. I'm here because Henry asked it of me. But also for mine own sake. He set me to spy on Perkin Warbeck and his household. Hush. You knew that. But I came to London because I thought that Perkin Warbeck might be my own lost brother. Listen.

My name, though you may never speak it lest you kill me sure as with an arrow, is Edward. Edward Plantagenet. Listen . . ."

She was very quiet when he was done speaking, and he'd spoken for a long time, uninterrupted.

Well-a-day, he thought with unaccountable merriness, though his body was suddenly cold, even entwined as it was with the warmth of hers, there was nothing to fear, after all. She only thinks I'm a madman now.

But she believed every word, however mad a tale it had been that he'd told. Life, as she knew too well, was not sane. She knew his story was true because he had told it.

She put her face into the crook of his neck and he felt the brush of her eyelashes as well as the first tears on the sensitive skin there.

"You cannot want me now," she said.

"I cannot?" he asked.

This time, when they were done, she knew a little more of the reason for his great urgency and for his sigh as he enfolded her in his arms again.

"I want you for more than that," he whispered, "and always shall. Because I need you. Even if I were to be king again, I would need you, and would have you—that I vow," he whispered. "My family is famous for wedding where love is, despite the consequences—just look at me." It may have been that he chuckled. "But I will never be king again. That's an incontrovertible truth. It's less terrible to me every day, although I suppose in a way that's terrible too. I'm not sure of anything anymore," he said, and knowing this to be the greatest confession of all, gripped her more tightly, so as to take the same solace from the closeness of her body as he did from her mind.

She held him as closely.

"Be sure of me," she said.

She stayed in his room with him until the sky lightened. Then he helped her wash away the evidence of their night, laughing at how she was embarrassed by his assistance as well as the need for it, and then saddened that it was so simple to erase the proof of his claim to her. He grew grave, thinking of what a poor, insubstantial claim that was: some blood he'd caused her to shed, some traces of his seed he'd shed for her—and that thought made him even more solemn, for he'd always thought that transparent evidence a residue of lust, and never as that of possible life, before.

"Let Clarisse think what she will. With her Matthew in disgrace, she'll not dare to say a word," he told her when he took her to her chamber door at last. "At that, it makes no matter," he assured her, kissing the tip of her nose as she gazed up at him. "We'll be wedded before the gossip can go around once. I'll see you in a few hours and tell you of the proceedings at the Guildhall then," he added, bringing her back to their real life again.

"No," she said.

When he frowned, she sighed, and explained.

"It's not my decision. We're all going to be there, as well. But I wouldn't want to leave you to that alone, either."

She wasn't with him when the sentences were pronounced, even though they stood side by side. But then, closely as they were all crowded in together, each man and woman in the vast hall stood apart and alone with his own thoughts at that solemn moment, when men might be told they were to be forfeit of their lives. When the prisoners were brought in for sentencing, Megan stared at Perkin Warbeck even more searchingly than her lady did, seeking evidence that seemed so clear now that she knew what to look for. Only then did her hand, all unseen by any in the crowded room, seek Lucas' and hold on to it tightly.

The sentences were read off and greeted by sobs, or sighs or silence, by those they concerned. Some of the prisoners were stripped of land and goods. Some were told that they would also be stripped of their lives, and then their bodily parts after, so that no part of them remained to offend the living. Lady Katherine looked to her husband with pride and a hauteur to match his own, even though he never spared a glance for her as he heard the charges against them all again, as well as the payments to be meted out for them. He stood before them like a chained Titan, looking down on the thin, sallow king before him. He looked at no other, although he didn't seem to actually see him even when the king spoke: to sentence him to death, by hanging and quartering, before the month was out.

22

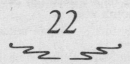

They passed each night together, locked in love, whispering it even as they recreated it. But Lucas and Megan were discreet. It was not the time to publicly declare their love, or plans for a more holy union. Not with the court so preoccupied with death. Their affair seemed to have escaped notice because of it.

Lady Katherine didn't care where her lady-in-waiting was each night, because her own nights began at dusk, with a sip of a potion to ease her to her pillow. Clarisse knew, but since her onetime suitor Matthew was in disgrace, she was more intent on restoring her good name than in blackening Megan's. And Henry Tudor, who knew everything happening in his kingdom, was so occupied with matters of state as the days of execution neared, that a love affair between one of his spies and another seemed to be of as little concern to him as it would have been to the rest of his court. Gossip about love was never so riveting as that about death. It was death that was on everyone's mind.

But Lady Katherine's trials embodied both. She was the one they discussed most, and was much admired. She seemed neither distraught nor drugged, but rather was so noble and forbearing in her grief that she stood as a symbol of suffering, and the coolness of it nearly broke Megan's heart.

"She smiles, she poses, it's more than the semblance of bravery. Does she not feel the horror that I do?" Megan whispered to Lucas in the dark. She could be honest about her feelings for Perkin now that she knew a greater love.

"She feels the horror, but she feels the majesty of it

369

more; she's never one to die for lost causes, or even lose her dignity for one. Yes," he answered, "she loves Perkin, but it is and never was the Perkin who is locked in the Tower now."

"Which Perkin, then?" Megan asked. But she never received an answer.

They only made love again, so that Lucas wouldn't have to think of the answer.

He loved her company as well as her body, and that was to say extremely so, for he'd found she'd a wellspring of desire to match the deepness of her mind. He found sharing a new joy, and closeness a heady one, and couldn't seem to get enough of her, mind and body. And so began to dislike himself for using her as Lady Katherine used her potions: as a drug to numb his own doubts.

It was more than the guilt and shame he felt for giving up his lifelong commitment. Or so he told himself in the darkness of each wakeful night hour when his love finally slept, exhausted, by his side. For he was no fool. He knew his pleasures would have to be paid for with guilt, for a time. But still, these nagging pains that bit at him when he was not dazed with desire, or repletion, had to be more than the stings of guilt and doubt. They were too urgent for that. And he began to think that he would sully this new and beautiful love if he used it to blind himself to them.

Or so he told himself on alternate nights.

"What is it?" she asked as he sat and stared out his window at nothing but the blind night.

"I'm only thinking," he answered with too bright a smile, catching her up and bringing her down to his side, "of us, and our future," and he took her lips and then bore her back to their bed, and kept her busy there until morning.

Perkin was to be hanged and quartered on the twenty-ninth of November—coincidentally, the Princess Margaret's birthday. Shall they wrap his guts up in gay ribbons and present them to her? Happy birthday, little princess, here is what remains of a traitor, possibly your uncle, whom we slew for you, Lucas thought bitterly as he lay on his back and stared up at the black ceiling in the early hours of another night.

"Why aren't you sleeping?" Megan asked softly.

"I'm thinking of Christmas coming, and how it will be to have a wife and a holiday together," he answered, and turned her on her back so that he could bury himself in her, mind and body.

Warwick had an appointment with the ax, and it would be quick, and merciful, but there was no mercy in it for Perkin, Lucas thought as he walked in the drear and empty winter garden.

"There are no roses left," he said when Megan stared up at him, her face pinched with the cold, and worry in her great eyes. "I'd snap one off for you, but all I'd get would be a handful of thorns. Let's go in," he said, and took her arm, gazing up at the sky to see how long it would be before he could take her to his bed.

"You must not," she said at last, one night when he reached for her.

She'd never said no to him before. It was not the time for her courses, and they'd not quarreled; her lips had been as warm as ever, and her arms still held him tight. He looked down into her face and saw tears.

"There is nothing you can do for him," she said. "I don't believe he is your brother, after all. How could it be? You want him to be, because you didn't want him to die. But he did. Long ago. And it is not wrong for you to live," she said, and then, weeping as he held her closer, she managed to whisper between great racking sobs as she stroked his hair, "and were he your brother, he would want you to live, wouldn't he? Let it be. Please, let it be."

When he had comforted her to the point that her tears ceased, she only said sadly, "I need you more than he does. But if he were your brother, I'd let you go. Don't go, Lucas."

She'd come so close that she knew his mind without his ever having spoken it. That thought made him as uneasy as the others did.

"I'm here, am I not?" he whispered, and held her until he thought she slept. Then he sat up. So that he could listen to the words again. The words that never stopped, the words that of late had come to accompany his every waking action, from the chewing of his food to the rhythm of love he set up with his love every night in this bed, to his own steady, unfaltering heartbeat: "Lead on—I'll follow." "Lead me to freedom—I will follow."

They were going to kill Perkin Warbeck in two days. And Perkin Warbeck might be his brother. It was one thing to give up an unreachable throne. It was another to give up a brother. He saw that proud, arrogant face over his own in his own love's eyes. He saw the sweet boy's face in his memory as clearly as he saw his love in his arms. And what if he had a son one day with just that face? Fate played such tricks. How could he look at his son with pride and honor, knowing he'd run away from the death of his mirror image once upon a time, in his cowardice—called caution?

But was it cowardice, or wisdom? What could be done for Perkin now, after all? Even, or especially, if he were truly Richard of York? No man in recent memory had escaped the Tower. He was, in truth, a traitor to this throne, if not his own. He was so altered by his pain and his coming martyrdom that he might well betray his own newfound brother, if he were told of him.

But if he were told, it might ease him. Even if only so that he'd know he'd a brother to carry on . . . what? Not even the name.

Men had escaped from the Tower in the past.

No man should die alone.

Henry Tudor could just as easily send another man to the gallows; there was always room in the cart.

Megan could not be left alone.

His own life was just beginning. . . .

Perkin Warbeck was to die in two days' time.

Megan gazed up at him. She put a hand on his bare hip; that was all it would take now, she knew. He turned to her in glad acceptance of her invitation, and bore her down beneath him, and almost killed her with the sweetness of his need, and love. But by now she was acquainted with such joys, and for the first time, at the height of love, some small part of her stayed alert to watch. And saw that he was never free of it for more than that one scalding moment now. For it all came rushing back to his eyes the heartbeat after he opened them again after it was done.

They lay quietly. If she told him she thought she was with child, it might answer, Megan thought. Because it could be true, even so soon, and he was, for all his guilt for his brother, a man who would love his son. But even if it were true, she didn't know if she could bear to live out her life with a husband she'd held to ransom. Or even with the man he'd be if he really believed he'd abandoned his brother. She was no Lady Katherine, to give up her love for what she saw as his greater glory. But it might be that she must give him up for the sake of his own soul.

She still could fight, though.

"No, no," he said with infinite sorrow when he felt her fingers come down so lightly to rest upon him again. "You don't want that now, my love. You could not. You're exhausted. You want me. And that you have, no matter what happens," he said, and she wanted to weep as well as rejoice because he'd known her mind so well.

"Don't, I pray you . . ." she said, and then fell still, for he knew what she would ask, and she hadn't the right, and knew she could say no more.

"I'll be careful, I'll be clever, I'll be sure, and I will never leave you, of my own will," he said. "If you must pray, than pray for my wisdom," he breathed, holding her as tenderly as a brother might, until they both slept for that last hour before dawn.

The letter he addressed to his father said that the Lady Megan Baswell was his affianced wife and that if anything should happen to him, she should be taken in as the daughter she already was to them in spirit. And if it should chance that she should be with child, it would be his, it could be no other's. Then it spoke as eloquently of his love for her as for them. Lucas finished it, sanded it, and put it in his wardrobe chest, where it would be discovered if and when his belongings were sent back to his father. Then he went out to walk in the gardens with Megan and wait for the night.

He told her that this night—this one night—it was her duty and only fitting that she remain with her lady, even if that lady slept like the dead man her husband would be in the morning. Megan accepted the truth in that. Then Lucas told her that he would be well, he would be fine, and he would see her in the morning. She never believed

him, but there was nothing she could say to that. He
kissed her as though he were going across the seas instead of just to his room again. She clung to him as
though it were a much longer good-bye. She was too
moved for words and too terrified for tears when they
parted, so only nodded, and went into her lady's rooms
to help her grieve and await the fatal morning.

And Lucas dressed all in black velvet and dark embroi-
dery, until he looked like an oddly festive hangman, and
put on sable furs against the cold ride ahead of him, and
left the palace as the sun set over it.

"You may follow in the shadows, but it's hardly necessary," he said to the air in the empty street where he
paused near the river. "It doesn't matter anymore. I go
where I must, and you say what you must and there's an
end to it, Philip. In the end, we all do as we must, don't
we?"

The rider came out of the shadows.

"I'll ride with you as far as you'll permit, sir. Then I'll
leave. Marry, at least I can say I followed until I lost you,
and mayhap won't come under so much censure that
way. I've a wife, and a babe coming very soon, and
would go home now, even if it means that by so doing I
won't rise as high as I'd planned. There are more important things. Or, at least this week, there are," Philip
said, his color rising to match his embarrassment for his
honesty, as he'd always complained that it did. "Howbeit, I don't think there's much even you can do at the
Tower tonight. I'll gamble, then."

"Then, go home. I never saw you after I lost you in the
maze of the city," Lucas said, and spurred his horse and
was gone down the crooked streets into the coming night.

He heard no horse follow, and saw no shadows slip
and slide in his wake. But as Lucas looked out to the
Tower, where the night had already been caught in the
highest turrets, he knew there were likely some who'd
see where he was bound. This was, after all, Henry's
England. And his own, he reminded himself, and a man
had to live in his world as well as his skin, or there was
no point to living at all.

They let him in, of course. Hundreds lived in the great
complex that was the Tower, even if some few unfortu-
nates also died here. And the gatekeepers didn't know

where he was bound to go. He barely believed it himself. He waited until full dark, standing by the water tower, walking along the docks, pacing, muttering in his mind as the menagerie beasts did in their throats, wondering what it was that Perkin was seeing out his window or in the depths of his soul, on this, the last night of his life. Mayhap, he thought as he waited, the condemned were the most fortunate, after all. If every man could know the hour of his death, and the way of it, he could even accounts with his loved ones as well as his enemies, say his piece and be done with it, make his peace with God, and not fear the unknown anymore. Yet, even knowing his own danger tonight, he himself hadn't done more than leave a note—because, he supposed, life was not meant to be lived in expectation of death. Why, even now, he thought as he scanned the sky, waiting for every last star to appear, he thought he had a chance to survive this. Even though it was likely madness of a sort, brought on by guilt, weariness, and the great loneliness that had been his life until he'd found Megan.

He would tell Perkin who he was.

If he was his brother, it would comfort him in his hour of need. If he was his brother! Why, then, after the rejoicing, he might even attempt some mad thing to free him, the very unexpectedness making it possible, at least in his thoughts. Or mayhap he'd only hold him in his arms until morning.

If he were not his brother, he'd see what was to be done; it might be that he'd have to bring on the results of the morning before its appointed hour. But what if he were his brother, and Perkin—Richard—became angry or exalted enough in his madness to proclaim it to the world? It was dark enough now for Lucas to see that it hardly mattered anymore. He yearned for the truth, at last, and here where it had begun was just as good a place as any for it to end. His only other thought was for Megan. He was glad he'd the wit and self-control not to have married her before this night. If he failed, she'd be free. Without his name, she'd escape all that he and those of his blood suffered. And if, pray God, she bore his child, it would be born without his glorious, damned name, and so also be free. And if by some mad chance he succeeded? But he didn't know what success meant anymore.

There ought to have been a dozen guards in a ring round the bottom of Perkin's tower. But there were only a few to be seen. He'd thought to come in by stealth, slinking up by a stair, inside or out—by climbing a swaying rope ladder, if he must, or even by employing his dirk, sharp side or blunt, in order to buy his entry when all else failed. Instead, the guard that took Lucas' gold did so without hesitation, though he never looked him in the eye as he did.

He was led up the stair and abandoned there, left with a swaying lantern in the silent night. He would not go to Edward, Earl of Warwick. He was here to see if Perkin was his brother, and not to break his heart. Lucas stood silent in the dim, dank corridor, scenting its stench of fear and impatience, feeling the weight and chill of this place seeping into his bones again, along with the memories, and for all the place and the time and the situation felt like a trap, he knew he was already held fast, trapped by the power of this place and his reactions to it.

Beginnings must have endings. He'd never really escaped this place. And if he could not now, he could not live, no matter how long they let his body live on. Lucas Lovat, born Edward Plantagenet, Prince of Wales, took in a deep breath and let it out with his last doubts, and stepped forward to Perkin Warbeck's cell.

The heavy door swung open at his touch. Perkin was not there. At least, Lucas thought, striding in, his heart pounding, he was not chained to the wall. But as he swung around the stony room, he calmed himself as his eyes adjusted to the dark. Perkin Warbeck lay at his length on a cot by the wall, sleeping.

The tall fair man looked down at the sleeping giant before him. Perkin's gold hair, dulcet in the dim light, was reduced by the night to Lucas' own indistinct shade of moonlight. The stubborn chin remained thrust out, even in sleep, though the soft, shapely lips were parted gently as a drowsy child's might be. And the lucid blue eyes were shuttered by a fan of long lacy lashes. In sleep, Lucas could swear that he at last saw the boy that had been, and his eyes filled with foolish tears as he thought of how late he'd left the admission that should have been made at the first. He dropped to his knees.

"Brother," he whispered, touching the warm, wide, undamaged shoulder that was nearest to him.

Perkin did not stir.

Lucas was doubly shamed at the signs of an innocence that would let a man sleep even as the hours ticked him down to his last sleep.

"Brother," he said again through his tears, as sorry to wake him to possible fear and pain as he was glad to arouse him to the truth at last. But Perkin didn't stir as Lucas' hands shook his shoulder, and did not so much as move behind his eyelids as Lucas touched his face to be sure it was still warm and living.

"He will not answer you," the voice said, soft, from behind Lucas' back. As Lucas sprang to his feet and wheeled around, dirk at the ready, the dark-cowled monk must have spread out his two hands, for two belled sleeves raised up before him in a gesture of supplication.

"He sleeps," Brother Robert said, "a blessed sleep, for he was most agitated, his nerves so overset he felt the passing breeze on his face as a slap. He stalked, he roared, he raged. Now he dreams of better things: kingship and triumph, perhaps," he said sadly, "and such is the draft I gave him that when he awakes, he'll still be sleeping, even as they walk him to the cart, even as they draw him to Tyburn Hill. He'll smile at the noose, and won't feel its pull, nor will he know the obscenities they perform when they cut him down, nor will he know he still lives then. My order is a mendicant one—we've traveling brothers who go to the far ends of this poor earth to spread the word of God and give surcease from pain. And so we know how to heal when there is no hope of healing.

"There are green and hot hells here on earth," the monk explained patiently as Lucas stared, "where men tear each other's hearts from their beating breasts to placate false gods. That's where they brew such potions, and God forgive us here in England, we've need of such here, and now. This is my cathedral, these are my flock. I've locked this cell, stoppered up the leaks in its walls, and sealed the door until morning to accomplish my ends. Perkin Warbeck sleeps, and will, until God receives him in his mercy. You cannot rouse him. Only the last trumpet can do that now."

Lucas stood still, as the words came clearer to him after they were spoken. Then he flung himself upon the monk and tried to beat him down in to the stones of the floor they stood upon.

"God damn you!" he cried. "This is no mercy! I must speak with him, you damned dog of death! You damned black and filthy knave!"

But the monk was surprisingly strong, and as resolute as he was fit, and Lucas was worn out with worry and debilitated by shock and hate. It wasn't long before the monk had captured his two hands in a tight grip, breaking his attack.

"Ah, don't grieve, don't, I pray you." the monk sighed, raising his other hand to touch Lucas' bright hair as he threw his head back and howled at the night. "Peace," the monk murmured. "Edward, Edward, be still, you break my heart."

Lucas froze. He shook his head, and the monk released his now-trembling hands.

"All this time, I believed it better you never knew," Brother Robert said softly. "For your own sake, so as to save you from mourning what had to be forgotten. To save you, in truth, from Perkin's own fate. For no one can be king in England save for Henry now. But now I wonder if I'm as much a man of God as I long to be, or only still what I once was—too much of this world, too much afraid of what you'd think. I never meant to do aught but save you. Was I saving my own last earthly vanity?" he murmured, as if to himself.

"Edward, my brother," the monk said slowly, his great belled sleeves rising to lift back his cowl, "I've loved you, I've never stopped. I've looked after you, as best I could. God forgive me, I'd have spared you this."

The cowl fell to the monk's wide shoulders. The dim light made the craters crawl with shadows. For it seemed the face exposed to Lucas' wide and shocked stare was composed of only pits and hollows, wormy tunnels and runnels wherein the tears gathered as they fell from the only recognizable human features: the clear, bright, lucent and shining blue eyes. Light, smooth fair hair framed the horror that was left of the face, for all else was pitted, scarred, and puckered: the remains of a face lost, when life was not, to smallpox.

The scarred hands began to raise the hood again, but Lucas' own smooth strong white hands stayed them, so he could stare, unblinking, into his brother's eyes.

The monk spoke again. "They say the son of a great Scots warrior, Gilligom, was crippled, bent in two by his enemies, who, finding him as a babe, cracked his back and let him live, knowing no clan would ever follow a disfigured leader. He became a holy father instead, and all mankind his clan. I would be so blessed. I was brought to the monastery to die. You were told I already had, because they fully expected me to and you had to be safely away. But I lived, though when I saw what had become of me, I tried to die. The brothers saved more than my foolish life. They saved my soul. They taught me I'd been spared for a purpose, as are all men—only I was fortunate enough to discover it.

"Don't pity me, Edward," he said, his smile making his skin writhe in the darkened light. "I was never born to be king, only to serve one. I do. I serve the only king, the greatest one, the one no mortal man can be."

"All these years . . . " Lucas said.

"But that didn't mean I gave up ambition for you," the monk went on, "for it wasn't mere ambition, you *are* God's anointed king. If you'd reclaimed your throne, you wouldn't need me—except, mayhap, in the background, where I've always stayed, watching you, protecting you, if I could. I do what I can, and try what I must, and hope to aid all men, and harm none. But you most of all, my brother."

"Our mother?" Lucas asked, not yet fully believing the truth he saw and heard.

"Knew, from the first. It gave her comfort and the ease she needed to accept and abide our sister's only road to safety. She, our sister, cannot be hurt by any man, even as she cannot be told the truth, for she's been touched by God. So have we all been. Go forth from here, Edward, and go free. Wed your lady, have children, and tell them the truth so that if ever this land needs those of our blood again, they will be ready."

Lucas looked down at the sleeping Perkin Warbeck. He gestured, being unable to speak.

"I do not know," Richard, Duke of York, said as he raised his cowl to become Brother Robert again. "Sometimes I think, when I wish to think the best of him, that he was one of those poor sacrificial youths coming up as we were going down that terrible night. It would explain much, even his remembered pain at losing a brother. But I don't know."

"And Warwick?" Lucas asked, reluctant to leave, but not knowing how to stay with this stranger, his brother.

"Has no need of my potions—he sleeps the sleep of an innocent heart. And welcomes the walk to the block, and its ending, for we've talked, and he's come to accept that his new home will be loud with the beating of many wings. I don't say it's just," he said, seeing the shudders course across Lucas' wide shoulders, "but it's unalterable. It will be a great sin on Henry's head, and he knows it, but I can't move him. His love for Arthur surpasses his love for his own soul. Mayhap, one day, that will be taken into account, and will lighten his punishment."

Lucas nodded, and moved to the door. Then he stopped. He looked at the monk, and he put out his arms.

"How do I leave you, now that I've found you?" he asked unsteadily.

The monk came to him and clasped him in his own two strong arms, and the two men hugged hard.

"Leave me with God, where I belong. But, marry," he said on a broken laugh, sounding very like a young man and not at all like a dark and cowled man of God, "it is good to hold you in my arms as I have in my heart all these years. He works in wonderful ways—it's good to have a brother, my brother, as well as a calling from God."

The two men held each other hard, and swayed, as if they were at some strange dance, while the man on the cot at the side of the chamber dreamed of crowns, and glory, and triumph.

They couldn't hear the sounds of the crowd from where they stood with Lady Katherine by the open windows. All of London was at Tyburn Hill this morning. The cheers that arose from hundreds of throats as Perkin Warbeck's intestines were ripped out, and those that rang out as his limbs were hacked off, even the great clamorous swell of joy that rose up when his head was taken off, at last—even that uproar could not be heard all the way from Tyburn Hill to Westminster Palace. No, it was quiet there—even the birds did not chirp so merrily in this winter hour—and so they only knew from the height of the sun, at length, that Perkin's heart had stopped beating.

Lady Katherine turned her head into her handkerchief and rested upon the queen's breast. Then she raised a proud head on an unbending neck.

"He will never be forgot," she vowed.

"No," Megan echoed, but her eyes remained dry because it seemed no part of her functioned now, save for her heart, which beat heavy and hard and slow.

She was too frightened to feel even grief. She'd not seen Lucas this morning, as she'd not last night. But Lady Katherine hadn't left her rooms until only recently, and now sat, stone still, waiting for the king to return from the kill.

It was past noon prayers when the king arrived, with most of his court, as festive and boisterous and ruddy as if they'd come from a great hunt. It was no small thing to see another man's slow and bloody death. It was a relief as well as an exhilaration that it was over. The sport of it had overcome the reality of it, as always, and walking away from it when it was done could not help but make a man feel more alive. They'd the grace to grow silent when they saw Lady Katherine. Prince Arthur, who'd entered seeming only pensive as he'd tarried at Brother Robert's side, looked close to tears when he looked into her eyes.

"Lady," Henry said as he came to Lady Katherine and she only at the last sank into her curtsy, "it is done, although with all my heart I'd have spared you the pain of it. But it is done, as it had to be. Stay on with us, madam. Our home is yours, and in time you may come to forgive us for doing as all stern but loving parents must. For it was for your own good, however harsh it seems."

She rose from her low bow, hot-eyed and cold. "Sire," she said without a quaver in her voice, "after his head has been displayed to the pleasure of your house, may I have him buried, before God?"

This, of course, was impossible. Perkin Warbeck's remains, those that hadn't been burnt, and which the dogs and ravens left, would be cast, with other offal, into an unmarked grave, as befitted a traitor. His widow's audacity was so great that many, hearing her, gasped. Then they looked to her with great admiration.

Henry paled. But it was the monk, Brother Robert, who spoke.

"God will receive all men, as he does their prayers," he said softly, reminding the listeners that it was said the monks of London came in the night and gathered up the remains of murdered princes, as well as traitors, so as to lay them mercifully in sanctified graves for God to judge, after men had done all they could with them.

"Look to the future, my child," Henry said, gazing at Lady Katherine as though he could not take his eyes from her, even in her grief, drinking in the sight of her light-and-dark beauty as if it were a salve to his spirit. "Make your home with us until you find another, worthier love. And you will," he promised in a softened voice.

Lady Katherine ducked her head at the tone of his voice, if not his words. When she raised it again, her bright, hard, glittering eyes had grown misty with easy tears. She relaxed, and sighed, and drew long lashes over her tears, to become as she was before all men, and especially this doting king: herself again, the soft and meltingly lovely White Rose of Scotland.

They stayed awhile and talked, before Lady Katherine was excused to go to her prayers. When she'd left with her ladies-in-waiting, the atmosphere lightened. For it was festival time because of the executions, as well as the princess Margaret's birthday, and one could hardly celebrate properly in the presence of a widow of one of the fellows one had enjoyed seeing rent limb from limb.

Megan stayed with her lady in the great abbey until she was sent away, for Lady Katherine was keeping vigil into the night, and wished to be alone with her prayers and her confessor now. Clarisse went to join the court, in search of a new suitor, as well as diversion. Megan went to her room, alone, as she'd been in her doubts all day.

She'd not seen Lucas return with the king. Or heard his name mentioned. But then, she thought, he owed nothing to her, after all. If his tale were true, he owed less than that. Even in exile, even nameless, a king merited more than she had to give. She'd known she'd cast away her future when she lay with him, or entrusted the whole of it to him then—it was the same thing. But it hadn't mattered then, or at least it had mattered too much to matter. Now it was done, and whatever it brought her, it was too soon to regret. She only worried for him.

And so when she saw him standing in her room when she entered it, she only cast herself into his arms, so grateful she could not speak.

He hadn't slept, nor had he seen Perkin's death or what had come before it; instead he'd walked into the sunrise and beyond it. Now he'd come halfway home.

"I've spoken to a priest, and to Henry. We're to be wedded as soon as this damned bloody week is out," he said. "I'll not feed my guests with cakes that have been baked to celebrate any man's death."

He put her at arm's length and gazed at her. His face was blurred with a golden stubble and his eyes were red-ringed and yet bright. She was muzzy with weariness, and her own eyes were drowned with sorrow, but he looked at her with growing delight before he drew her close and held her hard and spoke into her ear, "He was not my brother. But he was some man's brother, and so I weep for him. My brother lives, but is no longer my brother, but all men's. It makes no matter. I am free. I've sent for my foster father and mother. They're to come to receive new honors from Henry, a new title too. Whatever it is to be, my first one will be husband. Yours will be wife. You will come home with me."

But he asked that, instead of declaring it. And on that grace note, she wept, at last.

And of course, said yes, as many times as he permitted before he kissed her to silence.

They were married in the chapel at the White Tower. The assembled guests said they'd seldom seen a prettier pair: both so slender and graceful and gifted with beauty and charm. Lucas wore purple and sable, as though he were the princeling from a bard's tale that he resembled, and Megan's heavy satin gown was cream, encrusted with brilliant jewels, and she wore such a look of repletion and wonder that she looked less like a trembling bride than like the princess just awakened by a kiss.

They didn't have the customary feast or bedding at the palace, because they were bound for their estate in the south, and wanted to arrive there before the new year and the snows of winter did. But the look on the bride's face assured the court that the bedding was no longer necessary, just as the look on the groom's convinced them, as they whispered enviously, that it would be achieved, as it doubtless had been already, many times more on their long journey home.

The king volunteered to send a guard with them to ensure their safety, because the bride and groom and his parents, the new duke and his duchess, had been given so many gifts. Lady Katherine had given her former lady-in-waiting furs and jewels almost as fine as those the queen had bestowed on Lucas, on behalf of Prince Arthur, who, she said, had taken him in highest regard. But they'd their own men—a caravan, with riders as well as walking men to watch over their heavily laden baggage wagon. Lucas insisted he was capable of guarding his own. No one doubted him. Then, too, Philip de Lacey was accompanying them; now that his wife had given him a son, he jested, he was not needed at home for a while.

The couple left London only moments after they emerged newly wedded from the Tower. The king himself was there to see them off. It was a handsome sight. The lady was entirely enveloped in furs, but the cold sun glinted off Lucas Lovat's deceptively bitter blond hair. It was not so bright as the look in his eyes as he gazed at his new wife, nor half so warm. They bowed to the company and then mounted up double on a richly caparisoned horse, and left, riding out past the bridge, beneath the sightless eyes of the heads of Perkin Warbeck and Edward, Earl of Warwick, and all the other traitors that were left, gape-jawed and bodiless, to hang on poles there. But the newly wedded couple were seen to look only into each other's eyes as they passed, their hands linked as their gaze was. And so they traveled on, seemingly oblivious of the grim evidence of the king's betrayal.

"Hold hard," Lucas told Megan, "and look only to me."

"I will, I do, I always shall," she said.

Henry Tudor watched them go.

"A pretty lass. Lucas is well-served," Henry commented.

"As is she," Brother Robert said.

"Aye, you've passed much time with the pair of them of late, brother," the king said merrily. "I was beginning to feel neglected."

"They had need of me," the monk said.

"All men do," Henry said, staring at his monk. "I wonder, sometimes, are you already a saint?"

"I have far to go," the monk replied.

"If that is so," Henry jested, putting his arm around his son Arthur and shaking him gently, "then there is not much hope for the rest of us, is there?"

"But a saint would never know he was one, Father," Prince Arthur said seriously. Henry laughed, and then they all did, even Brother Robert, a little, for they heard it issue from beneath his cowl. It was such an uncommon, yet clear and lovely sound, that they paused a moment to look at him. Henry knew what was beneath the cowl, and Arthur had heard of it, yet this time, for the first time, they both wondered what it must be to be such a man. It was, naturally, not a thing a man wished to speak of, not even a king.

"I did well with the old man, and so, then, in time, with the younger one," Henry said instead. "A title is a lovesome thing, my son. We've been too mean with them in the past. It's time to award more; they cost little, and return much, in fidelity and honor, to us. But what a curious motto the old man chose for his house."

" '*Vincit Qui Partitur*' " Brother Robert quoted softly.

" 'He Who Endures, Conquers,' " Arthur translated perfectly.

"Nay, 'He Who Conquers, Conquers,' " Henry jested.

"No," Brother Robert said, "Only God conquers all. Men must endure."

"Well-a-day," Henry said, staring at the sight of the wedding party as it dwindled from his view, "true. But too sober a thought on a fair day. Let's to the palace, Christmas is coming, we've pageants and music to prepare."

"I must go to the Tower first, and then to Cheapside, men await me," Brother Robert said, tucking his hands together against the cold within his long sleeves.

"What? To the sewers instead of a festival? Marry, brother," Henry said, half-mocking, half-awed, as always,

with this, his most puzzling and yet most trusted counselor. Lesser men might be better guides to the salvation of
his kingdom, he'd wilier bishops and more politic priests,
but he never doubted or had cause to doubt this man's
care for his soul. "How can you desert your king for other
men?" he asked in a voice any other would take for a
command.

"I am always faithful to my one king," the monk replied.

"And brother to all men," Henry said, as chagrined as
he was envious of that, as ever, looking at his monk,
wishing he could see his face, even ruined as it was.

"All men," the monk replied.

But there was such tenderness in his voice, and it was so
low, that it might have been that he'd said "Amen" as he
watched the wedding party finally ride out of London,
ride entirely out of even the king's keen sight.

Afterword

Prince Arthur was finally married, in person, amidst much rejoicing, to Katherine of Aragon on November 4, 1501, when Arthur was fourteen. The newly wedded pair went to Ludlow Castle, where Arthur, always susceptible to illness, contracted a cold, which led to a lung infection, and he died at Ludlow on April 2, 1502.

Henry's queen, Elizabeth Plantagenet, died giving birth on February 11, 1503. The infant died a few days later.

Henry Tudor died on April 21, 1509.

His son, Henry VIII, married his brother's widow, Katherine of Aragon, in June 1509. She was his first wife.

Lady Katherine Gordon remained at Henry Tudor's court, not remarrying until the reign of Henry VIII, her second husband being a gentleman of the king's chamber, James Strangways. Her third husband, Matthew Craddock, was a wealthy landowner. Her fourth husband, Christopher Ashton, was also a gentleman of the king's chamber. She died a wealthy woman, in 1537. From her only child, Margaret, are descended the earls of Pembroke.

Lambert Simnel became a king's falconer.

Although not noted in historical texts, Lucas Lovat and his wife, the Lady Megan, retired to their estates in the south of England. Their descendants live there still.

Brother Robert, a grey friar, lived for many years in London, and then, in the manner of such anonymous and holy friars, was one day seen no more.

ABOUT THE AUTHOR

Edith Layton has been writing since she was ten years old. After getting a degree in creative writing and theatre arts, she worked for a motion picture company, a television production company and in the newsroom of a radio station. She has also written publicity and worked as a freelance writer for newspapers and magazines. But she has always been fascinated by the history of England as well as its language. She has three children, and lives on Long Island with her physician husband. She collects antiques, books, and large dogs.